"ISN'T THERE ONE SUITOR WHO'S CAUGHT YOUR HEART?"

Jack's dark eyes held Lilith's. "One only, who makes you breathe faster? Whose image won't leave your mind, but rolls around and around in your thoughts until you can think of no one else?"

"It doesn't matter who . . . who it is," she said, trying unsuccessfully to avoid his gaze, "so long as he is respectable."

Jack's lazy smile was belied by the glint in his eyes. "Anyone but me, then?" he whispered.

Lilith took a shaky breath. "Yes."

"And you've left nothing out of your little equation for respectability?" His breath was warm and soft against her mouth. "Happiness, maybe?"

"Respectability will make me happy, my lord."

"Are you certain of that, Miss Benton?"

"Absolu—"

He bent his head and captured her lips in a rough, hard kiss.

STOLEN KISSES

SUZANNE ENOCH

AVON BOOKS ◆ NEW YORK

This is a work of fiction. Names, characters, places, and incidents either are the product of the author's imagination or are used fictitiously. Any resemblance to actual events, locales, organizations, or persons, living or dead, is entirely coincidental and beyond the intent of either the author or the publisher.

AVON BOOKS
A division of
The Hearst Corporation
1350 Avenue of the Americas
New York, New York 10019

Copyright © 1997 by Suzanne Enoch
Inside cover author photograph by Cheryl L. Enoch
Published by arrangement with the author
Visit our website at **http://AvonBooks.com**
Library of Congress Catalog Card Number: 97–93016
ISBN: 0–380–78813–6

First Avon Books Printing: September 1997

AVON TRADEMARK REG. U.S. PAT. OFF. AND IN OTHER COUNTRIES, MARCA REGISTRADA, HECHO EN U.S.A.

Printed in the U.S.A.

WCD   10   9   8   7   6   5   4   3   2   1

For Meredith, who introduced me to Regency romances. Thanks for that, and for not making me the only girl in school who could tell a Bantha from a Jawa, and an Andorian from a Gorn. May the Force be with you.

Chapter 1

J onathan Faraday, the Marquis of Dansbury, looked up at the building before him and scowled. Depressingly respectable both inside and out, it stood in a section of London he rarely visited. And staying away from it this evening would have suited him perfectly well. He slid his gaze sideways to regard his mistress. "This is quite possibly the dimmest idea you've ever had."

"Nonsense," Lady Camilla Maguire soothed airily, though she wore the wary expression of a handler facing an irritated lion. "Anyway, I won the cut of the cards. You promised we would spend the evening wherever I wished."

"When I *allowed* you to win, I assumed that your idea of an evening out would consist of Vauxhall Gardens or one of Antonia's card parties." He leaned closer as he led their small party through the open double doors. "Or better yet, my bed chamber," he continued, breathing the words into her ear in a last attempt to change her mind.

"Stop it, you naughty thing," she chastised, with a smile that did nothing to disguise her annoyance at him.

1

"Whatever for? I had no idea you would be leading me straight to Hades."

"Jack, Almack's is not at all like Hades. Please behave." Camilla tugged at his arm to pull him into the coat room, her brown eyes regarding him with impatience from beneath carefully disheveled flaming red hair.

Jack raised an eyebrow at her. He had swiftly begun to weary of Camilla's narrow ambitions and predictable desires, as she had apparently tired of his sarcasm and pointed cynicism—her obvious reason for the evening's sojourn. Even so, keeping her about was less troublesome than going to the effort of acquiring a new mistress yet again this Season. He'd lost count already, after barely a month in town. "I beg to differ," he returned, in a determinedly amiable tone. "Almack's and Hades are barely distinguishable from one another. Damned souls wailing and swirling about, stacked to the ceiling and trapped for eternity."

Ernest Landon, the third member of their foursome, chuckled in his usual sycophantic manner as they entered the main room. "Well said, Dansbury. Damned wailing souls. Ha, ha."

Since London still remained locked in a midwinter chill, even in the middle of June, the blast of heat from the crowded, noisy assembly rooms ought to have been welcome. But as the smell of sweat followed close behind the warmth, Jack found it more a confirmation of his analogy to hell. Promise or no promise, the sooner he could make his exit, the better.

"Please don't be so difficult, Jack," Camilla pleaded again. "It's proper society."

He nodded. "I know. Disgusting, isn't it?" Stodginess and Almack's had ever been fast friends, and as Jack looked about the room he could see no evidence that the relationship had faltered. His presence had already elicited a few stares, which he returned in kind, and muttered comments, which he pretended to ignore. If he hadn't been titled, his scandalous little party would never have been allowed into the hallowed, foul-smelling halls.

Ogden Price took a silver box from his pocket and flipped it open. "You know, Dansbury, you might for once attempt to spend an evening in a socially acceptable manner," he said offhandedly, taking a pinch of snuff and inhaling. "It won't kill you, after all, and I doubt your reputation will be the least bit purified by the experience."

Jack began to reply, then stopped, his interest snared. Price cared for Almack's nearly as little as he did. It seemed that two of his companions had ulterior motives for being in attendance this evening. He eyed his friend, noting the shifting of the gray eyes and the way the snuff box seemed to have become inexplicably fascinating.

"Who is she, Price?" He stepped closer to be heard over the strains of a boisterous country dance and a hundred wagging tongues.

Price's gaze flicked over to meet his, then dropped. "No one," he returned too quickly, and snapped the box shut. "Simply a pretty face." The silver container disappeared back into his pocket. "One may admire, you know."

"Indeed, one may," Jack agreed, cheering considerably. If Ogden had found an *objet d'intérêt*, at least he could look forward to a bit of amusement before he fled back to the darker corners of London he preferred. "And does this admirably pretty face have a name?"

"Jack, dance with me," Camilla interrupted, sliding her arm around his, her warm closeness smothering in the sweltering room.

"No. I'm conversing with Price." He wished her well and Godspeed in her search for a less acerbic peer to keep her company, but he had no intention of looking the fool while she searched.

"I want to dance," Camilla insisted, rubbing her bosom against his arm.

The motion was more annoying than arousing. "A country dance? Not even your considerable charms, my dear, could entice me to step into that pit of hell."

"Brute."

She pouted, but didn't relinquish her grip. If the embrace hadn't been shockingly intimate for Almack's, he would have shrugged her off. Instead, he returned his attention to Price, intent on the hunt. "So, my boy—"

"Jack," she protested again.

"Come, Lady Maguire, I shall dance with you," Ernest offered, with more astuteness than usual.

Camilla humphed and airily took Landon's hand. "At least there is one proper gentleman present tonight."

"Better Landon than me," Jack drawled, watching her departure.

Lady Maguire may have wanted a night in proper society, but she certainly hadn't dressed for it. Her burgundy and gray gown stood out bright as blood amid the wan flowers in the pallid assembly, and her deep curtsey served to reveal most of her charms to her dancing partner—an effective advertisement for the services she offered.

Jack glanced back at Price. Although he was regarded with some fear, over the past few months he had felt in greater danger of succumbing to boredom than to a duelist's blade. Tormenting Ogden would provide some diversion, at least. "To repeat—who is your mysterious charmer, Price?"

"Leave off, Dansbury," Price returned, clearly irritated. "It's not worth the jest you'll make of it. And looking does not mandate desire, anyway. Admiring a woman is like admiring a statue; one may recognize a pleasing shape without wishing to make a purchase."

Jack lifted both eyebrows. "Now I am truly fascinated. I have never heard you utter the words *pretty*, *admirable*, and *pleasing* in conjunction with any single female. Do tell me her name."

With an annoyed glare, Price pointed at the noisy gaggle of young ladies gathered about the edges of the room, waiting to be asked onto the dance floor. "Go bother the babes in the woods," he snapped.

"The fox prefers hens to chicks," Jack said, amused. Simpering, witless things, they were naive enough to think his reputation romantic, and too stiff and awkward to be worth pursuing. "You'll need a better distraction, I'm afraid. This year's flock doesn't show any more promise than last year's."

"For God's sake, Dansbury. Have mercy," Price sighed.

"Never. Why don't you save us both the trouble of my wearing you down and point her out to me?"

"She's not even here." Price distractedly motioned to a footman laden with glasses of flavored ratafia. He took one and thrust a second at Jack. "I say, is that Lord Hunt over there? I thought him still in India."

Jack didn't bother looking. "He returned better than a week ago. I've already nicked him for nearly four hundred quid at hazard, and he still thinks he's having fun. Don't turn the subject. This chit is obviously the reason you joined our little jaunt into proper society, and the reason you refused to flee with me to Jezebel's Harem when the chance arose."

"No, she is not. You—"

"No? Then what's wrong with her? A squint, perhaps,

or an ill-placed mole?'' He grinned at Price's put-upon scowl. ''A prominent birthmark, an insufficient bosom, a lisp, stooped shoulders, a bald sp—''

''Sweet Lucifer, Dansbury! Leave off!'' With a look of inexpressible annoyance, Price jabbed a finger in the direction of the entryway. ''There—she's just arrived. Now, have your amusement and be done with it.''

Turning, Jack caught a glimpse of a white dress and offered his friend a brief look of mock horror. ''A debutante? For shame, Price, to become besotted with a young and inno—''

For the space of a dozen heartbeats, the clamorous country dance, the cackling laughter of Lady Pender behind him, the shuffle of dancers sliding across the slick floor, and Almack's itself simply ceased to exist. Emeralds, he thought silently . . . her eyes were the color of emeralds. She stood in the doorway and glanced about the crowded assembly room as though seeking a familiar face. And then, with a rousing shock nearly enough to rattle his teeth, the green, sparkling gaze caught his.

Jack drew a slow breath and stared back at her. As if in a daze, unwilling and unable to turn his eyes from hers, he took in the rest of her. Hair dark as blackest midnight had been pulled up into an intricate, fashionable tangle at the top of her head, while a few curling tendrils escaped to frame her high cheekbones. The ebony against the smooth cream of her skin was so striking it made her look almost sculpted, an artist's rendering of perfection. Her eyes, though, were bright, interested, and very alive. They seemed to hold his with the same startled intensity he felt in himself. A slight, blushing rose touched her cheeks, a smile curved her lips—and then the dancers obscured her from his gaze.

He blinked. '' 'Angels and ministers of grace defend us,' '' he murmured.

"*Hamlet*?" Price returned.

Jack jumped. "Beg pardon?"

"You were quoting *Hamlet*. You must be impressed."

"Ah." Jack resisted the urge to look in her direction again and instead took a sip of peach ratafia. Thankfully, it was truly awful. "Good God." He scowled and handed the glass to a footman. By the time he faced Price again his cynical expression was back in place, though anticipation and excitement ran hot just beneath his skin like a fever. "It's merely that you had me imagining all sorts of horrors. I hadn't expected anything remotely . . . attractive. Who is she?" Unable to resist, he turned to find her again.

"I . . . ah—"

"You said you didn't wish to make a purchase." This keen, humming interest was quite unlike him, but it was impossible to ignore. As she looked in his direction again and then spoke to a young woman beside her, he knew she must have felt it as well. If she possessed a beating heart and half a mind, she'd felt something. "So, who is she?"

"The Ice Queen," came from beside him. Camilla returned to slide her arm around his. "Look at her. She's got half the lords in London after her. Nance has already proposed, they say."

Apparently no wealthy gentleman had been interested in Lady Maguire's considerable charms, and Jack frowned, finding her continuing presence annoying now. He returned his attention to the girl. The crowd of gentlemen vying for a place on her dance card was rather large—and most of them weren't particularly young, either.

Another line from Shakespeare—something about a snowy dove trooping among crows—crossed his mind, but he sternly refrained from uttering it aloud. Perhaps he was suffering from a delirium brought on by the over-heated room. Yet he was alert enough to note that the delicate flowered pattern running through her ivory gown was the exact emerald of her eyes, and that the ribbon in her black hair and the soft-soled slippers peek-ing out from beneath her skirt were of the same rich color. And he was aware enough to know that he wanted to do more than simply look at her. Looking was for the other toads in the room. "Stuffy bunch of circling buz-zards."

"What do you expect?" Camilla returned, breathing the words into his ear, infinitely more interested in his companionship, now that he was looking at someone else. "Only the most respectable for Lilith Benton."

"That lets you out, doesn't it, Jack?" Ernest chuck-led.

"Lilith Benton," Jack repeated softly. She and her companion, a tallish girl with curly blond hair he vaguely remembered seeing last Season, stood speaking to their admirers and whispering together. "Who's the girl with her?"

"Miss Sanford, I believe," Ernest offered.

"Yes, that's it." Jack nodded absently as he extri-cated his arm from Camilla's. "Excuse me for a mo-ment. I believe I've done my duty by you for the evening, my dear."

Camilla snapped her fan shut with an angry crack but knew better than to protest as he turned to make his way across the crowded floor.

No doubt Miss Benton was receiving an earful of frightful details about his character from her companion. Though he could hardly dispute them, neither was he feeling particularly monstrous this evening. A few smiles and compliments were generally enough to put even the most seasoned lady at ease, and a schoolroom chit would hardly take that much effort. And schoolroom chit or not, she was exquisite.

Jack ignored the two men standing directly behind her, obviously her father and a brother, and instead stopped before the girl's companion. "Miss Sanford." He smiled charmingly and took the young lady's fingers in his.

She stared at him open-mouthed.

"How pleasant to see you again." He released her hand, and she snatched it back as though it had been scalded. "I was hoping you might introduce me to your lovely companion."

"Oh . . . I . . . you . . ." Miss Sanford stammered.

Although Jack could sense the girl beside him, he didn't want to look at her until he could speak to her and take her hand. He intensely wanted to touch her, could almost feel the heat coursing between them. He took a slow breath, welcoming the unaccustomed craving running along his veins.

"If you please, Miss Sanford," he cajoled.

"Yes—oh, yes," she finally managed, blushing a violent red. "Lil, the . . . um, the Marquis of Dansbury. My . . . my lord, Miss Benton."

Jack finally turned to look at her. She was smaller than he had realized, nearly a full foot shorter than he. Small-boned and slender, she was enchanting, with a bosom that seemed to beg for poetry to be written in its honor. His gaze traveled upward, taking in every inch of her as if she truly were a piece of fine art. At her lips he paused—not just because they were full and red and he wanted to taste them, but because they were drawn in a firm, straight line completely at odds with the enticing look she had given him earlier.

"Miss Benton," he said, as his gaze reached her eyes.

"I'm pleased to make your acquaintance." He reached for her hand, but with a slight start she put them both behind her and took a step backward.

Emerald eyes looked directly into his. "I am appreciative that your quite . . . thorough perusal of my person has deemed me adequate for you to converse with, my lord. However, I have perused your reputation—and find you to be someone with whom I do *not* wish to be acquainted. Good evening." She turned her back and walked away to rejoin her admirers.

Jack stood where he was for a moment, flabbergasted. The chit had actually *cut* him. Miss Sanford uttered something unintelligible, gave him a quick curtsey, and hurried away as well. The movement roused him, and he glanced down at his outstretched hand and slowly lowered it again.

His wild reputation generally made him a titillating guest for the more daring hostesses, on the rare occasions he attended their balls and soirées. Females might be wary of him, but *never* did they insult him to his face. The cut had certainly been seen; he could already hear the wave of quiet snickers and giggles going about the assembly room. Black anger and frustration burned deep in his chest and down his veins to his clenched fingers. She'd felt the attraction between them, too; he *knew* it. And she had just cut the wrong man.

Jack stalked back to his cronies.

Price took one look at his face and began shaking his head. "She's a mere babe, Jack. Leave it be."

"Why do they call her the Ice Queen?" the marquis asked Camilla tightly.

She gave a slow smile. "Much as you like to keep up on things, I can't believe you haven't heard of her. Her mother was Elizabeth Benton, Viscountess Hamble." She raised a painted eyebrow at his dark, unchanged expression. "No? Shame on you, Jack. Lady Hamble's the one who took up with the Earl of Greyton and ran off from her family six or seven years ago."

That explained his ignorance. "I was in France," he said. Camilla's smile faltered. "Continue."

"Jack," Price began again.

Landon snapped his fingers. "I remember. Greyton needed a bankroll to edge off the hawks—he was near bankrupt. Thought Lady Hamble was plump in the pockets and won her off. Turned out everything was in her husband's name, though, and she hadn't a feather to fly with. He left her in Lincolnshire and married Lady Daphne Haver a week later. She's hare-lipped, but her papa was so pleased to get her off that he bought Greyton out of twig."

"Lord Hamble pulled the family out of London," Camilla took up the tale. "When she came begging back, he turned her away. She died a few months later of some illness, but he hasn't been back in town since. Now that the Ice Queen's come of age, she's out to restore the family's good name." She snickered. "And believe me, she's the one to do it—Little Miss Respectable."

Jack looked across the room again. She was waltzing with the Earl of Nance, and Jack glowered as he watched the pair for a few moments. She hadn't so much as glanced in his direction since the cut, and he wondered if she thought she had disposed of him. Her second mistake of the evening. "Is that her father who came in with her?"

Lady Maguire nodded. "And the other's her brother, William."

"He's the one I took two hundred pounds off of at the Navy Club the other night," Landon supplied. "Boy

doesn't know a damned thing about cards.'' He grinned.
''I'm meeting him at Boodle's later.''

''Jack,'' Price pleaded again, ''for God's sake, d—''

''You said you weren't interested in making a purchase,'' Dansbury snapped. ''Has that changed?''

''Well, no,'' Price hedged, ''but you can't mean to—''

''Then leave off or go away,'' Jack continued blackly.
He forced a slight, dark smile. ''I've a game in mind.''

''I knew it,'' Landon chuckled. ''She won't be respectable for long.'' He turned to Price. ''One hundred
quid says the Ice Queen'll be warming our Jack of
Spades' bed by the end of the Season.''

''That wee small-breasted thing?'' Camilla laughed
gratingly. ''Jack wouldn't bother. Besides, she doesn't
want to be warmed. She hates mischief, and she's already worried that her brother's going astray in London.'' She tugged at Jack's sleeve. ''Let's go,'' she
cajoled. ''You hate it here, anyway.''

Jack's eyes flicked to the brother. The tall, tawny-
haired boy looked fresh down from university, and from
his expression was chomping at the bit to do something
bold and reckless.

''Astray and mischief are my specialties, my dear.''
He disengaged himself from Lady Maguire. ''Perhaps I
might lend a hand.''

''Jack,'' she wailed.

''Don't worry, Cam. Price will see you home.'' He
made a mental note to send her a diamond something-
or-other in the morning to quell any inconvenient feelings of jealousy and to keep her quiet until she found
her next true love.

Jack could be very patient, and he had every intention
of seeing to it that the Ice Queen was thoroughly melted
by the end of the Season. Another line from Shakespeare

crept into his thoughts, and he smiled grimly. " *'Cry havoc, and let slip the dogs of war,'* " he intoned, then winked at Ernest. "I'll join you and young William Benton at Boodle's, I think."

Chapter 2

"There's Mary Fitzroy," Penelope Sanford said, leaning over to whisper into Lilith Benton's ear. "Do you think she's heard about last night, yet?"

"Shh, Pen." Lilith kept her eyes directed toward the front of the room, where Lady Josephine Delpont played *Für Elise* on the pianoforte. The piece was a particular favorite, despite the mediocre interpretation. "I'm listening."

"But Lil, Mary will faint dead away when she hears what you said to the Marquis of Dansbury."

With a put-upon sigh, Lilith glanced at her friend. "I would be quite content if you never mentioned last night or the Marquis of Dansbury ever again," she said in a hushed voice. "It was simply a brief, unfortunate encounter, and it is over with."

"It was spectacular," Pen insisted stubbornly. "I wish I had been as bold."

"I was not bold," Lilith protested, scowling. On her other side, Aunt Eugenia sniffed and glared at her. Lilith quickly wiped the expression from her face and straightened. As her aunt had lectured her a thousand times, a

14

lady did not scowl during a recital, lest those present think her jealous of the performer.

When the piece ended Lilith joined in the polite applause, and Eugenia Farlane stood. "You girls may go to the refreshment table," she instructed, in her clipped, dry voice. "Nibble only, of course. I must go congratulate Lady Delpont on Lady Josephine's fine performance." A brief wince contorted her pale, thin features. "One can only hope the final piece is slightly more suited to her talents."

Lilith curtsied. "Yes, Aunt."

As soon as she was out of sight, Penelope tugged on Lilith's hand. "Come on, let's go find Mary."

"Pen, no," Lilith said, exasperated. "The sooner this is forgotten, the better."

Grinning, Pen clasped her hands in front of her like an opera diva. " 'My lord, I have perused your reputation and have no wish to converse with you.' Oh, Lil, I thought he was going to pull out a pistol and shoot you dead, right in the middle of Almack's."

Lilith glanced over her shoulder, but thankfully, Aunt Eugenia and Lady Delpont remained deep in conversation. Her aunt would have nothing but harsh words for gossip concerning someone of Dansbury's ilk. Since her mother had left and her aunt had come to live with them, Mrs. Farlane had had her share of harsh words for Lilith, as well. Stephen Benton had made a mistake in marrying Elizabeth Harding, and Eugenia made it her personal mission to see that the Benton name was restored. Sometimes Lilith wished she wasn't quite so religious about it. "I couldn't very well have him speaking to me, Pen, but shooting me?" she continued skeptically. "For heaven's sake, don't be so melodramatic. I imagine proper folk refuse to speak to him all the time."

"I don't think they do." Miss Sanford led the way

toward the crowded refreshment table. "Actually, I don't think he speaks to proper folk very often. I saw him only three times all last Season." She stifled a giggle beneath an embroidered handkerchief. "But then, I don't frequent clubs and gaming hells."

Finally Lilith smiled. "You're being completely silly, now. I truly don't wish to speak of him any longer."

"But you absolutely *cut* him," Pen insisted, taking her arm again, "and I must tell Mary about it."

"Oh, Pen, please don't," Lilith protested again, to no avail.

Mary seemed quite impressed when Penelope cornered her and animatedly related the tale. Lilith had heard stories about the marquis before she'd ever set foot in London: wild stories of duels and drinking and gambling and womanizing. Though she'd never expected to meet him, she had imagined him to be half panther and half devil, provoking stark terror in every proper female he approached.

Yet she hadn't been terror stricken in the least. Mesmerized, perhaps—at least momentarily. He certainly looked like a devil, wearing stark black with no ornamentation to speak of, drawing her attention simply by virtue of his dark, commanding presence and his dusky, bewitching eyes.

The Marquis of Dansbury was tall, with dark, wavy hair a little longer than the current fashion, high cheekbones, and curved, sardonic eyebrows. She had kept her hands clenched behind her back so he wouldn't see them shaking when he spoke to her in that deep, musical voice. And until Penelope had informed her who he was, she had very much wished to meet him. To her continuing vexation, she couldn't stop thinking about him, and wondering what it would be like to be the focus of someone as wild as he was.

"Lilith, you are so brave," Miss Fitzroy gushed, fanning her face. "I don't know what I would have done if he had approached me."

"It was nothing," Lilith insisted, growing a bit impatient with the continuing adulation. She glanced over her shoulder to see that Mrs. Pindlewide had just wandered into earshot. "And please don't tell anyone else what transpired," she continued in a hushed voice. "If they saw anything last night, they would merely assume that he asked for a dance and that I gave him my regrets because my card was full."

"But Lilith, weren't you terrified?"

Lilith furrowed her brow. "Why in the world would I be terrified?"

"Don't you know? He killed a woman once for slighting him."

For a moment Lilith froze, remembering the glitter of anger in those dark eyes. She forced a disbelieving smile. "I'm certain that's not true."

"Oh, but it is," Penelope put in. "In France, six or seven years ago. My cousin Samuel told me all about it. She insulted him, and he was very drunk, and he shot her dead."

Then he *was* the dark, amoral demon those stories made him out to be. A flash of disappointment surprised her. "I suppose I should be grateful that he wasn't drunk last night, then."

She wondered again what in the world had possessed her to speak to him in the first place. Simple silence or a polite nod and a greeting would have sufficed just as well—much better, in fact. Though from all accounts, the Marquis of Dansbury was not someone to be politely disposed of.

Why had she encouraged him to approach? She had no business staring at a complete stranger—but once

their eyes had met, it had been . . . extraordinary.
Though Lilith knew herself to be an intelligent, sensible
female, there had been nothing logical in the way her
pulse had begun to race at the mere sight of him. But
someone of his reputation could ruin hers merely by
looking at her in the wrong way. Thank heaven he had
left Almack's shortly after she'd cut him.

She shook herself. There were far too many other
things for her to be worrying over without the unfortunate confusion with the Marquis of Dansbury. Lionel
Hendrick, the Earl of Nance, had proposed again last
evening, and so had Mr. Varrick, Viscount Sendley's
son.

"Do you know anything about Peter Varrick?" she
asked, lifting a biscuit from the table and nibbling it.

"He's pock-faced," Penelope said promptly, wrin-
kling her nose.

"I know that. But have you heard anything about his
character?"

"You mean you don't care that he looks as though a
flock of chickens has been at him?"

"Of course I would prefer a pleasant countenance in
a husband," Lilith admitted reluctantly, wishing she
could grimace and scowl and giggle as Pen did. Instead,
as she had constantly been reminded since her mother's
flight, she must always remember herself. Too much
rested on her; she couldn't afford to indulge in impulsive
behavior, in manner or in speech. Or in thinking. "But
it's not necessary."

"Oh, Lil, he's ghastly."

"He has a fine, quiet reputation," she insisted.

"So does a tomb."

Lil looked back in her aunt's direction and lowered
her voice. "It's not as though I have a choice."

Penelope gave a small, sad smile. "I know. Apologies." Despite her gaiety, Pen had a strong compassionate streak, and Lilith felt fortunate to count Miss Sanford first among her friends. "Where's your brother this afternoon?" Pen asked, thankfully changing the topic. "If you don't mind my asking."

"Of course not. I imagine William's still to bed, sleeping off his amusement. He didn't return home until nearly six o'clock this morning. He told Bevins he'd acquired a fabulous new set of cronies, been allowed to see the inside of something called Jezebel's Harem, and lost ten quid. Which probably means fifty."

Her brother had been determinedly carousing since their arrival in London. Just out of a detested four years at Cambridge, and moneyed for the first time in his life, he was an easier mark than he liked to think. Restoring the family's honor was a gargantuan enough task without William's wild streak appearing.

"I'm certain it's completely innocent," Pen reassured her.

Lilith sighed. "Oh, I doubt it."

"So who actually has proposed to you so far?" Mary returned to the topic nearest her heart. "I've received only one offer, from Freddie Pambly—and my father says he's not plump enough in the pockets to make up for his fat head."

Lilith chuckled. "I have received my share of offers," she conceded, "but I don't believe it's polite to count."

"Oh, posh," Pen retorted, rolling her eyes. "She has four offers. The Earl of Nance, Mr. Varrick, Mr. Francis Henning, and Mr. Giggins."

"What of His Grace, though?"

Penelope's smile vanished. "Hush, Mary."

Lilith's amusement died abruptly as well, and a slight tremor ran through her. "I have received no offer from the Duke of Wenford. Please don't say anything," she murmured, "but I hope he chooses elsewhere."

Geoffrey Remdale, the Duke of Wenford, was the same age as England's mad King George, and it was rumored that the two men had been friends as youngsters. Lilith had difficulty believing His Grace had ever called anyone friend, that he'd ever laughed at a quip, ever smiled in acknowledgment of a witty riposte. White-haired, with steel-gray eyes above a curved hawk's beak of a nose, he had sought her out at Lady Neuland's dinner soirée, and asked her age, weight, and height, as though she were some sort of horse. Since then, Wenford had twice sought out her father at parties and they had spent several minutes in discussion. Her father had never revealed the topic, but only smiled when she asked whether he had heard anything of interest. His good humor made her nervous.

Wenford had been married thrice and had buried all three wives, none of whom had borne him an heir. Rumors were that after six months of marriage, his most recently deceased wife, half his age and still ten years older than Lilith, had gone to bed one evening with a glass of elderberry wine and hemlock rather than awaken another morning at Wenford Park. Fanciful and dramatic as the story was, it had stayed in the back of Lilith's mind ever . since those eccentric, half-mad eyes had turned in her direction.

"Lil?"

Lilith started and looked at Pen again. "Beg pardon?"

"You look in such doldrums. Don't worry. I'm certain His Grace will find some dour-faced widow who thinks he's the very picture of romance."

Lilith smiled reluctantly. "Yes, you're likely right. I imagine he asks the height and weight of all the debutantes." Her grin grew. "Preserving the standards of the realm, you know."

"Ladies and gentlemen," the butler intoned, though there were woefully few gentlemen present this afternoon. "If you would care to retake your seats, Lady Josephine is about to recommence."

With a sigh, Lilith turned to find her aunt. She and Penelope were halfway to the music room when someone behind them gasped. A wave of whispers began at the far end of the hall and swept toward them. Lilith turned around—and froze.

Topping the stairs behind a flustered-looking footman, and accompanied by another gentleman, was the Marquis of Dansbury. His companion wore a self-conscious look, his lips pinched in an ill-humored smile of apology. Dansbury looked completely at ease as he strolled through the gaping crowd of women. His stark black dress of the evening before had been exchanged for a forest green coat and beige trousers, but the lighter colors didn't at all lessen the impression that he was dangerous. Neither did his mildly amused expression as he stopped before Lady Delpont and took her hand.

"My lady, I do apologize for being so very late. I only just awoke." He leaned forward as if speaking in confidence, though he didn't bother lowering his voice. "I was completely cast away last night, you know. Absolutely sluiced over the ivories." His smile could have caused a nun to forget her vows.

Beside Lilith, Pen stifled an astonished giggle. Lady Delpont was a rabid teetotaler, and it was said she hadn't allowed a drop of the devil's drink in her house—or in her husband's gullet—in the twenty years they'd been married.

"I . . ." Lady Delpont opened her mouth, closed it again, looked around at her rapt guests, and pasted a smile on her flushed face. "Well, I'm pleased you've arrived in time to hear the last piece, my lord."

"Splendid." Dansbury gestured at his companion. "You know Ogden Price, don't you? Price, Lady Delpont."

With an uncomfortable nod, Mr. Price stepped forward to take their hostess's hand. "Lady Delpont."

"Mr. Price." Wide-eyed, as though in the midst of a waking nightmare, Lady Delpont turned to face her guests again. "Shall we?" With an unnerved titter, she motioned everyone toward the music room.

"What cheek!" Lilith hissed, as Dansbury placed their hostess's hand on his arm to escort her. Mr. Price trailed behind them, while the rest of the assembly herded forward so as not to miss anything.

"Do you think Lady Delpont actually invited him?" Mary asked.

"I'm certain she did no such thing. But how could she turn him away in front of everyone?"

"Come, Lilith," her aunt commanded from the doorway.

"Lil," Pen whispered, as they hurried inside to retake their seats, "what are you going to do?"

Out of the corner of her eye, Lilith watched as Dansbury dropped into a chair one row in front of her, several seats down. "I'm not going to do anything," she muttered back. "It's certainly not my fault that he's come here."

Lady Josephine stood at the pianoforte, her mother beside her, clutching her daughter's hand tightly. "My lords and ladies," Josephine announced in a quavering voice quite unlike her self-confident one of earlier. "For your . . . enjoyment I shall now play . . . play Mozart's *Piano Concerto No. 23 in A Minor*." She curtsied.

Dansbury led the applause as Josephine took her seat and straightened her music. He leaned over and murmured something to his companion, then glanced back at Lilith. His dark eyes caught hers, and she met his gaze squarely. For a brief moment something changed in his eyes, as though she had surprised him. Then a devilish, sensuous smile touched his lips, and he faced forward again.

Lilith's breath caught. She *was* the reason he was here, tormenting Lady Josephine and her mother. She glanced quickly at Aunt Eugenia, but her chaperon was whispering to Mrs. Hadlington. She sneaked another look at the marquis, to find his attention was on poor Lady Josephine as the poor girl badly mangled the concerto.

She couldn't imagine having the temerity to stroll into an event to which she had not been invited—and then announce that she was late because she had been out drinking all night! Yet there Dansbury sat, from all appearances enjoying himself immensely. How in the world had he known she would be here?

Lilith clenched her jaw. She was becoming obsessed with the scoundrel. It could be a coincidence. He and Mr. Price might simply have heard the music and wandered in, knowing they wouldn't be turned away. And he had merely been surprised to see her. That was it. A coincidence.

After all, she had done nothing wrong last night, she thought indignantly. He had been the one in error, to approach her so boldly and then look her up and down as though he were sizing up his next meal!

"Lilith," her aunt hissed.

Lilith blinked and turned to face her. "Yes, Aunt?"

"Do not stare at that man."

"I wasn't . . ." She *had* been staring, and stifled another frown. "Yes, ma'am."

"We have nothing to do with persons of that sort, members of the peerage or not. Is that clear?"

"Yes, Aunt Eugenia," Lilith answered stiffly. "I am aware of that. I have no desire to have anything to do with him."

"Good. Your father would be very disappointed if he saw you ogling such an infamous creature."

That wasn't fair; she'd only been glaring at the back of Dansbury's head and wishing he would go away. But arguing with propriety-obsessed Aunt Eugenia only caused more trouble. "Yes, ma'am."

Finally the concerto banged to a close. Again Dansbury led the applause, then went forward to congratulate Lady Josephine on her performance.

"Awful man," Aunt Eugenia muttered, and dragged Lilith by the arm toward the doorway. "Going about terrorizing young girls now, I see. Thank goodness your dance card was full last night."

Lilith nodded, more than happy to make her escape. She could only hope that the Marquis of Dansbury *was* just having a bit of fun antagonizing all the debutantes, and that she'd merely been last evening's selection. Even so, she imagined she could feel his eyes on her back as she followed her aunt down the stairs and out to her father's coach.

"Good God, that was horrendous," Price uttered, as they made their way out to the marquis's waiting carriage.

Jack turned from watching the vehicle carrying Lilith Benton disappear down the street. "Well worth the agony, I think." He waved on his own coach, preferring to walk. He needed to think, and couldn't do it while being jolted all over Bedlam. "Besides, I seem to recall that just last evening you said a jaunt into proper society would be good for me."

Price grimaced. "I said it wouldn't hurt."

"Well, you were wrong. Young Lady Josephine's playing sounds very like a caterwauling feline. But I accomplished what I set out to do."

"You never exchanged a word with her," his companion said, looking sideways at him.

"I know. It wasn't necessary."

Price shook his head. "You're mad," he muttered. "I said so ten years ago at Oxford, and you've only gotten worse since then."

They crossed the avenue onto Grosvenor Street. It had been some time since Jack had seen the inside of any of the homes along the way, belonging as they did to the oldest, most respected families in Mayfair. And it had been some time since any of them had come to call on him at Grosvenor Square. At least *he* still found it humorous that the most disreputable peer in London lived in one of its finest homes. He shrugged, swinging his cane easily in his hand. "Has it really only been ten years since we graduated? It seems a lifetime ago."

"Made me feel a hundred last night, listening to that fledgling going on about his adventures in London," Price said woefully.

"Young William Benton is a key piece in my game. Leave him to me, if you please."

Price sighed. "I do wish you wouldn't drag me into your insane schemes."

"Do you?"

"Yes. Particularly when they involve innocents, who don't know what kind of devil you are."

"Why, thank you, Price." Jack paused to sketch a bow and continued on his way. "And no one is innocent. Besides, she started it."

"Cutting you for good reason is a poor excuse to ruin a girl."

It probably was. He had decided last night, somewhere between the fourth and fifth bottle of port, that the cut was not what he had taken offense to. It had been her denial of the attraction between them. And there *was* something between them; he'd felt it again today when she'd met his gaze, damn her. "Miss Benton didn't seem to recognize you, Price," he said, turning the subject again. "How long did you say you've been pursuing her?"

"I didn't. As I recall, I said she was pleasant to look at."

And Beethoven's *Moonlight Sonata* was simply a piece of music. Jack supposed that to be part of the rub, as well. If she hadn't been the most exquisite thing he'd ever set eyes on, her repeated dismissals of him mightn't have been so . . . irritating. The chit needed to be taught a lesson she wouldn't forget. And if everything went as he planned, he would have an evening of very intimate acquaintance with her, to compensate for his trouble. "Where did our young informant say his sister was going tonight?"

"The opera. *Cadmus and Harmonia*, I believe." Price looked at Jack expectantly. "By Lully."

The marquis sighed. "Opera."

His companion nodded. "Opera."

"Damnation." Jack cracked his cane against his boot. "I still have a box, don't I?"

"Not that you've used it in the past two years."

"Yes, but it looks so lovely empty, don't you think? Especially with Tarrington yammering after it."

Price chuckled. "He's only been yammering since you invited his mistress to join you there."

"A captivating little thing, Amelia. And quite adventurous." He glanced sideways at his companion. "I don't suppose you wish to accompany me?"

"I'd rather contract the plague."

"I can't very well go alo—" Jack stopped, a slight smile curving his mouth. "Ha. Sometimes I am quite brilliant."

"What?"

"Antonia. I can introduce her to William, afterward."

"You're going to go to hell for this, you know."

Jack nodded unrepentantly, his mind already plotting the maneuverings of the evening. "I've already paved my way to Jericho. If you don't have the stomach for a bit of amusement, then go. But you won't be asked back."

Price shrugged. "Someone needs to remind you how badly you're misbehaving."

Jack laughed, genuinely amused. "I've all of London for that, m'boy." And one blasted chit in particular.

The theater box directly beside that of Lord and Lady Sanford stood empty. Given that *Cudmus and Harmonia* was Lilith's least favorite French opera, she couldn't help but envy the missing occupants of the adjoining box.

"Lilith, sit up straight."

She sent an annoyed glance at her aunt. "I am."

"Well, I should hope so. The Duke of Stratton is watching us right now."

Lilith lifted her fan and peeked around its edge. Up in a lavish box on the far side of the theater, a pair of opera glasses was aimed in her direction. She quickly returned her gaze to the stage. "I hate being stared at," she muttered. "It's so rude."

"Well, make a face at him," William whispered, leaning toward her.

From his seat at the rear of the box, Lord Hamble rapped his son on the back of the head. "Idiot."

"Ouch." William sank lower in his seat, gazing

around in an echo of Lilith's boredom. Abruptly he straightened and pointed to the adjoining box. ''Well, I'll be damned. Will you look at that?''

Lilith glanced over and stifled a very unladylike curse. The box was no longer empty—and apparently the Marquis of Dansbury enjoyed the opera.

Jack Faraday sat back in his seat, his eyes on the high drama being played out on stage. Next to him, wearing a blue plume that had no doubt cost the lives of several ostriches, sat a petite, dark-haired woman. A stunning necklace of sapphires twinkled in the dim glow of the stage's gas lights. Unmindful of the growing stares and whispers from the other boxes and the orchestra seats below, the couple spoke softly to one another as they watched the drama unfold.

Lilith kept one eye on the scoundrel, waiting for him to do something disreputable. Whatever miniscule interest she'd had in the opera vanished, and though she hardly considered that to be a pity, neither could she be comfortable with Dansbury so close beside her. Only a few feet of wood and open space divided them from one another, and she wondered that he couldn't feel her eyes boring into the back of his skull.

Intermission arrived before she expected it, and she stood quickly to move into the shadows at the back of the box.

''Lilith, what are you doing?'' her father grumbled, as she trounced on his toe.

''Apologies, Father.''

''Ah, Miss Benton!''

Lilith stopped, then slowly turned around. The marquis leaned across the edge of his box, completely unmindful of the long drop below him. His dark eyes took in her blue beaded gown with such intensity that it made her feel completely naked. "My lord," she said with a quick curtsey, and turned away again.

William stood, though, and hurried over to shake Dansbury's hand. "I say—"

"Do you mind?" Aunt Eugenia glared haughtily at the marquis.

"Actually, I do, but I don't suppose that will make you go away," he replied regretfully.

Lilith choked back a shocked snort. No one spoke to Eugenia Farlane that way—though she'd wished to on many occasions.

"Stephen!" Eugenia gasped, flailing her fan in her brother's direction.

"I don't want any trouble, Dansbury," the viscount said, rising.

"Neither do I, Hamble. I merely wished to give greetings to your daughter, and thank her again for her astute observation at the soirée last evening. It has quite turned my life around."

Lilith glared at him. "I did not—"

Her father took her by the arm and half-dragged her to the back door of the box. "Good evening, Dansbury," he grunted, shoving her into the narrow hallway and following her out.

"What do you think you're doing?" Aunt Eugenia's face was drawn tight with fury as she practically bounded into the back corridor. "You actually spoke to him?"

"He told a lie!" Lilith replied. "I did not speak to h—"

"That's enough," her father interrupted. "William, let's go."

William shook his head and stepped back toward their box. "I think I'll stay and see the end of the opera, Father. Quite interesting, really."

The neighboring door opened, and Dansbury strolled out into the hallway beside them. "Dear me, I have caused a ruckus, haven't I?"

Hamble clenched his fist, and Lilith—remembering Dansbury's reputation as a duelist and fearing her father might actually hit him—stepped between them. "Yes, you have, my lord. Good evening."

She stepped past him, her father and her aunt hurrying to follow her.

"Good evening, Miss Benton," came softly from behind her. "A pleasure to see you again."

Though she expected another tongue-lashing, her relations were silent as she led the way out to their coach. Apparently for once she had acted properly. Lilith frowned as she sat back in the cushioned seat, wondering who in the world that woman had been, who'd dared to go out in public with the Marquis of Dansbury, and whether he had given her those blasted lovely gems.

Chapter 3

Lilith sat eating breakfast when Bevins opened the front door to admit her brother. She looked up at the sound, then sighed and resumed spreading jam on her toast, thankful that her father and Aunt Eugenia were still abed. It was far too early for another round of arguments over William's carousing. At least now he'd be off to sleep, and by the time he arose Father would be gone on his "political" visits, trying to resume relations he'd cut off when he'd left London six years earlier.

"Lil?"

She looked up. The breakfast room door creaked open, but no one appeared through the narrow opening. "Good morning, William. No one else is awake."

"Thank goodness." The door opened farther, and her brother sauntered into the room. "I'm far too disguised to listen to Father bellow at me."

William's cravat was thoroughly wilted and hung listlessly down both sides of his collar, and his eyes were red and ringed with dark lines of fatigue. He positively reeked of liquor and cigars, and—unless Lilith was mistaken—women's perfume. Worst of all, he was grinning. That didn't bode well.

31

"I assume you had a good time last night?"

She poured her brother a cup of tea as he slumped into the chair beside her. Sometimes it was difficult to believe that William was three years her elder, for he had never been much for responsibility and common sense. Father said that he took after Mama, just as strongly as he insisted that Lilith would *not* do so. Lilith remained unconvinced of William's apparent foolishness, though; she thought he'd simply rebelled against applying himself. On occasion, she wished to do the same thing herself.

"Oh, it was splendid. You know, I don't think even the lads at school who'd been to town had any idea what sort of fun could be found here." He cradled the hot cup of tea in his hands and slouched further. "It all relies on becoming acquainted with the right people, you know."

"Ah." Lilith watched him out of the corner of her eye, less than enthusiastic. "And you have become acquainted with the right people, then?"

William chuckled. "Absolutely. They know everything about London, and all the cracks and crevices therein." He sipped his tea, then leaned forward to capture a slice of toasted bread. "Hell's bells, Lil, there are private card parties here that almost no one knows about, and even fewer people are invited to attend!"

"Really?" she said in mock amazement, and propped her chin in one hand. "Do tell."

"You can make fun if you want, but it was prime. And Jack says even Prinny attends Antonia's card parties at least once a Season."

Something very unpleasant wrenched Lilith's insides. "Jack?"

William nodded. "Jack Faraday. The Marquis of Dansbury. He knows everything about gambling, but I have a few tricks up my sleeve, as well." Her brother set down the tea and grinned. "I took him for thirty quid last night, and he never figured out how I did it."

"The Marquis of Dansbury," Lilith repeated numbly. William truly did have absolutely no sense at all. "The Marquis of Dansbury."

Her brother took her hand in his. "Don't fret, Lil," he cajoled. "Dansbury's a good sort. Really, he is. Top of the trees. He took me to Jezebel's Harem, night before last. He and Ernest Landon and Price."

"He took you to Jezebel's Harem."

"What's wrong, Lil? You're echoing, you know." William grinned again. "You need to have a bit more fun, I think."

"I need . . ." Lilith stopped when she realized she was continuing to echo. "William, do you have any idea what you've gotten yourself into?"

He furrowed his brow. "No idea. Why?"

"Dansbury is a very base character," she said earnestly. "He—"

William shook a finger at her. "Nonsense. You're only flying off because he overset you the other night."

"He did *what*?"

"You know, when he came up to introduce himself, and you went all wobbly on him." William chuckled. "Said he was afraid you might faint right there in the ballroom, but I told him you'd never do such a silly thing. You weren't much better at the opera, though, I must say."

That was simply too much. Lilith pushed to her feet. "I did not go all *wobbly* when Dansbury approached. He is completely disreputable, and I wanted nothing to do with him! *That* is what I told him. And you should do the same, before he drags you down with him, Wil liam. My goodness, why do you think he suddenly became acquainted with you? Because he wants revenge against me, for embarrassing him! And—''

William stood as well. ''You're all about in the head, Lil. You have nothing to do with us taking up together.''

''Taking up with whom, William?''

Lilith and William started as their father strode into the room. Despite the question, from Viscount Hamble's tight-jawed appearance, he had heard at least the last part of their conversation. Except for the lines across their father's forehead and the light hair whitening at his temples, Stephen and William Benton looked very much alike. In temperament, though, they stood as far apart as the earth's two poles. William was lighthearted and easygoing, while the viscount was sober and even more reserved than Lilith. It bothered her that she had so seldom seen him smile since his wife's adulterous flight six years earlier, and she could only hope that her success in society and in marriage would lighten his grave heart.

''Just some new cronies, Father,'' William mumbled. He stretched and yawned ferociously. ''Well, I'd best get some sleep if we're to attend the ball at the Feltons' this evening.''

''William, I'll say it but once.'' The viscount took a seat at the head of the breakfast table. ''Your comportment in London reflects on all of us. I trust you will use what intelligence you have to avoid disgracing this family any further. Is that clear?''

Stiffly William nodded. ''Yes, Father. Clear as glass.''

''Good.''

Lilith frowned at her brother's back as he left the breakfast room. She'd received a sounder scolding than that from Aunt Eugenia simply for glaring at Dansbury. William had spent two evenings carousing with the man, and was only reminded to behave himself! And her brother was so thrilled with his new cronies that he refused to see the real reason someone like the infamous Marquis of Dansbury would want to have a stripling like him about.

"Lilith, be certain tonight that you save a waltz for both Nance and Jeremy Giggins. Only a quadrille for that idiot Henning, and I think a country dance for Peter Varrick, unless they offer four waltzes for the evening." The viscount rang for a fresh pot of tea.

"But you've accounted for only three waltzes," Lilith pointed out.

"One must be kept free for the next most likely gentleman in attendance," her father answered, and glanced at the footman. "Bring me the morning paper."

"Yes, my lord."

Lilith looked down into her tea. "Have you decided about Lionel's proposal yet, Papa? It is the second time in a fortnight that he's asked your permission to marry me."

Her father nodded as the freshly ironed morning paper materialized at his elbow. "I could hope his holdings were a bit more noteworthy, but I've heard no ill spoken of him. I think he might do, though I intend to wait until at least the end of the week before I give my answer."

Though Lilith had hoped to be more excited about her impending marriage, at least her father seemed to have given up on the Duke of Wenford's suit. And she did like Lionel, for if he was a bit . . . solid, he was always kind and pleasant. "It will be a relief to have a decision made." She sighed and looked teasingly at her father. "Though I do wish Lionel was a more proficient dancer."

The viscount looked at her. "I don't believe that to be a requirement for a good match," he stated flatly. "He has an impeccable reputation. I don't give a damn whether he can dance or not."

"Yes, Papa," Lilith said, with a pained grimace. "I was only teasing, you know. Though I do like to dance."

Unexpectedly her father chuckled. "I wouldn't worry too much about that, my dear. As the Countess of Nance, you would have far too many duties to worry over missing a waltz or two." He leaned forward to touch her cheek. "Even so, don't turn away any of your other suitors until I've made my final decision. We can't risk insulting anyone."

She nodded at him. At least he was smiling again. "Of course, Papa."

The bitter wind was up, howling through the narrow carriage paths dividing the mansions just beyond Mayfair. The air smelled like rain again, though there was a board up at White's for those daring enough to wager on whether snow would fall this June. The Marquis of Dansbury had gambled on a full six inches, expecting to lose, but he was beginning to change his mind. Icy weather it was, fitting for his pursuit of an Ice Queen.

"Why do you think that is?"

Jack blinked and looked up at the woman seated in the overstuffed chair opposite him. "Why do I think what is?"

Antonia St. Gerard uncurled from the deep cushions and refilled her glass with brandy. "Why we never became lovers, Jack."

The marquis grinned and lowered his gaze to finish perusing the brittle newspaper in his hands. "Because we're exactly alike. Two battling tarantulas. We'd kill one another before we ever finished spawning, or whatever it is that tarantulas do."

With a soft chuckle, Antonia curled up again, catlike. In the firelight, her brunette hair looked the color of burnished copper. It hung down her shoulder in a single braid, curling a little at the end. "It is the female spider who kills the male after mating, is it not?" she asked in a faint French accent.

"Another splendid reason why I've not engaged in the process with you, my dear." Jack glanced up again, amused, and went back to reading.

"When you came calling, I didn't know you intended to sit about in my drawing room. I thought you at least wanted to play cards. Otherwise, I wouldn't have bothered rising yet. I didn't go to my chambers until after seven this morning, you know."

"You should keep more sensible hours."

"Ha," she scoffed. "If you left here at a more sensible hour, I would. One would think you never sleep."

He pursed his lips, continuing to read. "I don't."

Antonia gestured at the stacks of newspapers resting on either side of his chair. "Whatever are you looking for in those old things, anyway?"

"You're the only one I know who collects back issues of the *London Times*," Jack answered. "I'm looking for a death notice."

She shrugged, running her fingers along the rim of the glass. The fine crystal hummed an A-sharp in response. "One never knows what knowledge one may have use for later. Whose death notice?"

"Elizabeth Benton. Lady Hamble." He folded the paper, set it down on the stack to his left, and lifted the top issue from the even more substantial pile to his right. "No one could give me an exact date."

"Is this lady a relation to the handsome young man who joined us after the opera last evening?"

"His mother." Jack started to read again, then paused. Antonia was mercenary to the core and saw people only in terms of profit and power. Or so he had thought. He regarded her for a moment, lifting one eyebrow. " '*Handsome* young man,' Toni?"

Antonia smiled and stretched, which did some very enticing things to the low front of her dressing gown. That sight made him wonder if it would be worth risking death or dismemberment to know her on a more intimate level. Occasionally, especially after he'd consumed several glasses of port, that question became a complicated one to answer. This morning, though, he happened to be almost completely sober and knew better than to indulge himself with her.

"Handsome, yes. And wealthy as well, I assume," she continued, "from the fact that you actually let him win a few quid from you. You never bother reeling them in unless they are exceptionally well heeled."

The marquis looked at her speculatively for a moment, as a slow smile curved his mouth. He'd had a hunch that Mademoiselle St. Gerard would enjoy meeting his new companion. And it obviously would serve to further ensnare Lilith Benton if he held the key to both her brother's salvation and to his ruination. Antonia could do a fine job of ruination. He'd seen it before. "Perhaps I'll bring him by for you later."

She smiled and sipped her brandy. "Thank you, Jack."

"My pleasure." He began scanning the headlines of the paper he held. It was from nearly six years ago, in late May 1815, and the country—or London, at least—had been obsessed with Bonaparte and whether he would strike north from Paris and meet Wellington, or head west across the Channel and invade England itself. Jack wondered how many people knew just how close Bonaparte had actually come to doing the latter. Not many—or not many who were still alive, anyway.

"Something *intéressant*?" Antonia queried.

"Not really." He flipped the page. "Ah, here we go. 'Elizabeth, Lady Hamble, beloved daughter of blah blah blah, died of influenza on May 14, 1815, at the age of thirty and five'." He sat back. "Hm."

"What, 'hm'?" Antonia asked. "It says nothing."

"It says everything," Jack answered. " 'Beloved daughter.' Nothing about beloved wife or beloved mother. Her parents placed the notice." He snapped the paper with his fingers. "Nothing about 'she will be missed' or whatever contributions she'd made to her title or society or her embroidery circle."

Antonia chuckled. "What contributions have you made, my lord marquis?" She stood and glided over to his chair, sliding her warm arm along his shoulders. "What would your death notice say?"

" 'Jonathan Auguste Faraday, the Marquis of Dansbury, is dead. Thank God.' " He refolded the paper and dropped it back onto its pile. "*Merci*, Antonia." Jack finished off his glass of port, glanced down at his pocket watch, and stood.

"Aren't you going to tell me why you wanted to see this death notice?"

He shouldn't, because although he looked upon Antonia with some affection, there was a reason she collected people's pasts in newspapers, letters, and whatever else she could get her hands on. She'd never attempted to use anything against him, but then, he'd always made certain there wasn't much to find, beyond the general ill manners and aversion he displayed to all his fellows. "Just a point of interest."

"I see," Antonia said to his back as he headed for the door. "And does this point of interest have anything to do with a certain Ice Queen?"

Jack stopped. Given that Ernest Landon knew of his game, most of the more disreputable *ton* no doubt had a fair idea what he was up to. Jack wished, though, that Antonia wasn't quite so astute. "And where might you have heard that, my dear?"

She rose to join him in the doorway. "Simply because you have stopped seeing Camilla doesn't mean I have." Antonia smiled and ran a finger along the line of his jaw. "You are very angry at this girl, yes?"

"No. I am . . . irritated." And after seeing her again yesterday, even more intent on getting Lilith Benton into his bed. Ice Queen or not, she was stunning. But he had no intention of letting Antonia know that his lusts ran toward that vein. "But I am taking steps to remedy the emotion."

"I have no doubt you are." She smiled again. "Poor girl, I don't know whether to pity her or envy her. She hasn't a chance."

"That's the idea."

Antonia followed him as he collected his hat and greatcoat. "I have learned one thing about Miss Benton which you might find of interest, my dear," she offered.

Jack shrugged into his caped overcoat, wishing the damned weather would warm up before it came time for winter again. "And what might that be?"

"Her suitors."

Ah, the vultures. "Yes, there are several dozen, I believe."

"Did you know one of them is the Duke of Wenford?"

The marquis faced her again, myriad new possibilities and plots coming to his mind in rapid succession. He'd had no idea even the Ice Queen was that chilled. In an odd, unexpected sense, he was disappointed in her. "Oh, really?"

Antonia chuckled. "With your gift of young William, you many consider us even, Jack."

"Thank you, Toni. I shall." He tipped his hat jauntily. "I'll see you tonight. Late, I think. I've several things to take care of first."

"I thought you might."

The Countess of Felton liked to consider herself progressive, so she had requested four waltzes from the substantial orchestra she had hired for the evening's festivities. While the older guests were quick to declaim the large number of scandalous dances, the younger set in attendance voiced no complaints at all.

Lilith wasn't pleased, though. Not one bit. She nervously ground her palms into one another while Penelope pretended to admire a vase of sad-looking spring flowers. The poor things were likely the only ones from the countess's garden to have survived the late frost.

"What's he doing now?" Lilith whispered, pressing closer against the wall and wishing she'd chosen something more drab to wear so she could escape the duke's notice.

"Still talking with your father," Pen muttered out of the side of her mouth, peering through the flowers at the crowded ballroom.

"Oh, Pen, what am I to do? Why couldn't Lady Felton have scheduled two waltzes? Then they would have been over with before he arrived."

"Perhaps you could claim tired feet and leave early?"

Lilith shook her head. "Father would be furious." She sighed and braced her shoulders. "I shall simply have to do it. It's only one dance, after all."

When her father had told her to leave the fourth waltz open for a likely peer, she hadn't expected the Duke of Wenford to make an appearance. Or that he would ask her for a waltz, of all things. She hadn't even been aware that he could waltz, had never imagined he would have wanted to learn the steps to something so obviously modern.

"Oh, Lilith, I'm certain it's not as bad as you believe. Perhaps you are only overset by . . . well, you know, the Marquis of Dansbury."

"I am not overset by Dansbury," Lilith stated firmly. "I am annoyed by him and wish he would go away." She emerged from her hiding place. "At least he isn't here tonight."

"I still think his appearance at Lady Josephine's recital must have been a coincidence," Pen stated. She had been skeptical at Lilith's suggestion that Dansbury was hunting her in revenge.

Lilith shrugged. "I hope you're right. It hardly seems fair, with everything else I must tend to this Season." For nearly two months she had been dancing with, speaking with, and smiling at the most well-bred peers in London. Although she had heard the rumors that she was some sort of ice princess, she had tried to ignore them. If someone could point out a better way for her to make a match with an appropriate man, she would gladly try it.

"Miss Benton."

Oh, dear. Lilith locked eyes with Pen, then swallowed and turned around. "Your Grace." She smiled. "How wonderful that you decided to attend tonight."

The Duke of Wenford looked back at her, no expression on his angular, bony face. His gray eyes, sunken behind high cheekbones and severe slate gray eyebrows, assessed her, and she again felt like some sort of farm animal. For a fleeting moment she wanted to whinny at him.

"It is time for our waltz."

"Yes, Your Grace."

Her earlier encounters with Geoffrey Remdale had

been blessedly brief, requiring little conversation from her except for a few *Yes, Your Graces* and *No, Your Graces*. As they turned about the floor now, he again made no effort to engage her in conversation. Wenford danced adequately, though he moved with little emotion, as though he had simply memorized the steps. At least the Earl of Nance, while he tended to step on her toes, seemed to enjoy himself. The duke might have been reading dunning notices from his creditors, for all the enthusiasm he showed.

"You look well," he finally said.

"Thank you, Your Grace."

"You draw people's eyes," he elaborated. "You plan for your family's meals, your father says."

Lilith didn't like where this conversation appeared to be headed. "Yes, Your Grace, I do. But with just the four of us—"

"Have you ever planned for large occasions?" he interrupted in the same bored, gravelly tone. "Balls, dinner parties?"

"No, Your Grace. I have not." She was abruptly grateful that her father had kept them in virtual seclusion in Northamptonshire.

"I'll have someone teach you. If you're too stupid to learn, I'll hire someone. No matter. You look the part."

Lilith's heart and her feet faltered. The duke's lips tightened in annoyance as she stumbled, and she quickly gathered herself. "Your . . . Your Grace, I'm afraid I don't understand," she stammered. This was a nightmare. It simply couldn't be happening—it couldn't!

"No need. Your father and I have a few more points to settle, but I've little necessity for whatever pittance of a dowry you'll bring me. I doubt there will be any other complications."

Feeling abandoned by her wits, Lilith wished she was

one of those silly girls who could simply faint. "You—you take me by surprise, Your Grace. You must know that I cannot give my ans—"

"As I said," he interrupted impatiently, "it will be a few days before everything is settled. Until then, you are not to say anything about it." He frowned, the glowering expression the most natural she had yet seen on his face. "No need to stir up trouble with the damned wags."

The set ended. "Yes, Your Grace," she whispered through the applause. He returned her to the edge of the floor, then without a backward glance made his way over to join the group of older peers who had commandeered the warmest area in the room, before the fireplace.

"Well, at least that's over with," Penelope grinned, prancing up beside her. "Was it awful?"

Lilith was shaking. She kept trying to turn what Wenford had said, so that his words wouldn't mean what she knew they did. "He's going to marry me."

"What?" Pen exclaimed, then covered her mouth with one hand. Her eyes wide, she looked in the duke's direction. "He said so?"

"My pittance of a dowry doesn't concern him. He thinks I'd look an adequate duchess." Hysteria pulled at the edge of her mind, and she concentrated on breathing evenly.

"But Lil, surely your father won't make you. He's so strange and . . . awful!"

"Who's awful?"

"William!" Lilith jumped, and turned to see her brother standing beside her, two glasses of punch clasped in his hands. "Shh."

"All right, but who's awful?" he whispered, handing her and Pen the punch. Lilith took a long swallow, but it didn't help.

"The Duke of Wenford is," Penelope answered, when Lilith didn't.

"Old Hatchet Face?" William followed her gaze. "He'd send Beelzebub running. Why?"

"He's going to marry Lil." Penelope looked sorrowfully at her friend.

"What?" William lifted both eyebrows. "You're bamming me."

"I'm not. Really," Pen returned, blushing.

"Pen, hush," Lilith said urgently, hoping her father was nowhere near. "It's to be a secret until it's arranged."

"Perhaps I should pretend I didn't hear anything, then," a deep, musical voice said from behind her.

Lilith froze. Deliberately, she took another swallow of punch to steady her nerves and her wits before she turned around. The Marquis of Dansbury stood gazing down at her, his dark eyes dusky and cynical. His lips pursed in a faint grin, he handed William a glass of punch, keeping another for himself. Again his dress was plain, dark gray and blue, leavened only by an exquisite diamond pin on his cravat. He was truly handsome as the devil, and apparently at least as tenacious.

"I believe I made my feelings about speaking to you quite clear," she said stiffly. Remembering her aunt's warning about staring, she turned away.

"Seems you've little time for me, anyway," he said smoothly, "now that you have five proposals to sift through. A record at this early stage of the Season, I believe, though I'll have to check the wagering books at White's to be certain. Madeleine, the Marchioness of Telgore, may have had as many as seven before she finally settled on Wallace, but that was over the course of an entire Season."

Lilith sent him a disdainful look. "My state of matrimony need not concern you, my lord. And do stop following me everywhere.''

"Following you?" Far from slinking away, as he should have, the marquis took a step closer. "Following you," he mused again, rubbing his chin as though trying to decide what she meant. "Oh, of course. The opera. And Lady Josephine's recital, I suppose. Lovely girl, don't you think? Quite talented, though she seemed a bit nervous.''

"You are . . . evil!" Lilith blurted out, flushing.

"Lilith!" Pen exclaimed, wide-eyed.

"Oh, dear me, that does put my plans into some disarray.''

"What plans, Jack?" William asked unhelpfully.

Lilith clenched her jaw, determined to say nothing else to the scoundrel.

His gaze remained on her. "I had intended to throw my hat in, and become your sister's sixth suitor."

That was too much. "You?" she scoffed. "You would be wasting your headgear."

"Better you should tread on my hat than on my heart," he replied, looking at her from beneath dark lashes.

"You haven't one," she retorted promptly.

A wicked, twinkling amusement touched his eyes. "Only because you've broken it."

It was amazing that someone hadn't disposed of him in a duel long ago. "Would that the destruction of it had killed you.''

"But then we wouldn't be having this conversation. You know, I thought you weren't speaking to me. I do wish you would make up your mind." He chuckled. "Perhaps I should have offered to throw down my gauntlet, instead of my hat."

His laugh was as musical as his voice, and his

smile . . . "Lilith caught herself staring at him yet again, and shook herself. There was no excuse for her to be ogling this villain, however physically attractive he might be—or for her to forget either her temper or her manners.

"At least one of us is amused at your cleverness," she said coolly. "And it is not me, my lor—"

"Lilith," Penelope hissed, clutching her friend's arm, "he's coming back."

Indeed, Wenford had left his companions and was strolling in their direction. To speak with him again tonight would be more than she could bear. She needed time to discuss the situation with her father, to make her feelings of revulsion toward Wenford clear to him before it was too late.

"Oh, dear," she murmured.

The marquis had followed her gaze. "I suppose I should tender him my congratulations." He stepped around her.

"Don't you dare," Lilith gasped, paling. Wenford would think her a complete gossip, and her father would be furious.

Dansbury paused, grinning at her over his shoulder. "If we were speaking, I might be convinced to listen to you." He strolled toward the duke.

"William," Lilith commanded frantically, jabbing a finger in the marquis's direction, "stop him!"

"Ah, Lil, he's just looking for a bit of fun with Old Hatchet Face. It'll put him in a jolly mood, and I want him to take me to the Society tonight."

"William, he must not—"

"Wenford," the Marquis of Dansbury called in a carrying voice, "I hear that congratulations are due."

Cold gray eyes flicked in her direction before they turned to the marquis. "I'm afraid I don't know what you're talking about, Dansbury. As usual, you seem to be acting a complete fool."

The acid in the duke's tone surprised Lilith. Realizing that His Grace had as little liking for the marquis as she did was hardly a comfort, though. In fact, it almost made her look more kindly upon Dansbury. Beside her, Penelope watched the exchange in astonishment while William grinned in admiration of his mentor.

"Not as foolish as some," Dansbury replied, glancing down and brushing an imaginary speck of dust from the lapel of his blue coat. The motion brought the duke's, and their audience's, attention to the exquisite diamond in his cravat.

The Duke of Wenford flushed furiously. "You are a thief, boy!" he snarled, striding forward.

Dansbury gracefully sidestepped. "Now I'm afraid it is my turn to be baffled," he returned apologetically. "I thought the larcenist was you."

"That pin belongs to the Remdale family, and you know it, you blackguard!" Wenford shouted.

The orchestra raggedly halted, and the dancers on the ballroom floor turned two by two to watch the proceedings. The Countess of Felton stood by the refreshment table looking positively elated. Thanks to Wenford and Dansbury, her ball had just become the event of the Season.

The marquis looked down at the bauble, as though puzzled at all the commotion it was causing. "This diamond was purchased just this evening with an exceedingly fortuitous throw of the dice," he drawled. "It now belongs to the Faraday family."

"Damn them all to hell!" Spittle flecked the duke's lips.

"Do you think there'll be a duel?" Pen whispered excitedly.

Lilith shook her head regretfully. "From what I've heard of him, no one would dare challenge Dansbury—though I wouldn't complain if they killed one another."

Pen covered her mouth with both hands to smother her giggles.

"That pin has been in my family for generations," Wenford growled, coming another step closer to the marquis.

"Apparently your nephew places less value on its possession than you do. Otherwise he would have seen fit to carry more blunt with him to Boodle's, or he would have dropped out of the game when it became too rich for his blood. Never gamble where you can't win. 'Twas you who taught my family that lesson."

The duke's hands clenched, his color becoming an alarming crimson. "You—"

"Besides," Dansbury continued, glancing at Lilith, "you have another possession you're about to acquire anyway, do you not?"

"Oh, no," Lilith whispered, wishing to sink into the floor as half the rapt audience looked in her direction, the whispers gaining more volume. "That villain!"

"That is none of your bloody concern. Give me my pin."

Dansbury smiled at Lilith, and then with apparent reluctance returned his attention to Wenford. "I apologize, Your Grace, but I am quite late for an engagement." The marquis strolled for the door. Just before he vanished through the wide entryway, he paused. "Seeing Your Grace's attachment to the trinket, however, if you or your nephew would care to call on me tomorrow, I would be pleased to return it to your family for its table value."

"Which was?" Wenford sputtered.

"Twelve hundred seventy-seven quid," Dansbury returned, and exited.

For a moment the duke glared after him. Then, with an angry roar of commentary, his gray-haired cronies joined him in sending a chorus of black oaths in the marquis's direction.

William started as though coming out of a trance. "Od's blood," he murmured, shaking his head. "Isn't he top of the trees?" He handed his glass of punch to Lilith and strode for the door after the marquis.

"Oh, my," Penelope said wonderingly. "He's not afraid of anything, is he?" She fanned her face again. "And you were right, Lil. He *is* after you." She blushed again. "He wants to be your sixth suitor."

Lilith's pulse fluttered. "Nonsense. He's merely angry at me for cutting him, and this is his diabolical way of gaining revenge."

Penelope thought about that for a moment. "You may be right," she conceded, "though I think you're simply overcome. I know *I* am, and I wasn't even at the center of it."

"I wish I hadn't been. I have no desire to anger His Grace."

"Lilith." Her father stalked up to the two of them. "Your brother is a complete idiot."

"Yes, Papa, I know."

The viscount nodded stiffly at Penelope. "Apologies, Miss Sanford, but I must collect Lilith." He took his daughter's arm. "Best if we not stay about, with Wenford in such a foul mood."

Finally they were in agreement over the duke. "Papa, has His Grace spoken to you about—"

"We'll discuss it later, daughter."

"Lil," Pen said, taking her hand, "Mama and I've asked Lady Georgina Longstreet to the Vauxhall Gardens soirée tomorrow evening. Do come with us.''

Lilith had little liking for the rowdy crowds of the Gardens, and she started to decline. "I—"

"Will Lady Georgina's mother be in attendance?" Lord Hamble cut in.

"I don't know if the marchioness will accompany us or not," Pen replied. "She was invited, of course."

"Lilith would be delighted to attend," the viscount answered for her.

No doubt he wanted the *ton* to see her in the company of the marchioness and her daughter, especially after tonight's unpleasantness. And in truth, it would be more fun than sitting at home and having Aunt Eugenia deliver another of her endless lectures on propriety and etiquette, as though Lilith hadn't memorized absolutely everything by now. She smiled. "I'd love to go."

Aunt Eugenia waited for them at the entryway, outraged indignation on her thin alabaster face. "The nerve of that man," she snapped, "to practically assault His Grace that way. He's very bad *ton*, and I can't believe he's still allowed to roam free, after everything he's done." She glared at her brother. "And your own son is hanging after him like a dog looking for a bone. For shame, Stephen. Mrs. Pindlewide has already remarked on it, and her husband is very influential with Lord Liverpool."

"William's association with that blackguard will end as soon as the fool returns home," Viscount Hamble returned stiffly.

Lilith could only hope he was right. The more distance placed between Jack Faraday and herself, the safer she would feel.

Chapter 4

Nine o'clock in the morning was far too early for visitors, but the Marquis of Dansbury had a very good idea of who must be pounding at his front door. With a groan he sat up and rubbed his temples. William Benton had grumbled and whined to be taken to the Society club, and rather than listen to the continuous drivel, Jack had given in, little liking as he had for the snobberies there. His aching head was proof enough that his encounter with the Duke of Wenford had irritated him more than he had realized. The Remdale clan always seemed to bring out the worst in him.

His valet scratched tentatively at the door. "My lord?"

"Come in, Martin. I'm awake, and fairly civilized this morning."

Martin stepped into the room and handed over a cup of hot, strong American coffee, generally used to placate him when his mood was less civilized. Jack took a grateful sip as his valet headed for the mahogany wardrobe. His servants were a generally impudent bunch, which was how he liked it, and Martin would get around to telling him who was at the door in his own good time.

"Which demeanor do you wish to present this morning, my lord?"

Or perhaps he wouldn't tell. "Who's at the blasted door, Martin?" he growled.

"Peese says it's Randolph Remdale. He's waiting, quite impatiently, I believe, in the morning room. I had thought him a gentleman of good breeding, but to come calling at this hour, I must say—"

"The nephew, hm?" Jack interrupted, uninterested in Martin's tirade. It was only for effect, and they both knew it. "I thought so. Something conservative, I think. It will annoy him excessively."

The valet frowned. "Why would that—"

"I wish to make certain he remembers that I outrank him." He shrugged out of his nightshirt and tossed it onto the bed. He hated wearing the damned things, and if the blasted weather would warm up, he wouldn't bother with them. "At least, I do for the moment, anyway."

After he dressed in a stolid brown coat that looked better suited to a banker than a nobleman, he dropped the diamond pin into his waistcoat pocket and asked Martin to remain in his chambers. "I will be going out directly, and in something less . . . stiff."

"You look better in your worst than most do in their best, if I say so myself."

Jack grinned. "Compliments like that will get you an extra five quid in your pay envelope, Martin."

The valet bowed his long frame. "They always do, my lord."

As he made his way downstairs, Jack reflected that his little game seemed to be skittering a bit off the path. Last evening Lilith had been amusing, by God—five times brighter than any other debutante he'd had the misfortune to come across. He loved a challenge, and whether she intended it or not, Lilith had just raised the stakes. Knowing she had the wits for a battle would make her imminent downfall even more entertaining.

William, though, was another sort entirely. He'd never seen a lad so determined to earn a tarnished reputation since—well, since himself. It was actually quite enlightening to view the proceedings from the far end of the hell he had put himself through when he'd come into the title at seventeen. Of course, he'd been on his own then. William was far luckier. There was no more willing, or proficient, tutor than himself when it came to self-destruction.

Peese stood waiting for him at the bottom of the stairs. "My lord," the butler said, handing over Dolph Remdale's card, "I informed Mr. Remdale that you hadn't yet risen, but his reply was unrepeatable."

"So repeat it."

Peese grinned. "He said I was to get you and whatever plum-assed baggage you were rutting with out of bed and downstairs immediately."

"Hm. Did he want to see me or the baggage?"

"He didn't say, milord, but I assumed it was you."

With a fleeting smile, Jack examined the calling card. Finely inked and bordered with delicate swirls, its refined effect was spoiled by the sweat-stained, bent edges. Dolph Remdale was obviously not in a good mood. "Thank you, Peese. I will require breakfast in five minutes."

"In the morning room, my lord?" the butler asked in confusion.

Jack glanced at him. "If you insist."

Peese squinted, then gave up trying to interpret the remark. "Yes, my lord." The butler stepped down the hallway and opened the door to the morning room.

The heir presumptive to the Duke of Wenford stood

scowling out the front window. There was one thing for which Jack could be grateful to Lilith Benton: making trouble for the Remdales was something he would gladly do. Lilith was a damned fool to take up with Wenford, title or not. Then again, she'd been a damned fool for insulting the Marquis of Dansbury. For a bright chit, she seemed to make poor choices rather regularly.

Jack paused in the doorway to watch his guest. Antonia St. Gerard had on several occasions referred to Randolph Remdale as London's blond Adonis. It was widely speculated that the only reason he hadn't married was that he hadn't yet come across a woman grand enough to be the Duchess of Wenford once he inherited the title. Jack suspected his continued bachelorhood had more to do with Remdale's short temper and his unwillingness to share the mirrors in his home on St. George's Street.

"Good morning, Remdale," he drawled, strolling into the room. "Should I go through the pretense of asking why you're here, or shall we just—"

"This is beyond belief," Dolph snarled, turning to glare at Jack with his much-admired blue eyes. "I told you I would make good on that pin. There was no need for you to go about flaunting it in public."

Jack nodded, unmoved. The reason he had gone to the trouble of winning everything out of Dolph's pockets last night, and then suggesting the pin as collateral, was so he *could* go about flaunting it, after all. "I believe what you said was, 'Take the damned thing and be done with it.' " He reached over to adjust Sir Joshua Reynolds' portrait of his father. The old marquis hadn't quite managed a smile even for immortality. Thank God his wife had been imbued with sense of humor enough for both of them. "Or do I err?"

"Bastard," Remdale grunted, then pulled a bulging

leather purse from his pocket. "Here." He tossed the thing onto the table.

For a moment the marquis was surprised. "Where did you come up with the blunt?" Twenty-four hours ago, Dolph had been completely to let.

"None of your damned affair, Dansbury. Where's the pin?"

Jack casually pulled the diamond from his pocket and examined it. "Hm," he mused, "Uncle Geoffrey paying your gambling debts, now?"

Dolph's jaw clenched. "Give me the pin."

Jack tossed it to him. "In the future I suggest you not gamble with family heirlooms. Uncle Geoffrey seemed none too pleased to have it escape his clutches."

Dolph flushed, his face becoming the blotchy red which characterized Remdale rages. "You dog," he hissed. "I should call you out over this."

That sounded promising. If there was one thing experience had taught him about the Remdales, though, it was that they didn't begin fights they couldn't win. Not without a considerable push. But Jack would be pleased to push Dolph, or better yet, his uncle, all the way to hell.

Behind him, Peese scratched at the door and entered with his breakfast tray.

Jack's eyes lit on the bowl of marmalade, and on an impulse he snatched up the bowl and dashed the contents into Dolph Remdale's face. "Will this convince you to call me out?"

Dolph sputtered and stumbled backward, swiping at the sticky orange jam running down the front of his fine coat. "You damned blackguard!"

"So?" Jack returned, examining his nails. "I asked if you were going to call me out."

Dolph glared at him, uneasiness abruptly vying with

the fury on his face. Marmalade dripped down his perfect Roman nose, and he angrily wiped at it. "I'll do worse." He shoved past Jack and the silent Peese. "I'll ruin you. You will regret this." Remdale stomped down the hallway and out the front door.

"Blasted coward," Jack said calmly, looking after Dolph and licking marmalade from his finger.

"My lord?"

Jack turned to his butler. "Yes, Peese?"

"Was that why you wanted breakfast?"

The marquis snorted and replaced the bowl on the tray. "Would that I possessed such powers of premonition." He headed out the door, already anticipating his next encounter with Lilith Benton. Her brother would know her schedule for the evening. "Have the tray sent up to my chambers, if you please. And have Benedick saddled." He'd promised to assist William Benton with purchasing a new mount, and there would be several very expensive ones at the auctions today. Antonia was partial to black Arabians, something he would mention to the young cub. "As long as I've been dragged out of bed at this ungodly hour, I may as well try to get something accomplished."

The butler looked down at the orange globules spattered over the expensive and elegant Persian carpet, and sighed. "'Something accomplished'?" he muttered. "What does he call this?"

Vauxhall Gardens was a carnival of competing noise. In daylight, the pleasure gardens were uncrowded and quiet, one of Lilith's favorite places. In the evenings during the Season, though, the wild soirées and fireworks displays were legendary. If it hadn't been for Lady Georgina's presence, her father would never have

allowed her to attend. She was halfway to wishing he
hadn't permitted it, anyway.

"Lilith, do quit scowling. It'll ruin your complexion."

Lilith looked away from the sight of Lord Greeley and
Mr. Aames wading through the Gardens' central fountain, singing a ballad about some Scottish maiden with
whom they were apparently quite intimately acquainted.
"I'm not scowling, Georgina. I simply don't understand
how some people can behave so foolishly."

Her companion leaned over the side of their rented
box to get a better look at the gentleman. "My papa
says everyone is foolish." She giggled as the two men
waved at her. "Some are just less skilled at hiding it."

Behind Georgina's back, Pen wrinkled her nose. Lilith
stifled a smile. Georgina was a bit feather-brained, in
addition to being nearsighted, but as her dowry was pur-
ported to be ten thousand pounds, her intelligence and
her eyesight probably didn't matter. Lilith sighed and
looked toward the gazebo, where the orchestra played a
beautifully rendered piece by Haydn. She was aware that
she was considered to be a beauty, which meant she was
viewed as superficially as Georgina. No one cared if she
could wield a wicked metaphor.

A confectioner's cart rounded the hedge, and she
straightened. "I'm going to get a strawberry ice," she
declared, needing a rest from giggling nonsense for a
moment. "Does anyone else wish one?"

"No, thank you." Pen shivered. "It's too cold already."

When Georgina, the marchioness, and Lady Sanford
declined as well, Lilith stepped down from their box and
strolled over to purchase her ice. As she paid her shil-
ling, the Duke of Wenford's gravel-bucket voice
sounded from somewhere behind her. Lilith flinched.

With a stifled curse, not stopping to question her wisdom, she hurried toward the protection of the gazebo. She couldn't face Wenford without Pen or William there to help extricate her from any difficulties. The duke's voice came again, closer still, and she looked over her shoulder as she ducked behind the structure—and immediately crashed into someone.

"I'm sorry," she said, reaching out to steady herself and finding her elbow gripped. "How clumsy of—"

"Not at all, Miss Benton," the Marquis of Dansbury returned, looking down at her with dancing eyes. "How rude of me to be standing to one side of the path like that."

"What are you doing here?" she demanded.

At her jerk, he relinquished his grip on her arm. "Actually, I was listening to the orchestra."

"There are benches around front for that purpose." Belatedly, she stepped backward to put distance between them.

A male voice said something from around the turn of the hedge, and the Duke of Wenford answered. Lilith jumped again. She had thought to escape His Grace, and now she would be plunged into the middle of another confrontation between him and Dansbury!

"I didn't wish to risk my reputation by being seen sitting on a bench without a companion." Dansbury tilted his head, dark hunter's eyes studying her. "Perhaps you'd care to join me."

"You must be joking." She glanced over her shoulder.

He raised an eyebrow, following Lilith's gaze before he returned his attention to her. "Are you in some difficulty?"

"No."

"Not avoiding anyone, are you?"

Blast him, he was every bit as quick as William

bragged. "If I were, it would be you," she countered.

The marquis nodded agreeably as his eyes focused on something past her shoulder. "Just as a point of information, though, you might wish to know that your fifth suitor is coming around—"

Lilith whipped around, frantically trying to think of some way to escape Wenford's presence. Before she could react, Dansbury yanked her backward through a cluster of bushes.

"Don't you dare—"

"Shh," he chastised, putting his finger over her lips.

Lilith looked at him, startled at the touch, then slapped his hand away. She turned to stalk back out of the bushes, then heard Wenford on the other side of the gazebo—where he would have a clear view of her if she departed. When she turned around again, Dansbury was still watching her, his expression speculative.

"You truly don't want Old Hatchet Face's attentions," he said.

"That is none of your concern," she snapped as loudly as she dared.

He shrugged. "Then I shall depart," he told her, turning to walk away.

"Don't you dare leave me to follow you out of here, as though we've been up to something," she hissed.

He stopped and looked over his shoulder at her. "You request my company, then?"

"I didn't ask you to drag me into the shrubbery, and I won't have myself ruined over it." She narrowed her eyes. "But that's your intention, no doubt."

The marquis returned to stand in front of her, pursing his lips. "If I were trying to ruin you, we would both be wearing fewer clothes."

"Hah," she scoffed, trying not to blush. "Is this one of the subtle seductions you are teaching my brother? I fear, then, that he is doomed to celibacy.''

Unexpectedly, Dansbury chuckled. ''If you disbelieve my pure, good-hearted intentions, Miss Benton, then leave.''

''I will. As soon as you look and see whether His Grace is still there.''

With a slight bow, the marquis turned and parted the branches. ''He's still there, lecturing Greeley. Looks as though that idiot's been wading in the fountain again.''

''Again?'' she repeated. Lilith craned her neck to see over his shoulder, and instead caught herself studying the lean, rugged line of his jaw. When he looked back at her, his eyes seemed genuinely amused, the cynicism for once missing.

''Greeley seems to end up in some pool of water or other at least twice a Season. He is something of a toad, though, so I suppose it's not all that surprising.''

Greeley *was* somewhat frog-eyed, and a corner of her mouth quirked. ''That's not amusing.''

Dansbury contorted his face into an expression of mortified dismay. ''Oh, my, is Greeley a seventh suitor of yours? I had no idea. Please, let me tender my most sincere apol—''

''He is not a suitor,'' she said, beyond impatience. ''And neither are you, my lord.''

''But I can think of nothing but your heavenly smile,'' he protested, the picture of innocence as his own deucedly attractive smile touched his mouth, ''and tasting your sweet lips. How can you so callously banish me from your heart?''

''I am surprised you have any place for thoughts of me at all, with the amount of time you spend pursuing hazard, faro, port, and brandy,'' she retorted, unsettled. Not even Lionel had dared suggest he thought about kissing her. The evening's fireworks began close by, and she jumped at the sudden noise.

He laughed again, softly, and reached out to straighten the blue shawl draped across her shoulders. His fingers were warm even through his gloves as they brushed the base of her throat, and her pulse leapt in response. "You exaggerate. I almost never drink brandy."

"And this is supposed to redeem you, you scoundrel?" she countered in her most hostile voice.

"One can only hope." He took a step toward her, so only a few scant inches separated them. A white cascade of glittering light lit the night above his head and made his eyes sparkle. "Do you mean there is no charity in your heart for a poor, misguided soul such as myself?"

"You've guided yourself astray," she informed him, backing up, "and my poor brother, as well." Her thoughts and her wits seemed to have scattered, and she fought to keep an affronted expression on her face.

"Then he is safe," the marquis murmured, "for my path leads straight back to you."

That was what she was afraid of. She should simply turn and leave, Wenford or not, but the rogue was not going to have the last word. "You will find that the gate is locked, my lord."

"I'll jump the hedge."

Of all the things she had expected, Lilith had never imagined Dansbury could be silly. "I shall buy a large dog," she answered shakily. Why was the blackguard being charming when he knew she despised him?

He grinned. "Then I shall be bitten, whereas now I am but smitten."

"Smiting you would be my pleasure," she returned, her voice faltering a little at the end.

"Come now," he chastised. "You want me dead for approaching you to ask a waltz?" He reached out again, gently tucking a stray strand of hair behind her ear.

Lilith took a ragged breath, trying to regain control of her senses. "You know what I mean," she said, as soon as she regained control of her voice. If he would stop touching her and looking at her in that intense, heart-stopping manner, she would be able to give him the set-down he deserved.

"Please, explain it to me. I wish to know your thoughts."

"Very well. I want you to leave William alone."

"I can't do that," he answered promptly. "I'm quite fond of the lad."

"You're ruining him. And that will destroy my father, which will . . ." she faltered, not wanting to disclose something he didn't already know. There was apparently little, though, that the marquis didn't seem to know. "Which will . . . hurt me." She met his gaze. "Unless that is your intention, I beg you to stop."

His eyes searched hers. In the cold night breeze a lock of dark hair had fallen across his forehead, making him look boyish and far more innocent than she knew him to be. Finally he smiled, less innocently and more sensuously than before. "Will you not sacrifice something to save your brother from such evil as I apparently represent?"

She narrowed her eyes, thankful that she could rally her anger again. "You truly have no heart at all," she stated hotly. "A gentleman, anyone possessing *any* kindness, would not do what you are doing."

He grinned crookedly. "But you've already informed me that I have no positive qualities whatsoever. So how could I possibly make use of them? Perhaps I have sought you out as my last chance of salvation. You are as beautiful as any of heaven's angels, Lilith. Could you, would you, save me?"

Lilith's heart began to beat wildly in trepidation and something more as he leaned toward her, his gaze focusing on her lips. "I—"

"Miss Benton," a male voice called sharply, and she jumped again.

The Earl of Nance fought his way through the shrubbery to face the marquis. Thank goodness it wasn't Wenford, or any other of her suitors—Lionel Hendrick at least had some sense in his head.

"Has Dansbury offended you?" Nance demanded, glaring at the marquis.

Jack smiled lazily. "Yes, Miss Benton, have I offended you?"

She wanted to slap him for nearly kissing her, and for making her wonder what it would be like. Lionel, though, looked aggravated enough to push for a fight. She certainly had no wish to be involved in one of Dansbury's scandals, which he appeared to regard with such amusement.

Lilith shook her head. "I simply no longer wish to converse with him."

"Allow me, then, to escort you back to your friends, whom I discovered looking for you a few moments ago." Nance tucked her hand around his forearm.

"Yes, by all means," the marquis agreed easily. "But beware, Miss Benton. Your ice is melting."

She looked at him sharply. His gesture, though, was toward the strawberry ice she still clutched in one hand. She'd forgotten about it. Lilith glared at him for effect, then turned to Nance. "Thank you, my lord," she smiled sweetly, "for your assistance."

As they emerged from the bushes, she looked about warily. The duke was nowhere in sight, and she had to wonder whether the marquis hadn't made up the tale of Wenford's continued presence to keep her hidden with him. She glanced back to give Dansbury a cold parting glance, but he was gone, vanished in the dark as if into thin air.

The faint smell of brimstone from the fireworks drifted by as she and Nance returned to the Sanfords' box. Perhaps Jack Faraday *was* the actual devil. He'd already possessed William, and now he was after her. He would find, though, that she was not so timid and easily cowed as he believed. However charming he thought himself, this was one little game that the Marquis of Dansbury was not going to win.

"Jack, would you please explain to me once more what in God's name we are doing here?" Ogden Price muttered. He nodded halfheartedly at the shocked-looking cluster of women standing a short distance away from them.

"We are attending a tea-tasting," Jack said calmly, putting another biscuit on the small plate he carried. "And do try smiling, before you frighten the poor dears. You're becoming entirely bracket-faced."

"And you're becoming entirely demented," Price hissed back. "Why didn't you convince your sister or Antonia to come along, instead of dragging me into this hell?"

Jack's determinedly pleasant smile became more strained for a moment. "Antonia is nocturnal. And my sister's side of the family doesn't speak to me, remember? Besides, a little civilization is good for the soul."

"You haven't a soul." Price sighed. "Otherwise, you never would have done this to me. Pass me a damned biscuit."

Across the room, the tittering and whispering females looked like a flock of frightened hens herding away from a fox. To complete Jack's torture, Lilith Benton had yet to make her appearance. William Benton was going to find himself in considerable trouble if he was wrong about her plans for today. "Honey, or blueberry?"

"Honey, damn your eyes."

"If you please, Price, do watch your tongue." He took a bite of biscuit, smiled grandly, and addressed one of the women in the corner. "I say, Mrs. Falshond, these are marvelous. You must see that my cook receives the recipe. That spice I taste couldn't be cinnamon, could it?"

Mrs. Falshond perked up and ventured a few steps forward. "It is cinnamon, my lord. The secret ingredient of a very old family recipe."

Jack nodded and elbowed Price to try a bite. "I do hope you don't mind sharing it."

"Of course not, my lord." Their hostess preened like a peacock and playfully slapped her hand against his sleeve.

Evidently she'd decided he was harmless today, and though that was Jack's aim, her gullibility amazed him. "Splendid."

Mrs. Falshond clapped her hands imperiously. "Shall we proceed, ladies?" As she turned back, her smile brightened further. "Mrs. Farlane, Miss Benton. So pleased you could come. I believe you are acquainted with everyone present."

The marquis turned to see Lilith Benton wiping surprise from her face as she quickly looked away from him and took her hostess's hand. "Indeed I am, Mrs. Falshond. Thank you for inviting us."

Jack watched Lilith as she glanced once more in his direction, then quickly away. He felt it again—that queer lifting of his heart which seemed to coincide with her presence. He'd felt it for the first time last night—light, airy, and completely absurd—when she'd slammed into him at the Gardens. He'd canceled his weekly fencing bout to track her down and find out if it would happen again. He was both intrigued and consternated that it had.

Jack spent the next hour sampling teas from around the world, and charming a roomful of hostile females. Miss Benton remained uncharacteristically silent, but over the course of their several encounters, he had noted that she only seemed to voice her opinion when there was no one of import to overhear her. Evidently she considered him to be of no import—which was acceptable, if it provided him with the opportunity to continue speaking with her.

Something about the entire situation was askew, but that realization was as intriguing as was the chit herself. Finally he cornered her between a table and the fireplace, while Price unenthusiastically occupied Mrs. Falshond and Lilith's annoying aunt.

"Good afternoon, Miss Benton," he said, reaching over her shoulder for a teacake.

She started and then quickly glanced in her aunt's direction. "Lord Dansbury."

He smiled as she picked up a pastry, keeping her back carefully turned to him. She might think she was doing her duty by ignoring him, but she certainly made no other attempt to get away. "Have you tried the Madagascar blend?" he asked, brushing his hand down her sleeve as he indicated the nearest teapot.

"No." She stayed where she was, as though rooted to the spot.

"I recommend it," he continued, reaching for another teacake and trapping her between his body and the table. "Quite subtle, with a light tang of spice in the aftertaste."

"Really."

Lilith lowered her head to set down her plate, and Jack very nearly kissed the slender, curved nape of her neck. He took a deep breath, wondering for a fleeting moment just who was seducing whom. "Rather like you, I would imagine."

"Do go away," she whispered.

"Do face me when you're speaking to me," he returned.

Tightly she shook her head. "I'm *not* speaking to you."

"I beg to differ." She smelled of lavender and tea, and as his breath lightly touched her hair, she shivered. "You are speaking volumes."

Lilith's shoulders heaved with the breath she took, then she turned around and met his gaze directly. "*Now* will you go away?"

Price cleared his throat, indicating he'd lost his sway over the two hens.

"One day," Jack murmured to Lilith, bringing her hand to his lips and softly kissing her knuckles, "you will ask me to stay."

"Lilith," her aunt's stern voice came.

"I shall not, my lord."

He smiled and returned her plate to her hands. "We shall see."

Lilith and Aunt Eugenia headed directly from the tea sampling to join Penelope and Lady Sanford at their dressmaker's. Eugenia immediately plunked herself down beside Lady Sanford in the shop window. "Imagine my horror, Daphne," she said breathlessly, "at stepping into the room to see the devil himself there before us. The Marquis of Dansbury, pretending to be interested in sampling tea!"

Pen looked sideways at Lilith. "Dansbury was there?" she mouthed.

Trying to overhear the rest of her aunt's remarks, Lilith gave a small nod. As the conversation turned to a recitation of Dansbury's past duels and mad, drunken wagers, she impatiently stepped over to eye the nearly finished gown draped over a mannequin. "Are you certain it's not too daring?" she asked the dressmaker.

"*Mais non, mademoiselle*," Madame Belieu protested. "You will see when you try it on. It will be *parfaite*."

Lilith had her doubts. The emerald green silk was quite low-cut—something that the Marquis of Dansbury would no doubt find perfectly acceptable, but his standards were so low as to be practically invisible.

Aunt Eugenia scowled. "It's perfectly—"

"Lovely." Lady Sanford smiled approvingly. "It will show you off to fine advantage. And with the cold weather, dark colors are quite fashionable this Season. A splendid choice, Eugenia."

"Hm. Thank you, Daphne," Eugenia said, sending the gown another distasteful look.

Lilith smiled gratefully. The gown was truly beautiful, and she had never been allowed to wear such a thing before.

"I will have it and the gold one delivered to you tomorrow, *mademoiselle*."

She had been hoping for something new to wear to the Rochmont ball. "Thank you, *madame*."

While Aunt Eugenia asked Madame Belicu if the new French silks had arrived, Pen cornered Lilith. "So tell me, Lil—what did he do?" she whispered.

"Nothing." Lilith tried unsuccessfully to banish the provoking, handsome marquis and his dratted attractive smiles from her mind. "He sampled tea."

"Truly?"

"Shh. Yes, truly. Now stop talking about him. Please."

"But, Lil," Pen insisted, pulling her friend toward the far corner of the shop, "when I told Mary Fitzroy that the Marquis of Dansbury wanted to be one of your suitors, she—"

"Pen, you didn't!" She couldn't have stories like that going around! Such a rumor, especially after the supposedly coincidental meetings at the recital and the opera, might discourage Wenford—which would be the one positive thing about Dansbury's tormenting her. But it might also discourage the Earl of Nance and all her other suitors from continuing their pursuit.

"Mary won't tell," Pen insisted stoutly. "And she said he's never pursued anyone. He must truly be smitten with you."

"Nonsense," Lilith returned, her pulse jumping at the words. Suitors simply didn't behave the way the marquis did. Besides, she had handed him enough insults to discourage even the most ardent of suitors, and he had shown no sign of anything but amusement. "I seriously doubt he's smitten with anyone but himself," she said. "And I'm certainly not attracted to him."

"But he's so handsome." Pen batted her eyes and sighed.

That was the problem. Everyone should look as they truly were, she had decided last night when she couldn't sleep. It would be much simpler if rogues simply looked like rogues. Then she wouldn't be tempted by their looks and compelling presence before she knew their despicable character. "You're the one who told me he shot a woman. And everyone knows how disreputable he is. And he's ruining William. And he's only angry because I insulted him, so he's trying to get even. And—"

"Are you certain?"

"Of course I'm certain," she answered vehemently. "Why else in the world would someone like the Marquis of Dansbury concern himself with me?" Despite what he'd said to her, he certainly wasn't seeking salvation. She hadn't figured it out entirely yet, but he was somehow cleverly trying to arrange her ruination.

"Oh, I don't know, Lil," Pen admitted, shrugging. "But I find it hard to believe that anyone could dislike you, much less want to hurt you."

"His villainy knows no bounds," Lilith pointed out. "It may sound melodramatic, Pen, but you know it's true."

"Yes, I suppose I do." Her friend sighed. "It just seems so romantic, for a rakehell to set his sights on you and threaten your virtue."

"My virtue can do very well without being threatened," Lilith returned dryly.

The front bell rang, and a tall, dark-haired woman entered the shop in the company of her maid. Despite the pelisse and heavy wrap, her rounded belly proclaimed her to be several months pregnant.

Madame Belieu excused herself to greet her newest arrival. "Lady Hutton," she smiled, taking the young woman's hand and gesturing her to a chair, "you look *enchanteresse* today."

"Thank you for your kind lies, *madame*," Lady Hutton replied with a rueful smile that crinkled the corners of her eyes.

"I would have been pleased to send the dress over to you, my lady." The dressmaker motioned to one of her seamstresses to fetch the garment.

"Oh, heavens, no," the lady protested. "Richard is determined to keep me prisoner until the end of summer. This is one of the few places I'm allowed to escape to."

With a smile of her own, Lady Sanford stepped forward to shake the woman's hand. "Alison," she said warmly, "I don't believe you've met my daughter, Penelope, or Eugenia Farlane." She turned to indicate Lilith. "And Mrs. Farlane's niece, Miss Benton. Eugenia, Pen, Lilith, this is Lady Hutton."

Pen dipped a curtsey. "Pleased to meet you."

"Lady Hutton," Lilith seconded. Alison Hutton was lovely, with light brown eyes and an olive complexion that spoke of a French or Spanish ancestry. She had an easy smile, which appeared again as she met Lilith's gaze.

"Ladies. Forgive me for not rising, but it is easier to find one place and remain stationary, these days."

"Of course." Amused, Lilith smiled back at her.

Aunt Eugenia was nodding. "Your husband is a baron—Richard, Lord Hutton—is he not?"

"Yes, he is," Lady Hutton answered promptly, not seeming in the least offended by the direct question. "Do you know him?"

"You own the Linfield estate in Shropshire, then."

"Yes. How do you know Richard?"

"Lord Dupont, who used to live down the lane from you at Hawben Hall, was a friend to my late husband."

"Oh, yes. Richard's spoken often of Lord Dupont. Shortly before he passed away, he gave Richard and his mother most of his late wife's roses. They are astounding."

Lilith's ears perked up at the mention of roses. As though sensing her interest, Aunt Eugenia gestured at her. "My niece keeps a garden here and back at Hamble Hall. Little as we like her grubbing about in the dirt, the girl loves roses."

"Aunt," Lilith admonished, smiling reluctantly.

Mucking about in the dirt to tend roses was one of the few vices she insisted on exercising.

Lady Hutton looked at her and chuckled. "My husband has a mad passion for them, as well. I have friends who think it rather foppish of him, but my brother, at least, says it shows backbone."

"Exactly so," Lilith agreed. The seamstress appeared with a lovely green and violet–colored evening gown, and Lilith came forward to help Lady Hutton to her feet.

"You know, my husband would love to trade if you have anything unusual. You must call on us." Her expression turned rueful again. "I'm afraid that is a rather bald way of saying I could use another visitor. Being held prisoner isn't nearly as romantic or exciting as one might think."

Lilith chuckled. "I would be pleased to come visit you, Lady Hutton. Roses or not."

"William, when trying to drink someone under the table, the object is to become inebriated less quickly than they," Dansbury pointed out.

Even at two o'clock in the morning, the crowds at White's had barely begun to thin. Lady Helfer's soirée was tonight, but no one under the age of seventy was ever invited, and there were no other soirées or balls of note. Still, it seemed a large number of lords preferred smoking and playing cards to being at home with their wives. He grinned slyly as he spotted Viscount Davenglen. He knew for a fact that Lady Davenglen was anything but lonely this evening, because Ernest Landon had slipped off to pay his respects some hours ago.

"You're the one who keeps refilling the damned glass," William returned.

"And you're the one who keeps emptying it." When he had begun the task of leading William Benton to ruin,

Jack had expected the boy to be a slow-witted country dullard. What he was discovering was that although the lad lacked a little town polish, he also lacked town cynicism and the common predisposition toward judging one's fellows. That alone lifted him several steps above most of the London *ton*. William's naïveté was actually somewhat refreshing, even if it did tend to complicate matters further—as had Lilith's plea to spare her the pain her brother's destruction would bring about, blast her. That had actually bothered him, to the point that he'd led his cronies to White's rather than to Antonia's. Not that William had been the least bloody bit grateful to receive a night's reprieve from ruination.

"You're drinking as much as I am, Dansbury," William protested.

The table dealer stifled a smile as he dealt a hand. Across from him, Ogden Price was chuckling, but it appeared that Thomas Hanlon had as much need for the lesson as William, for he was asleep in his chair. Jack raised a finger at William. "It *appears* that I am drinking as much as you are."

Price's grin folded into an affronted frown. "You've been tossing your port?"

He smiled lazily. "Among other things."

His crony shook his head. "I'll be damned. For how long?"

"Whenever the mood strikes me." As it had tonight, for he needed at least some of his wits in order to get Lilith's schedule from her brother. Given her reaction to him at the tea sampling, he wondered whether she was beginning to soften toward him just a little. That would be all the edge he needed, and he wasn't going to ruin it by hanging William this evening.

"But I never saw you dumping your glass," Mr. Benton stated, leaning forward to eye Jack's sleeve.

"Actually, I've been using that potted plant behind you. I'm afraid it will have quite a head in the morning." Jack made a show of stretching. "I shall as well. I'm nearly all in."

"But I'm down two hundred quid," William protested, cursing and shoving his cards back at the dealer.

Jack looked at him for a moment, waiting for the tingle of conscience that would tell him his life was becoming far out of balance. He sighed. "How much were you willing to lose tonight, my boy?"

"About half that," William returned, after a hesitation. He banged his fist on the table. "I didn't think your blasted run would last all night."

"It's lasted for years, William," Price informed him. He tipped his glass at Jack and drank down the contents. "I don't believe in throwing away port, weak or not."

Across the room, a flurry of movement began in the entryway, and Jack looked up. The Duke of Wenford entered and was quickly ushered into the second gaming room. Evidently the proprietors of White's didn't want a repeat of the Felton ball incident in their parlors.

Dansbury forced a chuckle and raised his own glass. "Hate to waste the stuff, myself." He drained it. Price was correct; it was definitely watered down. He called one of the footmen over for a fresh bottle. "One of mine this time, if you please, Freeling."

The head footman bowed and headed off toward the kitchens.

"I still can't believe you keep your own store of port at every demmed club in town," William marveled.

"I've noticed you have no trouble drinking it," Jack returned dryly.

"And neither do I," Price put in. "William, do come with me to the Admiralty after we drink all of Jack's wine," he cajoled.

The marquis shook his head, Lilith Benton's damned threads of guilt still pulling at him. "He's already out two hundred pounds, Price. Leave us something to play with tomorrow."

William looked relieved, and the marquis reflected that with the help of Antonia and the other cronies in his circle, young Mr. Benton was probably dropping five hundred quid a week. Still, a few days ago he would have suggested the jaunt to the Admiralty himself.

"William, I would appreciate your taking this sage advice to heart: never, and I repeat, never, wager more than you can afford to lose. It puts you in debt to all sorts of disreputable people. Like me." Perhaps he was more swaggered than he thought, to be actually warning the boy off from himself.

"According to my sister, you're just about the worst thing that could happen to me," William noted happily, finishing off the last of their old bottle. "You're a devil, she says, and just this evening she called you a malignant Jack-a-dandy. Rather clever, don't you think?"

Jack looked at him, his amusement draining away. "She called me a *what?*"

"A malignant Jack-a-dandy."

"It seems the cold north wind is still blowing." Price studied the cards in his hand, refusing to meet Jack's angry glare.

So much for going to the effort of behaving himself. That obviously wasn't working. "You know, speaking of dear Miss Benton, last I saw her, she looked rather tired. It's been a busy Season for her, hasn't it?"

William nodded. "Father thought the same thing. He told Lil she didn't have to go to the Billington breakfast recital in the morning. Wouldn't let me out of it, though, dash it all.'' He gripped Jack's sleeve with his fingers. ''Do you go, Jack?''

The marquis scowled and twitched his coat out of William's grip. ''Breakfast and recitals have never much appealed to me, especially in conjunction.''

Price chuckled again. ''I thought only disreputables like Jack stayed away from Billington's famous breakfasts.''

''The whole reason I became disreputable, actually.'' Lilith Benton would be home, alone, tomorrow morning. It was well past time he stopped dancing about her like a schoolboy and made his next move.

''Dansbury,'' a gruff voice said behind him, and Jack stiffened.

''Your Grace,'' he drawled, turning. He wished that for once he could leave an establishment without becoming involved in some sort of imbroglio, unless he'd actually intended one. He noted that the diamond pin was back in Wenford's cravat, no doubt for all the *ton* to see that the duke had set things to right. Fleetingly he wondered how Dolph felt about being relieved of the family heirloom a second time.

''Just wanted to say that what's done is done,'' the duke said stiffly, and held out his bony hand.

It was a poor apology, and not nearly enough to compensate for the longstanding bad blood between the Faradays and the Remdales. Jack held the old man's gaze, then reached for the bottle of port the footman had just placed on the table and pushed it into the duke's waiting hand. ''My compliments,'' he said, and turned back to the game.

His Grace remained awkwardly beside the table, obviously trying to decide whether the slight was worth beginning another shouting match or not. ''Ah,'' he finally said, then cleared his throat. ''Very good.''

''You've got brass, Dansbury,'' Price murmured, as the duke turned and walked away.

''It was a bloody good vintage,'' Jack returned with a scowl, motioning for the dealer to proceed.

Chapter 5

"**I** truly don't mind going to the breakfast, Papa."
Lilith leaned against the door of her father's bed chamber while he finished his morning's toilette. She had already dressed, hoping he would give in and let her go to Billington's. It was one of the few events this Season she'd actually been looking forward to attending. The breakfasts were famous, and the duke held them only once a Season. Everyone who was anyone was supposed to be there.

She wondered if the Marquis of Dansbury would have managed to get himself invited to such a prestigious event, then determinedly cast the thought aside. Undoubtedly he hadn't even returned yet from his evening's rambles, and if there was one thing she knew about Billington's breakfasts, it was that no bad *ton* were invited. Ever. If William had begun his association with Dansbury a few weeks earlier, no doubt he would have found himself excluded, as well.

"Nonsense, Lilith," the viscount said over his shoulder, while his valet put the final touches on his cravat for him. "There's no need for you to be tiring yourself out. Especially with the Rochmont ball this evening.

79

Your aunt and I, and William, if he manages to stay awake through the meal, will make your excuses.''

Lilith sighed and fiddled with the pearl earring pinching her right ear. ''All right.'' She hesitated again. ''And Papa, I do hope you understand my feelings about His Grace. I simply cannot marry such a . . . dreadful man. As I said last night, I will happily wed anyone else you see fit to choose. I apol—''

He waved her off with one hand, picking up his gloves with the other. ''I heard you last night. Wenford is a highly respected man, and a joining of our families would have put us above reproach. But you, fickle girl, decide he has too many gray hairs on his head, and you won't have him.''

''That's not it, Papa. Truly.''

''Bah. With all those pretty words that've been whispered in your ear by every eligible lord in London, I've no doubt you have your handsome fool all picked out for yourself. Who is he, Lilith, some baron's third son?''

The accusation surprised her, for of course, no one had captured her heart. She hadn't been looking to find love. ''There is no one, Papa.'' He continued to look at her suspiciously, and she put a hand on his arm. ''I won't shame you.''

He turned his back. ''That's what your mother used to say,'' he muttered. ''Those green eyes of hers held nothing but lies.''

''I'm not Mama.''

''I keep praying my blood will be stronger in you than hers. William's already falling into her flighty ways.''

Although Lilith disliked the pain that showed in her father's eyes whenever he spoke of Elizabeth Benton, she did wish sometimes that he would remember that he wasn't the only one who had been hurt by Lady Hamble's flight. ''You'll see, Papa,'' she said encouragingly.

"I'll make you proud of me. Of our family."

He leaned over to touch his lips to her forehead. "I know you will. And don't trouble yourself about Wenford. I'm certain everything will work itself out."

Lilith smiled in relief. It generally took him ages to recover from the foul mood any discussion of her mother put him into. "Thank you."

William, still half foxed from whatever he and the Marquis of Dansbury had been up to last night, would have been more than happy to trade places with her, but it was clear that their father had no intention of letting him escape. Aunt Eugenia seemed none too pleased that Lilith was to remain, either, but when her father insisted that the girl needed her rest, the arguing finally stopped and Bevins let them out the front entry.

Once they were gone, Lilith wandered about the house for a few minutes, reveling in the quiet, for Wednesday was the day most of the servants were given leave to go about their own business. She headed outside to cut a bouquet of Lord Penzance roses from the garden. As she later arranged the flowers in the hall, someone began rapping at the front door.

It was too early for visitors, and she frowned as Bevins appeared to pull open the door. The Duke of Wenford pushed past the butler without so much as a by-your-leave. Lilith stifled a dismayed curse and turned to make her escape, but he spied her immediately.

"Lilith," he rasped, coming forward to take her hand and kiss her knuckles.

It was the greatest show of affection he had ever granted her, and because of what it implied, it was also the most frightening. "Your Grace," she exclaimed, forcing a smile and quickly pulling her hand free.

He was still in his evening clothes, the diamond pin back through the withered cravat hanging about his ca-

daverous neck. He or Dolph Remdale must have paid
Dansbury the money he had so rudely requested.

"I require a word with you," the duke said, reeling
as he reached for her hand again. His usually pale complexion was flushed and clammy looking, and Lilith realized that he was drunk. Very drunk. And whatever
he'd been imbibing didn't look to have agreed with his
constitution, though it had apparently served to render
him more amiable than she had ever before seen him.

"Of course, Your Grace. Except I'm not actually entertaining this morning." It was also far too early to go
calling; if this was a proposal, as she feared it must be,
Wenford's timing was inexcusable—for anyone but
Wenford.

"This is not entertainment," he returned, reaching for
her again. "This is business."

Lilith sidestepped. "Allow me to fetch my maid,
then." She gestured the duke toward the morning room,
but when she glanced over her shoulder, he was following close behind her. "If Your Grace would care to
wait?" she suggested, nervous and irritated.

"Your father is at Billington's," he stated.

Lilith leaned up the staircase and called for Emily, but
there was no answer. "I'm certain he'll be back
shortly," she offered stiffly. She'd forgotten; Emily
would be at her cousin's house for the day, visiting.

"Oh, I doubt that," Wenford grunted. "Billington's
breakfasts are splendid."

"Then don't you wish to partake?" Lilith suggested
hopefully.

"Stomach's rather spoiled this morning." He captured her hand again. "Besides, I wish to partake of
you." He tugged her closer. "A little premarital bliss."
Before she could react, he planted a stale, fetid kiss on
her lips.

His breath reeked of liquor and laudanum. "Your Grace!" Lilith frantically pulled free and ducked into the library.

There was no sign of Mrs. Winpole, the housekeeper, or any other female in the entire house. She was on her own. Nearly running, Lilith crossed through the library and into the morning room. Wenford trailed behind her mumbling incoherent snatches of poems, no doubt his version of wooing.

"You know my late wives died without giving me offspring, and a beautiful female of such well-bred stock as you should get me a fine, strapping boy or two."

Lilith felt ill. To be married to the man—to have him kiss her whenever he wished and to share a bed with him . . . "Your Grace, I believe you should first speak to my father again," she said cautiously, not wanting to anger him if she could avoid it.

"Don't tell me what to do, girl," he said, immediately annoyed again. "I know there are matters yet to settle. And I'll speak to Canterbury to get us a special license. No sense in putting off a wedding for no damned good reason."

This was growing worse and worse. "Well, that's splendid, but—"

"I must consider the good of the realm. If I were to pass on to glory without heirs, you have no idea what chaos England would be thrown into! No successor to the Dukedom of Wenford? I shudder to consider it."

Lilith shuddered for a completely different reason. He made another grab for her, but with his poor coordination she was thankfully able to evade him. If this was his attempt at seducing her, he was failing badly. Even the Marquis of Dansbury was more adept at seduction than Wenford. Much more adept. "What about your nephew?"

"Randolph?" he growled. "That dim-witted, gambling wretch? Never!" He drew a ragged breath and stumbled against the couch. "Fetch me a cup of tea, girl," he ordered, sinking down onto the soft cushions. "Show some bloody manners."

"Yes, Your Grace." Finally, a chance to escape! And if he thought she was coming back, he was a complete fool.

He grabbed her hand as she hurried by. "But first we shall get acquainted."

"Your Grace!"

Jerked off balance, Lilith fell hard against his shoulder. Wenford grabbed her chin and placed another foul kiss on her lips. With his free hand, he ripped open the front of her bodice.

"Let me go at once!" Truly frightened now, she struggled to her feet. He pushed upright after her and tangled his hand into her hair to yank her back up against him.

"Cooperate a little, damn you," he grunted, pawing her breasts through her thin shift.

"Let me go at once, or I will scream!" She shoved against his shoulder. No one had ever touched her like this, and she had no idea what to do. If she called Bevins, there would be a terrible scandal, but if she didn't, Wenford's actions left little doubt as to what he had in mind. She took a breath.

"Scream, little spitfire," he droned. "Then we'll see wh—"

The duke suddenly gagged and doubled over. When he straightened again, his face had turned a ghastly ashen gray. He clutched at her shoulder, and then, with a rasping wheeze, collapsed. His weight knocked Lilith backward onto the couch—and then the duke fell full length on top of her.

Lilith desperately punched and kicked at him. "Get off me!"

It took her a moment to realize that he wasn't moving.

"Get off!" Nothing. "Your Grace?" No answer. "Your Grace, get off. Please!"

She received no response to that, either. With a shudder of distaste, Lilith grabbed a handful of his gray hair and lifted his head off her shoulder and neck. His eyes and mouth were half open, a thin froth of spittle around his lips. She shoved with all her might, but only succeeded in further tangling his limp hand into her hair.

Lilith reached up to grasp the back of the couch and tried to pull herself out from under Wenford, but he was nearly twice her weight, and she couldn't budge herself an inch—which left her three choices. Call Bevins and risk an even more enormous scandal, or hope Wenford rose from whatever stupor he had fallen into and that he would climb off her before she smothered. Or, she could lie there beneath the duke until her family returned home, and hope that no one opened the door to the morning room until then.

The door rattled and opened.

"It's no worry, Bevins, I'll only be a moment," came the deep voice of the Marquis of Dansbury. "William made off with one of my gloves. I'm certain he left it in here."

Lilith shut her eyes, a wave of hysteria running over her. She prayed fervently that he wouldn't notice anything.

"Miss Benton? Your Grace?" he called. "I hope I'm not . . ." His voice trailed off. "Anyone here?" he asked. "Children, servants, small animals?" He chuckled. "Ladybirds? High flyers?"

"Go away," she said succinctly.

His footsteps approached the couch and then abruptly

stopped. "My apologies, Wenford, Miss Benton," he said after a moment, an odd edge to his voice. The footsteps turned away again.

"Stop!" she ordered frantically. He couldn't possibly mean to leave her there!

He stopped. "Yes, my lady?"

"Come back here and assist me, at once!"

A pause. "*Assist* you?"

"Immediately!" She held her breath, praying now that he had barged in, the devil wouldn't abandon her.

"I had no idea you were so adventurous, Miss Benton," he said coolly, both his footsteps and the hard cynicism in his voice returning. "I think I should tell you, though, I generally don't share." Jack Faraday's face appeared over the back of the couch. His dark eyes met hers, his expression unreadable. "However, in this instance . . ." Abruptly he frowned and reached down to put his fingers across the duke's neck. "Sweet Lucifer," he murmured.

She took a breath. "Is he . . ." Lilith couldn't finish the sentence. It was too terrible to utter aloud.

"Dead as mutton," Dansbury stated calmly. "Hopped the twig. Put to bed with a shovel. Tipped all—"

"Enough!" she demanded frantically. "Help me!"

The marquis strode around the front of the couch, leaned over to take Wenford around the waist, and hauled backward. "So this is why you decided to forgo Billington's," he grunted. The duke slid off her and onto the floor, landing with a dull thud. "You might have told me I was merely too young for your taste. If I'd known you preferred old men, I might have powdered my hair."

"I would only have found you old and loathsome," Lilith snapped, as she shakily climbed to her feet. Her heart hammering fiercely, she swayed unsteadily.

Suddenly the marquis was beside her, cupping her elbow in one hand. "Perhaps you should take a seat," he suggested quietly.

Her legs did feel terribly weak, and she didn't object when Dansbury's strong, warm hands guided her to the chair by the window and helped her into it. She shut her eyes, and his touch left her. No doubt the blackguard had fled out to the streets to shout his news to anyone who would listen.

"Here, Lilith," he said from right beside her.

Her eyes snapped open. Dansbury was squatting beside her, a glass of brandy in one hand and his eyes on her face. With a shuddering glance at the figure sprawled on the carpet, she took a long, grateful swallow.

"Better?" he asked after a moment.

Sputtering from the strong drink, she nodded.

"Not injured?"

"No. Are you certain he's . . . deceased?"

Dansbury nodded and stood. "Terribly sorry," he uttered, shifting the curtains aside to glance outside, "but you really should have known better."

"Better than what?" she returned, scowling at the sarcasm in his voice.

"Better than to throw up your heels for someone in such poor physical condition before you got him caught in the parson's mousetrap."

"Caught in the . . ." she repeated, her shock swiftly turning to anger.

He nodded. "Didn't your mother ever tell you to wed them before you bed them?"

Lilith stood bolt upright, her face flooding with furious crimson. "I did not—I was not—I had nothing to do with—"

"And here I was beginning to think you truly didn't care for Wenford. Good show, Lil," he interrupted, folding his arms across his chest, his expression distant. "I hadn't realized that any old pot would do, so long as he claimed a dukedom."

Though she was tempted to throw her brandy at him, Lilith carefully set down the glass before she stalked up to him. "The Duke of Wenford barged into this house, chased me while I went looking for a chaperon, and then attacked me. If you are so obtuse as to think I would welcome that . . . that *lunatic's* amorous attentions, then you are an even greater oaf than I believed! And I gave you no leave to use my Christian name!"

Dansbury looked at her assessingly. "Rather bold of you to rail at someone who holds your reputation in his hands—Miss Benton."

Lilith bit back a retort and eyed the tall scoundrel closely. "Are you threatening something?"

He shook his head and glanced over at Wenford. "Just an observation." He sighed, the picture of put-upon integrity. "Because to be honest, I don't exactly wish to be associated with this myself."

"No one asked you," she shot.

The marquis gave a slow, dry smile. "I seem to recall some sort of plea for assistance."

"Then just leave," she said testily, feeling faint again. "I certainly don't wish to inconvenience you by asking for any further aid."

The smile became genuinely amused. "Ah, playing on my sense of honor, are you? Not too wise a stratagem, considering you've informed me on several occasions that I have none." She began to argue, but he raised a hand. "On the slight chance that I am able to summon some sort of propriety," he continued after a moment, his eyes studying hers, "what would you ask of me?"

Lilith sat again, disguising her relief. Dead men in the

morning room had never appeared in any of her aunt's lessons in etiquette. It seemed much more in the realm of Dansbury's experience. "I really have no idea," she confessed. "I don't see what else to do but call for the watch. One cannot hide the death of the Duke of Wenford." Papa would be devastated, and there would be a horrid scandal, but at least she wouldn't be found trapped beneath His Grace. She did owe Jack Faraday for that.

"Hm," the marquis said thoughtfully, "I wonder."

Lilith frowned. "About what?"

"About whether it matters where, exactly, Old Hatchet Face expired."

Lilith's muddled brain refused to travel beyond the body on the floor and how her father would react. He would say that she was behaving just as her mother had, that she was a trollop and had intentionally encouraged Wenford's amorous attentions.

"Please explain," she requested, putting a hand to her throbbing head.

"I mean that perhaps Wenford might be placed elsewhere, and left for someone else to . . . discover."

She looked at him suspiciously. It was a good thing she knew that Jack Faraday couldn't be trusted. "This is very gallant of you, my lord. I'm surprised you're willing to go to such lengths to protect my honor." She folded her hands daintily in her lap. "If it *is* my honor you are concerned with."

He looked sideways at her. "Not much gets by you, does it?" he said wryly. "And unfortunately, you are correct. I have no doubt Dolph Remdale would use my presence at the site of his dear uncle's death to try to get me thrown into Old Bailey."

His offhand compliment surprised and pleased her,

but only for a moment. "Then the authorities should definitely be contacted."

The marquis actually chuckled. "*Un coup très palpable*," he said in perfect French. "A very palpable hit. You've wounded me with your wit."

"I believe one is supposed to quote Shakespeare in his native language," she noted stiffly. It irked her that he thought she might require the translation.

Dansbury pursed his lips, his eyes dancing now. "But Hamlet was Danish."

He did know which play he was stealing from. Interesting, though it certainly didn't leave her feeling any steadier. "Then why French?"

"I don't speak Danish. I do speak a little Italian, if you would prefer me to quote from *Romeo and Juliet*."

"Why would I wish that? I am not Juliet, and you, my lord, are certainly no Romeo."

The marquis was wearing his innocent, seductive look again, but with Wenford's corpse in the background, he was slightly easier to resist than he had been the last time he had waylaid her. "I suppose that would depend on whom you ask."

"I don't discuss you at all," she lied.

He grinned, real amusement in his eyes, and glanced toward the window again. "Miss Benton, it's still early. Why don't we simply put Wenford in your coach, drive him home, and place him on his front step?"

"What? What if someone sees?" It was too scandalous to contemplate. Yet at the same time, it was the best idea she'd heard all morning.

"No one will see. Everyone's at Billington's, remember?" Dansbury studied her for a moment. "It will be our secret."

Lilith abruptly understood why he was being so solicitous. "And I will be in your debt, yes?" she said slowly, meeting his eyes.

He didn't show any sign of being remorseful at all. In fact, he smiled. "Yes, you will. And make no mistake, my lady—I intend to collect." He looked down at his pocket watch, then glanced up at her from beneath his long, black lashes. "It is your choice, however."

There seemed very little choice, to her. Wenford left on the floor and a scandal, or Wenford gone and no scandal, but a debt to a blackguard. And with her family's, and her own, good name to consider. "I don't seem to be in a position to bargain."

Again he gave that sly, seductive smile. "No, you're not." He strode to the door and leaned out. "Bevins, Miss Benton requires the coach to be brought around front." He glanced back at her. "You trust your head groom?"

The rogue of a moment ago was gone, replaced by an efficient, intelligent man who, for a wild moment, she wanted to believe in. "Yes."

"What's his name?"

"Milgrew."

He turned away again. "Have Milgrew bring it himself."

Dansbury hadn't questioned her decision, hadn't second-guessed her; he'd simply assumed she would have an answer and had followed it. That abruptly made her very uncomfortable. "So, is this how you captured William, as well?" she said, to have something to say. "Some sort of blackmail?"

He laughed as he leaned back against the couch. "No. William walked into my demonic clutches quite willingly."

That stilled the comment she had been about to make regarding his demonic nature, so she clenched her hands together and cleared her throat. "You returned the Wenford pin."

Jack nodded. "Yes, to Dolph. Apparently, though, His Grace didn't see fit to leave it in his nephew's care."

"He probably decided it would be safer from you that way," she countered.

"If I'd wanted it, I wouldn't have given it back."

That stopped her. "Then why did you bother taking it in the first place?"

"I won it, Miss Benton," he corrected, faint humor touching his lips. "Because I could." Dansbury shrugged. "And because the Remdales are a detestable lot of scabs, and I felt like causing them trouble."

"You pulled me into it, as well. I don't know why you've decided to hound me, but I don't appreciate it."

"Come now," he said, "it wasn't hate at first sight between us, now, was it?"

"At . . . at first sight I had no idea what sort of scoundrel you were," she admitted, flushing.

"A scoundrel?" he repeated, grinning. "Only yesterday I believe you called me a malignant Jack-a-dandy. You are beginning to warm to me, I think."

"William told you," she gasped, furious at her brother.

"Oh, he tells me all sorts of things," the marquis returned.

Lilith flushed again. "I shall have to begin asking him for your secrets," she retorted, though it seemed a rather weak response.

Evidently he agreed, for he chuckled. "I have none. My dark side is on display for the world to shudder at."

Despite the bold words, she didn't believe him for a moment. "If you have no secrets, then tell me why you fear Dolph Remdale's anger."

His eyes narrowed. "I don't fear Dolph Remdale's

bloody anything. We had a disagreement the other day. That's all."

"And he wants you thrown in prison because of a disagreement?" she pushed, interested to see him lose his cool veneer of cynicism.

"He wants me thrown in prison because I threw a bowl of marmalade in his face at the conclusion of our discussion."

"That would make me rather angry, as well." She was surprised that Dolph Remdale hadn't immediately demanded that the marquis make amends. Despite the duke's description, Mr. Remdale had never seemed terribly dim-witted to her. Some five or six years older than Dansbury, he was quite pleasant featured, and he certainly had rosy prospects. She glanced at the duke. Especially now.

"Wondering if you'd like to marry into the family, after all?" Dansbury asked. She looked up sharply to find the cynical mask firmly back in place. "How very calculating of you. My congratulations."

"You buffoon," she growled, and stalked over to the window to watch for Milgrew.

"Hm. That hardly seems fair, considering the kind advice I was about to give you." He stepped over beside her.

He was baiting her; she knew it, but still she was unable to resist. "And what kind advice was that?"

The marquis shrugged. "Just that you might wish to change your clothes before we proceed any further."

"Change my . . ." Lilith trailed off, abruptly flushing and looking down to see her shift clearly exposed beneath her ripped bodice. She'd been half naked while she'd argued about propriety with Dansbury, and he'd never said anything! Well, he'd certainly taken his time about it, anyway. "Excuse me for a moment."

He sketched a bow. "Of course. His Grace and I don't mind waiting."

With a deep frown, Lilith slipped out through the library door and rushed upstairs. She swiftly pulled off her gown and slipped on a patterned peach muslin. Her hair was a shambles as well, and she quickly rearranged it. In just a few moments she rejoined the marquis.

He still stood looking out the window, his dark hair curling a little where it touched his collar. After a moment he turned to look at her.

"Very nice," he approved with a smile. "Now—is Bevins stiff as he seems?"

It took Lilith a moment to turn her thoughts from the marquis's second compliment of the morning. Bevins wouldn't like any of this, but she didn't think he'd say anything if she asked him not to. Her father would not look kindly upon whoever carried this tale to him. "Yes, but I think he'll do."

If the situation hadn't been so dreadful, Lilith would have laughed at Bevins' expression as Dansbury beckoned him into the room. "My word," the butler said faintly.

The marquis motioned him toward Wenford's feet. "If you please, Bevins."

The butler eyed him dubiously. "I don't believe this is at all the thing," he protested indignantly, turning to Lilith.

"We must get him out of here," she explained, as calmly as she could. "There really is no choice."

"Don't want Miss Benton ruined," Dansbury seconded helpfully.

Bevins looked down at the duke again. "Oh, very well," he grumbled.

Dansbury squatted to reach under Wenford's arms. "Sorry, old boy," he grunted, lifting.

They maneuvered the body through the door and down the hallway, while Lilith rushed ahead of them to pull open the front door. The coach stood waiting at the front of the house, Milgrew in the driver's seat. The groom jumped to the ground and hurried to assist the two men as they struggled down the shallow steps. "Holy Saint Mary," he exclaimed in his thick Scots brogue, grabbing onto the duke's coat and helping them heave Wenford up onto the floor of the coach.

Most of the drive was obscured by rhododendron bushes and maple trees, so it was doubtful that anyone had seen them. Lilith kept her attention on Dansbury as the marquis gracefully clambered up into the coach to haul the duke the rest of the way inside while Milgrew maneuvered him from the ground.

Bevins wiped distastefully at his hands and turned back to the house. Abruptly he froze, his complexion going pale. "Miss Benton?"

"What is it?" she asked in alarm.

"Your father." He hurriedly straightened his coat and neckcloth.

As Lilith turned, the other Hamble coach appeared at the foot of the drive, and she had to squelch the sudden desire to flee. Fainting was a greatly underappreciated art, she decided, wishing she had mastered it.

"Well, we can't have this," the marquis commented, his tone as calm as if he had been discussing the weather. He sat down in the coach and yanked the door shut.

Her father stepped down from his carriage and strode forward, barely contained anger in every line of his body. "What the devil is going on?" he scowled, glaring at the occupant of the coach. Lilith didn't care to contemplate what his expression would be once he discovered there were two occupants.

"Jack, thought you were riding to Bristol this morning." William grinned, helping Aunt Eugenia down from the coach and coming forward.

The marquis reached out to shake his hand, but made no move to release the door handle he held shut with the other. He smiled lazily. "I stayed out a bit later than I realized, and now I seem to have misplaced my mount," he drawled. "Poor Benedick, I hope he finds his way home."

"Blind drunk at ten in the morning, is what you are," her father said scathingly.

For just a moment Dansbury's expression changed, and then he favored them with a lopsided grin. "I would hope all that effort didn't go to waste," he agreed. "Anyway, I ended up here, and Miss Benton offered me a ride home." He glanced at her. "To get rid of me, I do think."

The viscount gestured impatiently at Milgrew. "Get him out of here."

"Aye, milord," the groom responded, and climbed back up onto the driver's perch.

Lilith could only stare, amazed, as the marquis sat back and in a slurring voice called for Milgrew to be off. He gave a sterling performance as a drunk, and she didn't know what to make of the story he'd concocted. He'd told Bevins he'd come to Benton House looking for a glove. Just before he passed out of sight, Dansbury nodded at her, and she came back to herself with a start.

"How was Billington's?" she asked, smiling sweetly and linking her arm through her aunt's.

"Everyone was there," Eugenia returned, "but Stephen insisted it was too crowded and that we should leave."

Her father glanced up the drive again, then shrugged, the affronted anger slowly leaving his face. "Far too many people were allowed to attend this year. I didn't get a chance to say more than two words to Billington." He turned on William, his expression darkening. "Now that blackguard is coming here when you're not even home. I told you I want you to have nothing further to do with him."

"But he's a good sort, Father, really," William protested. "Slap up to the echo. I'm learning everything from him and his cronies."

"That is precisely what I am afraid of."

As Lilith looked after the vanished coach, she reflected that she was rather worried herself. She had just placed her honor in the hands of a gamester and rakehell. And Dansbury would collect on the debt she owed him. He had warned her. She took a deep breath, her heart fluttering nervously.

He would *try* to collect.

Chapter 6

The Duke of Wenford had a damned lot of nerve.

"It's a bloody good thing you're dead," Jack growled at Geoffrey Remdale's remains, "or I'd have sent you to Jericho myself." He nudged his silent companion with the toe of his boot, turning the pallid face with its lifeless, staring eyes toward the opposite seat. Then he sighed and sat back to watch Mayfair roll by outside.

After going to the effort of discovering that Lilith Benton would be at home alone, and then convincing her stuffy butler that he actually had a legitimate reason for stopping by, Jack had not expected someone else to have beaten him to her. And he certainly hadn't expected it to be Wenford.

The anger that had hit him at the sight of Old Hatchet Face sprawled on top of Lilith, like a wrinkled old rutting ox, still surprised him. Whatever her reputation for coolness, he hadn't expected to find her lifting her heels for a duchy. He'd been severely disappointed in her. And then she'd asked for his assistance, and he'd suddenly become Galahad in shining armor.

Of course, his own plans for Lilith were a far cry from

Wenford's. His plan of seducing her into bed left her an out, if she managed to resist him. If she didn't—well, that would be her own poor choice, wouldn't it? After all, it was his game, and his rules, so naturally they favored him.

Which did not explain why he was currently taking the risk of being caught carting the corpse of a member of the peerage about London. And—more to the point—a member of the peerage with whom he was well known to have a longstanding disagreement. With his tattered reputation, marquis or not, it would be nearly enough to get him jailed.

Difficult as it was for him to believe of himself, apparently whatever temporary sentiments of chivalry Miss Benton had awakened in him were real. Of course, it could merely have been his eye for opportunity, deciding that putting Lilith in his debt was to his advantage. But whatever had roused this fleeting propriety, he needed to get Wenford safely planted somewhere to be found.

He couldn't say he was the least bit sorry to see the old boy gone. Politically, Wenford was hopelessly backward, and his absence from the House of Lords would be a relief. It was a pity, though, that his death would elevate Dolph Remdale to the dukedom. The conceited fool was already insufferable enough. Jack thoughtfully studied Wenford's profile again. Dear Randolph needed something to take him down a notch.

Milgrew knocked the handle of his whip against the door. "We're here, milord," he called down from his perch.

Jack regarded the Remdale manor through the trees that obscured the drive, then leaned his head out the window. "Milgrew, take the street around to the west side of the house." He gave a slow smile. "I have a better idea."

"Aye?" the Scot queried, leaning down to look at him and raising an eyebrow.

"Aye."

Waves of excited conversation buzzed through the Rochmont ballroom as Lilith and her family entered, and she steeled herself for what would follow. Word of the duke's death must have circulated around the *ton* by now, and she dreaded having to face everyone's speculation with pretended ignorance. She had practiced an expression of sorrow tinted with knowing regret all afternoon: after all, the Duke of Wenford had been quite elderly, and given to fits of near apoplexy . . .

"Lil, have you heard?"

Penelope Stratford tugged her arm, leading her across the floor to their waiting circle of friends. Lilith was glad to part from her father; he'd been glum and short-tempered all afternoon, and nothing she'd attempted had cheered him up in the least. "Heard what?" she asked, hoping the curiosity in her voice didn't sound forced.

"Only the most shocking thing—there, you see? I told you that you looked splendid in gold. And you said it wouldn't do."

Pen looked admiringly at the golden silk gown with the puffy lace sleeves Madame Belieu's shop had delivered earlier in the day. Lilith had thought it a trifle much, but at the last moment had become too fainthearted to don the emerald dress. Her father would never approve of it.

"What shocking thing?"

"Oh, yes." Pen leaned closer, covering her giggles with one hand. "The widow Mrs. Devereaux eloped last night to Gretna Green with Raymond Beecher."

"Oh, that's dread—What?" Lilith stared at her friend.

"But Mrs. Devereaux is ten years older than Mr. Beecher."

"And when the earl, his father, found out, he disowned Raymond on the spot," Jeremy Giggins finished, grinning as the two young ladies reached their group. "Beecher never had a pound of sense."

"And now he has no pounds at all," Lionel Hendrick continued. He took Lilith's hand and brought it to his lips. "Good evening, Miss Benton. You are stunning."

Lilith curtsied. "Thank you, my lord."

Her suitors seemed to have established a hierarchy of sorts, and no one contested the earl as he led her out onto the polished floor for the first waltz of the evening. Lilith wondered if he would be the one her father chose, now that Wenford was gone. He stood an inch or so taller than Dansbury, and unlike the dark-haired marquis's, his light brown hair was cut in the very latest style. Nance was certainly pleasant enough to gaze upon, but as he stepped on her toe and murmured an apology, it occurred to her that she really knew very little about him—or about any of her other suitors. She knew more about the Marquis of Dansbury—little as she liked the information—than practically every other man she had encountered in London.

Lilith abruptly frowned and glanced about the room. Dansbury had yet to make an appearance this evening. Of course, this very proper soirée was not his usual milieu and normally his absence would have pleased her no end. But any information regarding the Duke of Wenford's death seemed to be absent as well, and she couldn't help linking the two.

"Frightfully cold weather we're having this Season, isn't it?" Nance offered, smiling at her.

Lilith hurriedly smiled back at him, chastising herself for her inattention. That blasted Dansbury was a nuisance even when he wasn't about. "Yes, it is quite chilly, my lord. I do hope it will warm up before it comes time for winter again."

He chuckled. "Indeed. I have had to send for half my winter wardrobe from Nance Hall."

"I think we all have."

The earl cleared his throat, leaning closer. "You might be interested to know," he confided in a conspiratorial tone, "that my aunt on my father's side has just finished a complete tracing of our family tree. It seems I am directly related to Edward the Fourth."

"No," she exclaimed, sneaking a hurried look over his shoulder in the direction of the punchbowl. There were no games started upstairs yet, so if Dansbury was in attendance, he should be in the ballroom.

Nance pursed his lips, the resulting thoughtful expression much less sensual than when Dansbury did the same. "I am now thinking I should have my family crest changed to reflect this association," he continued. "My sister, however, believes this might be entirely too scandalous, as the York line is not universally liked. What is your opinion?"

Lilith barely caught what he was saying. *Where was that scoundrel?* "I'm certain you'll do what's best," she offered absently.

"For a member of the gentler sex, you are quite wise in matters politic. I have always said so, you know."

Though she wasn't entirely certain that was a compliment, she smiled and nodded anyway. For all the attention she was paying, it might very well have been an invitation to take her off to Belgium for the duration of the summer. "Thank you, my lord."

"You are troubled this evening," he stated, frowning.

"Oh, no," she returned quickly, trying to rid the dastardly marquis from her thoughts. "I am only worried a little, about . . . about my brother.'' She disliked discussing William's wild behavior, but it did seem wiser than admitting that Geoffrey Remdale was dead and that she couldn't figure out why she was the only one who seemed to know about it.

The earl nodded. ''I assume you refer to Dansbury and his crowd? His blood's blue enough, I suppose, though no one with any proper sense of status will have anything to do with him. The libertine cheated me out of a hundred and fifty pounds last week, and I never did figure out how he accomplished it.'' He sighed. ''Pray do not let him trouble your perfect brow, *mademoiselle*.''

''Thank you, my lord.''

''Would you like me to speak to your brother?'' He lowered his voice further. ''You know, I hear he has spent the last several evenings at Antonia St. Gerard's card parties, and that she seems to favor him. I don't mean to alarm you, but that association could do him more harm than Dansbury. Perhaps as a contemporary, I may be able to set him back on the straight path, as it were.''

His offer was unexpected, and though William seemed to listen to no one but the marquis these days, Lilith supposed it could do no harm. She herself had heard her brother mention this Antonia woman, and what Nance said certainly alarmed her. ''That would be very kind of you, my lord.''

Nance's smile broadened as he narrowly missed kicking her shin. ''It would be my pleasure. And I ask you again to call me Lionel. After all, I have asked your father for your hand in marriage.''

''I know,'' she acknowledged, feeling a bit harried.

''I heard that His Grace the Duke of Wenford has received permission to court you, as well,'' he continued lightly. "I do hope that hasn't hurt my own suit."

Lilith gave a slightly hysterical laugh. "Oh, no, Lionel. I don't think I could seriously consider His Grace," she tittered. "He is quite elderly . . . and probably not in very good health, and you know—"

Nance laughed as the waltz came to a close. "Please, Miss Benton, *I* am already convinced." He brushed her chin with his gloved fingers. "I am pleased that you are, as well."

Dinner and another complete dance set passed, and still no one had mentioned anything about the deceased duke. When a smiling Randolph Remdale entered the ballroom halfway through the evening, Lilith knew something was dreadfully wrong. And with the marquis continuing in his absence, she needed some assistance— even if it was rather haphazard.

Lilith turned to look for William, only to spy him waltzing with the woman Dansbury had brought with him to the opera. Perhaps three or four years older than Lilith, the woman wore her brunette hair tangled and twisted away from the restraint of two delicate French bone clips. Slightly slanted hazel eyes gave her an exotic look, wise and innocent at the same time. Her green and peach silk gown was demure enough, but she had a sensual, gliding way of moving across the ballroom floor that caught the eyes of more than one gentleman. Antonia St. Gerard herself, no doubt.

Lilith waited impatiently for the set to end. Finally she intercepted her brother as he went to fetch a glass of punch. If the dazed, puppyish expression on William's face was any indication, she had another problem she was going to have to deal with, and soon.

She sent a carefully gracious smile in the direction of her brother's companion as she stepped up and touched his arm. "I need to speak with you for a moment."

"Lil, I'm occupied," he protested.

"Please, William," she insisted. "It's important."

He must have read her expression, for he delivered the punch, excused himself, and followed her to the nearest alcove. "You ain't going to warn me off Antonia, are you?"

She scowled at him. "Not at the moment. William, something awful happened this morning, and I need to tell you about it."

Finally he gave her his attention, his expression becoming serious. "What awful thing happened?"

"While everyone was at Billington's, the Duke of Wenford came by to see me, to propose to me. And he . . . well, he assaulted me, and then—"

"Wenford *assaulted* you?" He blanched, his eyes widening. "Where is the bastard? I'll call him out right now and—"

"You're too late."

He faltered, his gaze snapping back to her face. "What?"

"He was . . . mauling me, and then he fell over dead." There was no point in telling him on whom Wenford had fallen, she decided, for that would only complicate matters.

"*The Duke of Wenford is dead?*"

"William, please be quiet," she hissed desperately. The marquis had been much more calm about the disaster. "Lord Dansbury removed His Grace from the morning room. But now—"

"Jack helped you? Ha! Old Hatchet Face was in the coach with him, wasn't he? By God, I told you he was a good sort."

"But why doesn't anyone else know about this?" she argued. "The marquis was supposed to leave the duke on the front steps of Remdale House."

"Well," her brother said slowly, furrowing his brow and obviously trying to grasp all the information she'd given him, "Wenford's house is open. Surely one of the servants would have found—"

"But they obviously haven't. And where is Dansbury?" she pursued.

"I don't know." William shrugged. "He doesn't usually come to this sort of milkwater rout . . . I say, you don't think Jack's got something to do with no one knowing about Wenford?"

"Of course he does," she retorted, completely exasperated. "He'll ruin everything. It's what he's been planning all along."

"You're all about in the head, Lil," her brother whispered.

Perhaps she was, but the explanation for the *ton*'s lack of knowledge lay somewhere between her front step and wherever Jack Faraday was. "He was the last one with the body."

Obviously William wasn't about to accept that his idol could be such a villain. "I'm certain it's all right, Lil. Perhaps there're things to be put in order before the announcement of Wenford's death is made. He was a duke, after all."

For a moment it made sense. "So it's to be kept a secret."

"Certainly," William soothed.

She shook herself, narrowing her eyes. "Even from his own family?" she countered indignantly. "From his heir? Look over there!"

"What are you talking about?"

Dolph Remdale stood laughing over some tale being related by his close friend Donald Marley. At that moment he looked toward her. Lilith froze, her fingers still waving in his direction. With a word to his crony, he strolled over. Lilith clutched William's arm, knowing with absolute certainty that things had just taken a turn for the worse.

"Good evening, Miss Benton, Mr. Benton," Dolph Remdale greeted them, showing his perfect white teeth in a smile.

"Good evening, Mr. Remdale," Lilith replied, trying to put a touch of surprise into her voice. After all, this was practically the first time he had even acknowledged her presence. She hoped her brother would have enough sense to keep his mouth shut.

"I noticed you looking in my direction, my lady. Is there something I can do for you?" he asked politely.

"Oh, no," Lilith gushed, cursing Dansbury all over again. This was all his fault. "I was simply telling my brother that his time might be better spent in finer company."

At that William stirred and opened his mouth, and she dug her fingernails into his arm. With a strangled cough he subsided.

Remdale nodded. "A wise counsel," he said, his eyes remaining on her. "Perhaps you'd care to join me at White's this evening, Mr. Benton."

"Don't care to, no," William said stiffly.

"William," she protested, blushing, and glanced at her brother. "My apologies, Mr. Remdale. My brother tends to speak before he thinks. We find it amusing, but at times it—"

"Lil, don't you apol—"

"Please, Mr. Benton, Miss Benton. There is no need to explain." The pale eyes held Lilith's. "Obviously your brother is under the influence of a rather—how shall I say—a rather unacceptable person. I hope he is able to pull himself free before permanent damage is done."

William opened his mouth, and Lilith tightened her grip on his arm. "Thank you for your concern, sir."

Dolph smiled. "Of course." With a nod, he turned away to rejoin his friends.

"Dash it, Lil, that hurt," William protested, pulling his arm free and rubbing it.

"You cannot go about insulting people like that, William! For goodness sake."

"Jack don't like the Remdales." Her brother frowned. "Don't see why I should, either."

"Yes, well, *that* Remdale obviously knows nothing about his uncle's death," Lilith returned, glancing after Dolph. "Now do you believe Lord Dansbury's done something?"

He scowled at her. "From what you've told me, it seems as though he saved your reputation so that you could go to your fine acquaintances and say shabby things about him behind his back."

"I do no such thing." That wasn't quite true, but she had never said anything that Dansbury didn't deserve, after all. "You must go find him. If he's done something foolish, it could make things worse for all of us. Thanks to him, everyone knows His Grace was courting me."

William sighed. "I'll fetch him in the morning. I'd wager a thousand quid that you're wrong about him, but something's definitely spotty here."

"Thank goodness you're finally listening to me."

She had been wrong to place an ounce of trust in the marquis. And debt or no debt, if Jonathan Faraday had as much to do with the disappearance of Wenford's body as she suspected, she would see him in Old Bailey prison herself.

"William," a smooth, faintly French voice cooed from behind her, and Lilith turned around.

"Antonia." Her brother beamed. "I'd like you to

meet my sister, Lil. Lilith, Miss St. Gerard.''

"Charmed.'' Miss St. Gerard nodded, smiling coolly and holding out her hand.

Lilith shook it. "Miss St. Gerard.''

"If you've as much a head for cards as your brother, Miss Benton, you're welcome to attend one of my little parties. One may meet all types of interesting people there.''

"No doubt,'' Lilith said stiffly.

With a smile, Antonia slipped her arm around William's and led him toward the refreshment table. Apparently Miss St. Gerard was something else she could thank Jack Faraday for. It was unfortunate that it was unladylike to thank someone with a pistol.

Chapter 7

Something damned peculiar was going on. Peese and Martin had been whispering together all morning. Irritated at being excluded, Jack finally reminded them what an odious habit gossip was. His valet finally confessed to hearing the news that Harriet Devereaux and Raymond Beecher had eloped the day before.

"Anything else?" the marquis prompted, straightening his arms so Martin could avail him of his coat. The elopement had to be an *hors d'oeuvre* to the news of Wenford's death, and he readied himself to make some cool, cynical comment regarding the duke's demise. After all, His Grace had been old as Methuselah, and pompous as a—well, as a Remdale.

"No, my lord," Martin returned, brushing at the back of the coat. "Not that I'm aware of."

"Hm." Jack picked up his beaver hat and kid gloves, turning for the door to mask his perturbation. "Well, if that's the case, I've an appointment with Hoby."

He'd made the appointment almost the moment he'd arrived in London for the Season. The Hessian boots he'd destroyed last winter, while pulling a trapped cow from a stream at Dansbury, had been his favorites, and he was growing damned tired of pinched toes. But seeing Hoby was more difficult than gaining an audience with Prince George.

In truth, Martin's gossip had troubled him greatly. First, it irked him when his servants got wind of any good gossip before he did. Second and more importantly, every other piece of news, however scandalous, should pale in light of Wenford's death. His servants, though, seemed to know nothing of it at all.

No one else appeared to know, either. As he rode Benedick to Hoby's establishment, he was actually relieved to see William Benton's sour expression when the boy intercepted him on his exquisite, and very expensive, new stallion. At least someone else found the morning troublesome. "Good morning, my boy. And how was Rochmont's stale little *fête* last evening?"

"Jack, thank God you're about. I was on my way to see you."

"So I gathered." Jack sighed and crossed his wrists over the cantle of his saddle. "Don't keep me in suspense," he said dryly. "You look as though you've swallowed a bug."

"Were you ever going to tell me about your rescue of Lil?" the boy returned. "Lord, what a caper, Jack."

The marquis attempted to hide his surprise. "Told you, did she?" That didn't seem particularly wise; it wasn't something he would have expected of the astute Lilith Benton.

"She didn't have a choice. Something's gone wrong, I think."

An image of Lilith Benton, pale and shaken and clutching his arm to keep from falling, crossed unbidden into Jack's mind, and he took a breath at the abrupt feeling of concern. "Is your sister well, then?" he asked offhandedly. It would never do if he ruined her by accident. The *dénouement* had to be as carefully planned as the rest of the steps in the game.

"Oh, she's fine. Don't know quite how to take you now, though."

"Really? She finds me heroic, then?"

"Hardly. Don't like being in your debt, I think. She glowers like a gargoyle whenever she mentions your name."

"She actually mentions my name? That *is* a surprise." Jack kneed Benedick into a walk. "I'm on my way to Hoby's, so if you wish to keep gossiping you shall have to accompany me."

William hesitated, then turned his black Thor to follow. "Where were you last night?" he asked as he caught up.

So the boy was going to feel abandoned every time he chose to go off somewhere on his own. Antonia obviously wasn't keeping William as occupied as either she or Jack intended. "Seeing a man about a dog," he said coolly. "Why, do you require a nursemaid? Or pointers in navigating a woman's boudoir?"

William flushed. "I do not need a nursemaid. And I don't know why you become so hostile whenever I ask you anything personal. I'm not the damned Spanish Inquisition, you know."

At least William's repartee had improved since he had taken the boy under his wing. "William, I have no intention of relating to you the intimate details of my existence," he said shortly. There were times he wished he knew nothing of them himself.

"Do you have any objection to telling me why no one seems to know Wenford is dead?"

"Keep your bloody voice down," Jack warned, abruptly unwilling to believe what he had suspected all morning.

William glanced about guiltily. "Lilith sent me to ask you what you're up to this time."

The marquis stared at his companion. "Lilith sent you? To me?"

William cracked a grin. "Amazing, ain't it? She's convinced you've done something scandalous with Old Hatchet Face."

"And you're none too certain, either, I assume?"

Actually, William's speculations did not bother him as much as the fact that Miss Benton was correct. He could only guess what she would think when she learned what he had actually done with Wenford's earthly remains. He'd been working too hard at this to let a misunderstanding set him back to the beginning.

Hoby's establishment came into view up the street. If he broke his appointment it would be another month, if he was lucky, before he got another. "Damnation," he muttered, then brought Benedick around. "Let's go see your sister."

"Is Father gone?"

Lilith jumped as William leaned his head into the morning room. Her brother had become far too proficient at sneaking about, and he was wearing that conspiratorial look on his face again. She frowned at him. "Yes, he took Aunt Eugenia to see Mrs. Higginson half an hour ago, after I spent twenty minutes convincing him that Mr. Higginson was personally acquainted with the Duke of Gloucester. Where in the world have you been?"

"Looking for Jack, of course."

"And did you find him?"

The Marquis of Dansbury reached past her brother to push the door open the rest of the way, and strolled into the morning room as though he owned it. He had donned a blue coat and tan breeches, and he still looked more like a pirate than a member of the peerage. "Indeed he did, Miss Benton." She watched him, unable to look away, as he swept a bow and sank onto the couch beside her without being asked. "And thank you for inviting me. I admit, it is an honor I never expec—"

"Why is it," Lilith interrupted, with what she considered remarkable composure, "that the greatest scandal of the moment is Raymond Beecher's ill-planned elopement with that fortune-hunting Harriet Devereaux?"

Before Dansbury replied, he took a moment to look about the room. "I say, it looks much more pleasant in here without a corpse on the floor." He nodded approvingly. "It is a scandal because no one can conceive that the two of them might actually have fallen in love. And Harriet is no gold digger. She's got more blunt than Beecher could ever have hoped to inherit."

"But I heard her late husband's will stated—" Lilith stopped herself, scowling, as the marquis looked at her, amusement in every line of his lean face. "You know what I mean," she continued, lifting her chin. "Why does no one know of the Duke of Wenford's unfortunate death?"

"Except for William, of course."

So he didn't approve her choice of confidant. "I don't require your approval."

The marquis glanced at William, who frowned at him. "Just pointing out a fact," he said.

"That's right, you don't want to upset your new disciple, do you?" she said sweetly, pleased to be on the attack for once.

He looked sideways at her and leaned closer. "You don't want to upset your rescuer, now, do you?" he murmured under his breath.

Lilith reluctantly stopped baiting him. He could do far more damage to her than she could to him, after all. "Suffice it to say that including my brother was necessary. Now explain yourself, Lord Dansbury."

The marquis hesitated. "I'm a bit baffled," he finally sighed, rising to go lean against the mantel.

"You're—where is the body of the Duke of Wenford?" she demanded.

"Didn't you put him on his doorstep, like you told Lil you would?" William questioned from his perch by the window.

"Not exactly."

"Where is he?" Lilith asked evenly.

The marquis met her gaze. "I found myself unable to resist a rather grand notion, and I convinced your groom to help me haul Old Hatchet Face down into his wine cellar."

She stared at him, what was left of her color draining away. "You didn't."

He shrugged. "I couldn't let my last chance at him go by untouched."

This was all happening too fast, which seemed to occur quite regularly when the Marquis of Dansbury became involved. "So you've hidden him in his wine cellar. What good will that do? Someone will find him eventually."

"You misunderstand me. I didn't hide him. I left him in the middle of the floor."

"And?" she prompted.

He gave a brief smile. "And I opened one of his bottles of wine for him. Not a very good vintage, I'm afraid—but no doubt everyone will understand his poor taste, given his condition."

Lilith shut her eyes for a moment. "What condition?" she asked faintly.

"His being naked and completely flummoxed in the middle of the famous Remdale wine cellar."

"*Naked?*"

William gave a shout of laughter. "By God, Jack. I wish I'd been there!"

Lilith took several deep breaths. "William, please go watch for Papa," she suggested tightly. Her brother wasn't helping matters in the slightest, and she certainly didn't want the two of them ganging up on everything she said. The marquis was more than enough for her to handle.

"You're not leaving me out of this," her brother countered, stubbornly folding his arms across his chest and frowning.

"William, be a good boy and do as you're told," the marquis unexpectedly seconded. "Your sister wishes to bellow at me in private. I'll catch you up later."

His scowl deepening, William stood and stomped to the door. "Dash it all, Jack, you'd better."

"Now, my sweet, you wished to speak to me in private?" Jack said softly. "You have my utter, complete, entire, undivided attention. I am yours to command, your willing slave in all things real—and imagined."

Lilith rounded on Dansbury, attempting to credit her speeded pulse rate to simple annoyance. "Why would you do such a thing? *Why?*"

"That is the most interesting topic you can come up with? Surely you can do better," he returned. "Perhaps we might decide how to settle the debt you owe me. I have several suggestions."

Lilith blushed, and tried to pretend that she had not. "Why would you leave His Grace in such a state? The scandal—"

His expression unexpectedly darkened. "The scandal is exactly why," he said shortly. For the first time, genuine, unmistakable anger touched his voice. "I have no idea how naive you may be, Miss Benton, and I don't wish to offend your delicate sensibilities, but I know damned well what Wenford was attempting to do to you when he popped off. The bastard may have taken away the opportunity for me to do something nasty to him while he was alive, but it was not too late to put him in his place. Now everyone will see him for what he was—a big, bloody buffoon."

Lilith had the disturbing sense that she'd just met the real Jack Faraday. It was unsettling, because for a second, she'd liked the man. "It's too late to embarrass him. It will be his family, and mine, who will suffer."

"Nonsense. Dolph, maybe—I hope so. You had nothing to do with it, or with him. No one knows anything but that he was courting you."

A moment ago he was insulting her, and now he was apparently comforting her. "Are you defending my honor?"

Jack gave a brief smile and looked away. "I don't know. Perhaps I am."

Lilith looked at his lean, handsome profile for a long moment. "Why?"

This time he chuckled. "You seem at such a loss," he returned. "Can't even admit you approve my choice of Wenford's resting place."

"How could I approve such a thing?"

He eyed her. "Don't you find it the least, tiny bit satisfying, Miss Benton? You were the one he was assaulting, after all."

"Under the circumstances, what I think about it doesn't matter," she said firmly. "I—"

"Only if you don't let it matter."

He'd misinterpreted her meaning, but his answer surprised her nevertheless. "My, aren't you enlightened?"

she said, with as much sarcasm as she could muster.

"I do try," he conceded, inclining his head. "And you're evading my question."

"I don't intend to answer it."

"That's an answer in itself, isn't it?" he pursued with a wolfish grin. "I believe silence is generally considered to be an assent."

"You, my lord, are extremely irritating." Lilith shut her eyes and massaged her temples with her fingers.

She expected an answer in kind, and it was a moment before she realized that Dansbury was being far too quiet. Lilith opened her eyes again, to see him studying her face closely, his own expression thoughtful. She liked it better when he was being flippant. At least then he was easier to decipher.

"What is it now?" she snapped. Thank goodness her father would never consider him a potential suitor, because it was completely impossible for her to keep her temper and her tongue in check around him.

"This is quite a trial for you, isn't it?" He folded his arms and leaned back against the mantel.

"Of course it is," she said haughtily, annoyed that he thought her helpless. "I am unused to dealing with dead dukes and devious scoundrels."

If she hadn't despised him so much, she might have thought his answering grin attractive. "I thought nothing rattled Lilith Benton."

She was actually feeling quite rattled at the moment, and not simply because of Wenford's death. "And what gave you that impression?"

"Why, you did." He looked at her from beneath his dark lashes. "Always so cool and calm—"

"I am not the Ice Queen!" she blurted. To hear his amused voice call her that name would be simply unbearable.

Dansbury straightened. "What do you call a female, then, who encourages six suitors—"

"Five," she snapped.

"—six suitors, and answers none of them? Are you waiting for an even dozen?"

"That is complete nonsense!" Lilith stood, then didn't know what to do with herself. She settled for stomping her foot and glaring at him.

"Come now, Miss Benton," he chastised, moving closer, "are you being prudent, or calculating?"

"That does not concern you," she retorted. "It concerns only my family."

"What does your family matter?" he said cynically. "Your family wouldn't have had to rut with Wenford."

She couldn't suppress a shudder at the image. "Family is all that matters."

He paused, looking at her with an intense curiosity that unsettled her even further. "Even so," he went on after a moment, as though conceding a point to her, "couldn't you turn down two or three of the least likely candidates? After all, there are other females looking for husbands this Season. It's not fair to monopolize every man of marrying age and inclination."

That hadn't been her decision, either. "I've turned you down," Lilith reminded him, so angry her voice trembled. At least she told herself it was righteous fury making her shake.

"But what of the rest?" He stepped closer, a slight grin on his face. "Other than Wenford, of course, who has taken himself out of the running."

Lilith backed away from him. His voice sent a shiver down her spine, and her breathing was keeping pace with the accelerated beat of her heart. As he continued to advance, her back came up against the bookcase, and she was forced to stop. "Papa favors the Earl of—"

"Nance?" he interrupted, scowling. "He's an idiot, and you know it. And I didn't ask you to name your father's favorite. Isn't there one who's caught your heart?" Dansbury stopped in front of her, his dark eyes holding hers. "One only, who makes you breathe faster?" He placed his hands on either side of her shoulders and leaned closer. "One whose image won't leave your mind," he murmured, "but rolls around and around in your thoughts until you can think of no one else?"

"It doesn't matter who . . . who it is," she said, trying unsuccessfully to avoid his gaze, "so long as he is respectable."

His lazy smile was belied by the glint in his eyes. "Anyone but me, then?" he whispered.

She took a shaky breath, wishing he would move away, look away, so she could muster whatever it was that gave her the courage to stand up to him. "Yes."

"And you've left nothing out of your little equation for respectability?" he pushed, his breath warm and soft against her mouth. "Happiness, perhaps?"

"Respectability will make me happy, my lord."

"Are you certain of that, Miss Benton?"

"Absolu—"

He bent his head and captured her lips in a rough, hard kiss. Everything stopped—her heart, her breath, all sensation except for the hot, sensuous feel of his mouth on hers. Her eyes closed, and her fingers tangled through his dark hair. Torn between wanting him to continue kissing her and horror that she felt that way, she frantically grabbed a handful of his hair and yanked his head back. He looked down at her in surprise, and she kicked him in the knee. The duke's kiss had felt nothing like this, like lightning shooting down her spine. "You . . . you scoundrel," she gasped.

Dansbury stepped back and bent to rub his knee, apparently unmoved by their embrace. "Sticks and stones may—"

"You blackguard! You beast!" She was angry—that's what she was. She was furious.

He straightened with an unruffled grin. "—break my bones, but names—"

Lilith snatched up a vase.

"Try this, then!"

She hurled the porcelain at him.

Dansbury nimbly ducked sideways, and the container crashed against the couch. "Well, well, well, Ice Queen." His eyes twinkling with amusement, he moved toward her again.

Lilith snatched up a ceramic candy dish and flung it at the marquis. "I am not a damned Ice Queen!" she shrieked.

This time her aim was true—the dish struck the side of his head. With a grunt, Dansbury staggered and fell to the floor.

For a stunned moment, Lilith stared down at him. Then she dashed over to kneel beside him. He remained motionless. "My lord? Dansbury?"

He didn't move, but lay with one arm draped across his face.

"Jack?" Alarm that she might actually have hurt him ran through her.

He slowly lowered his arm and eyed her. "Blast it! That hurt." He touched his temple with his fingers, and they came away bloody. He sat up, his dark eyes dancing. "I do believe you've proved your point."

"What point?" This man insisted on bringing out the worst in her, and she seemed completely unable to resist responding.

"That you're no damned Ice Queen, Lil."

"Miss Benton," she corrected, wondering why it mattered to her that she had convinced him. "And you deserved worse, you cad."

"I've had worse." He chuckled. "Though cracking me in the head does seem rather severe—it was only a kiss."

Only a kiss. Well, he might have kissed enough women that he felt nothing, but Lilith couldn't even put into words what he did to her insides. "Don't ever do it again."

He lifted an eyebrow. "I intend to kiss you as often as I can get away with it."

For a moment Lilith sat frozen on the floor, staring at him. "What have I ever done to you," she managed, "that makes you keep tormenting me?"

Apparently unmoved by her plea, he gave her a careless grin. "I've already told you how you infatuate me." He looked at her sideways. "And besides, you looked at me."

"I looked at you? I don't doubt there are at least a dozen other people in the world who have 'looked at you,' " she countered, wondering what game he was playing now. "Why don't you torment all of them instead?"

A slow, sensuous smile touched his mouth. "No, Miss Benton, you misunderstand. You *looked* at me. And then you pretended that you hadn't." He shifted closer to her, so that only a few inches separated them. "You were attracted to me. You still are."

"I am not." Lilith swallowed. "Perhaps for a moment I thought your countenance pleasant," she admitted reluctantly. "But that was before I learned of your poor character."

"Hm," he murmured, holding her gaze, "and why is it you think my character poor?"

"You know very well."

Jack reached out and gently touched her cheek with the back of his fingers. "You've made an accusation. I would like to hear your evidence."

Lilith shivered at his light touch. "Stop that."

"You're a sensual creature, I think," he murmured, letting his fingers trail down to touch the pearl necklace at the base of her throat. "Tell me."

Good Lord, she'd been in less difficulty with the Duke of Wenford—at least her sentiments toward him had been pure revulsion. Dansbury was much more complicated. The gentle tug of the silver chain at her neck as he fingered the single pearl made her take a quick, shallow breath. Dansbury was also a much greater threat. "I am not—"

Before she could finish, William slammed the door open and rushed into the room. "Father's carriage just turned the cor—" He stopped short, looking down at the marquis. "What the devil happened to you?"

Dansbury hauled himself to his feet. "I met with an accident," he replied with a short grin, and held a hand down to her.

Lilith allowed him to pull her to her feet. "I hit him with a candy dish," she elaborated.

Stifling what sounded like laughter, Dansbury squatted down, swiftly and efficiently cleaning up the broken pieces of pottery. No doubt he was accustomed to covering his scandalous doings on a regular basis.

William stood staring at Lilith, his eyes wide. "He's one of the deadliest shots in England, Lil. Are you mad?"

"Completely demented," the marquis supplied, before she could answer. "I'm beginning to wonder whether you didn't do Wenford in yourself, Miss Benton."

Lilith blanched. "Don't you dare say such a thing!"

"Lil, you shouldn't be talking that way to the Marquis of Dansbury," William argued.

"He shouldn't be talking that way to *me*!" She stomped her foot again, wishing for another item to throw at him. "Now, get out, before Papa sees you."

"Lilith!" William protested.

"Oh, do be quiet, William," the marquis unexpectedly interrupted, his expression annoyed. "I can fend for myself." He set the pottery into the waste basket, then touched the knot on his temple. "I'll have to think up an explanation for this, though."

"I'm certain no one would have the least bit of difficulty believing a woman had to defend her honor against your advances," Lilith said in amusement.

"I was hardly advancing," Dansbury returned.

"No," she agreed dryly, "I believe you were falling."

He laughed. "Only for your beauty, my dear."

Before Lilith could conjure another retort, he swept an elegant bow and gestured for William to precede him out the door. "Do show me out, will you?" He paused to look at Lilith. "Until next time, *ma chère*."

As they left the morning room, William chuckled. "I don't know why you'd think Lil might have done in Old Hatchet Face, Jack. I thought it was you. That bottle of port you handed him at White's wasn't full of strychnine, was it?"

"What?" Lilith asked sharply from behind them.

Jack stopped abruptly. "That is not amusing, William," he growled under his breath.

"I thought it was," William defended weakly.

"You gave Wenford a bottle of port before he expired on—on my couch?" Lilith said, eyeing him suspiciously.

"Oh, for God's sake," he snapped. He finally had the

chit thinking about him and kissing in conjunction. The last thing he needed was for her to have an excuse to return to her former contempt toward him. "I didn't want to shake his damned hand. I'm certain he's been given gifts by peers far worthier than myself."

"A less worthy one would be difficult to find," she returned haughtily.

"Look among your other suitors, Miss Benton," he retorted. "*Adieu.*"

He knew she wanted the last word, so he quickly shut the door behind him before she could respond. He wanted her to feel that things were unfinished between them—because they were. He followed William out the back way, where he had stashed Benedick. His skull throbbed, but as he'd told Lilith, he'd had worse, and for less reason. In this instance, it had been worth it.

The craving to touch Lilith Benton, to kiss her, had been driving him half mad, distracting him from the true goal of the game. He was saying things that were completely out of character, all to feel her mouth against his. And he was anything but cured of the desire to kiss her, to touch her, again.

"Where are we off to, then?" William asked, swinging up onto Thor.

"Believe it or not," Jack said, still annoyed at the boy, "I'm off to Parliament. You'll have to amuse yourself."

"You actually attend the House of Lords?"

"When I can find it." He pulled Benedick in when he sidestepped. "And I have a previous engagement this evening, as well."

William grinned as he dismounted again. "Who is she?"

"A young lady of fair countenance and bright eyes, with sweet laughter an angel would envy." Now seemed as good a time as any to forward his secondary plan. "By the by, I believe Miss St. Gerard is hoping a certain young gentleman will escort her to the opera this evening."

William brightened. "Antonia? Oh, Jack, that's . . ." A frown lowered his brow again. "That's awful. I have no box, and I can't very well have her sitting with the commons in the back."

Jack produced a piece of paper from his pocket. "Yes, but as you may recall, I have a box." He held out the note. "Enjoy yourself."

William reached up to take it, but Jack kept it gripped in his fingers. "And William, when the news of Wenford's death comes out, I would suggest you not mention that bottle of port again. Is that clear?"

"Hell's bells, Jack, it was a joke."

"William . . ."

"All right, all right, I swear. I won't mention the bottle of port again."

Jack released the note and nodded. "Good lad. Come by and see me tomorrow morning. I'll take you to Gentleman Jackson's."

In the meantime, Jack had more planning to do. His initial anger at Lilith Benton had evolved into something much more complex, and he had damned well better decide where he stood, before he took another step. Otherwise, he reflected with a grin, he might very well end up on his backside again.

Aunt Eugenia canceled their afternoon shopping excursion because of the frightful cold, ignoring Lilith's protest that she would welcome a chance to get out for a bit. Even shopping with Eugenia would have served to clear her head, to get the blasted Marquis of Dansbury out of her thoughts.

She filled her schedule with whatever useless projects and entertainments she could find around the house, but however busy she made herself, it did no good. Dansbury was definitely up to mischief, though she was no longer exactly certain what kind of trouble he was planning. She reached up and traced her lip with her fingers, then, with an exasperated sigh, went back to her sewing. Mainly, she wished to figure out why he kept reminding her of her debt to him, instead of collecting on it.

"Lil?" her brother called.

"What is it?" she said irritably, regarding the rather large hole she'd been jabbing in her embroidery with her needle.

William strolled into the morning room. "I thought I might go to the horse auctions. Care to come?"

She sighed and set aside her stitching. "I'd love to, but Papa would never approve."

Her brother leaned over the back of the couch beside her. "He never approves of anything, except finding old, sour-faced widowers for you to marry."

"William, hush."

"I know, I know. It won't do any good, and it'll only make him bellow at me. But it hardly seems fair." He picked up her embroidery hoop. "This is . . . interesting," he offered, studying it and experimentally lifting the needle.

"William, don't you dare. Give it back."

Silently he handed it over. "This Season's ruined for you, isn't it?" he said quietly. "Not that you ever had a chance of having any fun. But now with Wenford, and Jack, and me, and—"

"At least I won't be marrying His Grace," she interrupted with a smile. "And the Season's not over yet." Lilith looked up at his face, unused to seeing him somber. "I do wish you would be careful around the Marquis of Dansbury, though."

He gave a short grin. "Jack's all right. And I wouldn't worry about his proposal, either. Ernest and the others've been talking about how he's after some chit called the Ice Queen this Season."

Lilith blinked. "Oh?" Her heart began to beat faster again. "And what is he after her for?"

"To melt her, of course." He chuckled. "I don't give the poor gel much of a chance. Jack could burn the Devil's toes, if he had a mind to."

"No . . . no doubt."

He left a few moments later. Lilith sat where she was, trying to figure out why Dansbury would think that endlessly annoying her would make her look more kindly on him. Still more disturbing, she couldn't dismiss the scoundrel from her thoughts even knowing his arrogant, presumptuous plan. When Bevins scratched at the door, she started.

Alison, Lady Hutton, had sent over a note cordially inviting her and Aunt Eugenia to attend a party in honor of her daughter's fourth birthday that evening and apologizing for the short notice the letter gave them. Lilith smiled as she read it. The visit would provide a much better direction for her wandering thoughts than the recital at Lady Wickes'. Immediately she went to the desk to write out her grateful acceptance. The distraction was just what she needed.

"Miss Benton?"

It seemed no one could leave her in peace today. "Yes, Emily?" she said, looking up at her maid.

"Miss Benton, I . . . I can't find one of your earrings."

"Which one is it?" Emily had been her maid for

years, and she couldn't think for a moment that it had
been anything more than misplaced.

"The . . . your mama's pearls, Miss Benton." Emily
looked quite upset, and Lilith patted her hand while the
girl took a breath. "Jenny, the downstairs maid, she
brought up one of the earrings from the morning room
the day before yesterday, and I already put the necklace
in its box, but I've looked everywhere and I can't find
the other one."

"Day before yesterday?" Lilith mused, trying to recall what she'd been doing. The past week had been full
of tumultuous events, most of them involving Dansbury
or His Grace. Abruptly she remembered, and the blood
drained from her face. She had been wrestling with the
Duke of Wenford, and he had grabbed her hair. "Oh,
no," she breathed.

"What is it, Miss Benton?"

"Nothing, Emily." Lilith took a deep breath. Those
earrings and the matching necklace were the only me-
mento of her mother she'd allowed herself to keep. Little
as she approved of Elizabeth Benton's wild ways, and
much as her mother's abrupt departure had hurt, she
hadn't been able to bring herself to part with the baubles.
Perhaps Milgrew or Dansbury had noticed the duke gripping something when they'd placed him in the cellar.
Certainly Jack would have, for he noticed everything.

Emily offered to take another look through her wardrobe, and Lilith agreed, hoping her supposition was
wrong. She finished her missive to Lady Hutton and was
just rising to give it to Bevins when her father intercepted her. He wore the same dour expression on his
face he had since Billington's, and Lilith sighed. Hearing
of Wenford's death wouldn't serve to cheer him up.
"How was Mrs. Higginson?"

"Whining incessantly. Six years hasn't changed her

one spot." He gestured at the note. "What've you got there?"

"My reply to an invitation from Lady Hutton. She's giving a birthday party this evening, and I would like to attend."

"Hutton?"

"Her husband is Lord Hutton, from Shropshire."

"What land does he possess?"

"A barony at Linfield. What does that mat—"

"Only a baron?" The viscount frowned. "I thought you were attending Lady Wickes' event this evening. I heard Lady Georgina ask if you would sit with her there."

"But Papa, Georgina's so . . . light-headed," Lilith protested. "And I truly would like to see Lady Hutton again. Lord Hutton's grandfather was the Earl of Clanden," she added hopefully. Or so Penelope's mother had told them.

Hamble looked at her, his somber expression unchanged. "Flighty girl. Very well. Once you're married, you'll have no time for such nonsense, anyway."

"Thank you, Papa." Lilith braced herself. "Papa, about His Grace . . ." she began, hoping to convince him once and for all to choose someone else before Wenford's naked corpse was discovered and her father had to add embarrassment to his already keen disappointment.

"Yes," he returned with a distracted frown, "I've been meaning to speak to him." He headed back for the door. "I'll send over a card," he said to himself as he left the room.

"But I truly don't want to marry Old Hatchet Face," she muttered, going off to find Bevins and have her note delivered. "And besides, he's dead."

Chapter 8

"There are beautiful gardens in Paris," Richard Hutton conceded, "but no one grows roses like the English."

Lady Hutton, seated on the couch beside her husband, took his hand and patted it between her own. "Sometimes I think Richard believes God created English weather solely for the purpose of growing roses."

The twenty or so guests gathered in the Hutton drawing room laughed. As Lilith had suspected upon meeting Alison, the Hutton circle was rather boisterous. They had also been warm and generous, and thankfully none of her suitors were there. Aunt Eugenia had been gloomy until the Countess of Ashton's entry into the party, at which point she had cheered considerably, to her niece's relief. The occasion was a welcome respite from the pressures of the Season, and Lilith was in no hurry to leave.

"Well, all I know is it's too damned cold for me," Peter Wilten commented, handing over another gaily wrapped package.

"Mr. Wilten," Gabriella Wilten admonished, but the others laughed again.

131

Beatrice Hutton sat on the floor, surrounded by mounds of opened gifts. Even at four the girl was a beauty, with her mother's dark, curly hair and her father's gray eyes. Lilith smiled at her, gratified that the stuffed animal she had purchased seemed to be among the little one's favorites.

Aunt Eugenia laughed at something, and Lilith glanced over to see her animatedly chatting with the countess and with Lord Hutton's mother, who had also been acquainted with Lord and Lady Dupont in Shropshire. Richard's niece and nephews sat sorting through the pile of gifts on their cousin's behalf.

"Miss Benton, how many different varieties do you cultivate?" Lord Hutton asked, as Beatrice climbed into his lap and demanded help with a particularly difficult wrapping job.

Lilith looked up to find herself the center of attention. "I have fifteen bushes here, and another thirty or so at Hamble. Many are duplicates, so perhaps thirty-five different varieties."

"That's marvelous!"

Lilith smiled at his enthusiasm. "Thank you."

"You know, I've been looking for a Madame Hardy. Mine perished in a trimming accident." He glanced down at his daughter good-humoredly.

"I have a Madame Hardy at Benton House," Lilith replied, pleased to be able to render assistance. "I'd be happy to give you a cutting."

"I would be grate—"

"Where's my Honey Bea?" a voice called out.

Beatrice squealed and vaulted off her father's lap. Paper and ribbons flew from under her feet as she ran for the doorway. Lilith could only watch, stunned, as the Marquis of Dansbury strode into the room, picked Beatrice up, and swung her around in the air. Laughing, he kissed the girl soundly and then set her back on the floor. Beatrice promptly began tugging at his pockets.

"What's this?" Jack asked innocently. "What are you looking for, little girl?"

Beatrice giggled. "My birthday present."

"You told me what you wanted. Do you remember?"

"Yes, Uncle Jack."

"Do you think it would fit in my pockets?"

The girl spread out her arms. "Where is it, then?"

The marquis motioned behind him. A servant stepped into the room, a wiggling Irish setter puppy in his arms. Beatrice laughed happily as the marquis took possession of the puppy and squatted down beside her. "She's littler than you, Bea, so you have to be gentle. Understand?"

Beatrice reached out and carefully stroked the puppy's back while Dansbury cradled it. "Yes." She nodded.

"All right, Honey Bea, here's your red puppy. Happy birthday."

With a glance at the Huttons, the marquis set it down. It immediately jumped up on Beatrice and began licking her face. Her cousins crowded around excitedly to greet the four-footed arrival, as well. After a moment, Dansbury rose and strolled over to the couch. Halfway there his lazy, intelligent eyes passed over Lilith. For a heartbeat he froze, plainly astounded to see her there. She raised an eyebrow at him, pleased for a moment to have gotten the upper hand, as he continued on his way.

"Sorry I'm late." He smiled, leaning over to kiss Alison on the cheek. He glanced again at Richard. "Shall I stay?" he asked quietly.

"Of course," Alison said warmly, and tugged him down onto the couch beside her. "She told you she wanted a puppy?"

"She was quite specific. She wanted a *red* puppy."

Now that she saw them together, Lilith was surprised she hadn't realized before that Jack Faraday and Alison Hutton were siblings. They had the same dark, wavy hair and brown eyes, though Alison's features were softer and more rounded than those of the lean-faced marquis. Alison had even mentioned that she had a brother, and Lilith was disgusted with herself for not realizing sooner who it must be.

Dansbury reached across his sister to offer his hand to Richard. Unless Lilith was mistaken, the baron hesitated before he shook it.

"Still busy days for you, Richard?" Jack asked easily, accepting a glass of port from the maid.

Richard nodded. "The prime minister remains unconvinced that we've purged England of the last of Boney's spies."

"I still don't see what it matters, anymore. Bonaparte is dead. They have no one to report to."

Lord Hutton's eyes narrowed. "Try explaining that to Liverpool."

The marquis straightened. "As I recall, I—"

"Jack, have you met Miss Benton?" Alison interrupted hurriedly, and gestured at Lilith. "Lilith, my brother, the Marquis of Dansbury."

Jack rose to take Lilith's hand in his long fingers, and brought it to his lips. "We've met," he murmured with a smile, his dark eyes dancing. "Though I'm delighted to see you again, Miss Benton."

"My lord," Lilith responded, retrieving her hand from his warm, strong grip as quickly as she could.

Dansbury nodded amiably and turned away to chat with the rest of the guests—or at least, those who didn't seem unnerved by him. Lilith watched him closely. Charming and personable tonight, he still looked like a panther among house cats. It wasn't until he sat to spend several minutes talking with his sister, his cynical, guarded expression slowly easing into a soft smile, that Lilith thought she again glimpsed the real Jack Faraday.

He glanced at her, and she self-consciously looked down at the tea cup cradled in her hands. A moment later he had seated himself beside her. Lilith took a sip of tea before she met his inquisitive look. "I thought you would have business elsewhere this evening."

"I decided to leave your brother to his own devices tonight. You should be pleased."

She looked up to find his amused gaze on his niece and her red puppy. "Still trying to melt the Ice Queen?" she murmured.

He smiled as he turned back to her. "You've already made it quite clear that your temperature runs somewhat to the volcanic."

"And it took only one blow to the head to convince you."

"It took only one kiss," he corrected softly.

"You are a devil, my lord," she snapped, flushing.

Unexpectedly, the insult made him laugh. "Your eyes are flashing again, Miss Benton," he commented. "I have never seen such green, even in king's emeralds."

The flattery made her blush, which made her even angrier. He threw compliments about like daisies, and she knew better than to take any of it seriously. "Were these emeralds you speak of by any chance stolen?"

Again he chuckled. "So now I am a devil, a murderer of dukes, and a jewel thief," he whispered, leaning closer. "Are there any other dastardly deeds you wish to accuse me of performing this evening?"

"Not in polite company," she sniffed.

Slowly he ran his finger along the edge of her gown. "I was hoping you would say that. Perhaps we could go somewhere to discuss it in private, Lilith."

"Miss Benton," she corrected again, her eyes darting in his direction and then away. She wondered how many other women had received that same enticing smile, and tried to ignore her fluttering pulse. "And don't think any of your compliments will have the slightest effect on me: I've never had any use for your sort, and I never will. In fact, I've very nearly decided to wed the Earl of Nance."

He scowled. "I thought we'd been over this. Nance is completely wrong for you."

"Oh, really?" she replied, surprised at his sharp tone. "What leads you to that conclusion?"

Jack ticked the points off on his fingers. "He's an idiot, he's got no sense of humor, and he's stiff as a post. Premature rigor mortis." He smiled cynically. "Could say that about Jeremy Giggins, too. And Henning. And Varrick." He frowned. "*And* Old Hatchet Face. In fact, Miss Benton, it's difficult to tell how many of your suitors are actually deceased, and how many just don't know it yet." His smile cracked again. "Except for me, of course."

That hardly seemed fair. "They're all completely respectable. Except for you."

He looked at her for a moment. "And they're all completely unsuitable for someone who's no Ice Queen. Except for me."

The declaration was a rather direct one for Jack Faraday, and it was only fair that she answer in kind. "If you hadn't made such a waste of your life, I might agree with you."

She glanced over at Aunt Eugenia to see if she was ready to depart. Unfortunately, though, Mrs. Farlane seemed quite content to sit and chat all night. Apparently she had decided that with the Duke of Wenford's proposal nearly secured, even Jack couldn't harm things.

When Lilith looked back at Dansbury, his expression was solemn.

"Miss Benton, I would think that you, of all people, would be willing to admit that you have very little other than rumor and innuendo on which to base your perception of me—and that perhaps I am not at all the kind of man you imagine."

His seriousness surprised her, for she had expected neither honesty nor sincerity from him. "Just what kind of man are you, then?" she asked slowly, wondering whether he would answer.

They were interrupted by another guest, and Lilith stifled the desire to tell Gabrielle Wilten to go away. After an interminable moment, Jack turned back to her.

"What a piece of work am I?" he said softly, his voice low and intimate. " 'How noble in reason, how infinite in faculty. In form and moving,' " he ran a hand along the lapel of his magnificent blue coat, " 'how express and admirable. In action how like an angel. In apprehension—' "

" 'How like a god,' " Lilith finished. She smiled, shaking her head. For a rakehell, he was exceedingly well read. "And how modest, as well."

His eyes danced in the chandelier light. "Good God, you have a beautiful smile," he whispered.

It took Lilith a moment to gather her thoughts enough to continue. "May I ask you a question?" she ventured, reluctant to break the pleasant mood between them.

"I am at your service."

"Did—well, did you notice if His Grace might have been . . . holding something in one of his hands?"

"While I can think of several inappropriate comments, I will settle for asking for a description of what you think he might have been holding. I can attest to the fact that he had nothing in his pockets." He gave a slow grin. "He wasn't wearing any when I left him."

For a moment she'd nearly forgotten what a scoundrel Jack was. Thank goodness he'd reminded her. "Never mind." She didn't need to end up even further in his debt than she'd already landed.

"What are you looking for?" he repeated.

Lilith gazed at his stormy eyes, and then lowered her gaze and took another sip of tea. "An earring," she murmured reluctantly.

He sat forward. "An earring. You gave that gammon-faced goat an earring?"

Miss Gloria Ashbury looked in their direction, and whispered something to Lady Mavern. Lilith belatedly realized that she and the marquis were seated rather close to one another for mere acquaintances. Self-consciously, she shifted away.

"Do be quiet," she hissed. "You sound jealous."

He opened his mouth, then shut it again, his eyes glinting. "I am simply amazed that you would give such an old, ugly behemoth a token of your affection. Didn't you think to remove it from his possession while he was in your morning room?"

His voice remained hushed, but Lilith couldn't help glancing about the noisy room before she answered. "I didn't *give* him *anything*. And I didn't know it was missing then. He grabbed my hair when he fell, and I didn't notice it was gone until a few hours ago. I've looked everywhere . . . and then I thought he might still have it."

Jack looked at her for the space of several heartbeats. "I'm beginning to wish I'd come calling on you several moments earlier," he finally said.

"Because you don't believe me?" she returned, offended.

"Because I would have been able to save Wenford the effort of dying on his own."

Lilith swallowed at the dark, dangerous edge to his soft voice. It couldn't be jealousy, for of course he had no claim on her whatsoever. "I'm half convinced you had something to do with his death, anyway."

To her relief, he only sighed and shook his head. "It is times like this I wish I'd lived a more exemplary life."

It was the first time she'd heard anything like regret in his tone. "Then why didn't you?"

He looked down, shrugging. "There's no fun in it. And never fear, my lady. I'll go look for your damned earring later tonight."

Another scrap of honor. Dansbury was turning out to be full of surprises. "I wish I could believe what you tell me," she whispered, wondering if he realized she was referring to more than the search for her earring.

Beatrice ran over to tug at her uncle's hands, trying to pull him to his feet. "Show me a trick," she demanded.

"I wish you could as well, Lilith," he returned, then allowed himself to be dragged over to where the children were using furniture to make a pen for the puppy.

"Miss Benton," she murmured after a moment, following him with her eyes.

"*Uncle Jack* is not a proper name for a female pup," Uncle Jack explained patiently, while behind him Alison didn't even bother stifling her laughter.

"It's her name," Beatrice insisted, trying to keep the wriggling mass of legs and tail and ears confined to her lap.

The last of the Huttons' guests had departed only a few moments earlier, and Jack was exceedingly pleased to note that, despite her aunt's belated urging, Lilith

Benton had been among the last to leave. "But don't you realize how very confusing things could become?" he pursued. "How will your puppy know if you're speaking to her or to me?"

"I know who I'm talking to," his niece explained, looking at him as though he were a complete idiot.

"What about Lord Hutton?" he suggested, in a last effort to preserve for himself at least a scrap of dignity.

"Oh, thank you very much," Richard muttered from the doorway. It was the most he'd said to his brother-in-law in over an hour.

"She's *Uncle Jack,*" Beatrice argued, beginning to pout.

Jack squatted down to ruffle the dog's ears. "All right, Honey Bea. Uncle Jack it is." Richard wouldn't like the reminder of his presence in the Hutton household, but he'd be damned if he'd make Bea cry over the choice of a dog's name.

Fanny, Beatrice's governess, appeared from the direction of the stairs, and Jack stood as that formidable woman prepared to take charge.

"Time for bed, miss," Fanny informed the girl.

"I don't want to go to bed," Beatrice protested, but she reluctantly followed her governess out.

"Jack, come sit with me," Alison said from across the room.

He strolled over to sink onto the couch beside his sister. "Thank you for inviting me. I wasn't certain you would."

"And I wasn't certain you'd come if I did."

"Well," Jack said slowly, examining his fingernails and very aware of Richard lurking across the room, "though I admit to having been rather remiss in my familial obligations in the past, I have never yet missed Bea's birthday."

"Only very nearly," Richard commented, and left the room.

"You know," Jack commented, looking after his brother-in-law, "I do believe Richard's beginning to warm to me again. A year ago he couldn't even bear to be in the same room with me for longer than five minutes."

"Yes, you were quite civilized tonight. I rather like you that way."

He couldn't very well tell her that he was only behaving as a ruse to lure a skittish young lady, so he settled for sitting back and crossing his ankles. "Hm."

Alison smiled and rubbed at her rounded belly. "So tell me, big brother, how long have you known Lilith Benton?"

"Miss Benton?" Jack repeated innocently, giving a slight, calculated scowl as though trying to remember when the acquaintance had begun. "I am friends with her brother, I suppose."

For a long moment Alison looked at him, and he gazed coolly back at her. She was better at reading him than anyone else, but he was determined that she would see nothing.

"You fancy her, Jonathan Auguste Faraday!" she exclaimed.

Jack lifted both brows. "I don't really—"

His sister began applauding. "I never thought it would happen—that you'd be soured by all those high flyers you pretend amuse you. I'd given up hope."

"Alison, I think you're—"

"Oh, how the mighty have fallen!" she crowed.

This was becoming rather annoying. "Leave off, Alison. She wants nothing to do with me."

His sister's smile faded. "Why not?"

"She's after a respectable title. And she thinks I've

made a waste of my life, and that I'm spooning off her brother and mean to ruin him and take his fortune.''

"Oh, Jack," Alison sighed, reaching up to tug at his hair. "Why do people think such awful things about you?''

He shrugged, taking a swallow of port. "Because they're mostly true."

"Jack . . ."

He set the glass aside and stood. "So don't get your hopes up, my girl. Miss Benton's obsession with respectability makes her amusing. Barely. Goodnight, Alison." He headed out into the hallway to collect his hat and greatcoat. "Goodnight, Richard!" he called in a louder voice, though he didn't expect an answer.

He didn't receive one.

Though Jack had planned to continue the evening at Boodle's club, Lilith Benton's smile seemed to be occupying too much of his thoughts—particularly if he intended on gambling. She had given him another task for the evening, anyway, though it certainly wasn't one he looked forward to with much relish.

When he returned to Faraday House in order to change into something more appropriate for skulking about Wenford's wine cellar, he found William Benton sitting on the front step, elbows on his knees and chin in his hands.

"Did you lose something?" he asked, stepping around the boy as Peese pulled open the door.

William rose and followed him into the house. "No. Not exactly. I came to ask you a question, but your . . . your butler there wouldn't let me in.''

Jack glanced at Peese, who stifled a grin as he shut the door behind them. "No, he generally doesn't." He headed up the stairs, and noted that William hesitated in the hallway. "I don't have time to sit about and chat."

"Might I accompany you wherever it is you're going, then?"

"I hardly think . . . ." Jack paused, turning to look down at the boy. After all, this venture was his sister's fault, anyway. He shrugged. "Why not? I'll be down in a moment."

In his bed chamber, Jack pulled off his coat and tossed it on the bed. Martin appeared within moments and clucked his tongue in annoyance as Jack dug through the less-used portion of his mahogany closet.

"My lord, do you require assistance?"

Jack glanced over his shoulder. "Where are my old things?"

"Old things, my lord?"

"The French ones. Old and dark."

He felt Martin hesitate behind him. "Is there some difficulty, my lord?"

Jack sighed. "Not yet. I just need something I can crawl about in and still pass for half a gentleman."

The valet headed into the dressing closet and came out a few moments later with a dark brown coat. "Will this suffice?"

The marquis wrinkled his nose. "Did I ever wear that?"

"Once, I believe. In Paris." Martin paused again, and looked at the garment. Jack watched him, curious, as the valet's brow furrowed and he lifted the coat toward his nose. Immediately he paled and lowered it again. "No, not the thing at all. I'll get you another."

"What is it?" Jack asked, stepping forward to intercept the valet.

"Nothing, my lord. I merely—"

Jack took the coat from Martin's hands and lifted it to his face. He breathed in, expecting mildew, or ale. At the light scent of a French perfume, he blanched. In the same heartbeat he thought he detected the sweet odor of stale blood, though it was entirely possible that he was imagining it.

"Quite right," he muttered, returning the coat to Martin and rubbing his palms on his thighs. "Won't do at all."

"My lord—"

"Get me another damned coat, Martin. I'm in a hurry. And burn that one."

The valet swallowed whatever he had been about to say. He returned to the closet and emerged almost immediately with another coat of French design. This one was black, and Jack yanked it from Martin's grip and pulled it on. It was obviously five years out of style, with the tighter waist favored in Paris at the time. At least it merely smelled musty.

"So, where are we off to?" William queried, as Jack returned downstairs. The boy eyed his less-than-fashionable attire curiously.

"A little necroscopy," he answered, pulling on his gloves.

"Nec—you mean Wenford?" William asked, an unholy gleam of anticipation entering his green eyes.

"Hush," Jack admonished, as they reached the front entry and Peese pulled open the door for them. "If you can't keep your blasted mouth closed, you're not invited."

William took the warning to heart, and he was silent as they rode the mile or so to Remdale House. Jack could tell the lad didn't like the constraint, and that he was bursting to discuss something, but the marquis was too distracted even for William's amusing chatter. Coming back here was idiocy. By lucky chance he'd escaped notice in executing the original prank, and he had no more wish to be connected with it now than he had before. But Lilith Benton had smiled and asked him, and he'd acquiesced like a drooling idiot. She'd pay for it later. That was the only consolation, the only reason he could give, for taking the risk.

Approaching the house in the overcast dark was certainly easier than it had been in daylight, but once they reached the outer door leading down into the wine cellar, things became decidedly more difficult. With a quick glance around to be certain none of the stable hands was out for a moonlit stroll, Jack pulled a knife from his boot and squatted down at the foot of the cellar door.

"Are you certain you know what you're doing?"

Jack looked over his shoulder at William, cowering in the shadows beneath the elms, and scowled. "I told you to be quiet and keep your eyes open."

"Yes, I know," William whispered. "But I thought you'd done this already."

"That was during the day, and without a damned annoying pup whining every blasted second."

Jack was actually able to count to seven before William spoke again.

"Do you ever think of getting married?"

For a moment the marquis stilled his fingers on the rusted lock. Evidently Antonia's charms were beginning to have an effect, after all. "I said to be quiet," he repeated with less heat.

"I heard you," William whispered. "But Nance cornered me this evening at the theater, and warned me all about libertines like you. And then Antonia—"

"Oh, he did, did he?" Jack interrupted. Lionel Hendrick was a stuffy, self-centered boor, and he wished he'd overheard the conversation.

The boy nodded, his teeth showing in the dark as he grinned. "So do you? Ever think of getting married, I mean."

"Here's a piece of advice for you, William." Jack leaned to one side so his body wouldn't block the scanty moonlight while he went back to work on the heavy padlock. "Never give your heart to a female. When they're finished with it and hand it back, you may not recognize the wretched thing any longer."

The boy's silence and disapproval were almost palpable, but under the circumstances Jack didn't much care that he might have offended William's tender sensibilities. At least later no one would be able to say he hadn't been warned.

"But you proposed to Lil," William finally pointed out.

Jack scraped his knuckles. "Damn. As a joke, boy." At least that had been the idea. There seemed to be some confusion in his mind about his motivations lately. "Her feelings toward me have been well documented, I believe." He twisted the tip of his knife blade again, and the lock gave. "There. I told you I could do it."

"Took you bloody long enough. I'm freezing."

"Be grateful for the cold," Jack grunted, as he pulled the door up and open. "Otherwise you'd be smelling Wenford before we ever set eyes on him."

"That's rather gruesome."

Jack paused as he started down the steep stairs into the cellar. The lad had certainly never gone through anything like this before. "Perhaps you'd best wait out here."

"Nonsense. After what he did to Lilith, seeing Old Hatchet Face dead is certainly not going to offend my sensibilities."

"I hope not." Jack lifted one of the lanterns off the wall and lit it. Racks and shelves of wine bottles, illuminated by the yellow flicker, spread out in all directions in the substantial cellar. Moving silently, he carefully guided William along the wall and down an aisle. "Rather clever of your sister to send me off on her little errand while she gets a good night's sleep, don't you think?" he muttered.

"It would hardly be seemly for her to be creeping about the Duke of Wenford's house in the middle of the night."

"Just as well," the marquis murmured, turning his head at a slight rustling off to his left. "I'm nearly out of ammunition today, and I don't think she means to take prisoners." A faint meow sounded behind the shelving. Thank goodness Wenford kept cats down here to stop rats from chewing his corks, or the sight they came upon might have been a good deal less palatable than William was prepared for.

"Lil's not so bad, you know. And it's not her fault, really."

They rounded the end of the shelves. Behind him, William made a small sound in his throat and stopped. Wenford lay where Jack and Milgrew had left him, sprawled on his back in the altogether, a bottle of bad wine clutched in one hand. His clothes lay in a neat pile between his feet. With a sigh, Jack handed the lantern to William and squatted down beside the naked corpse.

"Good God," William whispered, the lantern wavering in his hand.

"Hold the damned light still," Jack hissed. The earring was in neither of the duke's hands, nor was it among his clothes. Jack spent several minutes looking about the dirt- and straw-covered floor. He found two pence which had likely fallen out of Wenford's pockets, but no pearls. "So tell me," he said over his shoulder, as he began working his way along the base of the nearest racks, "why isn't Miss Benton's concern with respectability her own fault?"

"You've likely heard the story about our mother and the Earl of Greyton, yes?"

"I seem to recall something about it."

"Well, I suppose it was all true. Mother was quite a bit wilder than Father was comfortable with. It was an arranged marriage, you know. To be honest, I don't think he had a clue how to deal with her. When she abandoned us for Greyton—well, Father swore he would never forgive her. And he didn't."

"And he pulled you out of London over it."

William nodded. "Lil was twelve. And from that moment, he made certain she knew that Mother's blood was tainted and that it was *her* duty to redeem the Benton name. Lil took it all very seriously. She used to make herself sick with seeing that everything was just so. And Father and that old stick Eugenia would damned well point it out if she missed anything."

Jack turned one of the coins in his fingers, then pocketed it. "Seems a great deal of responsibility for a little girl."

"Too much," William agreed promptly. "But she's never stopped trying. And with me for a brother, I sometimes think regaining the Colonies would be an easier task."

The floorboards above them creaked, and Jack lifted his head as a light shower of dust drifted down around them. Compared to him, William was a saint. He sighed in the near dark. "Which would place me somewhere between Falstaff and the Devil himself."

William chuckled. "Closer to the latter, I think."

That explained a great many things he'd observed about Lilith Benton. No wonder she came near to throwing a blue fit every time he approached. He threatened to collapse the carefully constructed respectability she'd worked nonstop for six years to build. On the other hand, he couldn't forget the way she'd responded to his kiss, or the way she'd shivered at his light caresses. She liked being touched. She liked *his* touch. Jack gave a slight smile. Perhaps the angel secretly wondered what it would be like to be in the devil's embrace. The devil certainly wondered.

"What now?"

Jack glanced up again. "Wait here a moment. If anyone comes, hide."

"Where are you going?"

"Upstairs. There's something I need to check."

"Jack . . ." the boy protested, as the marquis headed for the stairs leading up to the kitchen.

"I'll be right back," he said over his shoulder.

The duke had been missing for two days now, and he half expected the house to be in an uproar. Everything seemed quiet and peaceful, however, as he crept down the hallway and made his way to Wenford's private office. Nothing looked as though it had been touched, so no one had been by to look for clues to the duke's whereabouts. In the second drawer of the antique oak desk, he found the account ledger he was looking for.

More than a dozen entries over the last two pages were for debts he knew came from Dolph Remdale, including one of the final notations, for twelve hundred and seventy-seven pounds. The blunt for the diamond pin *had* come from the uncle. From the look of it, Dolph lost regularly, and heavily, at gambling, and no doubt Wenford made his nephew plead for every penny he required to make good on the losses.

Jack sat back in the chair. Old Hatchet Face certainly had picked a convenient time to end up dead. A week or two later and he might have been wed to Lilith Benton, and even possibly have an heir on the way—and Dolph wouldn't have been able to inherit. Now, as soon as the death was discovered, Dolph Remdale would become a very wealthy, and very powerful, individual.

Admittedly, it was likely nothing more than wishful thinking to hope that one of the Remdales had done the other in. Wenford had been old and given to fits of rage, and there was nothing odd in the idea that he would simply expire from it. On the other hand, Jack had never been one to discount luck. And that was why he took the account ledger and moved it to one of the bookshelves, where he stuffed it behind a volume of Aristotle. No one would think to look for it there—at least, not for some time.

He slipped back out and through the kitchen, making his way into the darkness of the cold cellar. "William?" he whispered, looking about blindly.

"Thank God," came the muttered response from almost directly behind him.

He spun to see William lowering a bottle of wine, and snatched it away from him. "This bottle is sixty-five years old," he hissed. "If you're going to crown someone, do it with a bad vintage."

"Sorry," William grumbled. "Did you find what you were looking for?"

"One can only hope. Let's go."

Chapter 9

Lilith awoke with a dreadful headache, her sleep destroyed by dreams of dead dukes, and dark-eyed demons with charming smiles and deep, seductive voices. And the ache in her head didn't ease in the least when William appeared in the breakfast room to inform her where he had spent a portion of the evening.

"You went where?" she gasped, setting aside her knife lest she should be tempted to damage her brother, or herself, with it.

"Jack needed someone to hold the lantern." Her brother shrugged, unperturbed, and reached for the platter of ham.

"I can't believe he would involve you in this," she sputtered, then considered what she was saying. "Yes, I can believe it," she amended. "Blast him."

"I volunteered," William countered, loyal to the last.

Something else which Jack Faraday had no doubt arranged. "Was there any sign of commotion at Remdale House?" she asked, uncertain whether Jack had mentioned the earring to her brother, and unwilling to explain to William the particulars of how Wenford might

151

have come to have it in his possession, if he didn't already know.

William grinned. "Only when Jack nearly took my head off for trying to crown him with an expensive bottle of wine."

"Whatever did you try to crown Dansbury for?" she exclaimed.

"It was dark. I couldn't bloody tell who was creeping back down into the cellar."

Lilith looked at him. Something was missing from this tale, and she didn't think she would like knowing what it might be. "Exactly where was the marquis creeping back from?"

"Jack went looking for something or other upstairs. I don't know what it was about, and as usual, he didn't care to inform me."

"Perhaps you *should* have crowned him with the bottle, then." She hated not knowing what that scoundrel was up to, especially with so much of her own well-being and peace-of-mind at stake.

William snorted and shook his head. "Said it was too good a year, and next time to crown him with a bad vintage. Never even seen Jack near a bad vintage. He keeps his own store of port at half the clubs in town. Even the bottle he gave Wenford that night was first class, and he don't—didn't—like Old Hatchet Face."

Lilith's breath and her heart stopped, and then began again painfully. "That bottle was from his *own* stock?" she whispered.

She'd only been teasing before, when she'd suggested that Jack had been more directly involved in Wenford's death than he let on. But abruptly it wasn't so amusing. The problem was that after the splendid time she'd had last night, she wasn't certain she wanted to believe the worst about the Marquis of Dansbury any longer. He'd been so charming and witty, and even generous, and the Lord knew he was handsome as sin itself. Whether that gentleman was just another pose he'd fancied for the evening, or whether the true Jack Faraday had made a rare appearance, she had no idea. She started when Bevins scratched at the door.

"Miss Benton," he intoned, holding out his tray with a card deposited on it, "Lord Hutton asks if you have a moment to spare."

"I say. Hutton? That's Jack's—"

"Excuse me, William," she interrupted. She owed enough of her reputation to Bevins' silence, and had no wish to trust him with any more than absolutely necessary. Lilith smiled as William looked at her suspiciously. "I promised Lord Hutton a cutting of my Madame Hardy rose. I hadn't realized he was so anxious for it." She rose and playfully patted William on the head. "I'll be right back. Stay out of trouble, if you please."

Richard stood in the hallway, admiring the vase of yellow-pink roses she had set in the vase there. "Lord Penzance," he said.

"They are particular favorites of mine."

"Mine as well." He took her hand. "I apologize for hurrying over like this, but I happened to be coming this way, and I thought—"

"I'm delighted you came by," Lilith said warmly, grateful for the distraction. Outside the Marquis of Dansbury's presence, Lord Hutton showed much of the same warmth that she had appreciated in his wife. "Do you wish a cup of tea?"

He shook his head. "I really haven't enough time, but thank you."

"Then let me show you my treasures."

The admiration Lord Hutton showed her rose garden was quite gratifying. In addition, his presence could serve another, more useful, purpose. "I hadn't realized the Marquis of Dansbury was a relation of yours," she said, rubbing her hands together against the cold, and attempting to stifle the inner voice that said she was being sneaky and manipulative. One must fight fire with fire, after all.

"Yes," he answered shortly, glancing up at her before he went back to his selection. "Jack actually introduced me to Alison. Might I possibly have a cutting of your Anne of Gierstein?"

"Of course." Lilith handed him her clippers. "He seems a very . . . independent individual," she ventured.

"I'll give him that." Richard winced as a thorn pricked his finger. "Jack's ruffled more feathers than a fox in a pigeon coop."

Apparently Jack had considerably ruffled Lord Hutton's feathers, as well. "He and the Remdales certainly don't seem to get along."

He glanced at her again. "No, they don't. It goes back a long way—something about a piece of land Jack's grandfather lost in a wager, and now the Remdales won't sell it back. Not likely to, either, with Jack antagonizing Wenford all the time."

Lilith suddenly wished Richard hadn't been so forthcoming. Perhaps Jack Faraday did have a motive for disposing of Wenford, after all. It was unthinkable, but neither could she ignore what she'd learned, especially in conjunction with the bottle of port.

That latest bit of information continued to disturb her all morning and most of the way through her luncheon with Pen and Lady Sanford, despite the warming weather and the lovely outdoor café they had discovered.

"Oh, that's Darlene McFadden." Lady Sanford looked across the avenue and smiled. "I hadn't realized she was in London this summer," she continued, eyeing the tall redhead entering a hat shop. "I'll be right back." She picked up her reticule and hurried across the street.

"She'll be gone for an hour," Penelope giggled, looking after her. Abruptly she straightened. "Isn't that William?"

"Where?"

Pen pointed out at the street. A phaeton emblazoned with the Hamble crest passed by, with William holding the reins. At the sight of her brother's companion, Lilith groaned. "He said he was going picnicking, but I didn't know it was with Antonia St. Gerard."

"That's Antonia St. Gerard?" Pen said, looking after them with a downcast expression. "I heard that she never comes out of doors in daylight."

Lilith sighed and picked up her napkin. "Apparently he was able to convince her. He makes me so angry sometimes, the way he gets an idea in his thick skull and runs off before he considers anything."

"I think he's quite nice," Penelope countered, spooning sugar into her tea. "He always makes me laugh."

Lilith looked at her friend. "Do you fancy my brother, Pen?" she asked, surprised.

Penelope blushed. "Perhaps." She held her napkin over her mouth. "A little."

"Well, I hope he comes to his senses, then," Lilith said feelingly, as she watched the phaeton disappear down the street. "He's been behaving like . . . like a rakehell, since he was captured by Dansbury."

Pen gave a small frown, and Lilith nodded. "I don't hold out much hope for his reputation, or his pocketbook, unless I can free him from Jack Faraday's talons."

"Does that make me a bird of prey, or a dragon?" The marquis's deep voice came from behind her, and she realized why Penelope had been frowning.

She blushed as he pulled up a chair and sat. He was

obviously amused at her insults, and she began to fume. "Definitely a fire-breathing dragon," she returned hotly.

"Hm," the marquis murmured, looking at her with enigmatic eyes. "Dragons are rather fond of . . . virginal young women, are they not?"

"Oh, my," Pen whispered, blushing bright red and fanning her face.

Lilith refused to be shocked. "That's rather weak-hearted prey for such a fearsome beast, don't you think?"

"Only if you equate virginity with timidity." He planted his elbow on the table, and chin on his hand, gazed speculatively at Lilith. "I have no doubt you could slay a dragon, if you wished."

"Actually, I've been considering something very like that, Lord Dansbury," she returned, narrowing her eyes. She wished that for once he would quit playing these blasted games and let her know what he was truly thinking.

"Lilith!" Pen exclaimed.

"Oh, it's all right, Miss Sanford. I'm quite used to it. Miss Benton and I have a rather unique bond."

"You do?" Pen asked hesitantly, glancing over wide-eyed at her friend, who sat stiff-backed as Dansbury signaled for a cup of coffee.

"Oh, yes. One of the many curious aspects is that she never asks me questions directly," the marquis continued, turning to meet Lilith's gaze, "but rather goes to my relations to pry into my personal affairs."

So he had found out that she had spoken to Lord Hutton. "What the marquis doesn't realize," Lilith said to Pen, though her gaze remained on Dansbury, "is that if he were as forthcoming as he claims to be, no one would need to go elsewhere for potential . . . evidence."

She used the word intentionally, and was pleased to see a muscle twitch in his cheek.

Dansbury took a swallow of his coffee and gazed into the cup for a moment. "You were much friendlier last night."

"Last night, I was not aware that a certain bottle of port came from a private stock. I have also been enlightened as to a disputed piece of property."

"Richard is a damned gossip." Jack scowled.

"So you say. What is your explanation for the bottle?"

Pen looked from one to the other, obviously mystified by the conversation. That was just as well, for Lilith didn't wish her friend involved in what could still be a gargantuan scandal.

Jack shook his head and leaned forward, brushing the back of her hand gently with one finger before she shivered and pulled it away. "What I think, Lilith," he said softly, "is that sooner or later you are going to run out of excuses about me. And then what are you going to do?"

A faint blush crept up her cheeks. "You can play at words all you like, my lord. It changes nothing."

"There are other things I'd rather play at," he responded suggestively.

"Cards, I would assume?" Lilith was half-surprised that her voice remained steady, confronted with those eyes that saw so much more about her than she wanted to reveal.

He reached over to pick up one of her biscuits and took a bite. "Not exactly what I had in mind, but I suppose it will suffice. For now."

"Go away, you scoundrel!" Furious and disconcerted, Lilith clenched her glass of ratafia.

Apparently remembering the candy dish, the marquis

stood. "Perhaps we may continue this later, Miss Benton." He dug into his pocket to pull out a five-pound note, which he tossed onto their table. "My compliments for the biscuit and the conversation," he said, grinning down at her. He walked away, but after a few steps paused and looked back. "By the way, there were no pearls before that swine." With a nod at Pen, he turned and strolled off down the street, whistling cheerily.

"Do you still think he's trying to ruin you?" Pen asked, watching after him. "Because it didn't seem that way to me."

"Because he didn't wish it to." Lilith set her glass back on the table carefully, so Pen wouldn't see that her hands had begun to shake. He'd taken the trouble to go look for her earring and then had sought her out to let her know he'd been unsuccessful. No one could upset her equilibrium like that dratted man!

"I know you don't like that he's become friends with your brother, but don't you find him attractive?" Pen pursued. "He's quite handsome, and so very . . . scandalous." She shuddered delicately.

"And you find that attractive?" Lilith queried, refusing to look after him.

"Don't you? The way you were talking together, it seemed as though you were absolutely going to devour one another! I hadn't realized you could be so ferocious."

"Is that supposed to be a compliment?" Lilith shot back, angry that Pen might think her behavior improper.

"It was meant as one," Penelope answered, obviously hurt. "I wish someone would look at me the way he looked at you."

Lilith paused, very curious as to what her friend had seen in the Marquis of Dansbury. "How did he look at me?"

"As though he was absorbing everything about you, inside and out."

A cascade of shivers ran up Lilith's arms. She turned to look in the direction Dansbury had gone, but he had vanished. This time, she was disappointed. Wenford had best be found soon, for she couldn't stand much more of the emotional confusion the last weeks had awakened in her.

Jack stood and stretched, then strolled over to the nearest window to look out at the rain, falling steadily outside in the darkness. Behind him the noisy game of faro resumed without him, and he sighed as he leaned against the wall and sipped his glass of port. He'd been losing slowly but steadily all evening, to an altogether poor group of opponents. And he had a damned good idea why.

"You are quiet tonight," Antonia commented, coming up behind him and sliding her arm through his.

"I am being reflective," he corrected, not looking down at her.

"A dangerous pastime for one such as you. Unless you are plotting someone's demise?"

"Nothing so devious, I'm afraid. Merely thinking." And contemplating endlessly the face, the features, and the voice of a petite, black-haired beauty whom he desired more with each passing moment.

"This thinking. Is it about anyone in particular?" she crooned.

Either Antonia had gained the ability to read minds, or he was being frightfully obvious. In neither case did he wish her to know how close she was to the truth. "Just general ruminations on the sorry state of mankind."

"Hm. Allow me, then, to turn the subject for you."

"Not necessary."

"But I haven't heard anything of your little game with Miss Benton lately," Antonia pursued, "except that you've been spending a considerable amount of time in proper company." She paused. "I thought you detested proper company."

She was fishing for information. "As that is where Miss Benton may be found, it makes sense I would be there, don't you think?" he countered, trying to keep the annoyance from his voice. "I would hardly expect to find her here, for example."

"Oh, for shame, Jack," she pouted. "There is no need to be insulting."

He glanced at her again, then returned his gaze to the dark street outside. "No, there isn't."

"Well, not to interrupt your foul mood, my love, but I do have news you might be interested to hear." Practically purring again, Antonia leaned her cheek against his arm and rubbed her fingers along his sleeve.

"I wait with bated breath."

"I find it so delightful. William Benton actually mentioned the word *marriage* today on our lovely little picnic," she murmured.

He looked over his shoulder, but William was occupied with losing a fair-sized purse to Lord Hunt and the Marquis of Telgore. "It doesn't count if you were unclothed when he said it," he pointed out softly. "I believe you're aware that a man will utter almost anything in the . . . heat of passion, shall we say."

She chuckled. "Yes, I know. I have found it to be very useful, in fact. But no, it was well after that. 'Antonia, have you ever been in love?' he asked me. And then he wanted to know whether I considered marriage to be a worthy institution." Antonia sighed. "He has five thousand a year, you know."

"So he does." Jack straightened, recognizing the predator's edge to her voice. "You aren't seriously considering him, Toni, are you? A virginal country pup?"

"Not so virginal as he once was." She smiled silkily. "And he hasn't actually asked me yet, of course. But I have thought that five thousand a year would be a very nice bit of pin money to play with."

It would kill Lilith. Jack was as surprised at the thought as he was dismayed at its implication. He wasn't supposed to care what happened after he had her. He certainly wasn't supposed to care what she felt—considering what he was going to do to her. Jack took a deep breath. She had started it; everything that happened afterward was her fault.

"Have at it, then," he muttered brusquely, and turned back to his view.

Antonia started to reply, but stopped when Price and Ernest Landon entered the room. They were highly agitated about something, and as they immediately hurried in his direction, Jack had a very good idea what it must be.

"Dansbury, have you heard?" Landon chortled, obviously highly amused over his news.

"I've heard a great many things. Did you have something particular in mind?"

"You look as though you're going to burst," Lord Hunt commented with a grin. "Out with your news, man."

Landon chuckled. "You'll never guess. Well. Ahem." He cleared his throat. "It seems—"

"Price?" Jack cut in, lifting an eyebrow.

"The Duke of Wenford is dead," Price said succinctly.

"Damnation, Price!" Ernest protested, "you've no sense of drama at all."

Hunt stood, quickly followed by the Marquis of Telgore. *"What?"* they demanded, almost in unison.

Jack sipped his port. "Do tell," he murmured.

William turned a bright red, and Jack hoped the idiot would have enough sense to keep his mouth shut.

"It gets even better," Price said.

"Oh, no, you don't," Landon countered. "I'll tell the rest—leave me some amusement."

"Unless you intend to do it in pantomime, I suggest you get on with it," Hunt demanded.

"All right, all right. Do get me a glass of port, though, if you please."

Antonia impatiently motioned to one of her servants. "We eagerly await your news," she purred at Ernest.

"Apparently, one of Wenford's footmen sneaked down into his wine cellar to steal a bottle of the duke's finest. And what do you think he found down there?"

"Wenford?" Jack suggested smoothly.

"Yes, but in what condition?"

"Dead?" Price contributed with a short grin.

"Yes, but—"

"Landon, get on with it," Hunt repeated darkly.

Ernest sighed at the unappreciative crowd surrounding him. "He was lying there, holding a bottle of the cheapest bloody wine you can imagine, already gone to vinegar, it was, and he was completely in the altogether."

"In the altogether what?" William asked, sending him up a point in Jack's estimation.

"He was naked," Landon explained impatiently, shaking his head. "Clothes in a neat little pile at his feet."

"By God," Hunt muttered. "Are you certain?"

Price nodded. "Carriage came to White's to collect Dolph Remdale. While they were waiting, his driver told mine the entire story."

"How delightful," Antonia murmured in Jack's ear.

"The tale'll be all over London by morning, I would wager." Price smiled. "Or so one would hope."

"Mr. Benton," Peter Arlen said from a table in the far corner, "wasn't your sister nearly betrothed to His Grace?"

William paled, his eyes darting in Jack's direction.

The marquis turned to face Arlen and chuckled. "I believe she's nearly betrothed to every unattached male in London."

Arlen and most of the others in the room laughed, and William scowled at him. What the idiot didn't realize was that if he had tried to protest her innocence he would have gone too far, and could very likely have gotten them all in a great deal of trouble. Lilith, at least, would have enough sense to distance herself from Wenford without causing any suspicion.

The news effectively put an end to any more gambling for the evening, but Price cornered Jack before he could gracefully make his exit. "Dansbury."

"So, you've taken to joining Dolph Remdale at White's, have you?" Jack commented, trying to put his friend on the defensive to evade any less pleasant topics of discussion.

"I've simply been avoiding you," Price countered. "I have no wish to be dragged to another tea sampling." He glanced about the room. "With the news I had, though, I thought it unfair if you should not be among the first to know."

Jack nodded. "I appreciate it. Though it was only a matter of time, I suppose; Wenford was older than Northumberland."

"He was that," Price agreed with a chuckle. "Do you think Dolph will wear the title with more . . . aplomb, shall we say?"

Jack shrugged. "I don't really care. All Remdales are a waste of air, as far as I'm concerned."

"You'll get little argument from me. But tell me, how goes your game? Any results yet?"

"I am moving in the right direction," Jack admitted, reluctant to discuss Lilith Benton with Price. It cheapened the game, somehow—though it was laughable to think that he was doing anything remotely noble. It was only that justifying the end, even to himself, was becoming difficult. And coming up with a different reason why he continued to pursue her was something he refused even to contemplate.

"My God," Viscount Hamble groaned, his head in his hands. "My God. All this time, and he's been dead."

Eyes downcast, Lilith stood quietly beside her father's desk as he lamented the passage of the Duke of Wenford. She could have told him several days ago. She probably should have. And yet, for the past few days she'd felt almost free.

Since no one else had known her most-favored suitor was completely out of the running, they left her fairly alone. Except for Lionel, of course, who had just moved into primary position by default—and Jack Faraday, who seemed determined to insinuate himself into her life without any regard for propriety at all.

"It was bound to happen sooner or later, Papa," she soothed. "After all, His Grace was quite elderly, and given, I believe, to near fits of apo—"

"He might have waited to expire until after you were wed," the viscount growled, cutting her off. "And until after he'd given you an heir to ensure your continued status in the Wenford household."

Lilith frowned. "But Papa, you said I wouldn't have to marry him."

He lifted his head to look at her, then abruptly turned his gaze away. "I had hoped to change your mind."

That made sense. He would never have given in to her request and turned down Wenford, unless he thought eventually to bring her around. "Well, I told you I would marry anyone else you chose," she reminded him, though the face that came to her mind for a disturbing moment was not on the approved list of suitors.

He looked at her, then slowly nodded. "Yes, I suppose there's no reason to delay our own plans." The viscount straightened. "In fact, we should get you out and about immediately. We don't want to give the impression that you are in any way mourning His Grace. If he had died in a more respectable manner, a show of regret would be appropriate, but in this instance, the sooner we distance ourselves from Geoffrey Remdale, the better."

Jack Faraday, then, had done her a double service by seeing both to Wenford's resting place and the manner in which he was laid out. "I had planned to attend the Doveshane ball this evening," she suggested.

"Yes, splendid." Her father eyed her critically for a moment, then abruptly stood. "You know, I have just hit upon the perfect idea."

Lilith shifted, less than pleased at the information. She was beginning to think that his ideas were nothing but more work and strain for her. "Whatever is it?"

"This can't displease even your high ideals for a good marriage," he continued. "How to go about it, though . . .?"

"Go about what, Papa?"

"About seeing you married to the *new* Duke of Wenford, of course."

Lilith froze. The idea had never even occurred to her,

except as a jest from Jack Faraday. "R-Randolph Remdale?" she stammered.

"Randolph Remdale, indeed," he agreed. "You can't have any complaints about him. Handsome man, and well mannered—and now, thanks to his uncle's demise, a very powerful individual." He sat down again, obviously contemplating his strategy.

"But . . . but won't Dolph—His Grace—be in mourning?"

"Haven't you heard anything, girl? Wenford's will forbade it. He wanted no time wasted in such nonsense."

That didn't sound like Geoffrey Remdale, especially not from their last conversation. He seemed to think that the world revolved around him, and that complete chaos would reign upon his death. She stifled a surprised smile. That part had been true, thanks to the Marquis of Dansbury.

With her father distracted with forming his plans, Lilith slipped upstairs to the drawing room. She'd only just sat down when Bevins opened the door to announce that Jack Faraday was requesting to see her, in private. It seemed a measure of how far things had decayed in the household that Bevins didn't even lift an eyebrow at the idea of her entertaining Dansbury without a chaperon. No doubt the butler considered it part of the entire scandalous affair with Wenford's body, but Lilith had to wonder at herself. A very short time ago, the thought of seeing any man alone, much less the marquis, would never have occurred to her. Now she actually welcomed the opportunity.

"Are you armed?" Dansbury asked, stepping into the room as Bevins shut the door behind him.

"Not at the moment," she retorted, glancing at the

nearest bookshelf. "There is an abundance of ammunition to hand, however."

He grinned. "I shall keep that in mind." He looked at the bookcase, then strolled over to examine the contents more closely. "Yours," he asked, glancing over his shoulder, "or part of the family heirlooms?"

"Most of them are mine," she said. "Father keeps the heirlooms in the library." She studied his profile. "I'll warn Bevins to keep you out of there."

He chuckled as he lifted a book down and opened it. "Greek mythology." He flipped through the pages. "An odd choice for a young woman determined to marry well."

"Why do you say that?" she demanded, rising.

Dansbury shrugged. "Seems to me you're setting yourself up as a pretty bauble—a gentleman's showpiece. A bit of advice, my dear: peers on the whole are a stupid lot, and they don't like their wives knowing more than they do. But I imagine you can disguise that, if you've a notion."

Another of his insults flipped into a compliment, so that Lilith had no idea how to respond. "What are you doing here?" she demanded instead. "This early, I thought you would barely have returned home from your gambling, or drinking, or . . . whatever else it is you do all evening."

"I assume you mean whoring?" he asked offhandedly, returning the book to its place and choosing another.

Lilith blushed. "Whatever you choose to call it," she replied flippantly.

"Ah. Well, for your information, I haven't been doing any of that 'whatever you choose to call it,' lately. I was at a friend's last evening when I heard the news of Wenford's demise, and I could hardly contain myself until a decent hour when I could come and determine your family's and your own reaction to the news.''

"It's still too early to be a decent hour," she informed him. "William hasn't risen yet, and neither has my aunt."

"You, however, have risen. Jane Austen?" he read, looking at the spine of the book he held. Jack lifted an eyebrow. "A romantic, as well, are you?"

"Yes," she admitted.

"Another odd choice for a gel marrying for a title. You are full of contradictions, sweet one."

She realized that she had made a mistake in admitting that the books were hers. Now Dansbury thought he had unlocked some sort of treasure chest to her mind and soul, and was invading it with a single-minded curiosity, as he did everything else remotely connected with her. "Do leave off, will you?"

Immediately he returned yet another book to its place and turned to look at her.

Unsettled, Lilith wondered how Alison's eyes could be so humorous and gentle, when the same shape and color was so cynical and darkly sensual in her brother.

"Very well," he replied. "But do tell me how your father reacted to the news."

She walked over to the window. "Badly." She had no intention of telling him about the viscount's decision regarding Dolph Remdale. The scoundrel would find out soon enough, and she had no desire to be hounded and teased about it. Not by him.

He followed her. "And?" he prompted, obviously sensing that she was leaving something out.

"And nothing. Go away now."

"But I've been polite this morning, haven't I?"

So he had. "That doesn't matter," she returned. "Your reputation precedes you."

"Hm," he murmured from beside her. "But that's what you like about me, isn't it, Lilith?"

"I did not give you leave to call me Lilith!" Half out of her mind at his antagonisms, and completely out of patience, she turned to slap him.

He intercepted her hand and yanked her against him. Before she could take a breath, he bent his head and kissed her.

Lilith shoved her hand against Jack's chest, only to find her fingers wrapping around his lapel. She pulled herself closer against him, shivering as she kissed him back with a passion that stunned and startled her. She groaned against his mouth as he reached up to brush the sensitive hairs at the back of her neck with a feathery light touch. Finally he released her mouth and stepped back, a look of surprised triumph in his eyes.

"You . . . you," she stammered, finding that her eyes kept wanting to focus on his lips. "Stay away from me."

He stood gazing at her closely for a long moment. "No throwing things this time, Miss Benton?" he murmured. "That was inexcusable, after all."

"Everything about you is inexcusable," she agreed hotly, managing to meet his gaze, and for an insane moment wishing he would kiss her again. She was as bad as her mother, falling into the first passionate embrace offered her.

He nodded, a slight smile briefly touching his sensuous mouth. "Yes. I agree."

She eyed him suspiciously. It was completely unlike Jack to allow her to beat him without an argument. "Don't you have something insulting to say?"

He pursed his lips. "Yes, I'm afraid I do."

She folded her arms, hoping he wouldn't notice that she still trembled. "Well, get it over with, then."

"Will you save a waltz for me at the Doveshane ball?"

The request almost sounded sincere, but Lilith refused to believe it. He was never sincere. "Absolutely not! I would sooner dance with . . ." She trailed off as his hand rose beside him, something silvery and flowing dangling from his fingers. "Give me back my necklace this instant, you thief!" She reached for it, but he stepped backward, eluding her. Just to be certain he wasn't trying to trick her, she reached up and felt her throat. Her necklace was definitely missing. "Give it back!"

"Dance with me," he cajoled softly.

"I'll have you arrested for doing something foul to Wenford. That's what I should have done days ago."

"No, you won't," he countered, examining the bauble.

"And how do you intend to prevent that?"

"If you have me arrested, I'll have you arrested for the same thing."

"I don't—"

"Come, Miss Benton, you gave Old Hatchet Face your earring. Don't begrudge me a w—"

"I did no such thing."

He swirled the necklace in his long fingers. "One waltz for one trinket, Lil." His eyes studied hers intently. "That's all I ask."

Lilith was furious, and at the same time oddly exhilarated. No one had ever gone to such lengths to receive permission for a mere waltz. "You are asking quite a bit, Lord Dansbury."

He gave a slight smile, his eyes dancing. "You have no idea," he whispered. "Promise me."

Now he was asking for promises. "You have my word," she answered.

"I'll take it."

"Now, give me my blasted necklace."

He reached out and handed her the necklace, gently draping the delicate silver chain over her palm. "That wasn't so bad now, was it?" he asked, running his fingers up her wrist.

"This changes nothing," she returned, her breath catching at the light touch. "You have a waltz. Nothing more."

He lifted his hand to stroke his knuckle along her cheek. "Nothing more yet, you mean," he murmured, then turned and was gone.

Dansbury had a great deal of nerve to assume that she was falling for him, that she liked him because he was scandalous. And even if she was, even if she did, Papa would never allow his suit anyway. It was preposterous!

Lilith slowly reached up and traced her lips. They still felt warm from his touch. Perhaps tonight she should wear her new emerald gown. That low-cut creation should impress . . . Dolph Remdale and Lionel Hendrick. They would be there, and for her father's sake, she should look her best. Fastening her necklace back on, she hurried upstairs to summon Emily.

Chapter 10

❦

Four of Lilith's surviving suitors were at the Dove-shane ball when she arrived, all of them full of compliments, vying with one another like a pack of hungry wolves to receive her hand for one of the three waltzes to be played that evening.

Lilith was more concerned over the whereabouts of her so-called fifth suitor, who was nowhere to be seen. She forced a smile and doled out one of the waltzes to the Earl of Nance, as her father had instructed, and held another in case he should be able to speak with Dolph Remdale and convince the new Duke of Wenford to dance with her. The third waltz was supposed to go to Jeremy Giggins, but with a guilty glance over her shoulder at her father, Lilith refused the request.

"Come now, Lilith, we know you've at least one waltz left," Francis Henning cajoled. "Don't deny me the pleasure of your sparkling company."

"You may have a country dance or a quadrille," Lilith returned, unmoved by his protests. Though Jack Faraday had criticized all of her suitors, she agreed that Francis Henning had something of a puddle for a brain. "The waltzes are promised."

"To whom?" Nance said with a slight smile, looking down at her. He was annoyed, though. She could see it in his light blue eyes. "You must tell me who has commandeered the first waltz of the evening from you."

Lilith frowned. That sounded possessive, especially since she hadn't accepted his proposal. She had selected the first waltz for Dansbury, to get the deed over with so she could enjoy the remainder of the evening. If Dansbury followed his usual habits, he would be late and miss it anyway, and it would be his own fault.

"Yes, to whom did you promise this waltz?" Peter Varrick demanded.

"She promised it to me," Dansbury said, materializing at her elbow. "Do you have any difficulty with that?"

Lilith flushed as the titter of conversation rose around her, with the names "Dansbury" and "Benton" intermingled. She heard Mrs. Falshond's distinctive voice recite to Mrs. Pindlewide how the marquis had pursued Miss Benton to her very own tea sampling. Next, Lilith knew, would be the speculation over whether Dansbury's frequent association with her would ruin her chances for a good match, and oh my, wouldn't her father be heartbroken?

She tried to stifle the sudden fast beating of her heart as she glanced up at him, but her tingling excitement had more to do with remembering his kiss and his embrace than with the trouble he continued to cause her.

"Lilith, I must protest," Nance immediately put in, stepping forward. "You can't mean to—"

"Protest all you like," Dansbury interrupted coolly. "We'll be dancing."

The orchestra struck up the waltz, and the marquis offered her his hand. She hesitated only a moment before she took it, and he gracefully swept her out onto the floor. He was all in dark gray, tall and lean and handsome. The glint in his dark eyes seemed more amused than cynical, and she wished again that she knew nothing about him except for what he had told her. The real Jack Faraday, when he made a rare appearance, was quite attractive.

"Why are all of your other suitors able to call you Lilith, when you deny your permission to me?" he asked.

"I like them," she returned. She wasn't the least bit surprised that he was a graceful dancer; Dansbury seemed to have mastered anything that could be considered or used as a vice. Even knowing that, waltzing in his arms was like being in a dream. "And I don't like you," she added for good measure.

"What if I told you that you are breathtaking?" he queried softly. "And that the only emerald more lovely than your gown is found in your beautiful eyes?"

She blushed. "It would have no effect whatsoever," she lied, pleased that he had noticed and approved of her new dress. It took some of the sting out of her father's disapproval of her attire.

"Or that your eyes—blast, I already told you about your eyes and king's emeralds. I hate repeating myself. What if I said your lips are the color of rubies, and—"

"No, they're not," she scoffed, chuckling at his unaccustomed silliness.

"—and that your hair is black as darkest midnight? Shall I continue? I do warn you that while I am not out of compliments, I am running out of acceptable features to admire. My next compliment, though sincerely meant, may earn me another slap."

Lilith laughed at him, and her heart gave a queer flop as he smiled back easily. She liked this version of the man, and wondered how close it was to the truth. "That will do, Lord Dansbury.'' She took a breath, knowing that she shouldn't say what she was about to. ''You may call me Lilith.''

''Thank you, Lilith.''

Lilith glanced away and saw her father glaring at her, arms crossed. ''I'll never be able to explain this,'' she groaned.

''Explain what?'' Jack followed her gaze, then sighed. ''Ah. How about saying, 'Father, I wanted to dance with Jack Faraday'?''

''I did not want to dance with you,'' she corrected. ''You tricked me into it.''

''Whatever,'' he said absently, studying her face. ''Do you take after your mother in looks?'' he asked. ''Your father does not have your cheekbones, nor your bright eyes or wit, I think.''

Lilith narrowed her supposedly bright eyes, not liking the line of questions. She was in London to emphasize the differences between herself and Elizabeth Benton, not the similarities. ''I'll answer that if you'll tell me why Richard Hutton dislikes you.''

His jaw clenched, the old, cynical Jack Faraday instantly back in place. ''The same goddamned reason everyone else does, my dear. But I make it a rule not to gossip about myself, so you'll have to go ply some nasty old wag for my dirty little secrets.''

''So,'' she said coolly, a bit shaken by the bitterness in his tone, ''you ask difficult questions, but you won't answer them. That hardly seems fair, Lord Dansbury.''

He pulled her closer in his arms, her skirt swirling about his legs and his hand and arm firmly caressing her waist. ''I am never fair,'' he murmured. ''All you need to remember, Lilith, is that I don't *lose.*''

Lilith put more distance between them. ''A rather bold statement, my lord, even for such a renowned gambler as yourself. Why are informing me of this incredible luck you apparently have?''

He smiled, surprise and pleasure touching his eyes for just a moment. Not that she cared what he thought of her.

"No reason," he chuckled. "Just something to keep in mind."

The marquis rarely said things for no reason, but she didn't press him. "I had no reason to trust you before, and your revelations have certainly not inspired me to change my opinion."

"Oh, I don't know about that," he smiled, turning her easily in his arms. "A scant few weeks ago, you wouldn't even converse with me."

She loved to dance, and had never had a more skilled partner. Or a more disreputable one either, unfortunately. "You shouldn't remind me."

For a brief moment his grip on her fingers tightened, and she thought she had angered him. His gaze, though, was directed at one side of the room. Lilith glanced in the same direction, and saw Dolph Remdale talking with her father.

"He's not in black." Jack frowned. "Not even a black arm band."

"The old duke's will forbade him to go into mourning," Lilith said, looking back at him. "Didn't you know?"

"I didn't," he answered. "Convenient, don't you think?"

"It's not for me to question Wenford's state of mind when he drew up his will," Lilith answered.

"Why not? It's damned convenient, and highly unlikely. Wenford would've ordered all of England to wear black bombazine if he could have managed it."

She hated agreeing with him, even though she'd

thought the same thing herself. "So Dolph didn't want to spend six months out of society. It's not the first time it's been done."

Jack reluctantly nodded. "True," he conceded. "But why—"

"There was no need to demand a waltz from me, if all you wanted to do was to belittle Dolph Remdale. You could have merely forced your way into my drawing room again to pester me for that," she interrupted.

"Pester you?" he repeated darkly.

"Pester me. And I might have saved this waltz for someone more respectable."

He opened his mouth, then snapped it shut again. "Ah," he said finally, "just so you realize that you've left me with nothing to discuss but my attraction to you."

Lilith's heart skipped a beat. "Don't you mean your antagonism toward me, my lord?"

"Is that what this seems like to you, Lilith?"

Thankfully, the waltz ended, and she abruptly came to a stop. Jack's arm remained about her waist for several heartbeats too long before he released her. Then, tucking her hand about his arm, he started to return her to her aunt's care.

"I can find my own way, thank you." Lilith pulled her hand free, continuing on without him.

"I want to kiss you again," Jack murmured from behind her.

Startled, she looked over her shoulder at him, but he was already making his way over to join William and Mr. Price. Lilith forced herself to keep walking. He was only trying to shock her and fluster her, of course—but that didn't explain why she, too, wished him to kiss her again, why she could scarcely keep from smiling at the mere thought of it. It was simply because he was the only man who had ever kissed her, she swiftly decided; for she refused to consider what Wenford had done to her to be any sort of proper kiss. Not that Jack Faraday's kisses were the least bit proper, either, but they were very . . . stimulating, as was the man himself. Then again . . .

"Lilith!" Aunt Eugenia hissed, grabbing her by the elbow and dragging her over to a chair. "What in the world do you think you're doing?"

Lilith blinked and tried to keep her balance. "Hm?"

"Dancing with that . . . that man," her aunt continued, beating her fan furiously against her thigh. "Now that you've lost your opportunity with the old duke, you have to watch yourself even more carefully. And you've been warned about the Marquis of Dansbury—several times."

"I was asking him to cease associating with William," Lilith improvised.

"That is hardly your affair, child," Eugenia returned hotly. "A woman's reputation is far more fragile than a man's. Let your father worry about William's acquaintances."

"Yes, ma'am."

"Now behave yourself, and be especially nice to Mr. Giggins, since the waltz should have been his."

Lilith nodded as Jeremy Giggins approached for their country dance. "Yes, ma'am."

She did exert herself to be especially pleasant to Mr. Giggins, and even to Francis Henning for their quadrille. Most of her attention, though, was occupied with wondering why Dansbury remained at the soirée. He did not go out to the gaming tables when they opened, nor did he monopolize the liquor at the refreshment table. Neither did he ask anyone else to dance. Instead, he leaned against the back wall and watched her. William and his other friends talked with him when they weren't engaged with dancing or gambling, but Jack Faraday didn't budge. She could feel his eyes on her, and was surprised she wasn't nearly as dismayed as she'd once been.

"Miss Benton, good evening."

Lilith turned from thanking Francis Henning for the dance. Behind her, in the latest Parisian-style blue coat with cream waistcoat and black breeches, a slight smile on his handsome face, stood Randolph Remdale. Acutely conscious of her role in his uncle's embarrassing death, she didn't quite know what to say to him. "Good . . . evening, Your Grace." She curtsied politely.

"Forgive my boldness, but I wanted to compliment you on your appearance this evening. That gown is lovely on you."

"I thank you, Your Grace," Lilith returned. "You are very kind."

"Not at all. Your father suggested that you might be amenable to sharing a waltz with me. I ask, though, that you give me a waltz at the Cremwarrens', night after next, instead. To dance tonight, considering my uncle's demise, would be unseemly, I think."

Lilith smiled, relieved. "Of course, Your Grace. It would be my pleasure."

He nodded, and glanced in Dansbury's direction before returning his gaze to her. "A word of advice, Miss Benton, if I may. I have heard whisperings that Jack Faraday is pursuing you. This cannot bode well for the reputation of a proper young lady."

Lilith was unaccountably annoyed at the unwanted advice. "Thank you, Your Grace. I shall keep that in mind."

Dolph looked at her for a moment, the expression in his blue eyes darkening for just an instant, and then he bowed over her hand. "I shall see you at the Cremwarrens', then."

"You shall."

Lilith sighed as the new Duke of Wenford made his way over to join his cronies. He was nice enough, she supposed, if a bit dull and pompous. Not at all like her supposed fifth suitor. With a slight smile she turned to find Jack again, but he was gone.

Unaccountably disappointed, Lilith made her way over to Penelope. Mary Fitzroy was there as well, her eyes wide as she whispered something in Penelope's ear. As Lilith reached them, Pen gasped. "Oh, my!"

"What is it?"

Mary giggled. "I heard Ben Collins tell Lady Francine Walkins that Lady Pender overheard Donald Marley and the Duke of Wenford—the new Duke of Wenford—talking, and they think that the old duke's death wasn't an accident."

The blood drained from Lilith's face. "They do?" she forced out. "Whyever would they think that?"

"I don't know," Mary admitted in a low voice, as she glanced about. "But they think a certain rakehell known to hate the Remdales might be involved. And we all know who that is."

Yes, everyone did. "Do they have any proof?" she asked, trying to sound skeptical and incredulous. Lilith was abruptly very angry at the accusation. It couldn't be true. She didn't know all that much about the Marquis of Dansbury, but she couldn't even begin to believe him a cold-blooded killer.

"Oh, I don't know. But can you imagine? What if it's true? Do you think they'll hang Dansbury?"

Lilith scowled at the unpleasant image. "What I think is that Dolph Remdale was embarrassed by the state his uncle ended in, and he's trying to put it off on someone else."

Mary looked at her slyly. "And *I* think you're trying to defend a certain someone you're in love with."

Lilith snapped her jaw shut, shocked. "*I beg your pardon?*"

"Everyone knows. Dansbury's been following you everywhere, like a big, tame panther."

"Do be serious, Mary," Pen put in with a chuckle. "Lilith's brother is friends with Dansbury. You know precisely how Lil feels about the marquis. She's complained about him often enough."

"Well, yes," Mary agreed reluctantly, then grinned. "But you should have seen the look on your face, Lil."

"Please don't even suggest such a thing again, Mary."

Even so, Mary's words had begun a swirl of thoughts that Lilith couldn't stop. Of course she wasn't in love with Dansbury—that was absurd! But she certainly didn't view him with the same contempt and disdain that she had a few weeks ago. She tried to see him as the same scoundrel she knew him to be upon their first meeting, but everything was becoming so twisted and confused in her mind that she didn't know what to think. For all she knew, he was only pretending to pursue her to assuage his own bruised pride. One thing was certain, though: she needed to locate Jack and inform him that Dolph was spreading rumors. It would be terrible if the good deed Dansbury had done for her led him into trouble.

When she tracked down William, though, her brother didn't know where the marquis was. "He went off somewhere," he said testily. "Something set him off. Probably you. Before long you'll drive him off, and then I won't have any friends."

"I am not responsible for Dansbury's ill manners or his black moods," Lilith said stoutly. "And if you're in need of friends, why not Nance or Wenford?"

"Dull as dead rodents, Lil," he retorted, and stalked off.

By the time Aunt Eugenia finally came to collect her for the evening, Lilith was exhausted, physically and mentally. All night the rumors had continued circulating, growing worse moment by moment. And Jack Faraday hadn't a clue.

The Duke of Wenford watched Lilith Benton and her party exit the Doveshane ballroom. She was lovely—his uncle had been right about that. He reached into his pocket, as he had several times during the evening, and fingered the pearl earring he had deposited there. It had been found beneath his uncle, and Dolph was blessed with a precise enough memory to recall who possessed such a unique little bauble. It seemed Miss Benton had been with his uncle at the time of his demise. And the lovely thing had another splendid merit, in addition to her beauty: Dansbury apparently found her fascinating.

Dolph smiled to himself. That knowledge alone would have been enough to convince him to set his little plan in motion, but he happened to know a great deal more about the circumstances of his uncle's death than one earring provided. In fact, he had it on the best authority that the mysterious illness which had killed Wenford would not have given him time to disrobe, neatly fold his clothes, pop the cork of a very bad wine, and lay himself out flat on his back before he expired. No, given the connection of the earring as added evidence, it had all the signs of a prank of Dansbury's. And Dansbury was going to pay for it. He was going to pay for everything, and he was going to pay very dearly.

Chapter 11

"Don't you think setting Dolph Remdale after Lilith is a bit . . . macabre, Father?"

"Don't you question me, boy," the viscount admonished, glaring at William as his son followed him down the stairs toward the breakfast room. "If His Grace doesn't feel the need to mourn, then neither should we. And he's finally the man who fulfills all of my requirements, and all of Lilith's."

Lilith stood on the landing, wishing they would stop arguing over Dolph, so she could think of a way to get her brother over to Dansbury's to warn the marquis of those awful rumors.

"And what requirement could Lil have that Dolph meets?" William asked skeptically.

"Oh, you know, she's looking for someone handsome who dances well." Viscount Hamble rolled his eyes and twiddled his fingers in the air in an overblown imitation of a country dance.

Lilith was beginning to be quite frustrated at the way he turned everything she ever mentioned, even in jest, against her. "Please don't say such things about me, Father. You know they're not true."

183

He stopped and turned to face her. "I am merely trying to think of an explanation," he said in an angry, controlled voice, "as to why you would grant one of your waltzes to Dansbury last night. Your desire for a handsome and pleasant dance partner seems to be the only excuse as to why you would dare defy me in this."

"He is William's friend," she defended herself. "If I were rude to him, it might have consequen—"

"Dansbury's consequences don't interest me in the least. Half the proper folk of London won't even speak to him. That should be reason enough for you never to dance or converse with him again."

Lilith clenched her jaw. "Yes, Papa."

"I told you what your father would say," Aunt Eugenia seconded unhelpfully from the foot of the stairs. "I warned her and warned her, Stephen. But she's so headstrong, and—"

"I am not headstrong," Lilith protested. "I said I was sorry, and that I won't disobey you again. Now, please— may we go have breakfast?"

"Yes. A splendid idea."

Her father and her aunt headed off, but Lilith took William by the arm and pulled him to a halt. "I need to speak with you."

"You almost stood up for Jack there, you realize," he said with his engaging grin. "Best watch yourself, sister."

"It's Dansbury I need to ask you about. Can you get a message to him?"

"Of course." His expression became speculative. "Why?"

Lilith scowled. "William, for the first and last time, I am not in love with Jack Faraday."

Her brother flushed. "I didn't say—"

"I barely tolerate him," Lilith snapped, knowing she

was overreaching, yet unable to stop her protest. "But I owe him a favor, and I am trying to make good on it. Please tell him—"

"William!" their father bellowed from the morning room. "Before you attempt to sneak off anywhere, please remember that you are accompanying me to Denson's this morning!"

William rolled his eyes. "Yes, Father!" He squeezed Lilith's hand. "Can your message wait until this evening?"

"No, I don't think it can." She felt responsible enough for Jack's involvement in the Wenford fiasco that she needed to be certain someone warned him of the rumors being aimed in his direction. And the sooner, the better. "I'll take care of it myself, then."

When Lilith and William entered the breakfast room, she made a show of gasping and whirling to look at the clock sitting on the sideboard. "Oh, no!" she exclaimed, putting her hand over her mouth.

"What now?" the viscount grumbled.

"Aunt Eugenia, today was the day we were to brunch at the Sanfords'. Pen's been talking about how her mother has been looking forward to it for the past week!" And the Stratford mansion was only three houses from Dansbury's residence.

"I don't remember any such invitation. We are to lunch with them tomo—"

"No, no, we changed that ages ago," Lilith replied, pulling her aunt's chair back from the table and trying to ignore William's obvious amusement at her antics. "Please? If we hurry, we can still be on time."

"Lilith," her aunt sighed, eyeing the platter of sliced ham and biscuits that sat before her.

"Please, Aunt Eugenia?" Lilith begged.

"Oh, very well." Eugenia muttered, and pushed away

from the table. "Give me a moment to freshen up."

"Of course."

Lilith took that moment to dash into her own bed chamber, scribble out a note detailing what she had heard last evening, fold it over, and stuff it into her reticule. With Pen's home so close to Dansbury's, it wouldn't be difficult to have Milgrew stop by and give the marquis's servants a note while she and Aunt Eugenia ate with the Sanfords. It was a sterling plan, if she said so herself.

Or it would have been, if her father hadn't commandeered Milgrew for his own excursion, forcing her and her aunt to take the barouche with young Walter at the reins. She would never trust the boy to deliver the message without telling every other household servant about the deed. So she was left with a piece of paper in her reticule, and the need to let Dansbury know what it said.

Lady Sanford came to the door as her butler pulled it open. "Good morning," she said, smiling, but obviously surprised to see them there.

"Good morning. We've been looking forward to brunch," Eugenia said.

Behind her, Lilith grimaced sympathetically and shrugged. Her aunt would be furious if she ever realized she was being played for a fool, but Lilith didn't feel the least bit guilty about it. Aunt Eugenia had never uttered a kind word about her or William that she could remember. And lately, what little tolerance she had for the unrelenting harshness was beginning to fade.

"Well, of course," Lady Sanford said immediately. With a wink at Lilith, she ushered them inside. "So have we."

Pen, her expression puzzled as well, came downstairs as they stood chatting in the hallway. "Good morning."

"Lilith and Eugenia have arrived for brunch," her

mother said, giving her a small nod. "James, please inform Cook."

The butler nodded and disappeared toward the kitchens.

Pen's smile brightened. "Of course."

The two older women stepped into the morning room, but Lilith caught Penelope's hand. "Pen, I need to tell you something," she said, forcing a giggle.

Lady Sanford smiled indulgently at them. "Off with you, then."

Lilith dragged Penelope into the library and shut the door.

"What is it?" her friend asked, blushing. "Is it William?"

"Pen, I need you to keep a very big secret for me," Lilith whispered, afraid to speak aloud even with the doors closed.

"Of course," her friend answered immediately. "What is it?"

"I need to deliver a message to the Marquis of Dansbury."

For a long moment Pen looked at her. "Dansbury?" she finally repeated faintly. "You mean Mary was right? You *are* in love with him?"

"I . . ." Lilith couldn't lie to her friend, and she swallowed back the flip answer she had been about to make. "I don't know. But this is important. Will you help?"

"Of course," Pen exclaimed, clapping her hands together. "What do you wish me to do?"

Lilith smiled, relieved. "I need to sneak out your library window. I'll only be gone for a few moments, but you must promise you'll stay in here until I return, as though we've been chatting the whole time."

"Oh, how romantic," her friend breathed. "Yes, go."

Her heart beginning to beat in a queer combination of

anticipation and dread, Lilith gave her friend a quick hug and then unlatched one of the tall library windows. "I'll be right back," she whispered again, and hitched up her skirts to climb out into the back garden.

There were only two low brick walls between the Sanford and the Faraday mansions, and despite her skirts, Lilith was able to navigate the first one fairly easily. Her shoe caught on a vine as she scrambled over the second, and with a curse she'd learned from William, she fell into the small Faraday garden on her backside. Luckily the garden couldn't be viewed from the street, so her clumsiness would at least go unseen by any passersby. She had never even dreamed of calling on a man before, and she hesitated at the servant's door at the back of the house. She had come this far, however, and so she squared her shoulders and knocked firmly.

It opened immediately, though the man standing there did little for her ebbing confidence. He might have been dressed like the butler of a fine household, but with a terrible scar along one cheek and a missing finger on his left hand, he seemed more like a street hoodlum than a gentleman's attendant. Then again, Jack Faraday was barely a gentleman. Or so everyone had been telling her.

"Yes, miss?" he inquired in a rough voice.

"You work for the Marquis of Dansbury?" she asked uncertainly, her voice cracking.

"That I do."

"I . . . I need to leave a message for him," she said, reaching into her reticule for the note. "Can you see that it is delivered to him right away?"

"Aye, miss," the butler answered, and motioned her into the house.

"Oh, no," she returned, backing away and further scandalized at the thought of entering Dansbury's home.

If anyone saw, her reputation would be destroyed. "I
need only to leave the note."

In a flash the man stepped forward, grabbed her arm,
and yanked her inside. Before she could scream, he
clamped one hand over her mouth, and with the other
slammed the door and then pinned her arms to her sides.
"My lord!" he yelled, wrestling her through the busy
kitchen and into the hallway while she kicked and
thrashed, frightened half out of her wits.

"What is it, Peese?" came Jack's easy voice. A book
in one hand, he stepped into the hallway from a side
door. "Why all the bellow—" He froze as he spied
Lilith. "Let her go at once!" he demanded, striding forward.

"Jack," she sobbed, and flung herself against him,
beyond relief.

He dropped the book and wrapped his arms around
her, holding her safe. "What in God's name were you
doing, Peese?" he snapped, rocking her slowly while
she regained her composure.

He smelled of tea and shaving soap, and she buried
her face into his chest.

"She was acting suspicious, and I didn't want her
getting away," the butler grumbled.

"I was not acting suspicious," Lilith returned in a
muffled voice from the haven she was surprisingly reluctant to leave.

"Delivering a note to the kitchen door," Peese argued. "Wouldn't say who she was, milord, so I—"

"What note?" Jack interrupted, lifting her chin with
his fingers so he could look into her eyes.

Lilith straightened. "I have news, and William
couldn't come, and . . ." She glanced over at the butler.

Jack nodded and took her by the hand, pulling her
through the nearest door and shutting it behind them.

"Why couldn't William come?" he asked.

"Papa dragged him off somewhere. You need to know—"

"And how did you get here?"

Lilith sighed, thinking what a terror Dansbury must have been as a child, never satisfied with the easy answer to anything. His tutors must have hated him, but Lilith found his single-minded intensity rather . . . intriguing. Especially lately. "I was supposed to go to the Sanfords' for luncheon tomorrow, so I convinced Aunt Eugenia that it was to be brunch today, and then convinced Lady Sanford and Pen that Aunt Eugenia had been mistaken about when to come." Lilith watched his lean face closely, curious as to what he thought of her hastily constructed plan.

The marquis chuckled, his eyes dancing. "How devious of you," he congratulated her.

"I don't like being devious," Lilith retorted, though the compliment pleased her.

"A pity. I think you may be a natural."

"I—"

"Why didn't you think to send Milgrew over here, though?" he asked.

"That was my original plan, but Papa took him along on his errand."

His lips twitched. "And your aunt?"

"Chatting with Lady Sanford, I assume."

"Ah." He studied her face carefully for another moment. "So tell me your news, my sweet one."

"There were rumors going about last night, after you left. It seems—"

"You and Dolph looked quite chummy," Jack snapped, his mood darkening. He glared at her, then strode over to the window. "Very heartwarming."

She started to reply in kind, but closed her mouth

again. If she told him of her father's plans for her and the new duke, she would never get him to listen to anything. "I couldn't very well cut him," she said instead.

"You cut me," Jack reminded her. His expression eased, though, and she thought that the memory had amused him. "By the by," he continued, "why is your, ah, posterior dirty?"

"What?" She glanced down and blushed, brushing at her skirts. "Oh, I had to climb two walls to get here without being seen. And you have all sorts of wretched vines growing on yours. There's no other way I could have called on you, so stop complain—"

The marquis gave a shout of laughter. "So, first you abandoned your aunt on an errand you invented?"

"I suppose. What—"

"Then you climbed walls and scrambled through gardens? To visit me?"

"Well, yes," Lilith admitted, affronted. "I can't fly, you know."

"By Jericho, you are a constant surprise," he chuckled, his eyes merry.

"Do you wish to hear my news, or not, Dansbury?" she asked, beginning to become deeply annoyed.

He swept a bow. "Beg pardon. Please, my lady."

"Several people were discussing how Dolph has begun to suspect that perhaps his uncle did not die of natural causes, after all."

Jack nodded. "That's to be expected. He's got to be as embarrassed as hell at the circumstances."

"There's also speculation that a certain rakehell who's always hated Wenford might be involved."

He was silent, those dark, mesmerizing eyes studying hers so closely it made her wonder if he could somehow read her thoughts. As confused as her thoughts concerning him had been over the last few days, she hoped he could not.

"And you went through all this subterfuge just to tell me that, Lilith?"

She hesitated. "I didn't want you to think that you had made a mistake in helping me. It was a good thing that you did, and I appreciate it. Now even more than at first."

For just a moment he closed his eyes. "Do you?" he asked, looking at her again.

"Yes. I do."

"And do you think I had anything to do with Old Hatchet Face's demise?" He took a step closer. "I would appreciate an honest answer. You have spent several conversations accusing me, and rather to my surprise I . . ." He hesitated, the first time she had seen him at a loss for words. "I find that I value your opinion," he finally finished, then gave a rueful grin. "You have a considerably better grasp on honesty than I do."

He wanted her opinion. She carefully considered her answer while he waited. "I think," she began slowly, "that I don't know enough about you to answer that question one way or the other."

Jack started to speak, and instead turned to pull aside the curtain and gazed outside. "I don't know why I expected anything different from you," he said, half to himself. Abruptly he turned to face her again. "I'll make you a bargain."

She wrinkled her brow suspiciously. "What sort of bargain?"

"You may ask me any three—and only three—questions, and I will answer them honestly and succinctly. That is, so long as you promise me that my responses never leave this room."

It was an intriguing suggestion, and much harder to

turn down than she expected. "And what is the catch?"

He gave a brief grin. "For every question you ask, you must allow me to kiss you."

Lilith lifted both eyebrows, trying to ignore the tingle that ran down her spine at his words. "Kiss me?"

Jack nodded. "One question equals one kiss. For a total of three. Do we have a bargain?"

He expected her to say no, she realized. What he didn't know, though, was that she had been able to think of little else but kissing him again since their last embrace. "Agreed," she answered clearly, her heart hammering.

She had the pleasure of seeing Jack's surprise. "Please. Proceed."

"All right." Lilith tapped her chin, seeking her first question. "Why do you dislike the Remdale family?"

Before he answered, he closed the distance between them, leaned down, and covered her mouth with his own. Not snatched by surprise, this kiss was different than the others had been. Lilith had time to feel the lips that were soft and firm at the same time as they caressed hers with a gentle, possessive touch that seemed uniquely Jack Faraday. And uniquely . . . stirring.

Slowly he lifted his head. "One," he murmured.

"And . . . your answer?" she asked, already seeking another question, not because she wished for a response, but because she wanted another kiss.

His fingers caressed the sides of her face. "One of Wenford's pieces of property is Hanfeld Hall—a small, rarely used hunting park that borders on Fencross Glen, one of my smaller, rarely used estates. There's a meadow dead center between them, a pretty little spot with a gazebo in the middle which floods up to the floorboards with every spring rain. It was on Fencross land, but rumor has it that it was also the place where

Wenford . . . acquired the consent of his first wife.''

"He did the same thing to her that he tried to do to me, you mean," Lilith said quietly, studying the serious brown eyes before her.

Jack's jaw clenched. "That's the rumor. Anyway, the buffoon decided he wanted to buy the meadow—probably thought the whole bloody thing was romantic. But my grandfather refused to sell. So Wenford offered to put up his prime hunting lodge in Surrey against the damned gazebo. My grandfather liked the odds, and agreed. They played a round of hazard over it, and Wenford won.''

"But what's so terr—"

"The hunting lodge, it was later discovered, was entailed. Wenford didn't have the legal right to give it away, so he had nothing to lose by wagering. And besides," and Jack lowered his head briefly, "he said some rather insulting things about the Faraday bloodline in the process of forcing the wager. My grandfather was a very proud man.''

"As you are, I think," Lilith whispered.

Jack looked at her. "I lost most of my pride some time ago, sweet one. And you have two questions remaining.''

"All right." Lilith took a deep breath that shook a little. "How is it that you are so adept at sneaking about, and that you always seem to know everything about what everyone is up to and why?''

"That's actually three questions, but as you are devastatingly attractive, I'll accept it as one," he said with a slight grin.

"Thank you," she said, a pleased smile touching her own lips. She couldn't recall ever being called devastating before, and certainly not by someone of Dansbury's experience.

His mouth touched hers, feather light, and then he leaned still closer and deepened the embrace of their lips. He teased her lips open, and slid his tongue along her teeth. The touch was shockingly intimate, and Lilith felt a shivering tingle running down her spine to the warm, secret place between her legs. This was what kissing was supposed to be like.

Slowly he lifted his head again. "Two," he whispered.

By then Lilith had forgotten her question, but the clock chiming faintly from the hallway reminded her abruptly of something else. "I have to go," she said in a rush, pulling free of his embrace. "Pen's waiting for me in the library. I can't—"

"I used to be a spy," he said succinctly, stopping her flight.

"What? You . . ."

"When Bonaparte retook Paris, Richard and I were recruited by Wellington as his envoys. We spent most of the war mucking about Paris and the surrounding countryside, trying to separate rumor from fact. Peese, my very rude butler, and my valet, Martin, were part of our team. Richard's still with the war department. I left."

"Why?"

He paused, looking at her. "Is that your third question?"

Sensing his hesitation, she met his gaze. Nothing else in his expression gave anything away, but that small flick of his eyes, the short breath, had been enough. "You don't want to answer that one, do you?"

Jack pursed his lips. "Is *that* your third question, now? I'm not answering anything until you decide."

There were things she wanted to know about him, about his feelings rather than his past—but with Wenford's death and the rumors surrounding it, it seemed more important to determine Jack Faraday's character once and for all. Learning whether he truly liked her or not would have to wait. "I want to know why you left the war department."

He turned away. "Surely you've heard the rumors, Lil. Take them as your answer and ask me something else."

"You said anything, Jack," she reminded him softly. "I want to know about this woman they say you killed."

Jack looked over his shoulder at her, then made his way over to lean against the mantel in a pose that looked easy and relaxed, until she looked into his eyes and saw the tension and reluctance there. "Her name was Genevieve," he said in a cool, distant voice. "Genevieve Bruseille. Yes, we were lovers. Yes, I killed her. With a knife, though. Not a pistol. No, I was not drunk at the time, and it was not an accident." He shook his head. "It was definitely not an accident. Do I regret it?" Jack looked over at her, the dark expression fading from his face as he regarded her. "Yes. Now, at this moment, more than ever."

Lilith studied his face, the myriad emotions running across his lean features. What she saw there—the regret, the momentary vulnerability, the desire for her—seemed to render his words less significant than the emotion that had driven him to confess.

"Given what I know at this moment, my lord," she said slowly, not daring to turn her eyes from his, "I do not think you had anything to do with Wenford's death."

"Thank you." He walked over to the window again and gazed outside for a long time. "You know," he said quietly, almost to himself, "embarrassed as Dolph might have been, he could have simply downplayed the entire event. Some other scandal would have come along in a fortnight, and everyone would have forgotten it. There was no need to bring in the suggestion of murder. Accusing a peer, even one as disreputable as I am, could have disastrous repercussions on the accuser if they were unfounded.''

"They were only rumors," she reminded him.

He turned to face her again. " 'Only rumors' can do a great deal of damage. I believe your family is well aware of that.''

Lilith bowed her head. "Yes, we are."

Immediately Jack came forward and tilted her chin up again with his fingers. "I never thought to hear myself say this," he murmured, "but perhaps you should go. I'll make a fight over something with William, and you'll be free of me and any unsavory connections should the rumors grow worse. Which they likely will.''

"So you are chivalrous, now?" she asked quietly.

"Apparently so. I have recently discovered several unexpected facets to my personality. It's a bit unsettling, actually.'' Jack placed his hands on her shoulders and looked into her eyes. "Do keep one thing in mind, Lil. If my theory is correct, and Dolph began those rumors to turn suspicion on me, then he is trying to turn it away from himself.''

She blinked. "You think Dolph Remdale killed his uncle?" she asked incredulously. "And you were warning *me* about rumors?''

"I admit I may be completely cork-brained about it," he returned softly. "But be careful around him. I don't want anything to happen to you.''

London's most disreputable peer was turning about to be not at all what she had expected. She reached up to touch the side of the marquis's face. "Now you only want me to be safe.''

"Yes, I'm full of contradictions today. It's only that of all people in the world, you were the last person I expected to see on my doorstep, Lil. I am a bit befuddled, I think."

"I doubt you are ever befuddled. In fact, I doubt you are ever surprised."

"Today, I was surprised," he countered, smiling jauntily. "As I continue to be, every time I encounter you."

"Shh," Lilith breathed. She pulled his face down toward her. Tentatively, very gently, she touched her lips to his, and his eyes closed. His hands drew slowly about her waist, and the pressure of his mouth on hers increased. Her arms slipped around his neck, crushing her chest against his so that there was no space between them. His lips parted hers, so it was as though they were breathing the same air.

This time it was she who tentatively explored his mouth with her tongue, moaning at the intimate, arousing sensations running through every part of her being. Gently he took her lower lip in his teeth and bit. Lilith gasped and pulled away a little, though she kept her arms about his neck. For a long moment they stood that way.

"What did I do to deserve that?" Jack murmured.

"You forgot the third kiss."

"Did I? That was rather stupid of me. How—"

She covered his lips with her fingers. "And besides, I like this Jack Faraday," she whispered, and pulled his face down to kiss him again. He returned the kiss roughly, running his hands up her back from her hips and down again. She knew she had taken several steps too far, but neither did she wish him to stop kissing her, touching her. She felt so alive when he touched her.

Jack walked her gently backward until she came up against the couch, his mouth trailing down from her lips to the base of her throat. His hands shifted, pulling her hips closer against his, while his mouth sought hers again—his kisses hot, and intoxicating, and very, very dangerous. Lilith forced her eyes open and drew a ragged breath that was half yearning moan and half protest. Oh, God, she wanted to let him continue . . .

"Jack, stop!"

Dazedly he lifted his head and regarded her. "What on earth for?"

"Please, please," she begged. "I can't . . . now . . . I—"

He looked at her. "Not now, or not me?" he asked quietly.

"I . . . I don't know." She shook her head, her fingers still wrapped about his lapels so he couldn't pull away. "I must go." Lilith tried to regain her breath and slow her heart before it exploded from her chest.

He ran a thumb slowly along her cheek. "You know, in a way I'm envious of Wenford."

"And . . . why is that?" she managed, relieved that he wasn't angry.

"There's nowhere I would rather expire."

"Oh, stop it," she protested. Jack Faraday was the most exhilarating, stimulating, annoying man she'd ever encountered. "This is simply your way of getting revenge on me, isn't it?" she demanded, releasing him. "Do you even bear me any affection at all, or do I just amuse you?"

He regarded her with an expression that made her want to slap him and kiss him again at the same time. "That's a fourth, fifth, and sixth question," he answered. "So what do we do, Lil?"

"Do? About what?" Lilith pushed his hands away from her waist and stepped aside.

"About Dolph Remdale possibly killing his uncle."

"How can you—" Lilith snapped her mouth shut. If he could still think in a logical manner, he must not care a fig about her. She could barely keep from throwing herself on him again.

"How can I what?" His hands returned to stroke softly along her arms.

Lilith drew a ragged breath. "Nothing. We have no proof that anything foul at all occurred, and you know it."

"Not yet." He smiled, cupping her cheek softly in his hand as though he was unable to keep from touching her. "Don't worry. I'll think of something."

"Don't. Don't think of anything. Don't try to drag me into another one of your games, Jack. My family couldn't withstand it—and neither could I."

Jack sighed. "I shall attempt to behave for a little longer, then. If you'll save another waltz for me at the . . ." He scowled. "What's the next damned society rout, anyway?"

"The Cremwarrens', tonight," she supplied, amused. He really did have little to do with proper society, and whatever his motives, it seemed that she was his lure. As Penelope had pointed out, it was very enticing to be a scoundrel's weak point.

"I think I was invited," he mused. "Will you waltz with me?"

Her father would be furious. "All right," she said. "If you promise there'll be no more talk of Dolph and murder."

"If there is no proof, I will not mention it again," he swore solemnly, then reached for her again.

"Oh, no, you don't," she protested, but couldn't help smiling as she backed away. "I truly have to go before Pen and I both end up in trouble."

"Yes, my lady," he said reluctantly. Jack walked to

the door and pulled it open for her, then followed her out the way she had come. The two of them walked together through his garden to the vine-covered brick wall.

After a hesitation, Jack leaned down and touched his lips to hers. A lightning pulse raced up her spine, and she kissed him back before pulling away to be certain none of his neighbors had seen them.

He chuckled. "No one out here but us criminals, my sweet."

"We are not criminals," she retorted. "At least, I'm not."

"You are the soul of honesty and purity," he agreed, then gave a wolfish grin. "At least one of which I hope I am able to change."

Truly shocked, she blushed. "Jack!"

" 'Twas your own imagination led you to that conclusion, Lil," he continued softly. "I told you that you were a sensuous creature."

She took a steadying breath. "I am not."

Surprisingly, his expression became serious again. "Don't ever tell yourself that, sweet one. Never." He put his hands about her waist and helped her up onto the wall, then held her hand as she jumped down to the other side.

She started to turn away, but he didn't release his grip. "I have to go," she whispered, glancing over her shoulder.

"Yes," he answered. "I do bear you some affection." He let her go and waved her off toward the Sanford home. "Be careful of Dolph."

"I will," she said, abruptly elated, and hiked up her skirts to hurry back to Pen's library and her waiting aunt. "You be careful, too, Jack Faraday."

"I will."

Chapter 12

Jack stood in his garden for some time after Lilith Benton disappeared over Lord Tomlin's well-manicured wall.

She had come to warn him. She had risked scandal simply to tell him that his reputation might be in jeopardy—a prospect so trivial it was almost laughable. Except he wasn't laughing. He was wishing. He wished she had stayed with him. He wished his reputation wasn't in such tatters that he didn't dare call on her in a proper manner, and he wished she didn't become upset and embarrassed every time he approached her in public.

"What a damned, bloody mess you've made of it, Black Jack Faraday," he muttered, absently shredding a twig in his fingers. "You don't know what in damnation to do with her any longer." He scowled, gazing up at the overcast sky and feeling the slight, chill breeze blowing through the maple and elm trees which bordered the north edge of the garden. "And even if you did know, you couldn't do anything about it, because no one—least of all you—would ever believe it. You're an idiot. That's what you are."

Jack threw aside the remains of the skinned twig and

strolled up the carriage drive to the front door. Lilith had accused him of having a few stray scraps of honor left to him, and while he couldn't quite call that an insult, it was certainly unsettling. And not just in regard to her.

There were certain things about Wenford's death that had begun troubling him more than they should. In light of Lilith's professed liking for the "real" Jack Faraday, whoever he might be, Jack was suddenly uncertain whether he could continue ignoring the little bits of information he kept acquiring. Wenford's paying of Dolph's debts, the supreme lack of affection between the members of the Remdale clan, and the old duke's dying just in time to prevent his marrying and begetting an heir to supplant Dolph were probably all coincidental. But now Dolph was apparently hinting that the death had been a murder. It was a dangerous course to take, but not an illogical one for a man desperately trying to pretend that he was innocent.

The whole thing was both intriguing and extremely vexing, particularly when he had to plan his own path so carefully. If he weren't behaving as though he were half addle-brained over a proper chit, he could proceed in a much more direct and less conventionally approved manner to forestall Dolph's damned rumors.

Jack paused at the foot of his front steps. He was more than simply *acting* addle-brained over her. Otherwise, he never would have lost his temper over the idea of her giving an earring to a mad old man. She'd kissed him this morning, and it had been unlike any of the other thousand kisses he'd ever received. Her soft, warm lips, the yearning for him he felt in her, had been so damned arousing, he'd nearly started ripping her clothes off there in his morning room.

"Let me guess," a caustic voice came from behind

him. "You're too drunk to make it up the front steps on your own."

"Richard," Jack acknowledged, starting. "How kind of you to come all the way to my humble home to inquire over my health."

"Don't give a damn about it," Lord Hutton returned brusquely. "You're allowed about at birthdays, and at Christmas and Michaelmas. But you've been to my home twice in the last two days. You've abused the privilege."

"I will see my sister whenever I choose to do so," Jack answered, finally turning around. Anger and hurt coursed through him, clenching his jaw and tightening the muscles across his back. Perhaps Richard had better reason to dislike him than anyone else in London, but lately the unrelenting hatred had begun to wear on him. Yet Alison was apparently acquainted with Lilith, and he wanted, needed, to know as much about the chit as he could. She had been what had tempted him to return to the Huttons', when nothing else over the past five years had been able to do so.

"I don't want you about Beatrice," his brother-in-law said flatly. "She'll have enough to live down with you as her uncle, without picking up your disgraceful ways."

"She's four, Richard. I'm not likely to teach her gambling or drinking."

"She worships you."

Jack sneered. "Jealous?"

Richard started to reply, then turned his back and stalked away toward his bay gelding, pointedly left waiting outside the gates bordering the short drive.

"Perhaps she's the closest I'll get," Jack called at his former friend and partner, though he didn't know why he bothered to speak. Richard wouldn't care.

The baron stopped. ''The closest to what?'' he asked, his back still firmly turned but his voice touched with reluctant curiosity.

''To what you have.''

He turned and climbed the shallow steps, and Peese pulled the door open as he reached the top. Jack didn't expect a reply, and was surprised when Peese's eyes shifted past him to look back out at the drive.

''*I* didn't take the chance from you, Jack,'' Richard's voice came in a more even tone.

The marquis paused. ''No. I did.'' And all it had left him was a game of revenge against a chit ten years his junior and a hundred years behind him in ruin. And though the game was proceeding splendidly, he was losing the stomach to continue playing it.

Jack continued on into the house, then bent to retrieve his book and a piece of paper lying on the hall floor. In Lilith's graceful writing, the note warned him of terrible rumors for which she in part felt responsible. A slight, unexpected smile touched his face as he lifted the letter and breathed in. It smelled of lavender. It smelled of her. Jack put the letter in his pocket and returned to the morning room and his book of poetry. Whatever else happened, at least the game had left him another waltz at the ball tonight.

Lilith spent the afternoon renewing her efforts to be a dutiful daughter, attempting to put all thoughts of the Marquis of Dansbury out of her mind.

It had been intoxicating, maddening, and exhilarating to be in his embrace. He was everything she had been raised to despise, and it was frightening to realize how much she craved seeing him, talking to him, and touching him again. When it was just the two of them, with no one about to chastise her or remind her to watch her tongue and her manners, she felt so free, as though she could say or do whatever she pleased. And the things that were coming to her mind were far from anything she should even be contemplating.

Deliberately she dressed in her most conservative and demure gown and occupied her mind with as many sober thoughts as she could conjure. Unfortunately, most of those thoughts seemed to center around making polite conversation with the new Duke of Wenford. Jack had repeatedly cautioned her to be careful of him, but she felt in more danger of being bored by Dolph's dull wits than of falling into his supposedly nefarious clutches.

Lilith stifled a smile as she descended the stairs to join her family. Now she had the ruined gentleman warning her about the proper one. She already knew which she would have more delight in dancing with, but it would have to be her last dance, and her last encounter, with Jack. Neither her heart nor her reputation could withstand prolonging the acquaintance any further.

The annual rout at the Cremwarrens' was famous, and as she entered the crowded ballroom, Lilith had difficulty keeping her aunt in sight, much less watching for any of her acceptable and unacceptable suitors. She sighed as she waved at Mary Fitzroy. It was no use denying that she was more eager to see Dansbury than any of her perfectly proper suitors—or, for that matter, anyone else she knew. Preoccupied, she jumped when her elbow was gripped.

"I hope this next waltz will be mine," Dolph Remdale said, smiling warmly at her.

"Of course, Your Grace." They stood for a moment, looking at one another and trying to avoid being jostled by the other guests. Lilith felt supremely awkward, and she shifted uncomfortably. After all, she had known of the old duke's death for a week before his own nephew had been informed of it. "I was sorry to hear of your loss, Your Grace," she finally offered. "Your uncle was . . . he will be missed."

It wasn't very smooth, but with a nod of his blond head he seemed to accept it. "Thank you for your condolences. Uncle Geoffrey was somewhat eccentric, but I believe he was rather fond of you."

The music began, and he offered her his arm to lead her out onto the floor, polished to a perfect shine with half a dozen layers of beeswax. He danced with nearly the same grace as Dansbury, though the new duke seemed more reserved about it—or at least, more proper. With the marquis, she had the wild sensation that he might sweep her off her feet, or try to kiss her or whisk her out onto the balcony on a whim. Unable to help herself, she glanced about the room to find him. After a moment she spied him, standing beside her brother and watching her while he spoke.

His dark eyes glinted as he met her gaze, and she wondered for a brief, thrilling moment if he might be jealous. William had better not have told Dansbury about her father's plans for her and Wenford—though, knowing her brother, he'd probably been gabbing about it from the moment the marquis entered the room. Whatever Jack might think, however, didn't matter. She couldn't let it matter. Resolutely, she looked away.

"I see you looking at Dansbury," Dolph said unexpectedly, and she hurriedly returned her attention to her waltzing partner.

"He was staring at me rather rudely," she improvised, "so I returned the favor."

"It might be wiser for you simply to ignore him," the duke advised mildly. "Those he dislikes tend to meet with unpleasant fates."

Lilith's breath caught. Surely he wouldn't voice his

suspicions about Dansbury to her, of all people. Not when the marquis and her brother were known to be fast friends. "Were you speaking of anything in particular?"

He nodded. "I don't like to gossip, but for your own safety, perhaps it's best that you know. There was a woman in Paris who humiliated him, and he shot and killed her. After he returned to London, there were rumors of at least two men killed in duels. He has a black temper." Dolph paused, once more looking in Dansbury's direction. "In fact," he continued in a more thoughtful tone, "I almost wonder whether he had anything to do with my own uncle's demise. His hatred for Uncle Geoffrey was quite well known. And my uncle's . . . the circumstances of his death were both unfortunate and very out of character."

When Jack had spoken of the woman, Genevieve, who had died in France, she had heard the regret in his voice. He'd tried to disguise it, but she was coming to understand his expressions and his moods, and she had to fight the abrupt urge to defend the Marquis of Dansbury's tattered reputation. "Rumors will abound, I'm certain," she returned stiffly, "but I have always preferred to judge for myself."

"A useless exercise." The duke smiled down at her.

Lilith knitted her brow. "What do you mean, Your Grace?"

He chuckled. "You are a beautiful woman. Anything else is a waste. A woman knows only matters of the heart, I always say."

Stunned, Lilith stared at him. Offense and anger swiftly followed. Wenford knew nothing about her— how dared he insult her intelligence! "If that is Your Grace's opinion," she said stiffly, flushing, "then perhaps we should—"

"Don't bother being offended," he said patronizingly,

his good humor vanishing. "Just smile and look lovely. That's all that's required of you." Before Lilith could think of a caustic response, the duke glanced at Dansbury again. "Speaking up where speech is not required can only get you embroiled in all sorts of idiotic nonsense."

"Then I shall not converse any further with you," Lilith said through clenched teeth.

Dolph shrugged as his much-admired blue eyes returned to her. "You'll speak in the flattering manner for which you are known, I believe, to excel. All the gentlemen of the *ton* discuss the esteem with which you regard them. And the loftier the title, the more pleasant you apparently are. And your father, as well. He finds my title quite fascinating, I think." He tightened his grip on her hand. "And in truth, I find *you* rather fascinating, Miss Benton. I can't seem to help myself, despite your unsavory relationship with Dansbury."

"I have no relationship with Dansbury. But even so, I find him to be far more appealing than you, Your Grace," Lilith snapped, all patience gone. This man was worse than his uncle.

"Mind your manners, girl," he grunted, the expression in his eyes turning briefly ugly, "or someone will mind them for you."

As she looked into Dolph Remdale's light blue eyes, Lilith was frightened for the first time. Frightened, and worried. She had promised her father she would wed anyone he chose. And he had chosen the new Duke of Wenford.

Dolph's slight smile widened. "It seems you learn quickly. Pity." He glanced in Jack's direction again, then as the dance turned them, his gaze found her father. "Your dear Papa looks so hopeful. Do let's make him happy, Lilith. Shall we?"

"You . . . you can't be serious," she stammered, white-faced. She wanted to scream, to faint, to pull free of his grip and run from the room.

He shrugged again. "Why not? I'm bound to marry sooner or later, and I'd rather have you in my bed than any of those squint-eyed chits waiting along the walls." Wenford tugged her closer, so that his breath was in her face. "I can't wait to have you, Lilith," he murmured.

"Never," she hissed.

"Shall we wager on that?" he returned conversationally, his mood changing again with lightning speed.

The waltz ended, and Lilith tried to pull free. He kept a firm hold, placing her hand over his arm and holding it there tightly enough to bruise.

"Let me go," she muttered, tugging at his grip.

"Smile, my love," he returned in the same tone. "You don't wish to cause a scene, do you?"

He was right. However much she feared and loathed him, there was little that could be done in such a public place. In private she would speak to her father and let him know what kind of monster Dolph Remdale was, and they could quietly decline his attentions. Lilith glanced up at the duke as he stopped before Lord Hamble. He hardly knew her. This was only the first dance, and the first real conversation, they'd ever had. He couldn't be serious. He couldn't be.

"Hamble," the duke said, smiling warmly at Lilith, "your daughter is exceptional."

"Thank you, Your Grace." Her father beamed. "I have done my best to raise her well."

"I shall have to speak to my man of business, of course, and the dozens of solicitors my uncle seems to have found it necessary to retain," the duke said, as though discussing the purchase of a coach or a cart mule, "but I see no real obstacle. Will you call on me tomorrow so we may finalize the arrangements?''

For a moment even the viscount seemed taken aback by the swiftness of the proceedings. He blinked a few times, then smiled broadly and offered his hand. ''It will be my pleasure, Your Grace.''

Dolph shook her father's hand, then forcibly took her own fingers and lifted them. Lightly he brushed his lips across her knuckles, and then finally released her. Lilith immediately took a step back. She desired to do nothing more than turn and run, but was prevented from it only by Aunt Eugenia's elated hug.

''Oh, my dear,'' her aunt gushed, beaming, ''what wonderful news!''

''Yes,'' Lilith agreed hollowly, pulling free, ''thank you. Excuse me.''

Hardly aware of what she was doing, Lilith turned to make her way through the jostling, stiflingly hot crowd. More than anything, she needed air, a chance for a moment of quiet. Everything was a nightmare. It couldn't be true! It couldn't really be happening. Her father had looked so ecstatic, so pleased, and she couldn't imagine what he would say when she told him she couldn't—wouldn't—marry Dolph Remdale. Finally she reached the balcony and grasped the railing to breathe deeply of the crisp night air.

''Congratulations.''

Lilith whipped around to see Jack standing in the shadows a few feet from the doorway. The breath which had caught in her throat began again raggedly. Jack would know what to do. She stepped toward him, but he lifted one hand to stop her.

''Well done,'' he continued, in the same soft tone.

She stopped. ''Jack—''

''A duke, even,'' he went on. ''I owe you an apology.''

"For what?" This was the Dansbury that she didn't like—the cold, cynical, arrogant one.

"I was wrong. You are an Ice Queen."

"How can you say that?" she whispered, stunned and shocked for the second time that evening.

He shrugged carelessly, but his eyes glittered in the moonlight as he looked at her. "How can I not?" he murmured, his voice icy with cynicism, but edged with a dark, heated anger. "You've made a very successful match with a monster. Don't you recall how we were discussing that he may have killed his uncle for the title? Oh, but he is respectable, isn't he? You must be so pleased."

Lilith clenched her fists. "I suppose it's true," she said with feigned calm, when she wanted to shout and hit him and tell him she'd been counting on him for support and help. "He may be a killer." She pointed a finger at his chest, willing her hand not to shake. "You, however, are a self-confessed murderer."

At Jack's quick, angry breath, she knew she'd scored a hit.

"True," he returned in a biting voice, "though where you're concerned, that would hardly seem to stand against me. It's only confessing to it that you find offensive, isn't it, Lil?"

"It is you I find offensive," she shot back at him, furious and hurt.

"The feeling is mu—"

"How dare you!" she interrupted, taking another step forward, tears streaming unnoticed down her face. "You're so damned selfish, you think everyone else cares only for their own amusements, as well. Not everyone is a self-centered boor like you, Dansbury. My actions affect my family, for better or for worse. My family wants me to marry Wenford. I want to please my family." Lilith didn't know whether she was trying to convince Jack or herself, but he didn't leave her time for reflection.

"And when your family is safe and happy back at Hamble Hall, and Dolph is sweating and rutting inside you at grand Wenford Park, will you be pleased?" He grabbed her hard by the shoulders. "You're not a fool, Lilith," he hissed, shaking her, "and you're not blind. Open your eyes, for God's sake, before you get yourself killed. Or worse."

Abruptly he released her, and without a backward glance returned to the lighted, noisy ballroom. Lilith staggered, and with a sob, returned to cling to the balcony's stone railing for dear life. She hated him. She hated Dansbury and his stupid, self-centered arrogance. Which didn't explain why she felt as though her last, best, and only hope of escape from Wenford's nightmare had just abandoned her.

Jack Faraday sat in his library before the fire roaring in the gilded fireplace, his legs stretched out in front of him and crossed at the ankles. Slowly he held up a playing card. The three of diamonds. Carefully he squinted down the length of the card, then flicked it in the direction of the fireplace. With a sucking hiss the card burst into flame and vanished. Methodically he lifted another card and repeated the process, with the same results.

He was halfway through his second deck, and none of the black anger coursing through his veins had lessened in the slightest. "Fool," he muttered, sending the five of clubs into the flames. "Idiot." The nine of hearts followed. "Halfwit." The ten of clubs became cinders.

Someone scratched at the library door.

"I'm not home," he called, and resumed the destruction of the cards.

"I know, my lord," Peese returned, his voice muffled by the sturdy oak door, "but if you were home would you be willing to see Mr. Price, who is waiting in the foyer for your reply?"

"You're fired, Peese," Jack said.

"Yes, my lord," his butler answered patiently. "But Mr. Price?"

"No."

"Very good, my lord."

Two more cards had been consumed before Price opened the library door and stepped in. "Yes, I know, you're not home, and if you were, you'd be in a very foul mood if anyone barged in on you." He shut the door behind him, then paused as another card sailed into heated oblivion. "My, my," he continued more quietly, and took the seat to Jack's right. "I haven't seen this for a while."

Ignoring him, Jack picked up the last card of the second deck. The queen of hearts, of course. He looked at it, trying to make it signify something, but the red, flat-faced monarch had little to do with the black-haired enchantress who'd just slipped from his fingers and into the arms of a snake. Scowling, he released the card, but instead of landing in the fire, it curved at the last moment and landed, face up, on the edge of the hearth.

Beside him Price leaned forward, looked at the card, and sat back again. "Female troubles, I presume?" he commented, sliding a third deck of cards from the pile on the table toward Jack's reaching fingers.

"No."

"Ah." Ogden cleared his throat. "Wouldn't have anything to do with Miss Benton's betrothal, then."

"Is she engaged?" Jack forced out, glancing briefly in his companion's direction. "Hadn't heard."

"Liar." Price picked up another of the decks and be-

gan absently shuffling the cards in nimble fingers.
"Doesn't really matter to me, anyway, except that I've
apparently won the hundred quid Landon wagered me.
I told him you'd never bed her."

*And Dolph Remdale will be able to take her whenever
he pleases.* "Season's not over yet," he ground through
clenched teeth.

Price lifted an eyebrow. "Perhaps you could use—
how shall I say—an evening with a pliable female companion."

"Probably." A meaningless wallow with one of the
new Italian divas gracing the opera stage was likely what
he needed. It had been weeks since he'd broken with
Camilla, and there'd been no one since then. He'd been
concentrating all his efforts and all his energies on Lil
Benton—and all because what had begun as a petty revenge had now evolved into something he couldn't put
words to, except to acknowledge that he was a damned
fool for thinking any woman would ever choose to follow her heart over her per annum, and that—even more
frustrating—he wanted her more now than he had at the
onset of this idiotic little game.

"You're not going to go find one of the fashionable
impures, though," Price commented after a moment.
"Are you?"

"No."

Price cleared his throat again. "Well, perhaps I'd best
leave, then." If he was expecting a request to stay, he
didn't receive one, and finally he stood. Even then he
continued to shuffle about from one foot to the other,
while Jack continued to ignore him. "The actual reason
I came by," he finally said, "was to mention that after
you rather abruptly left the Cremwarren soirée, some
speculation began that old Wenford may have been poisoned."

Jack paused in mid-throw and looked up at him. "So that's how I did it, then. I was wondering." The nine of clubs cascaded into the fire.

Price clasped his hands behind his back. "Yes, apparently with the bottle of port you gave him. The empty bottle was found upstairs in his study."

It hadn't been there when Jack had visited Wenford's study, the night before the body was found. If it had ended up there, it hadn't done so until after the duke's unfortunate demise was discovered. "Ah," he said noncommittally.

Price studied his countenance for a time, then nodded once more and turned for the doorway. "Well, good night, Dansbury."

"Price."

For a long time after Price left, Jack sat where he was and stared into the fire. He'd seen the speculation in Price's eyes, the wondering whether Black Jack Faraday might truly have had something to do with Old Hatchet Face popping off. And Price knew him better than most.

The marquis scooted off the chair to squat before the fire. Idly he began gathering the few cards that had escaped incineration, tossing them one by one into the flames. He'd erred on two counts. He'd badly misread Lilith Benton, had even begun to think that he was becoming more than just a scandalous novelty to her. Second, he'd spent so much time chasing Lilith that he'd forgotten about Dolph. And Wenford had outmaneuvered him.

Because he'd miscalculated, he was about to be in for another unpleasant bout of rumors and innuendo, being cut and ignored by the good *ton*. Jack lifted the queen of hearts again. It hurt to know that he'd been wrong about her—though even if he'd been right, he'd long ago lost any chance to earn her respect and consideration. With a scowl he crumpled the queen and threw it into the fire. "Damnation," he swore, shifting to sit cross-legged on the rug before the fire. Restlessly he ran his hand through his wavy hair. "Damnation."

Chapter 13

"My sister, the Duchess of Wenford." William grinned, bowing grandly as Lilith descended the stairs toward him. "Who would have thought? Father was right, after all. You have, by God, caught the highest title in London. Dullest, too, no doubt."

Lilith swallowed, determined not to begin crying again. She'd done enough over the past two days to last a lifetime. "I'd prefer not to speak of it at the moment, if you don't mind," she said haughtily. "I'm going shopping. I've an engagement ball to prepare for." In another two days, when her engagement was officially announced, it would be too late for everything. Though it had probably been too late for her from the moment her mother had vanished without a word six years ago.

William looked up at her for a moment, clearly trying to read her expression, then shrugged. "All right."

"Thank you." With a nod she stepped past him to collect her gloves from Bevins. She heard William hesitate before he turned and followed her, and she steadied herself for whatever he might say next.

"Lil, have you ever heard of Jezebel's Harem?"

She glanced over her shoulder. Her brother wore his clowning expression, the one that generally accompanied his attempts to cheer her up. For once, she was not in the mood to listen to his silliness. "Does that sound like a place I would have heard of?" she snapped.

A heroic smile touched his lips, then faded. "I suppose not," he continued gallantly. "But I wish you were a gentleman, so I could take you next time I go with Jack. We went there again last night, and there're these women, wearing nothing but veils all over their bodies. They didn't hide very much, though. One of 'em kept sitting in Jack's lap, but he was more interested in emptying his bottle of brandy." William gave a mock frown. "Jack turning down a chit wearing nothing but a few handkerchiefs. Odd, eh?"

Lilith flinched at the mention of Dansbury's name. "William, I do not wish to hear about it," she informed him coolly. Looking into the hall mirror, she placed her bonnet over her hair and tied the ribbons beneath her chin. Her brother's face appeared over her shoulder.

"What's gotten into you? Jack's antics always send you flying up into the boughs."

"Haven't you heard?" she returned, pulling on her gloves. "I am the Ice Queen."

"No, you aren't, Lil," he protested. "Stop it."

She turned to face him. "Why?"

"Because you aren't, that's why. If you don't want to marry Wenford, then just tell Fa—"

"It's a good match," she interrupted, patting him on the cheek and smiling as best she could, though it couldn't possibly look authentic. "And I'll be a duchess, as you said. Who could ask for more?"

Before he could reply, Lilith turned away so Bevins could help her on with her heavy shawl. She was halfway out the door, heading toward Milgrew and the waiting carriage, before her brother finally spoke.

"Jack doesn't like to talk about *you* anymore, either," he offered in a quiet voice.

Lilith faltered, and tried to hide the motion by straightening her shawl. "I don't care," she said without turning around, and Milgrew helped her into the coach.

Thankfully Lady Sanford seemed to realize that Lilith and Penelope wanted a chance to talk in private, for after Milgrew stopped for the other two ladies and then drove them to Bond Street, Pen's mother became very interested in a particular hat shop, and refused to leave until she'd found something to wear. Lilith and Pen stood outside in the wan sunlight and waited for her.

"I know you aren't happy," Penelope said quietly, glancing about the busy street, "but His Grace is handsome and wealthy, Lil. Doesn't that count for something?"

To her father, it did. "It doesn't matter, Pen," she returned, gazing uninterestedly at Lady Phoebe Dewhurst as that formidable woman and her retinue of footmen arrived, laden with packages, at the Dewhurst carriage. "It's been decided. He and my father shook hands on it, and their solicitors drew up some sort of agreement about my dowry. And in two nights, Aunt Eugenia will welcome everyone to Benton House for my engagement ball."

"Why so soon?"

"His Grace wished it," Lilith returned, not willing to reveal the exact conversation. "No dawdling," her father had said upon his return from Remdale House. "That's what he wants. To be wed and done with the nonsense. And so we shall be." The look he'd given her had stopped any protest in her throat. He'd wanted this marriage for six years, if not for his entire life.

"His Grace must truly be in love with you," Pen

offered, though neither her voice nor her expression seemed very enthusiastic.

"He must be," Lilith agreed tonelessly. "Do let's speak of something else." She'd tried to convince herself that she'd misheard Dolph at the ball, or that he'd been nervous about proposing and so had spoken poorly. She hadn't seen him since that night, but he had absolutely no reason to be cruel to her. They barely knew one another.

"All right," Pen agreed, scrunching up her nose in concentration. Finally she brightened. "Was the Marquis of Dansbury devastated at the news?"

"I doubt he possesses the ability to feel such a thing," Lilith said flippantly, glancing at her friend and then away. She'd figured Jack Faraday out, as well. He'd realized he'd lost whatever game he'd been playing with her, so he had yelled and stomped his feet and gone off to pout, and she'd never see him again. Good riddance— and he was *not* the reason she'd gone to sleep weeping for the past three nights.

"You truly did like him, didn't you?" Penelope asked.

"Not a bit. He's a scoundrel and a rakehell and a gambler, and if I never see him again, I will be quite happy, I assure you."

"You left out murderer."

Lilith blanched. "What?"

"Haven't you heard? Everyone says he actually killed old Wenford. That he gave the duke a bottle of wine, and it was poisoned." She leaned closer. "They even found the bottle, I hear."

"That's . . . that's nonsense," Lilith protested. "Awful as Dansbury is, he'd never murder anyone. It's absurd."

"But what about that woman in Paris, Lil?"

"If you think he's a killer, then why were you so excited when you thought he was pursuing me?"

Pen shrugged. "Because you don't think he's a killer."

"I—"

"And because you seemed to like him."

Just how much she *did* like him had become painfully clear when he'd abandoned her. Jack Faraday brought something to her life that she'd never had before—a sense that she didn't need to watch herself, that she could do as she chose. With a ragged sigh, she caught her daydreams and pulled them back to the ground. The reality was, she could do anything she chose, so long as her highly uncharacteristic behavior amused him. Well, he'd made it perfectly clear how he felt about her, and she was glad the silly, stupid pursuit he'd pretended was over with.

She looked over at Pen. "I was wrong."

Jack narrowed his eyes as Price looked about the crowded parlor at Boodle's, avoiding Jack's gaze as he had been for the past five minutes

"Go, then," he murmured, and lifted his glass, draining the brandy it contained. "I didn't expect to see you again after the other night, anyway."

Price sat back. "I've an engagement," he said emphatically and for the third time, as though volume and repetition made his excuse more believable. He glanced about again and leaned toward Jack. "I don't know what in hell you think you're accomplishing by sitting here, anyway," he continued in a lower tone. "Is being cut by your fellows another part of your game?"

"I am not being cut," Jack stated, refilling his snifter to the brim. "*They* are being cut. By me. And so are you. Go away."

The tables immediately on either side of him were empty, despite the evening's crowd, and he knew without looking that he was being widely discussed by the other patrons. William was at Antonia's. He'd nearly gone there himself, but he didn't feel up to Mademoiselle St. Gerard's smooth prying. Neither had he wanted to attend White's or the Society, knowing whatever snubbing he was going to receive was bound to be worse there. Boodle's had seemed safe enough, but even here he could feel the suspicion and the tension in the air. He didn't care. All he wanted to do was to get drunk enough so he could sleep without that damned chit's face and eyes taunting him through his dreams.

"Jack, go home," Price implored, then stood and left.

Jack didn't bother watching him depart. Dolph Remdale was doing a fine job with his rumors. Ernest Landon had failed to appear at all tonight, and he'd heard that Thomas Hanlon had been called to the country to visit an ailing relative. His cronies were fleeing like rats from a sinking ship. William Benton was the only one who'd actually offered to spend the evening with him, but William was Lilith's brother, and thereby far too much of a reminder of his own idiocy.

When Price hesitantly sat opposite him again a few minutes later, Jack didn't bother looking up at his companion. "The only thing worse than a coward is an indecisive one," he said. "Bugger off, Price, before I kill you, too."

"They say confession is good for the soul," a very different voice said from where Price was supposed to be sitting. "But given the setting, it's likely not the best way to defend your reputation."

Startled, Jack looked up and waited for his eyes to focus. "Richard."

"Well, that's an improvement," his brother-in-law

continued in the same low tone. "You're not blind drunk, anyway."

An encounter with his sister's shining hero was exactly what he didn't wish for the evening. "I haven't been near your precious family," he hissed, sprawling forward across the table and nearly spilling his glass in the process. "I haven't spoken to my sister, or to my niece, or to your damned dog or your damned wash maid. So leave me alone."

Richard examined his fingernails, then looked up again. "I would, except that Alison told me to find you and make certain you were all right."

"I'm splendid. Good night."

"Look, Jack, I don't want to be here any more than—"

The marquis jabbed a finger in his brother-in-law's face. "*You* look, Richard. I don't want you here. I did quite well the last time you turned your back on me. So don't think I want whatever charity you've decided to dole out."

Richard was very quiet for a moment. "I turned *my* back on *you?*" he repeated slowly. "Is that what you said?"

Jack should not have been speaking. He knew better than to begin rattling on about something he was angry about when he was this drunk. But he was so damned tired of it all. He was tired of himself, of Black Jack Faraday. "You heard me." The footman approached again with another bottle, but Jack waved him away. "Family is everything. Did you know that?" He downed his glass, and without pause poured himself another. "Don't embarrass your family, don't disappoint your family, and don't put yourself before your family." Jack glanced about the room, but he was still being given a wide berth by the rest of the patrons, damn them all.

"What she doesn't know anything about, though, is what your family is supposed to do for you." He leaned back and took another drink, beginning to doubt he'd make it out to his carriage without assistance. It would serve him right if he ended up on his face, out in the gutter. "They're using her. That's all." He sat forward again and pounded his fist on the table. "You know, maybe she does realize about family. She's afraid if she disappoints them, they'll turn away from her. You know all about that, don't you, Richard?"

From Richard's expression, Jack's speech had sounded as garbled as it felt. "Who is 'she'?" he finally asked.

Jack shrugged. "Just a chit I've been trying to ruin."

His disapproval palpable, Richard's lips tightened. "Lilith Benton, I presume?"

Jack glanced at him. "Don't worry. I've returned my attention to drinking and gambling and whores, where it belongs."

From Richard's expression, he remained skeptical, but Jack didn't much care. If he never set eyes on Lilith Benton again, he would be perfectly happy. Or at least, just as happy as he was this evening.

"She's made a good match politically," Richard offered quietly.

"Who? Oh, Miss Benton. Yes, Dolph Remdale's a fine, upstanding gentleman. I'm certain she'll be perfectly happy." He couldn't help the bitter tone, for even the words tasted sour on his tongue. Damn her for playing such havoc with his mind.

"She invited Alison and me to her engagement ball."

Now Richard was just fishing, to see whether he'd bite. "How wonderful for you. My invitation seems to have been lost in the London mail. Blasted shame, I'm sure."

"I would hope that didn't surprise you. Perhaps you might consider worrying about your own reputation for a moment, rather than ruining someone else's."

"I told you, I don't need your advice." The footman approached again, and Jack glared at him. "I'm leaving. Have my coach brought around."

"Yes, my lord."

Richard grabbed his arm. "Don't you realize, Jack," he said urgently, "there's talk that you murdered—*murdered*—Wenford? How can you sit about making a spectacle of yourself?"

Jack yanked free and lurched to his feet. "Apologies if I've embarrassed you, Richard. Just turn your back again, and no harm will come of it. Everyone knows we don't speak, anyway."

"That's the second time tonight you've accused me of turning my back on you," Richard snapped, blocking Jack's path. "As I recall, you were the one who took it upon yourself to kill Genevieve. I wasn't in the room."

"Someday, Richard," the marquis said, stepping around his brother-in-law and jabbing an accusing finger at him, "someday I'll tell you what really happened that night."

"Tell me now."

"Go to the devil."

To his surprise, Richard followed him to the door. "Jack, I know you don't want to listen to me, but the Duke of Wenford is pressing for a formal investigation into his uncle's death. If you could manage to lie quiet for a few days, it might blow over."

Jack glanced over his shoulder at his brother-in-law, trying to summon a careless grin. "Where's the fun in that?"

*   *   *

"Miss Lilith, should I put more rouge on your cheeks?" Emily asked, looking critically at her mistress's face.

Lilith examined her reflection in the mirror. Emily had already put more blush on her cheeks than she normally preferred, but even so, the face that looked back at her was wan and pale. "No, Emily. Any more and I'll look like a stage actress."

"Yes, ma'am."

Besides, it wouldn't cover the cold dread that made her hands shake, or the apprehension she saw in her own eyes. She'd begged Aunt Eugenia to wait before holding the engagement ball, but her aunt had insisted they not lose the momentum of Wenford's interest. Which meant her family was likely worried that Dolph would change his mind, and wanted to strike while the proverbial iron was hot. She wished with all her heart that he would change his mind, but in the two times they had met since his "proposal," he had been civil and polite and had not given any indication that he regretted his hasty decision. Of course, they had barely spoken, for she'd made every effort to ensure that they weren't left alone together for even a moment.

Perhaps it was her, and she was making more of her worries than she should. After all, Dolph was handsome and wealthy. And though he didn't have the depth of respectability granted his uncle, he was well liked and well mannered, and in time might even surpass old Wenford in power and influence. It was only what he had said that night while they were dancing, and the look in his eyes while he'd spoken, that sent shivers down her spine. And the fact that Jack Faraday had warned her about him, and that she had come to place a great deal of credence in anything the Marquis of Dansbury had to say. Even when it was about her own betrothed.

Lilith sighed miserably, finally admitting that she missed Jack. She missed seeing him, and bantering with him, and best and worst of all, she missed having him plot for ways to see her and steal kisses as though they were great prizes to be sought and won. He would never kiss her again, now, and because her family had chosen Dolph Remdale for her, she would likely never even see him again.

Her door opened, and Aunt Eugenia, resplendent in a flowing emerald and ivory gown, stepped regally into the room. "It's time, Lilith." She smiled. From the sparkle in her eyes and the high color in her cheeks, she was ecstatic about the hostess role she would be playing tonight.

Lilith remained rooted in the chair, her legs abruptly refusing to move. "Aunt Eugenia," she said, her voice shaking, "I'm really not certain about this. It's so sudden, and I hardly know—"

"It's just nerves, dear," her aunt soothed. "I hardly knew Walter when I married him, and you know how splendidly that match ended up."

Poor Uncle Farlane drowned in his fishing pond a year after you were married. "Yes, but—"

"Lilith, come along. You must be prompt for your own engagement ball."

"But I don't want to marry him!" Lilith finally shouted. She began sobbing, and lowered her head into her folded arms to hide her face.

In the shocked silence, Emily gasped.

"You are an evil girl, Lilith!" her aunt spat. "Evil! I'll see to this." With a rustle of skirts, Aunt Eugenia hurried from the room.

"Miss . . . Miss Lilith?" Emily's hesitant voice came a moment later.

"You may go, Emily," Lilith said, her voice muffled in her arms.

"Yes, ma'am." With even more haste than her aunt, her maid sped out the door.

For several minutes, Lilith could only weep. She'd already told her father she would marry anyone he chose, so long as it wasn't Geoffrey Remdale, and now she couldn't go through with his next choice, either. He would be so angry and disappointed. But she couldn't! Lilith took a sniffling breath. She could tell him again that she would marry anyone else he chose, but after this she doubted he would believe her.

"Your aunt says you don't want to get married."

With a start, Lilith sat bolt upright. "Your Grace."

She'd expected her father, and a rush of dread ran down her spine. Little as she wanted to face his anger, she knew how to deal with her father. The Duke of Wenford was another story entirely.

"I explained to the dear woman that you were suffering from a case of the nerves, and that you only needed to have me reassure you that you were making the right decision."

Lilith wiped her eyes and stood. "Your Grace, this has all simply happened too quickly. Surely neither of us wants to be left with any doubts about—"

Dolph took a slow step closer. "I have no doubts at all."

"But you hardly know me," she protested.

The new Duke of Wenford reached into the pocket of his gray evening coat. "I think I know you quite well," he said, lifting his hand.

Dangling from his fingers was a single pearl drop earring clasped by silver. *Her* pearl earring. Lilith stared at it for a moment, blanching. "I'm . . . I'm afraid I don't understand," she stumbled.

"Oh, I think you do," he returned. "As soon as I saw my uncle, I figured that Jack Faraday was responsible for his ending up where and how he did. No one else would have the gall. Imagine my surprise, though, when I discovered *your* pearl earring beneath Uncle Geoffrey's body."

"Your Grace, I—"

"Let me finish!" he snapped. "You are going to marry me. If you don't, I'll make certain everyone knows that you and Dansbury are lovers, and that the two of you conspired to murder my uncle."

Again Lilith could only stare. The rumor alone would kill her father. "Why?" she whispered, shock turning her hands cold.

He smiled. "Because Dansbury wants you."

She took a step forward, surprised at the mingled excitement and dread those words sent through her. "Then you've already won, because my family would never allow me to marry Dansbury, even if I wanted to."

"Which you don't, of course," he prompted.

"Which I don't," she repeated stiffly.

"Which doesn't matter," Dolph continued in the same tone. "You are a beautiful woman of good background, in spite of your mother's unfortunate lack of restraint." He examined the earring for a moment, then looked back at her. "And no doubt you will work doubly hard to be a quiet and complacent wife." He smiled, the expression not reflected in his eyes. "And every time Dansbury looks at you, he'll know he lost. To me."

"This is madness," Lilith protested, more than horrified now. She edged toward the door. She'd heard of marriages for title, convenience, money, or, as in her case, respectability. But to wed simply to win some sort of game of one-upmanship was unbelievable.

"If I want your opinion, I'll ask for it," Dolph replied, ugly anticipation coming into his eyes again. "The only pity is that Dansbury will likely be arrested before our wedding. We'll have to visit him in prison."

This was all wrong. And it wasn't just Wenford's sick motivation for marrying her, but also in the way he was using his uncle's death. She could almost hear Jack coolly pointing out that Dolph hadn't even bothered a show of grief, not even for propriety's sake. And if Wenford had been truly concerned about the cause of his uncle's death, he wouldn't have kept her earring hidden until he could use it to force her into submission.

"So, my dear, do you join me in your ballroom? Or do I go alone and express my opinion regarding this earring and the Marquis of Dansbury?"

"You are a monster!" she spat, glaring at him.

"I think you'll grow to like it," he returned, smiling again. He stepped forward and cupped his big, soft hands on either side of her face, then leaned down and kissed her.

It was horridly wet and sloppy and cold, and Lilith recoiled. Jack's kisses were so different, so exhilarating, that she could hardly believe the same physical action was involved. Which meant one of two things—either Jack was a stupendously proficient kisser, or she was in love with him.

"Don't think too hard, girl," Dolph said, obviously not reading her thoughts. "Your answer should be obvious, even to a female."

She needed time to sort out this disaster, and to determine how and if she could possibly escape from it. She needed to talk to her father, to figure out how she could warn Jack about Dolph and the earring, and to untangle her own growing suspicions about the old duke's death. Slowly, trying to hide her repulsion, she held out her hand. "I shall go with you," she stated.

"Good girl."

The evening was a nightmare of familiar faces congratulating her and wishing her well—friends and acquaintances who had no idea how little she wanted to be there, or how much she detested her newly betrothed. From the cold and heartless manner in which she had entered London, determined to find the most respectable match available, they had no reason to doubt her happiness. And now that she had realized what she *didn't* want in a husband, it was too late.

Or perhaps it wasn't. As the evening finally began to wane, she spied her father standing beneath the garden window, basking in triumph. The moment her betrothed was occupied with his cronies and the crowd had thinned enough for her to make her way over to her father without being intercepted, she approached him, trying to decide how much she dared tell him about Dolph and the late duke's death.

"Papa."

"You have made me a happy man, daughter." He smiled, taking her hand. "Wenford's talking of getting a special license so you can be wed by the end of the Season. Perhaps by the end of the month."

"That's what I wanted to talk to you about," she continued.

"Your aunt told me about the fit you threw earlier." For a moment his countenance darkened. "You might have ruined everything. Be grateful that His Grace was so understanding."

"Papa, he . . . he frightens me."

Her father lifted an eyebrow. "Frightens you? Don't be ridiculous. He's a true gentleman. And he dotes on you."

Lilith took a breath. "Might we go somewhere private for a moment?"

"Lilith . . ." he warned.

"Just for a moment, Papa," she insisted. "Please."

He scowled. "All right. All right." With obvious reluctance he gestured her into his private office. As soon as he closed the door, he rounded on her. "So what is it this time? You don't like His Grace, but you'll marry anyone *else* I choose?"

She'd known he wouldn't be easy to talk to. All she did know was that she absolutely did not want to marry Dolph Remdale. And that the man who had caught her heart was the last person in the world she could ever hope to marry. "I know I don't—"

"You tried that already!" He lifted a book and slammed it down on his desk again. "Do you intend to give me the same promise until you've gone through every unmarried lord in London? This is nonsense! You are engaged to His Grace, the Duke of Wenford, and you *will* marry him!"

"But I truly don't like him!" Lilith shouted back.

"You are an evil, flighty girl, just like your mother! If old Wenford hadn't been murdered by Dansbury, *he* would have made certain of things. I knew you couldn't be reasoned with."

Lilith opened her mouth—then, suddenly suspicious, shut it again. "You promised me I wouldn't have to marry old Wenford," she said slowly.

He glared at her for a moment, then looked away. "You would have changed your mind," he muttered.

Abruptly Lilith remembered her father's puzzled and disappointed search of the drive the morning Wenford had expired and Jack had carted off the body. "You expected him to call on me that morning, when you dragged William and Aunt Eugenia off to Billington's breakfast and gave the servants the day off," she accused, hardly believing she was daring to speak to him so, much less what it meant.

"You would have been a duchess," he growled. "And it's arranged so you *will* be a duchess. And that is final. Now, say goodnight and go up to bed before you cause any more mischief. I swear, you're worse than William."

Lilith wanted nothing more than to escape from the party, and she hurried upstairs. The evening had begun as a nightmare and had only grown worse. Her father had known what the old duke was like. By leaving the two of them alone together, he had also known what would transpire. She would have been compromised, and would have been shamed into marrying Old Hatchet Face rather than admit to having been ruined! It was in essence the same thing Dolph threatened her with. Marry him, or let everyone think she had become Dansbury's lover.

She shut her door and sat on the edge of her bed. All the proper men she knew in London were turning out to be monsters, and the only one who seemed to care for her happiness, the only one who ever listened to what she had to say, was Jack Faraday. Lilith sighed, heartbroken. Whatever did or didn't lie between them, Jack had no idea that Wenford had her earring. Nor was he aware that he might actually have been correct in his speculation that Dolph knew more about his uncle's death than he confessed to.

She paced restlessly about the room. If she told William about it, her brother would try to take care of things on his own, and likely would ruin whatever hope she had of escaping from this insanity.

Lilith paused, hugging herself and looking out the window into the dark streets of Mayfair. Maybe escaping wasn't such a bad idea.

Chapter 14

"**M**y lord," Peese said patiently, as he balanced two lamp shades and a chair in his arms, "spring cleaning is, I believe, supposed to be done in the spring."

"Shut up, Peese, before I hand you your papers again," Jack said absently, as he opened another of the half a hundred trunks stored in his substantial attic. "Take those downstairs and add them to the rest. I'm certain Father Donaldson will find a better use for them among the poor than they've found in the damned attic."

"But some of these are heirlooms, my lord."

"And they've been looming over my head long enough. Downstairs, Peese. And tell Frederick and Peter that I have noticed their absence and I expect them back up here posthaste."

"Yes, my lord."

For the past three nights, Jack had spent a great deal of time and energy drinking. And still he'd been unable to forget Lilith. Tonight, considering the events going on at Benton House, the idea of drowning himself in brandy had little appeal. Tonight was her engagement ball, and all the good *ton* would be there. He must still have some pride remaining, for he simply didn't want to be seen out among the bad *ton*, whether that was what he had become or not.

So he'd spent the last three hours burrowing through his attic, cleaning out years of accumulated heirlooms which had been of little purpose when they were acquired, and were absolutely useless now. Donating them to charity felt right, though admittedly it was a very small step toward salvation for a man with both feet firmly planted in Jericho. It did keep his nearest neighbors guessing about whether he was packing to leave the country, which at least provided some amusement. He straightened to stretch his back, slapping a layer of dust from his buckskin breeches. It must be past two in the morning, but he certainly had nowhere to be. And nowhere to go.

"My lord?"

"Peese, if I don't see Frederick and Peter upstairs in two minutes, I will—"

"My lord, you have a caller."

"I'm not home."

"Yes, my lord, but it's a female."

Jack paused and turned around. "Antonia?" he asked, hoping it was not.

Peese shook his head, and unless Jack was mistaken, he hesitated for a moment. "The other woman, my lord."

"Damnation, Peese, can you narrow it down somewhat?"

"The one who came calling last week, my lord. The one you took into the morning room."

Jack froze, his heart hammering. "Lilith?"

His butler nodded. "I believe that was what you called her, my lord."

The marquis swallowed, the thoughts coursing

through his mind having nothing to do with how angry and disappointed he'd been with her, and with himself for becoming so caught up with the cold chit. Probably because she wasn't cold, and he didn't want to see her wed to Dolph Remdale. He strode out of the attic and hurried down the two flights of stairs. Something must have gone very wrong for her to be here under any circumstances, and at two in the morning, he couldn't even imagine what might have happened. But if Dolph had hurt her, he was dead.

The drawing room door burst open, and Lilith turned with a start. Jack stared at her, his expression intensely worried. He was out of breath and covered with dust, his dark hair disheveled as the rest of him. He was without his cravat, and coatless, his shirtsleeves rolled halfway up his arms. Dansbury was breathlessly handsome, and she couldn't have taken her eyes off him if she'd wanted to.

"Jack," she whispered in relief. She'd been so worried he'd be at one of his clubs, or worse, that he'd refuse to see her. Tears filled her eyes and ran down her cheeks. "He . . . has my . . . earring," she managed. "He said he'd . . . he'd use it to . . . to tell everyone—"

"Wenford has your pearl earring?" Jack interrupted sharply, shutting the door behind him.

Lilith nodded. "I don't want to marry him!" She sobbed harder. "But he'll ruin me, and he'll get you hanged. He said he would."

His expression changed for a fleeting moment, but he moved no closer. "Allow me to guess. I told you I killed Genevieve, and now you come to me expecting that I will do you the favor of dispatching dear Randolph."

She shook her head, horrified that for a moment the idea tempted her. "No! I came here to—"

"Why not? Half the *ton* thinks I killed Old Hatchet Face, anyway. May as well dispose of the other Remdale while I'm at it."

"Oh, stop it," she snapped. "Don't you think I feel horrid enough that you're being blamed for old Wenford? Don't you think I wish I could tell everyone that you were only helping me?"

She put her hands on her hips. "But I was not the one who suggested that you strip Wenford and make him look like a drunken fool before his fellows. It had to be either Wenford himself, or someone with no fear of anyone who did it—and since Dolph seems quite assured that his uncle didn't render himself naked, who else would anyone suspect but you?" Her anger deflated. "And now me, because of that deuced earring. I'm beginning to think Dolph truly did have something to do with his uncle dying, Jack. That's why I came here."

For a long moment he was silent. "To warn me?" the marquis finally asked in a quieter voice.

She nodded. "And because I could think of no one else who could possibly help me."

"Help you?" he repeated. "*Help you?* Me?" Jack folded his arms across his chest and leaned back against the wall, the image of cynical disdain, but she saw the hope in his eyes. "My dear, hasn't anyone told you by now that I don't help people? I play with them, I amuse myself with them, and if it suits me, I ruin them."

"Considering you might have ended the speculation over your involvement in Wenford's death simply by telling everyone you found him dead on top of me in my morning room, I would have to say, Lord Dansbury, that you are somewhat in error about yourself."

"I told you, the incident amused me," he retorted. He tilted his head again, and looked at her for a long time. "How about a bargain, Lilith?"

"What sort of bargain?" she asked warily.

"I'll agree to help you be rid of Dolph Remdale, if you will agree to share my bed for one night."

Her breath caught. Dolph had threatened the same with her, and she had been revolted and nauseated. If anyone had even seen her at Jack's front gate tonight, she would be ruined beyond redemption. But the duke had already voiced the opinion that she and Jack were lovers. Lilith looked at him, exhilaration and anticipation running along every nerve. That had been the problem with Jack Faraday all along. She had craved the sound of his voice, his touch, his attention, from the moment she'd set eyes on him. He was everything she could never be—free, and unafraid of what anyone else might think or say about his actions and his opinions.

"No answer for me, Lil?" he pursued, the cynical tone coming into his voice again. "Then you should likely return home before—"

"I agree," she said, her voice trembling.

He shut his mouth. "Beg pardon?"

"I agree to your bargain," she clarified in a stronger voice.

Something vulnerable and elated crossed his features, then he turned back to the window and slowly shook his head. "Poor girl," he muttered, "you must be desperate. Go home. I'll find William tomorrow, and we'll see what can be done."

"But I agreed."

"I just wanted to see how you would answer, Miss Benton," he said, too quickly. "I'm not that much a monster." Slowly he turned to look at her again. "In fact, I find I am beginning to envy those men the world calls respectable. At least they may dance with you."

"My father became angry at me this evening, and he accidently mentioned that he knew Wenford was going to call on me that morning. He knew that the duke was going to . . . persuade me to accept his suit in a manner I would not be able to refuse.''

Even Jack looked shocked. "He *knew* he would be leaving you alone with that perverted rattle-brain?"

Lilith desperately hoped it was anger and jealousy she heard in his voice. Coming to find him in the middle of the night had taken every ounce of courage she possessed. If he turned her away, she had no idea what to do next. "He wanted a respectable match for the family, even if I had to be raped for him to receive it. So you see, Jack, I've had my fill of respectable men. From my experience, they are the monsters. Not you.''

"Lilith . . .''

Again tears gathered in her eyes, but this time Jack stepped forward to brush them from her cheeks with his thumbs. She shut her eyes at the gentle touch, and he kissed her eyelids. Lilith tilted her head up, and his mouth touched her lips—first gently, then, as she responded, more roughly.

He teased her mouth open, and she gasped at the raw sensuality as he slowly ran his tongue along her teeth. At her reaction he immediately pulled back, until the grip of her hands around his arms stopped him.

"For God's sake, run away, Lilith,'' he whispered. "Go home, where it's safe.''

"I feel safer here,'' she returned, lifting one hand to touch his lips. "Kiss me again.''

"I want to do far more than kiss you, Lil,'' he murmured, pulling her against him. "Unless you tell me no.''

Whatever else happened, she wanted Jack to be the first one to touch her, to hold her—whether his motivation was simple lust, or something closer to what she had begun to feel for him. "Yes.''

He took a deep breath. "Far be it from me to warn you that you're being foolish," he whispered, then bent to sweep her up effortlessly in his arms. "I think we'll avoid the couch," he said, and headed for the door.

She turned the handle, and pulled it open. And gasped.

Jack's butler stood in the hallway, a pair of candelabras in his hands. He lifted an eyebrow as Jack stepped out into the hallway.

"These, my lord?" he said in his rough voice, hefting the brass candle holders.

"Put them out with the others," the marquis said nonchalantly.

"Jack," Lilith whispered, hiding her face against his shoulder, deeply embarrassed.

"And Peese," Jack added, "send everyone off to bed, will you?"

"With pleasure, my lord." With another bold, speculative glance at her, the butler nodded and disappeared into the depths of the house.

"Jack, won't he—"

"He's trustworthy," Jack returned, lowering his head to kiss her deeply as he started up the stairs with her.

They entered his bed chamber, where the covers of the huge bed had been turned down, and a fire burned brightly in the fireplace. It hardly appeared to be the den of iniquity she had once imagined, but little of Jack had been what she'd expected.

He set her on her feet before the fireplace, and kissed her again. Slowly his mouth trailed down the line of her jaw to her ear, and Lilith half-closed her eyes, swaying a little toward him at the sensation. When he took the lobe of her ear between his teeth and gently bit down, she gasped again. He moved behind her, running his fingers lightly along the nape of her neck, his lips following. He loosened the clips in her hair, letting it tumble in a black wave down her back. His long fingers toyed with the tresses, caressing and lightly tugging, while his mouth nibbled at her other ear. Lilith's breasts tightened, and she felt a sudden, unexpected warmth between her legs. Unable to help herself, she moaned.

"You are a sensuous creature," his low voice murmured in her ear. "I knew you were, Lilith."

"Jack," she whispered shakily. Her breath came very fast, almost as fast as her heart's pounding.

"Tonight you're free to do whatever you choose, Lilith. Anything you choose."

His lips brushed the back of her neck, his breath warm in her hair, and his hands slowly captured her waist. Against the small of her back she could feel him, could feel his desire for her, and another moan escaped her.

His fingers shifted to the back of her gown, and the rhythmic sound of the dress fastenings coming undone was a further seduction. When he had finished, he moved in front of her. Slowly he slid the dress from her shoulders, his mouth caressing the bare skin he had exposed.

Finally Lilith stood before the fire in nothing but her shift, her dress puddled on the floor at her feet. She looked up into his dark, smoky eyes. Despite the warmth of the flames and the fires burning through her body, she shivered. As his fingers slipped under the shoulders of her shift, she trembled again.

"Are you cold?" he whispered.

"No," she said breathlessly. "Actually, I'm rather warm."

His chuckle sent another tingle down her spine. "So am I, truth be told."

Her shift slid silkily to the floor with her gown, and Lilith took a ragged breath. Only her maid had ever seen her naked. Self-conscious, she moved her arms to cover as much of herself as she could. His eyes took in every inch of her, from her toes to the top of her head, and the warm tingling down her spine settled between her legs.

"Glorious," he murmured, triumph and desire in his eyes. "You are glorious."

For the first time in her life, as Jack looked at her, Lilith felt glorious. Shaky, torn between desire and terror, but beautiful. His eyes holding hers, he touched her shoulders, then slid his hands slowly down so that his fingers just brushed the outside of her breasts. Lilith drew another ragged breath, wondering how much more of this she would be able to withstand before her knees buckled.

Everywhere he touched seemed to come alive, so that she was aware of the slightest whisper of air in the room against her skin. His mouth followed his hands, and she moaned again.

"Jack, please," she murmured helplessly.

"Please what?" he asked, reaching down to take her hands and pull them away from her body. He stepped into the circle he'd made and kissed her again, more roughly this time, and she realized that he wasn't quite as calm about this as she had thought.

"Please," she repeated, not certain what she was asking for, or at the least, not certain how to ask for it. "I want to be with you."

"You are," he said, "and you shall be."

He trailed his hands down to her breasts. Shivering, she watched his expression, fire burning through her at his expert touch. He ran his thumbs across her nipples, and they hardened in response. Breathing hard at the sensation, she arched her back toward him. He dipped his head and took one of her nipples into his mouth, sucking lightly.

"Oh," she gasped, as sensation unlike anything she'd ever felt stormed through her.

Jack's lips trailed over to her other breast, and he ran the tip of his tongue around the aureole, then suckled her again. Lilith tangled her hands in his hair, holding him against her.

He straightened and kissed her. "Now you undress me," he suggested in a soft murmur.

Lilith lifted her hands to cup the sides of his face and kiss him as he had kissed her. Her shaking, eager fingers fumbled over the buttons of his waistcoat. Jack didn't make the task any easier, for he was caressing her breasts again with his long fingers and kissing the nape of her neck. "Jack, you must stop," she ordered unsteadily, as she accidently pulled off one of his buttons. "I can't think straight."

"You're not supposed to be thinking," he said huskily, his eyes on her hands as they ran over the front of his shirt. "You're supposed to be feeling."

"I am." She smiled breathlessly.

Taking pity on her, he helped her with the waistcoat. She clumsily pulled his shirt free of his breeches, and he helpfully lifted his arms so she could pull it off over his head. Her fingers shaking, she reached out to run her hand along his hard, smooth chest. His skin jumped beneath her touch.

"You're not so poorly made, yourself," she offered, hesitantly sliding her hand down his flat, well-muscled abdomen.

"Perhaps I'd best see to the rest," Jack muttered. He swiftly pulled off his Hessian boots, then disposed of his breeches.

Lilith's gaze wandered lingeringly down his lean, hard

body. Finally she saw his aroused manhood. "Oh, my," she said faintly, her heart skittering with desire and nervousness.

"Is that good or bad?" he asked with a lopsided grin.

Naive as she knew herself to be, Lilith also knew that he was magnificent. "You're more beautiful than the statue of David," she whispered.

Jack closed the distance between them. This time, when he lifted her in his arms, she could feel the fast beating of his heart against her skin, and the slight tremor of his muscles as he laid her on the bed. He sank down beside her.

Lilith felt as though she was humming with tension, that she needed something only Jack could give her. As his lips found hers again, she shifted restlessly closer to him. While he kissed her, his hand wandered languorously down to her breasts, along her stomach, and then lower. As he slowly slid his fingers between her legs, Lilith gasped and tensed.

Jack smiled, though the motion of his hand against her never stopped. " 'If I profane with my unworthiest hand this holy shrine, the gentle sin is this, my lips, two blushing pilgrims, ready stand to smooth that rough touch with a tender kiss.' "

She tilted her head back and moaned, all sensation narrowing to where Jack's hand caressed her most private place. "You're a romantic," she declared shakily, her hands tracing the hard muscles of his back as he leaned closer.

He kissed her deeply again, and let his mouth once more travel down to her breasts. "You inspire me," he murmured, shifting so that the length of his body covered hers.

With his hand he coaxed her legs further apart, then settled his own between them. Lilith gazed into the dark eyes that seemed able to look deeper inside her than anyone she'd ever known.

He kissed her again, and at the same time entered her slowly and carefully. She gasped in mingled pain and surprise and wonder. "Jack," she whispered, digging her fingers into his back.

"It's the last time I will ever hurt you. I swear."

"It doesn't hurt," she protested shakily, gasping again as he moved. She watched his face, saw from his expression how careful he was being, and what a strain it was for him. "Really."

"How's this?" he asked, shifting and slowly deepening the embrace of their bodies.

He was right; the pain was nearly gone, replaced by a flooding, tightening sensation all through her that she'd never felt before. "Better," Lilith groaned, arching her back.

"I thought so."

Slowly and gently at first, then faster and harder, he entered her again and again. Lilith felt tension building inside her, and wanting him still closer, wrapped her legs about his thighs. She lifted her hips to meet each stroke, her fingers pressing into his back, and he groaned, half closing his eyes. He slowed his movement and deepened his strokes, watching her expression intensely, almost ferociously. Something more was happening inside her, and Lilith cried out his name and threw her head back as the tension exploded. Jack quickened his own movements in response, then shuddered, holding himself hard against her. After a moment he lowered his head against her shoulder, kissing her ear. Slowly and carefully, breathing as hard as she was, he settled himself down on top of her.

"Sweet Jesus," he muttered unsteadily.

Lilith didn't want to say anything, just wanted him to

hold her, wanted to feel the beat of his heart against hers. His weight on top of her felt so intimate and comforting, and she didn't want him to move. Ever. He seemed to sense that, for he stayed where he was, gently toying with her hair, for a long time.

Just as he was beginning to grow heavy, he shifted off her. He looked down at her, a slight smile on his handsome face, and his eyes dancing in the firelight. "Lil," he whispered, and sinking down beside her, slid his arm about her waist and pulled her against him. "You are definitely no Ice Queen."

Loath to separate herself from him, Lilith cuddled against him, twining her fingers with his while she curled her back against his chest. That way she could feel his slow, steady heartbeat. A clock out in the hallway somewhere chimed faintly half past three, and she knew she should gather her clothes, and her wits, and go home. There was still time, though, before she had to go back to the nightmare, back to tomorrow. *I love you, Jack,* she thought. Content in his embrace, Lilith sighed and closed her eyes.

Something was extremely peculiar. Jack had been mulling it over since Lilith had fallen asleep in his arms. With elbow crooked and head propped up on his hand, he looked down at her. Long, black hair, still wavy from being held in its clips, spread out on the pillow around her head like a dark halo. Not wanting to wake her yet, he leaned down and kissed her cheek.

There had been a time, a few years ago, when he had been even less disposed to care about the feelings of others. For a variety of reasons, including wagers and extreme intoxication, he had bedded a number of virgins. They had been awkward and nervous, hardly worth the tears and hysterics that generally followed, and what he had felt most was contempt at the silly things for giving in to a man they knew meant them no good.

He sighed as she stirred and tightened her grip on his fingers. All Season, since he'd set eyes on her, he'd intended to bed Lilith Benton. He'd told himself it was because she had insulted him, and she needed to be taught a lesson. Well, he'd taught her, but her passionate reaction, and his own, had left him feeling like the student. She'd wanted him as badly as he'd wanted her. As he still wanted her. And it was even worse than that. He wanted to protect her, to make things right for her, to see her smile, and to hear her laugh.

The hall clock chimed the quarter hour, and he scowled. Making things right for her would not include having London know she'd spent the night at Faraday House. "Lilith?" he murmured, brushing a strand of hair from her face.

She sighed and smiled, pressing her back against his chest. Then, with a start and an exclamation, she sat bolt upright. "Oh, my God!" she exclaimed, staring at him.

Jack sat up and wondered if she intended to indulge in hysterics, after all. "No, it's just me. And we're not often confused, I might add." It was a poor attempt at humor, and she didn't smile.

"What time is it?" she continued frantically, diving from the bed for the pile of clothes lying before the nearly dead fire.

Jack took a moment to admire her bare backside before he leaned back against the headboard. If she hadn't been so obviously distressed, it almost would have been amusing to see the proper chit dashing about like some frantic maiden in a burlesque comedy. "Fifteen minutes of six," he answered.

"Oh no, oh no," she cried, trying to pull on her shift. "I've ruined everything!"

The marquis continued to watch her curiously. "Worried about offending Dolph?" he asked offhandedly, clenching his fist in the sheets to disguise the sudden burst of hatred and jealousy that ran through him. This dementia of his was becoming extremely serious and troublesome. The thought of any man but himself—and Dolph in particular—touching her was enough to put him into a blind fury.

She was having a difficult time with her ball gown, and a tear ran down her cheek as she struggled to yank her arm through the short, puffy sleeve. "Oh, I'm just like her," she sobbed. "How could I?"

Jack abruptly realized what she was ranting about. "Your mother, you mean?" he asked quietly. Silently he rose and pulled his robe from the back of a chair. He put it on and stepped over behind her. "Don't do that to yourself." He reached out to hold up the other sleeve so her groping hand could find it.

"I've done the same stupid thing she did," Lilith said bitterly, "and now everyone else will pay for it, just as we did with her."

"Nonsense." She stilled as he pulled her hair free and draped it over her shoulder. "I have several adjectives in mind to describe what we were up to, and 'stupid' is not one of them." He swiftly fastened up the back of her gown. "Your father had no right to put you through this. And Dolph Remdale is a bloated ass."

"It doesn't matter," she said stubbornly. "I made an agreement."

"Did you? Seems to me it really wasn't left up to you at all."

She turned to look at him, and her frantic expression softened into inexpressible yearning for a moment as he held her gaze. "Jack," she whispered.

Perhaps he could set things right for her. He was disreputable, of course, but that could change, and he was titled, after all. Jack swallowed at the enormity of what he had just rather effortlessly talked himself into. "Lil, I—"

"Please promise you won't tell," she cut in, reaching out to touch the robe where it covered his heart. He took a quick breath to cover the tremor that ran through him at the caress. "It's still early. If I can get back—"

"London's most proper young lady, in the arms of the town's most notorious rake?" he said softly, so she wouldn't know how deeply she'd just wounded him. She was ashamed of him, of course. "Who would believe me, anyway?"

He tilted her chin up, meaning to brush the tears from her face, but he was unable to keep from leaning down and touching his lips to her. She didn't resist, and in fact, pursued his mouth as he straightened, wrapping her arms about his neck and leaning against him. He put his arms around her, holding her close. At least she still seemed to desire him. It was almost as if both of them had been drawn to this, to be together, against all better sense and reason. If this was a punishment for his past misdeeds, he was willing to pay the price.

"I would believe it," she said more firmly, and even managed a smile. "You're not so terrible, I think, whatever everyone else says."

"In that case, answer me two questions, will you?" he asked, handing over one of her hair clips and then heading for his dressing closet.

"It depends on what they are."

Apparently she felt steady enough to be defiant again. She might be afraid of scandal, but Lilith Benton was not the least bit faint of heart. "Do you truly think Dolph killed Old Hatchet Face?" Jack dug into the closet for a shirt and breeches, then leaned out the doorway to look at her when she didn't answer.

She had paused, her gaze on the smouldering fire. "Yes, I think he might have," she finally answered, looking over at him. "What is your second question?"

"What do you wish to do about it?"

"What do you mean?"

He pulled on his breeches, cast aside the robe, and shrugged into a shirt. "I mean, do you wish to ignore what you know and marry the murdering bastard, or do you want to do something about it?" He wasn't quite able to disguise the jealousy in his tone, and her expression became more speculative as she looked at him. "You don't have to decide now, of course," he forced himself to continue in a more even tone, "but before I go to the gallows for the deed would be nice."

He immediately regretted having spoken, for that would only remind her that he was rumored to be a killer. His jaw tightened as *she* jolted into his mind. Beautiful Genevieve, red-haired and eager to turn him over to Napoleon in exchange for a bag of gold—he *was* a killer.

The clock began chiming again, and he grabbed for his waistcoat. "Let's get you home."

Despite the early hour, Peese was already up and waiting for them in the foyer. "I took the liberty of hiring a hack," he announced, handing Jack the caped cloak Lilith had arrived in.

Jack glanced at his butler. He'd barely mentioned Lilith Benton to either Martin or Peese, but they both seemed to sense that she was not one of his typical late night trinkets. "My thanks," he said, and helped Lilith on with her cloak.

"A hack?" Lilith asked, still looking warily at the butler.

Peese held up his greatcoat, and Jack shrugged into it. "No Dansbury crest emblazoned on the doors," he explained. "Shall we?"

Lilith was silent as they traveled down Grosvenor Street toward Savile Row. For once Jack wasn't in the mood for idle chatter, either. Too much had happened that he needed to decipher, and she was too lovely sitting there trying not to look back at him.

He had instructed the driver to stop around the corner from Benton House, and Lilith started as they bumped to a stop. "You don't have to come," she said hurriedly as he rose and pushed the door open.

"I am fairly proficient at sneaking about," he answered, knowing he was just trying to prolong their encounter. He leaned out the door, looking at the fog-dimmed lane. No one was in view, and he stepped down and held a hand up to her. They quickly walked up the street, then pushed through a thin spot in the hedge into her garden. The stables behind them were silent, and the only light in the house came from the single kitchen window at the base of the wall. "Did you come down that way?" he asked, gesturing at the rose-covered trellis climbing the wall up to the roof, close to the window he knew belonged to her bed chamber.

"Are you mad?" she whispered. "I left through the servants' entrance. I think I can get in the same way."

"The trellis would be safer, if you don't wish to meet anyone."

"I have no wish to be thorn-bitten," she retorted, then gave an exasperated smile. "Thank you, Jack, for seeing me home."

He took a step closer. "Is that all?"

"I . . ." She met his gaze, the passion and yearning of the night before touching her emerald eyes. "I think it has to be," she said quietly.

Jack pushed her hood back from her face, cupped her cheeks in his hands, and leaned down to touch her lips softly with his own. "For now, perhaps," he murmured. "I don't think I'm ready to give you up yet, Lil."

"Jack—"

He covered her lips with his fingers, not wanting to hear her protest that they would never suit because he was an unredeemable scoundrel.

"I'll see you soon," he said. He kissed her again, and her return kiss gave him hope that she had no real wish to end this, either.

"Excuse me."

Jack jumped and instinctively stepped between the voice and Lilith. The Bentons' groom stood at the edge of a bed of geraniums, his expression curious.

"Milgrew," Jack acknowledged stiffly, his hand clasping Lilith's. "Fine morning for a stroll."

"Aye," the groom agreed slowly, still glancing from one to the other of them. "Bit chilly, though. I had thought to go into the kitchens and get myself a cup of tea," the Scot continued in his light brogue. "Thought perhaps Miss Lilith might wish to accompany me— t'make sure that certain . . . busybodies ain't awake yet."

Jack relaxed and smiled. "Splendid idea. My thanks."

"Thank you, Milgrew," Lilith echoed, and looked up at Jack again. "I have to go."

"Be careful," he said quietly, reluctantly releasing her fingers. "And stay away from Dolph, if you can. Until we know. Or until you decide."

She nodded. "I'll try."

Jack watched Lilith and the groom slip through the servants' entrance at the back of the house. Slowly he turned and made his way out of the garden, and back to the coach.

"Back where you came from," he instructed the driver.

The hack bumped into motion, but Jack hardly noticed. Lilith was probably already doing her best to forget the evening they'd spent together, and regretting that she'd ever left her engagement ball. For his part, he doubted he'd ever be able to forget. Nor did he wish to.

It was useless and idiotic to deny it any further. He was in love with Lilith Benton, had likely been in love with her since the moment he had set eyes on her. She was the only woman he'd ever met who seemed able to make him remember that he did possess qualities of decency and good-heartedness, however hard he'd tried to forget and deny them. And he couldn't have her.

Even so, she felt something for him. Though she had tried, she couldn't hide it from him this morning, and she'd certainly been enthusiastic enough last night. He'd be damned before he'd let Dolph or any of her other blasted swains have her. He wanted her for himself, and he wanted her forever. Which meant he had to accomplish two things: find out what, exactly, had killed old Wenford; and prove that Dolph, and not he, had done it, before the Crown saw fit to confiscate his lands and ship him off to Australia.

Jack was aware enough of the odds against him to be worried, and cynical enough to be amused at himself. It was a damned good thing he enjoyed a challenge—and turning his life right-side up again for the sake of London's most proper young lady looked to be the most difficult one he'd ever faced. It was also the one he most needed, and most wanted, to win.

Chapter 15

❧⟡❧

For someone unused to lying and subterfuge, Lilith was suddenly becoming very adept at it. She was even coming to enjoy it a little.

All along, she'd been assuring everyone that she felt nothing for Jack Faraday but disdain. And this morning she'd told the only lie she regretted—she'd told Jack she preferred to have nothing further to do with him. That was the wisest course, certainly, but it was not the one her heart wanted to follow. In fact, a good portion of her had wished he would whisk her back into the hack and take her away.

After that, the rest of the lies became progressively easier. She lied to her maid when Emily appeared to help her dress for breakfast, explaining that the reason she hadn't been found at bedtime was that she'd been sulking in the library. Then, in answer to her aunt's grating prompting, she admitted that she had come to her senses and that she was looking forward to her marriage with the Duke of Wenford. She even pretended that she didn't feel betrayed by and furiously angry at her father, and agreed with him when he said that the Marquis of Dansbury was a damned scoundrel, and that hanging him

255

would be performing a service to mankind. And the entire time that she was being pleasant and cooperative and telling the most outrageous lies, she was thinking of Jack.

Last night *had* been a mistake, undoubtedly the most foolish thing she'd ever done. And the most wonderful. When Aunt Eugenia insisted they go immediately to have her fit for the most wondrous wedding gown in history, Lilith stood through Madame Belieu's fitting session hardly noticing anything, answering only when spoken to. In her mind and in her heart, she was with Jack, feeling his touch, hearing his voice; wishing for things that could never be, and hoping that he would come up with a plan to get her out of this mess.

She might have spent the day dreaming if Penelope Sanford and her mother hadn't joined her and Aunt Eugenia as they strolled through Hyde Park.

"You look happier than you did last night," Pen smiled, tucking her arm through her friend's.

"I feel happier," Lilith admitted, wishing she could tell Penelope why.

"I'm glad. I was worried for you, you know. You seemed so distressed."

"I panicked, I suppose." Realizing just how little she meant to either her father or Dolph had sent her fleeing to the one man who'd seemed genuinely concerned about her. A risky choice, certainly, but she had been unable to stay away. And he hadn't disappointed her.

Pen looked at her for a moment, then glanced over her shoulder to be certain Aunt Eugenia and Lady Sanford couldn't overhear. "Have you heard from Lord Dansbury?"

Lilith jumped. "Why would I have?"

"Lilith, you sneaked out of my library to go see him, and when you came back you couldn't stop smiling.

Why do you have to pretend to me that you don't like him? I would never tell.'' Her friend squeezed her arm. "You do like him, don't you?"

Lilith sighed, leaning her head against Penelope's. "It's worse than that, I'm afraid."

"Worse? How?"

"I love him, Pen."

Penelope grinned. "Oh, Lil, that's won . . ." She stopped abruptly, frowning. "That's terrible. You're engaged to His Grace."

A shudder coursed down Lilith's spine at the reminder. "I know. But even if I wasn't, Papa would never let me marry Jack. Not even if he wanted to marry me."

"Does he? Does he love you?"

"Oh, I don't know. Sometimes I think he does." A blush touched her cheeks at the memory of his passionate touch. "Other times, I have no idea what in the world he might be thinking or feeling. But it really doesn't matter, because nothing can come of it."

Pen looked down, kicking a pebble out of their path with the toe of her shoe. "So you're just going to marry Dolph Remdale."

"Pen, I don't want to marry him, but I don't have any choice! It's been announced, for heaven's sake!"

"You could elope with Lord Dansbury," Penelope insisted stubbornly.

"And live forever disgraced in Scotland or America, I suppose?" Lilith retorted skeptically, trying to ignore the nervous, excited flutter of her heart at her friend's suggestion.

"At least you would be happy."

Lilith started to answer, then closed her mouth again. An unbidden image of her lovely, wild mother came to her, sitting alone in their morning room and gazing out the window. She'd looked so sad, Lilith remembered, though at her entrance her mother had turned away from the window and smiled and said she was only thinking of some silly thing or other. That had been a month before she'd fled with the Earl of Greyton.

For the first time, it occurred to Lilith to wonder what Elizabeth Benton's motivation for leaving them might have been. "Bad blood," her father had always said, and she'd been hurt enough at being abandoned that she'd never really questioned it. But if someone was happy, wild or not, they didn't flee into someone else's arms. Certainly if she'd loved Dolph instead of Jack, she never would have gone to the Marquis of Dansbury, and would certainly never have gone to his bed. It wouldn't have occurred to her to do so.

"Lilith," Pen said quietly, looking at her. "What are you thinking?"

Lilith sighed and gave a small, sad smile. "About what people will do to be happy. Even for a few moments."

Jack glanced at his pocket watch, then at the overcast sky, and then at the figure kneeling in the garden beyond the low stone wall and the sheltering row of bushes. He was nervous, which was both irritating and annoying. The more calmly and coolly he conducted himself in what was to come, the more success he was likely to have. Not that success was likely under any circumstances.

Finally, with one last glance at his watch, the marquis snapped it shut, dropped it into his waistcoat pocket, and approached the low gate in the fence. "Weeding?" he said, leaning against the wooden post.

Richard Hutton glanced up over his shoulder, and then stood and brushed dirt off his loose gardening breeches.

"Planting roses," he replied after a moment, picking up another short branch from the bucket it was soaking in and moving over several feet to dig another hole.

"Lilith Benton's roses?"

"Yes. Do you have a reason for being here?"

Jack kept a rein on his temper. Beginning another fight now wouldn't help. "Actually, I do, but it's not going to make you any more fond of me."

"Then go."

The marquis shook his head, hurt by the anger still in Richard's voice—anger that five years had done little to erase. "Richard, this isn't easy for me either, you know. I've been lurking out here in the bloody cold, waiting until Bea went inside, just so she wouldn't see me."

"I'm touched." Hutton started to say something else, then paused and glanced toward the house. "All right," he said grudgingly, and straightened. He walked over to lean against the wall a short distance away. "What is it?"

After a hesitation, Jack opened the gate and strolled over beside him. "I seem to be in a bit of trouble."

"I know."

"I'd like to discuss it with you, if you can stand to listen."

"Alison wagered me that you might come by," his brother-in-law commented, pulling off his gloves and setting them beside him on the bricks, "though I thought it considerably naive and optimistic of her. I'm listening."

The marquis looked across the garden for a moment, not seeing any way to make his news more palatable. "I was the one who left Wenford to be found in his wine cellar."

"*You what?*" Richard gasped, his fair complexion going even paler.

Jack nodded. "And stripped him naked. And left the bottle of wine in his hand."

"Good God." Richard looked over his shoulder as though to make certain they were not being overheard. "Did you kill him as well, then?"

Jack eyed his companion, then glanced away. "No— but I suppose I deserve that. Let me start from the beginning."

"Yes," Lord Hutton agreed faintly, "please do."

"Dolph Remdale lost to me at hazard, couldn't pay, and offered up a diamond pin to cover his wager. I took the bauble, though I suspected it wasn't his to give. So I made certain Wenford then saw me with it. He agreed to make good on it so he could get it back."

"I recall hearing about a bellowing match between the two of you a few weeks ago," Richard said. "Just for once, you might attempt to handle things in a conventional manner."

Jack shrugged. "At any rate, Dolph came by the next morning, we traded insults and the pin, and he swore he'd ruin me. I was rather hoping he'd call me out, but the coward didn't take the bait."

"That was wise of him," the baron commented, "considering your history of dueling and his future as the Duke of Wenford."

"Yes, I'm getting to that. A few nights later, I was at White's when Wenford came by to make amends. Still feeling rather aggrieved at His Grace, I offered him a bottle of port from my private stock, rather than my hand. Early the next morning I went to the Bentons'. I had . . . left my gloves there. Wenford had gone there just ahead of me to see Lilith, and expired on her floor in the midst of proposing to her."

He hoped Richard would swallow the slightly skewed tale. In the past, Jack would have been highly amused to relate the entire sordid incident. But not where Lilith was concerned.

"And for some perfectly valid reason you are about to explain to me, you didn't go to the law, and you didn't inform me," his companion grunted.

"Lil was there alone. I was completely at sea, and decided to save her from the scandal Wenford's death would cause her." He looked sideways at Lord Hutton. "And you and I aren't speaking, so I would hardly have come here."

"Ah."

"Therefore, I took charge of the remains and disposed of them as I saw fit—and in a manner which everyone in London has by now discussed in detail."

"If I may ask a question?"

Jack nodded.

"If you and I still aren't speaking, then why are you here now?"

Jack was accustomed to keeping things to himself, either solving or ignoring his own problems. Coming out and explaining himself and his circumstance was supremely difficult. He took a breath. This was his first, last, best, and only chance to have Lilith for himself. "I came to ask for your help, Richard."

"Why, did you kill another peer and need another convenient cellar to dump him in?"

With some difficulty he ignored Lord Hutton's sarcasm. "As we were removing Wenford from the Bentons' floor, Lil dropped an earring. Dolph found it with Old Hatchet Face's remains in his cellar."

Richard's brow furrowed. "I haven't heard any such thing."

Jack nodded. "That's because the only one Wenford's shown it to is Lilith, to force her to wed him." The baron would have interrupted, but Jack raised a hand.

"It strikes me as rather odd that a man who's hell-bent on claiming his uncle has been murdered would manufacture a bottle of port, and then hide the one true piece of evidence of possible foul play."

Richard's expression sharpened. "What do you mean, he 'manufactured' the bottle of port? You said you gave it to Wenford."

"I gave Old Hatchet Face *a* bottle of port. Not the one found in his study."

"And you know this is an entirely different bottle because . . ."

"Because when I broke into His Grace's study the night before his body was discovered, the bottle wasn't there. I don't think Wenford even returned home between White's and calling on Lilith. More likely, he trundled off to his nephew's and informed him that he was going to marry Lil and get a son, and would no longer be paying Dolph's gambling debts."

"You broke into . . ." Richard trailed off and shook his head. "I don't even want to know." He bowed his head, turning the trowel absently in his hands. "You think Dolph killed Wenford, don't you?"

"Yes, I do."

Slowly Richard blew out his breath. "You're going to have the devil of a time proving anything. It will be Wenford's word against yours. And you most definitely have the more spotty reputation."

"Thank you," Jack replied caustically. "I'm already aware of that. Do you have any more helpful ideas?"

"Considering what I heard this morning, I'm not certain there's anything that can be done."

Something in Richard's expression warned Jack that he wouldn't like what was coming. "And what did you hear, pray tell?"

"That the port remaining in the bottle in question was tested on a handful of rats. They died."

"So Dolph put arsenic in a damned bottle of port and left it in his uncle's study," Jack exploded, then swore. "It's so bloody obvious, it's pathetic."

"It's obvious to you. To everyone else, you're a blackguard who's already killed a woman. What's one ill-liked duke added into that equation? Especially one who's stolen a piece of land from you?"

Jack clenched his jaw and fixed his gaze on the long row of roses. "Not much."

Richard looked at him and sighed. "Miss Benton might come forward and attest that Wenford died in her presence and at a very early hour. It would put the bottle issue into dispute."

The marquis shook his head. "No."

"Why not?"

"She hates scandal." And he hadn't helped the issue by rendering Wenford naked, though he still had a difficult time regretting the action.

"Jack, I'm not certain you appreciate how serious this is becoming. The bottle clearly contained poison, and you were seen by numerous witnesses handing it, or an identical one, over to the old duke. You could go to trial for this, and then the true circumstances would come out anyway."

The marquis shook his head. "No, they would not. I'll not put her through that."

"You'd rather let Prinny get his hands on Dansbury and see you off to Australia in chains, then? Our dear Majesty has been lusting after your estate for years, you know. It's closer to London than Brighton, and it'd be considerably less expensive to convert into his idiotic 'pleasure palace.'"

"I'm aware of that. And yes, I would rather see Dansbury gone than break my word to Miss Benton.'' Surprising as it was to him, it was the truth. He'd rather die than hurt Lilith.

For the first time, a slight smile touched Richard's face. ''I see. Just how badly do you have it?''

Jack shrugged uncomfortably. Being in love was new and precious enough that he didn't wish to discuss it with anyone. Certainly not with someone who hated him. ''Badly enough, I suppose.''

''I owe Alison another ten quid, then. She said you were addle-brained over Miss Benton.''

''I am not addle-brained,'' Jack stated, annoyed. ''Now, do you mind if we return to determining how I am to clear my name without involving Lil?''

Richard cleared his throat. ''Does she know about . . . your past?''

''She knows I killed a woman, yes.''

''Damnation, Dansbury,'' Richard exploded, ''I keep throwing bait at you, and you simply ignore it. For the last time, will you tell me what happened that night?''

The marquis looked at him for a long moment. He wanted to, and for the first time, he thought Richard might actually listen. ''After we come up with a plan,'' he hedged.

Richard threw up his hands. ''That's simple. Get Dolph to confess he killed his uncle to gain the inheritance. Short of that, I don't think you have a prayer.''

Jack straightened. ''That's what I thought. My thanks. Good day.'' He started to offer his hand, but wasn't certain the baron would take it. Instead, he headed for the garden gate.

''Jack?''

The marquis turned to face his brother-in-law. ''Why did you decide to speak to me today, Richard?''

He shrugged. ''The other night, at Bea's party, I saw

you with Miss Benton. Your good side was showing. I simply hadn't seen it in five years, and I'd forgotten you had one."

Jack nodded again and continued to walk away, then on impulse stopped. Lilith was so concerned with the importance of family, and it seemed foolish that he was barely allowed to speak to his. Little as he cared to admit it, he missed their easy companionship from time to time. And there were occasions when he actually disliked being alone.

"That day . . . in France—when I broke down the hotel room door to capture Genevieve, she went mad. She screamed and grabbed a knife, and came after me. I kept trying to shove her away, to get the knife away from her, but she wouldn't stop screaming. She was making so damned much noise, shrieking bloody murder, and I was afraid those two blasted soldiers with her would come crashing in any moment . . ."

"So you stabbed her."

Dammit, Richard. "They came close enough to hanging me the first time she betrayed us. I didn't know where you were, and I couldn't risk letting her get away—"

"Why didn't you tell me it wasn't just revenge?"

"You didn't give me a chance."

Richard hesitated. "I suppose not. Blood all over the room, all over you, the look on your face, soldiers pounding up the back stairs . . ."

"You had enough time to call me a damned murderer, as I recall." Jack looked at his brother-in-law and shrugged. "You were my friend, Richard. After everything we'd been through . . . I was too hurt that you'd believe I could have done . . . that, for revenge. And then later, I suppose I was too proud."

"Jack—"

He yanked the gate open. "But you were right. I *am*

a murderer. I didn't have to kill her, I should have found some other way.''

Richard didn't say anything, just watched him as he swung up on Benedick and rode back toward the middle of Mayfair.

Jack's next task looked to be at least as difficult, but just as necessary. It took some searching, but finally he found his quarry in one of Bond Street's more exclusive rare gem establishments. ''William,'' he said, grinning, and slapped his young companion on the back.

For once, William looked less than pleased to see him. ''Jack, what brings you here?'' he asked stiffly, quickly placing a diamond-studded necklace back onto the velvet bag which had held it. ''I'm not supposed to be seen with you any longer. This morning Father spent twenty minutes preaching the gospel of avoiding the Marquis of Dansbury to Lilith and me. And poor Lili's got enough to worry about, marrying that bore Wenford.''

Jack glanced at the necklace. A thousand quid worth of stones, at least. ''You bring me here, *mon ami*. I've been neglecting you, I fear. I intend to make it up to you. An evening at the Society, I thought.''

''I'm occupied tonight, Jack,'' William returned, still obviously distracted.

Jack slipped an arm around the boy's shoulders and edged him toward the door, away from any prying ears. ''William, might I ask you a question?''

''I'm rather busy right now. Perhaps we could—''

''Have you ever engaged in sexual intercourse with anyone besides Antonia?'' he interrupted casually, tightening his grip when William tried to break away

''Well, of course,'' William answered indignantly, flushing. ''I've not had as many conquests as you, I'm certain, but—well, what bloody business is it of yours, anyway?''

"Intimacy tends to sway one's heart when one is un-used to it," Jack said easily. "I've known some young fools, much less intelligent than you, who have misinterpreted lust for love, and offered for the first chit they bedded. Just wanted to be certain you know what you're up to."

William pulled free, his expression angry as he shrugged his coat back into place. "I know what *you're* up to, Dansbury. I'm not an idiot, even if I don't have memberships at half the clubs in town. At least I can still get into them."

Jack kept his expression neutral. "I'll overlook that, William, because your sister seems to find your repertoire amusing. But if you want to remain friends with me, I suggest you not continue in that vein."

William swallowed, then took a breath. "I love Antonia, Jack, and I'm going to ask her to marry me. Whether you like it or not."

Jack nodded. "I'm not saying you shouldn't. I'm only saying you should make certain you've seen the true Antonia, not just the pretty face she's painted for you. Answer me this. Have you ever disagreed with her? About anything?"

"No," William boasted, his face still flushed. "We agree on everything. That's why we're so perfect for one another."

"Have you ever known any two people who know each other well and who don't argue?" His and Lilith's various encounters immediately came to mind, and he stifled a smile.

"Well, of course—"

"I'll wager you one thousand quid, William, that you can't *make* her disagree with you. That she'll voice no opinion that is not yours."

"And what would that prove?"

Jack shrugged. "Nothing in particular. It might make you a fair wedding gift if you win."

"I could lie about it and say we did argue."

The marquis gave a slight grin. "You won't. You come from the same blood as your sister. You won't lie."

William grimaced, glancing over at the bauble on the counter again. When he looked back at Jack, he was wearing his sly, self-confident expression. "When—*when*—I win this wager, you'll purchase that necklace for me to give to Antonia. Agreed?"

Jack nodded. "Agreed. But if I win, you have to consider what I've said here. After that, you do as you see fit."

They shook hands, and then the marquis strolled back out into the street, so pleased with the way things were going that he barely noticed the Countess of Devale cutting him. If Antonia St. Gerard reacted as he predicted, that was two down. Merely half a hundred to go.

Jack turned Benedick toward home. Lilith would be at the Mistners' this evening, and luckily they'd sent him an invitation before the latest rumors had caused the stream of cards that flowed to his door to dry into a miserable trickle. Before he proceeded with anything against Dolph, he wanted her permission. If she had truly decided to marry the buffoon, he would . . . well, he supposed he would flee to Spain or to America and then get himself killed in a duel, unless he could convince himself to kidnap her and make off with her to Gretna Green. Jack smiled a little. By God, he was getting soft-headed.

With her forbidden to see him, he'd have to be careful tonight—the stakes of the game had been raised considerably. This wasn't for amusement anymore. This was for forever.

*   *   *

Though Aunt Eugenia had been certain His Grace would attend the Mistners' with them, apparently Lilith's prayers had been heard. The Duke of Wenford sent his regrets, but he had a meeting with his solicitors he couldn't escape. It seemed almost too convenient, and Lilith spent the coach ride to the ball worrying that Dolph was out causing more trouble for Jack. After last night, Jack's troubles concerned her at least as much as her own.

She nearly tripped over Lionel Hendrick's foot when, halfway through her waltz with the earl, she spied Dansbury. He stood just inside the doorway, talking with Ogden Price. Those nearest him had pointedly moved away, but he didn't appear to have noticed. Lilith knew, though, that he had. At that moment, he glanced in her direction, offered her a slight smile, and returned to his conversation.

He should not have come. She had heard with dismay the news that the bottle in Wenford's study contained poison, so he must know about it as well, and would know that no one would wish to speak to him, no woman would want to stand up with him for a dance. No woman except her, of course—and she didn't dare. And yet he had come.

"Lilith?" Lionel looked down at her, and she blinked. His smile was a bit strained, as it had been since her engagement, but at least he had been a gentleman about the whole thing. "I do hope when the invitations for your wedding go out, that you will not choose to exclude me. I think that we have remained friends."

Of course he wouldn't wish to be excluded from the event of the Season. "I would not think of excluding you," she answered, returning his smile.

His expression brightened. "I am pleased to hear that."

Pen was waiting for her as the waltz ended and impulsively grabbed Lilith's hand as she approached. "I think he does care for you," she whispered, "because otherwise he would never be here tonight."

"Or he's just very stubborn," Lilith supplied, trying to keep reality and her dreams from becoming even more tangled with one another.

"It's so romantic," Penelope continued. "Like Romeo daring to visit the house of Capulet to see Juliet."

"Romeo went to the Capulet party to cause mischief," Lilith corrected with a slight smile, her gaze automatically going to Jack. He was looking at her again, and with his chin gestured off toward the back of the house. At least she thought he might have—it was such a slight motion that she couldn't be certain. "He'd never seen Juliet before that night."

"Spoilsport," Pen retorted. She glanced at the marquis. "I think he's trying to catch your attention," she continued in a low voice.

"You think so, too?" Lilith asked. "But I don't know what he wants. I can't very well dance with him."

Pen squeezed her hands, then released them. "I will find out for you."

"Pen!" Lilith exclaimed.

But her friend had already smiled directly at Dansbury, and then strolled over to the table to accept a glass of punch from a footman.

Jack looked from Penelope to Lilith, who gave a slight nod. Jack excused himself from Price and moved through the crowd toward the refreshment table. Belatedly realizing that she was staring, Lilith turned her back to earnestly contemplate a potted plant. It seemed an eternity before Pen came up beside her again. Her friend's color was high, and her pretty hazel eyes held an excited light.

"Lord Dansbury," she said under her breath, joining Lilith's study of the plant, "thinks you might enjoy the Thomas Lawrence portrait of Lord Mistner which hangs over the mantel in the drawing room." Pen stifled a giggle. "And that you might like it best of all at half past midnight."

Lilith looked over at the nearest clock. It was nearly that now. A shivering thrill went through her at the thought of speaking with him. She should not, she knew. She should forget him, ignore him, and make the best of what would hopefully be a marriage where the couple had as little to do with one another as possible. Arranged marriages happened all the time among her peers. Her own parents' marriage had been arranged. Lilith grimaced, then glanced at Pen. "Thank you," she whispered.

At precisely twenty-eight minutes after midnight, she approached a harried-looking Lady Mistner. "My lady," she smiled, hoping no one could sense the rush of excitement running through her, "I heard that your husband was painted by Thomas Lawrence. I am a particular admirer of Mr. Lawrence, and I wondered if I might see the portrait?"

Lady Mistner glanced about her teeming ballroom and motioned to a servant to bring in a fresh platter of confections. "My dear . . . Miss Benton, I should be delighted to have you over to show you our newest treasure," she smiled, commanding another footman to bring in more wine.

Lilith stifled a scowl. This was supposed to be simple. "Oh, I don't mean to inconvenience you," she protested. "I can go look at it on my own, of course."

Her hostess sighed, obviously feeling put out. "I wouldn't hear of it. This way, my dear."

"Thank you, my lady, but really . . ."

Lady Mistner hurried off down the hallway, and with a muffled curse, Lilith quickly followed behind her.

"I assure you, my lady," she continued in a loud voice as they reached the door, "I don't wish to take you from the rest of your guests."

The lady looked at her like she was some sort of oddity, then crinkled her eyes in another forced smile. "Nonsense, dear." She pushed open the door. "If I do say so myself, this is among Mr. Lawrence's finest works."

Lilith looked frantically about the room, ready to exclaim her surprise at finding the Marquis of Dansbury there before them. He was nowhere to be seen. She frowned; then, as she noticed Lady Mistner turning in her direction, she quickly looked at the portrait hung above the fireplace. "Oh, my," she gushed, clutching her hands together in admiration—and to disguise their trembling. "It's magnificent." She leaned over to look behind the couch, but Jack wasn't there, either. "Quite stunning. The way he's used the light . . . I do believe you're right. This may be his finest piece."

Lady Mistner's smile warmed at the flattery. "I told Malcolm it was well worth the time spent sitting for it."

"Oh, yes," Lilith agreed. "He has captured the true essence of Lord Mistner, I do believe."

"Lady Mistner?" Penelope leaned into the doorway, her swift glance at Lilith. "My apologies, but did you wish the musicians to have a break now?"

The lady blanched. "No! Not before the second waltz!" She turned to Lilith, who put out a hand.

"Please, do go. I'll be along in a moment."

"Oh, thank you, dear." With a bustle of skirts, Lady

Mistner hurried out the door. Pen winked at Lilith and pulled the door shut as she followed their hostess.

"My goodness," Lilith breathed, fanning at her face and dropping onto the couch.

" 'The true essence'?" a deep voice said from the direction of the window, and Lilith bolted to her feet. Jack stepped in through the half-open window and pushed it shut as he hopped down to the floor. "The true essence of Mistner has a great deal more belly and jowl, I believe."

"You were outside?" she asked, incredulous.

"On the second blasted floor, I might point out." He grinned, strolling toward her. "Thank God it wasn't raining." The sensual hold of his dark eyes was as palpable as the memory of his arms around her in the night. "What the devil was she doing with you?"

"I asked her permission to see the portrait. I didn't expect her to accompany me." Indignation colored her cheeks, and at the sight, Jack's grin broadened.

"I didn't mean you should *ask* to come in here," he murmured. "Proper chit. If you hadn't bellowed outside the door, things might have become awkward."

"I don't bellow." Good Lord, she was pleased to see him, and to talk to him again. It felt like forever, instead of a mere day, since they'd been together.

"You did a fine imitation, then." He closed the distance between them, and she shivered as he ran his palm slowly along her cheek. She wanted him, she craved him, but when he leaned his face down toward hers, she turned away.

"Don't," she whispered.

For a moment he was still, his hand encircling her waist. Then he released her and stepped back. "You came in here," he said, his tone almost accusing.

"I . . . feel responsible for the trouble you're in," she responded, not daring to look at him.

"I'm responsible for my own damned troubles," he growled. "Always have been. And I . . . worry . . . that my stupidity is what's gotten Wenford engaged to you."

"It's not your doing. My father would have sold me to have a dukedom," she said bitterly. "Remember?" Slowly she turned to face him, to find that he was looking at her with mingled frustration and concern in his intelligent eyes.

"We are a shambles, you and I," he whispered. She wondered if he could see in her eyes how much she loved him. "Lil, answer me a question."

"I'll try. But please hurry. If we're seen—"

"I won't let that happen." He smiled softly. "I promised I wouldn't hurt you ever again." She blushed again at the memory the words conjured, and he gently touched her cheek again. "If, hypothetically speaking, you could avoid marrying Dolph, would you?"

He would leave, she sensed, if she told him that she intended to marry Dolph. But this was the true Jack Faraday standing before her, the one who had held her last night, the one who allowed uncertainty and vulnerability to show on his lean, handsome countenance. "There is no way to avoid it," she began.

"Lil—"

"But, if there was a way, then no, I would not marry him."

He relaxed a little. "If he could be proven to be a murderer, and thus an unsuitable match for Miss Benton, would you wish for that to happen?"

"Jack, if you can clear your name, for heaven's sake, do it. I won't have you hung if you have proof that Dolph actually killed—"

The marquis shook his head. "Don't interrupt me, Lil;

I'm attempting to be gallant and proper. I have several suspicions and hunches, but no proof. I can likely weather this, even if I have to spend a year or two in Scotland or Italy before it blows over. For once, worry over yourself. What do *you* want, Lil?''

'' 'For once,' '' she repeated, her laugh brittle. ''I'm all I ever think about. Will *I* be happy with what my family needs? Do *I*—''

''Lilith,'' he said, his tone and expression so suddenly angry that it startled her, ''I daresay the only selfish thing you've done in the past six years was to share my bed last night. It's not a crime to want to be happy, for God's sake!'' He glared at her. ''Now answer my damned question. Do you want me to proceed against bloody Dolph Remdale?''

She shut her eyes, trying to shut him out. It would be easier to stop her heart from beating. ''Yes,'' she said quietly. ''I want you to proceed.''

Slowly she opened her eyes again. His gaze held another emotion entirely now. ''One more question,'' he murmured, sliding his hand about her waist and pulling her close against him. ''If I were, say, Galahad, would you consider me as a suitor?''

She couldn't believe he would even ask the question. But looking into his eyes, neither could she convince herself that this seasoned, cynical rakehell was only teasing.

''If I were not engaged to the Duke of Wenford, and you were Galahad, yes, I would allow you to court me,'' she answered, trying to be flippant and knowing her heartache must sound in her voice. If only it were so. For a few moments early this morning, she had been able to imagine a happiness that would last through the rest of her life. A happiness that had nothing to do with who or what she should be, and everything to do with whom and what she wanted. "But you're not."

"Pretend."

This time when he leaned down toward her, she rose up on her toes to meet his mouth with her own. For an insane moment she wished she had the courage to lock the drawing room door and let him continue. Though it was her mouth he touched, every part of her seemed alive and aware of him. She slipped her arms around his neck, pulling him closer.

"Jack," she murmured, "I love you."

He froze, a hundred emotions touching his eyes. "Beg pardon?" he whispered.

There was no taking it back now, and she didn't think he was entirely displeased to hear it. "I—"

"Mrs. Farlane," Penelope's voice said, gratingly loud and right outside the door, "I'm certain I saw Lil out with Mary, on the balcony."

The blood drained from Lilith's face. If Aunt Eugenia caught them together, everything would be ruined. Especially her.

"Good God," Jack muttered, and pulled away. He strode for the window and yanked it open. At the last moment he looked over his shoulder at her and grinned, his eyes dancing. "I'll be hanging about, if you need me. And Lil, don't get too attached to your betrothed. He's about to be finished with you, one way or another."

The door opened as he vanished, and Lilith whirled toward the painting. Just as quickly she made a show of starting and turning to see who had entered the room. "Aunt Eugenia." She smiled, indicating the portrait. "Have you seen this? It's magnificent, don't you think?"

Her aunt scowled. "What I think is that the future Duchess of Wenford should not be skulking about in drawing rooms, when Lady Fenbroke is organizing a card party for a few select guests.''

''Oh, splendid,'' Lilith forced out, and gestured her aunt to precede her from the room. As she left, she glanced back at the half-open window and the darkness beyond. Confident as he'd seemed to be, Jack could likely use some assistance. And who better to render it than Wenford's own betrothed? She gave a small, private smile. *Who, indeed?*

Chapter 16

William shifted on the deep, soft couch and nervously fiddled with his cravat, which Weems seemed to have tied rather too tightly this evening. Beginning an intentional row with Antonia was idiocy. Damn Jack Faraday anyway, for suggesting such nonsense. The blackguard knew full well that no one would be able to resist such a challenge. Lord knew he couldn't stop thinking about it, even though he'd already resolved that Dansbury was completely at sea and that Antonia was hiding nothing. Glass clinked over his shoulder, loud in the unusual silence of Antonia's drawing room. He jumped at the sound, and with a last tug, stopped pulling at his neckcloth.

Antonia St. Gerard glided into view, a brandy snifter in each hand. She curled up beside him and handed over one of the glasses, sipping at her own and watching him over the rim. William had been hoping she would have something for them to chat about, something to keep his mind off Dansbury's damned wager, but she'd been quiet all evening.

He cast about for a topic they might discuss, but the only conversation that came to mind involved him telling her how beautiful she was. That was how their chats usually began, and they always seemed to end in her bed chamber. Not that he had any objections to that. Damn Jack and his meddling, playing his deuced games. William sighed irritably. Perhaps simply to satisfy his own curiosity, he might have a go at starting a small argument, and then he could apologize and they could go upstairs. Jack would have to buy that necklace, and William would laugh at him.

"William," Antonia purred, running her hand slowly up his thigh and reminding him forcibly that there were better things he could be doing than trying to think up a topic for argument. "I might have held a card party tonight, *mon amour*. I had not thought we would spend the evening in my drawing room. Do tell me why you wanted me to yourself."

He took a breath and slowly let it out. "I don't want you to hold any more card parties, Antonia," he rushed. That should take care of it.

For a long moment she looked at him. "Do you have something else in mind?" she asked softly.

"I . . . I don't like it, all those men looking at you, and—well, you know," he stumbled.

She shifted to lean against his arm. "Thinking they own me?" she suggested, curling the tip of her finger around his ear.

"Yes. So no more card parties." Jack had told him that Antonia had been holding them since she'd come to London, and that he'd never known anyone with a love of gambling and games of chance so deeply imbedded in their bones. Of course she would protest.

Antonia sighed. "As you wish, my love. But I must have some way of paying my bills."

"Ah . . . don't worry about that," he returned, disappointed. He searched for something about which she would be more likely to contend, though if he had any sense he would simply give up and lie to Jack tomorrow. "And I don't think it's seemly for you to own a high-perch phaeton," he decided. "Deuced improper, you know, for a lone female to go gadding about London in a phaeton."

She pursed her lips, her gray eyes watching him, and took another sip of brandy. "Oh, William, I have been meaning to give it up. All of this terrible cold weather—who wants to go about anywhere in an open carriage, *n'est-ce pas*?"

William cleared his throat. "Quite right." This was becoming damned difficult. He gestured at her snifter. She loved a brandy in the evening. "And women drink Madeira or ratafia. Not brandy."

She looked down at the glass, then set it aside. "I am a teetotaler," she breathed, and removed her finger from his ear, only to replace it with her tongue.

He swallowed. "And I won't have you speaking that damned French anymore, either," he said desperately, shifting away from her.

Antonia leaned along his shoulder and lifted a perfectly sculpted eyebrow. "I am an Englishwoman," she murmured. "*Now* are you pleased?"

"I'd be more pleased if you'd quit playing lip service to everything I say to you," he grumbled, exasperated. "I'm serious, you know."

"I am whatever you wish me to be," Antonia continued, slipping her hand down his chest, and then lower.

Frantically William struggled to his feet. "Dammit, Antonia," he growled, backpedaling as she uncurled from the couch and followed him, a cat's canary-eating smile on her face. "Stop treating me like a fool."

"William," she chastised, stopping, "please do not be cross. I have agreed to everything you said."

"But why?" he demanded.

"Why did you ask them of me, my love?"

He scowled. "Oh, damned old Jack said I wouldn't be able to pull you into an argument. Said you'd painted a pretty face for me, or some such nonsense, and I said he was mad. Only you've agreed to every deuced thing I've said all night." He flung his arm out. "For God's sake, Antonia, I asked you not to speak French, and you didn't even blink."

Her expression became dark, almost feral, for a brief moment, but the look was gone so quickly that it might have been a trick of the lamplight. She smiled like dawn's first light. "Oh, William, I thought you were only worried that we wouldn't suit, and I was trying to reassure you." She glided closer, wrapping her hands into his lapels and pulling him toward the door. "I knew you would never seriously forbid me to speak French, *mon amour.*"

William smiled. "Thank goodness," he breathed, relieved. Jack had it all wrong. For someone who claimed to know women, sometimes Dansbury hadn't a clue.

"Now, come with me where we can apologize to one another," she murmured, turning to lead him out the door and up the stairs.

Once her back was turned, Antonia's expression slid into the venomous scowl she'd nearly let her naive lover see. Jack Faraday had turned on her, it seemed, and was undoubtedly trying to impress his little Ice Queen by warning her brother away from evil Antonia. Well, the Marquis of Dansbury didn't need William Benton's five thousand a year—she did. And he wouldn't stop her. She knew things—things that could get a certain arrogant marquis into a great deal of difficulty. Antonia smiled. Five thousand a year.

*   *   *

Peese frowned and watched his employer pace impatiently across the breakfast room floor. "Perhaps if you could be more specific, my lord," he suggested.

Jack paused to glare at him, then continued on his way. He'd lain awake nearly all night, trying to think of a way to save his neck and stretch Dolph's, and wishing Lilith would come calling on him again. Even though she had said she loved him—those words still rolled about thunderously in his heart, smashing apart little dark parts of him with every beat—he had far from won her.

"I don't know how damned more specific I can be, Peese. What do you know of Dolph Remdale's household?"

The breakfast room door rattled and opened, and Jack turned angrily to order the intruding servant out. When Martin stuck his head in the door, the marquis snapped his mouth shut and gestured the valet inside.

"About bloody time you joined the party," Jack growled.

Peese glanced at Martin and shrugged. "My lord," the butler began patiently, obviously trying to appease his tempestuous employer, "households is like the masters of them. You don't have anything to do with His new Grace, and we don't have anything to do with his servants. So if you could tell me exactly what you're wanting to know, per—"

"If I knew what I wanted to know, I would know it already!" Jack exploded, weariness and frustration eating at him. "I can't believe that with all the gossip the two of you collect, you haven't heard anything!"

"Neither has anyone heard anything about this household," Martin pointed out more quietly. Jack turned to pin a glare at him, and the valet sketched a short bow. "My lord."

Peese took a step forward. "Nor will they," he concurred proudly.

"I was about to say," Martin went on, "I heard a rumor several months ago that one of Mr. Remdale's—before he became a duke, of course—one of Mr. Remdale's housemaids broke her arm falling down the stairs."

Jack frowned. "It's unfortunate, of course, but not all that unu—"

"He had the girl sent off to one of his uncle's estates. Or rather, old Wenford had her sent away."

There was obviously something missing, and Jack had a fair suspicion what it might be. "And the infant's name was?"

Martin gave a short grin. "Don't know that part."

"You know," Peese broke in, "now that you mention it, my cousin's husband's sister was hired on there about three years ago, and she gave her notice after a fortnight."

Finally. "Why?"

The butler shrugged. "She said Mr. Remdale frightened her. Said some of the other girls there had bruises."

Fury and alarm coursed through Jack. "You mean, he beats and abuses his female staff?" And that bastard meant to get his hands on *his* Lilith.

Martin nodded. "T'would seem that way, my lord."

"You might have remembered that when I first asked you," he grumbled.

The butler assumed a hurt expression. "I said you should be more specific, my lord."

"If you'd pay attention to happenings in your own household, you'd have known what he was asking," Martin interjected haughtily.

Jack pinned the valet with a glare. "And what is that supposed to mean?"

Martin had the temerity to grin. "I'd not answer that on pain of death, my lord," he said.

The marquis decided it would be best to let the subject go. From their behavior the night Lilith had come calling and the morning after, both Martin and Peese knew there was something unusual about her, and the lot of them hadn't stayed alive in Europe during Bonaparte's damned war because they were fools. "I trust none of us will have to suffer through that."

Immediately both servants became serious. "That lout wants you hanged, my lord, no doubt about it," Peese growled.

"No, none at all." Jack gave a quick grin. "Let's see that it doesn't happen, though, shall we?"

The butler gave a grim smile himself. "We might beat him to the point, my lord."

The marquis shook his head. "I've thought about that. However clever we were, they'd still blame it on me." He sighed. "No, we'll have work within the law this time."

"That's a bloody shame," Peese grumbled.

"Yes, well, if everything goes as I . . . as I hope, we may have to get used to more propriety about the household, anyway." Jack looked at the two men, daring them to ask anything, and then headed for the door. "Peese, you're with me. Martin, you seem to have better information regarding the Remdale household. Find out as much as you can."

Martin came to attention and sketched a salute. "Aye, Major."

When Jack and his butler arrived at White's, he was somewhat surprised that the law hadn't been there already. His private stock of port remained locked in the cellar, and, according to the head footman, had not been touched. Apparently rumors weren't quite enough to stir

Bow Street against a member of the peerage. Not yet, anyway. He posted Peese to keep everything tidy and rode to get Richard.

"You realize what a chance you're taking," his brother-in-law pointed out as they removed the offending crate from the club's cellar and set it down on the largest kitchen table. As it was early evening, the main salon was beginning to fill with the usual midweek crowd. All the footmen, though, stood crowded about the large kitchen.

"I haven't much choice," Jack answered dryly, and motioned at Peese. "Bring it into the salon."

"Jack," Richard warned, stepping back as the legion of footmen crowded behind Peese.

"Come along," Jack said with a jaunty bow, as a wave of ill-tempered protests began inside the posh, crowded room. "You might enjoy this."

Peese set the crate down in the middle of the table occupied by Lord Dupont and his party, crushing their game of faro beneath its weight.

"What is the meaning of this, Dansbury?" Dupont growled, leaving his chair as Jack reached over his shoulder for a bottle.

"Good evening, gentlemen." Jack nodded to the assembly at large, then turned his attention to the port in his hand. The wax stopper remained in place, and it looked untouched. Though with cork it was difficult to tell, it didn't look as though it had been pierced with anything. He turned to find the head footman. "Freeling, you're certain no one's been near my store since I last asked for a bottle?"

The tall, thin footman inclined his head. "I'm certain, my lord. No one has touched it."

Jack studied the man's countenance for a moment, while the crowd muttered around them. Coin could make a lie, but it couldn't necessarily make a good one. And Freeling had always seemed an upright individual.

"Well, then," he sighed, and gestured at Peese, who came forward and uncorked the bottle.

"I don't suppose you thought to bring any rats," Richard murmured. He had looked over the storeroom as carefully as Jack had, and if the marquis hadn't known any better, he would have called his brother-in-law's expression concerned.

"Hate to waste good port on rats." Jack grinned, lifted the bottle, put it to his lips, and took a long swallow.

"Jack!" Richard bellowed, belatedly trying to snatch the bottle away. "Are you mad?"

"If any poor rats perished, I'd hang for it as well." Jack studied Freeling's countenance again. The footman looked as startled as the rest of the spectators, and nothing else came to his expression to indicate that he knew more than he claimed. He looked at Richard again. "How long does it take one to perish from arsenic poisoning?" he asked out of the side of his mouth.

"Under the circumstances, I believe you'd know you'd been poisoned by now," Richard said shakily. His face was gray. "My God, Jack."

Jack shrugged, trying to make light of what he'd done. If he'd acted the least bit concerned, they would all have interpreted it as guilt. Lilith would likely murder him herself, if she ever found out what he'd done, but he'd rather have died of poison than have Dolph Remdale laugh while he swung from the end of a rope. Slowly he took another swallow, and then set the bottle aside. "Now, Freeling."

"Yes, my lord?"

"Did I request a particular bottle that evening?"

"Not that I recall, my lord."

"And for what purpose did I request the bottle?"

Freeling cleared his throat. "You said you didn't want to drink any more house swill, and you'd have one of your own, my lord."

Jack turned back to Richard and lifted an eyebrow. "Shall I have a drink from each of them?"

"Fifty quid for each bottle he lives through!" Lord Hunt called, the wager swiftly taken up by others.

The bet seemed a sound one, and Jack wouldn't have minded putting a few pounds on himself. "Why not?"

Richard hurriedly shook his head and motioned for Peese to collect the crate. "No. Let me take the rest to an alchemist. I'll round up some more witnesses, and we'll test the remainder in a more scientific, if slightly less spectacular, manner."

Jack put his hand over the case before Peese lifted it. "And you won't let it out of your sight?" he said softly, catching Richard's gaze, making certain he knew just how much trust Jack was placing in his brother-in-law.

Richard looked straight back at him. "I'll not let it out of my sight," he confirmed.

The marquis stepped away from the table. "All right, then. Goodnight, gentleman."

Another point to his favor, and before he continued the battle, Jack admitted to himself that he wanted to see Lilith again. It was almost puppyish, his craving to be in her presence the way a bee craved flowers. The Lord knew he'd been foolish before, but for the first time he felt as though it might be for the right reason. And if nothing else, he needed to warn her about Dolph Remdale's way of dealing with women. If the bastard laid a finger on Lil, he would be lucky to live long enough to regret it.

*   *   *

Having become something of an aficionado of irony since beginning her acquaintance with Dansbury, Lilith looked up into the cloudless skies above Hyde Park and smiled. It seemed that the darker and more confused her own life became, the better weather London was having. She leaned forward to pet the withers of her mare, Polly, and sighed, trying for a moment to forget how much trouble both she and Jack were in.

"What did you say to your aunt this morning?" Penelope asked from beside her as they toured the Lady's Mile. Milgrew waited in the shade a respectful distance away. "She was absolutely beaming."

Lilith shrugged. "I said I would gladly accept His Grace's invitation to a picnic tomorrow." She wondered if that wasn't the main reason for her raised spirits this morning. Finally she was doing something, instead of merely agreeing to what everyone else expected of her. True, everyone might think she was still being dutiful and proper, because no one else knew precisely why she wanted to spend more time with Dolph Remdale. And hopefully he wouldn't realize it, either—at least, not until she had discovered for certain if, how, and why he had killed his uncle.

"You said *what?*" Pen asked, lifting both delicate eyebrows. "Last night the thought of ever seeing him again made you ill. And what about Lord Dans—"

"Hush, Pen," Lilith admonished. "I know what I'm doing." At least, she hoped she did.

Pen was shaking her head. "I don't know what's gotten into you, but . . ." She trailed off, looking over Lil's shoulder. Penelope blushed, a smile lighting her face and her eyes. "Good afternoon, Mr. Benton," she said.

"Miss Sanford," William returned.

Lilith turned around to see her brother rein in beside them. He was mounted on that monstrously expensive black stallion Jack had convinced him he must own. Now that Lilith looked at Thor with a kinder eye, though, she had to admit that he was a magnificent beast.

"I thought you'd be occupied with your cronies," Lilith said, looking at her brother curiously. He seemed distracted about something, though she had no idea what it might be. She was well aware, though, that the only thing that seemed to distract him lately was Antonia St. Gerard.

"My cronies have scattered to the four winds. The only one I can ever find is Jack, and Father'll thrash me if I speak to him again."

That was nothing compared to what their father would do to her if he ever found out about her and Jack. "What about Miss St. Gerard? Last week it was picnics and horse races every day."

"Antonia's nocturnal, mostly," he answered, his distracted look deepening.

"Is something wrong?" Pen asked him before Lilith could.

William looked at Penelope. "Hm? Oh, nothing. Just got my mind a bit occupied, is all."

"Is there anything we can do to help?"

"Gadzooks, no," William answered, flushing. Abruptly he pounded his fist against the pommel of his saddle. "Sometimes females are just too agreeable," he blurted out.

Lilith and Pen looked at one another, and Penelope giggled. "Any female—any person—who is *too* agreeable is after something," Pen said.

William tilted his head to look more closely at her, his expression changing a little. "You're never cross, Miss Sanford," he pointed out.

"I am frequently cross," Pen countered easily. "I am merely cross at the correct times."

"But how is anyone supposed to know—"

A commotion began across the clearing, and Lilith turned again. A bay gelding came charging toward them, riderless. Polly shifted nervously, and Lilith sternly reined her in. "What in the—"

"That's Jack's bay. Benedick," William said, turning Thor and kicking him in the ribs.

The stallion snorted and sprinted off toward the gelding. The horse stopped as soon as her brother leaned over to catch the dangling reins, and in fact looked almost relieved to do so. Lilith looked about in alarm, her breath catching, to see where Benedick's rider might be. Finally she spied him, strolling toward them through the park, unmindful of the other pedestrians moving out of his path to avoid him.

"My thanks, William," he said in a carrying voice when still some distance away. "I was chatting with Lady Henry, and the old boy got away from me."

"You are unhurt, then?" Lilith asked, trying to keep her voice cool.

He glanced in her direction. "Quite, Miss Benton." Lord Dansbury accepted the reins from William and swung up into the saddle. As he brought Benedick around, he passed close by Lilith. "Leave your window open tonight, m'dear," he murmured, and with a grin and a jaunty wave of his hat at Penelope, he was gone back across the park.

"Benedick got away from him, my left bootstrap," William muttered, looking with some awe at his former idol. "That horse is closer to human than some of the fellows I've played against." He shook his head. "Wonder what the devil he's up to this time."

"Perhaps he misses you," Penelope suggested, though when Lilith looked up, her friend's gaze was not on her brother. "Seems everyone's abandoned him."

"Not necessarily by choice," her brother grumbled, then sighed and straightened. "May I buy you ladies an ice?"

"I'd love one." Pen smiled, and William settled Thor in beside her mare while Lilith followed behind.

Her heart was racing and her mind tumbling about incoherently. If she had any sense left at all, she would lock and bar her windows and doors tonight. She smiled a little, knowing she would do no such thing. Jack was coming by.

"That brings back some memories," Martin commented soberly, stepping back to survey his employer.

Jack lifted his arms and turned, eyeing himself in the dressing mirror. The dark breeches and coarse black shirt and coat brought back memories for him as well, most of them unpleasant. Telling Lilith that he and Richard had "mucked about" the French and Belgian countryside did little justice to the work they had accomplished in the name of God and country. And while it had been necessary, much of it had been bloody awful. Some of it even worse than that.

"Yes, it does," he said, picking up his heavy, dark gloves and glancing toward the window. With the night, fog was beginning to roll in. That would make creeping about in the dark easier, for he had no wish to be seen climbing into Lil's window. "Any word from Peese?"

Martin shook his head as he straightened up the dressing table. "I think you wounded his pride, my lord, when you said he should have known more about His Grace's household. As soon as he returned from his assignation with Lord Hutton, he went off and said he'd be back tonight."

"He picked a splendid time to go wandering off," Jack grumbled. "The last thing I need is for my butler to be discovered peeping through Remdale windows, or under the skirts of Remdale housemaids.'' He made his way to his study, where he took one of his pistols from its case and loaded it. So far Dolph had been satisfied with rumors and cheap theatrics, but Jack had no intention of going about alone in the dark without some protection. The old duke had been mad, and he'd seen no reason to believe any differently of Dolph.

''And what might you be about, my lord?''

Jack spun, pistol gripped in his hand, as Peese leaned into the doorway. ''Information. And where in damnation have you been?'' He stalked past the butler into the foyer, set down the gun, and waited for Peese to help him into an old, patched greatcoat.

''Getting some information of my own,'' the butler replied, returning the pistol to Jack, who dumped it into his deep pocket. ''The butler's gone.''

Jack paused, then looked over his shoulder. ''What? Whose butler?''

''Wenford's. About four days ago. No one belowstairs knows where or why. And no one's daft enough to ask His Grace where Frawley might be.''

''What sort of gentleman was Frawley?'' Jack asked slowly.

The butler pursed his lips thoughtfully. ''Cook said Mr. Remdale hired Frawley because he was an old stuff, tighter than the former Wenford's purse.''

''The kind of fellow who might not enjoy being employed by someone doing something underhanded, you might say?'' Jack pursued.

Peese grinned. ''Unlike ourselves, of course.''

It made sense. Dolph would hire London's stuffiest butler for the prestige. The fact that such an upright individual had disappeared without a trace could mean that Frawley had discovered some information that either

Dolph or the poor butler was uncomfortable with him having. The whole supposition was mostly guesswork, but they had little else to chase after. "Do you have any idea where this Frawley might be?"

"Not yet. I will."

"Splendid." Jack turned for the front door.

"My lord, are you certain you don't wish some company?" Martin asked.

"No. And don't wait up. I'll be back late."

"His Grace wants you dead, my lord," Peese insisted earnestly. "You shouldn't be going anywhere alone."

"He said he wanted me ruined," Jack pointed out.

"Hanging'll do that."

Jack gave a short grin. "You saved my life once already, the two of you. I'll be fine."

Peese frowned. "You couldn't have known Genevieve Bruseille was going to turn traitor on you like that. Me and Martin and Lord Hutton, we trusted her, too."

The marquis wasn't in the mood to discuss his past errors of judgment, particularly when he was likely headed directly into another one. "That was five years ago. It's done and ended. Now, open the door, man." He started forward again, then paused. "And if I should fail to return, tell Richard I was on my way to see William Benton. Nothing more."

"My lord?"

Jack shrugged and stepped through the door. "If I'm dead, it'll be too late for me to enjoy the scandal, anyway." With a nod at his servants, the marquis headed out into the darkness.

On the off chance that Dolph was having Faraday House watched, Jack left his property by way of the garden wall, as Lilith had done several days ago. The heavy pistol thudded against his thigh as he walked down the street in the night shadows, further reminding him of late nights in the fog of Paris.

Not only had he trusted Genevieve, he had been stupid enough to think himself in love with her. And she'd betrayed him to Bonaparte, though whether it was for blunt or out of fear or patriotism, he'd never discovered. What he did know was that what he'd done that night—and what he'd done over the subsequent five years trying to forget it—had left him with a reputation so tarnished, he still couldn't believe Lilith Benton had ever dared speak to him, much less willingly become his lover. Even now, he wondered how far she would let him carry this before she turned him away and gave in to her father's wishes.

A few lights still shone in Benton House. He slipped onto the property through the garden hedge and then made his way around to the rose trellis fastened to the south wall. Carefully he began to climb, stifling a curse as the damned thorns cut through his gloves and snagged his greatcoat. *Why couldn't Lilith have chosen violets or some bloody geraniums as her favorite flower?*

At the top of the trellis he stepped onto the roof and scrambled quietly across the eave. Lilith's window was halfway open, and he peered inside, caution and a nagging sense that he had absolutely no right to be there making him pause. The bed was made and the room dark. He gently pushed the glass open the rest of the way and stepped over the sill.

"Lilith?" he said softly into the darkness, pulling off his gloves.

"I'm here," she said, and stepped forward into the moonlit pool before the window.

She was in her nightgown, her long black hair hanging loose down her back. In the dark, the delicate lavender scent of her hair was sweeter than any perfume, and almost without thinking, he reached out to pull her against him by the front of her nightgown. Jack bent his head to capture her soft, warm lips with his own. With a sigh he tangled his other hand through her silky tresses, feeling her immediate response to his embrace, and very aware of his own. And half the bloody *ton* thought her an Ice Queen.

"Jack," she breathed, pulling away a little, "please tell me you didn't actually test those bottles of port by *drinking* out of them?"

The anger in her tone pleased him. "I only drank out of one of them," he corrected.

She curled her hand into a fist and hit him in the chest. Hard. "That was stupid, Jack!" she hissed. "If Dolph had thought to change the bottles, you'd—"

"I needed to show a little confidence, Lil. If I'd hesitated or flinched, or tried to make off with the crate, it would only have made matters worse, whatever the results."

Lilith looked up at him. "Your being dead would have been worse than anything else," she said softly.

He held her emerald gaze, wondering what in the world he'd ever done right in his life to make himself worthy of even a few moments spent in her company. "Why, thank you, my dear," he murmured, instead of informing her that he would gladly give his life to save her. He kissed her again.

As she moaned and began placing feather-soft kisses along the line of his jaw and his throat, it would have been easy to forget why he had come and just sink to the floor with her in his arms, but that would do neither of them any good. The bottles might not have been poison, but it very nearly was, at least to her reputation.

"So, what we do know," he said with some difficulty, her kisses making it rather difficult for him to concentrate, "is that Dolph suggested poison as the cause of death, and that it happened someplace between White's and your doorstep."

"That's going to be nearly impossible to prove," Lilith noted, her own voice unsteady. "Dolph was already the heir. He had no reason to kill his uncle."

"Lil—"

She put her fingers over his lips and folded against his chest. "That's what they'll say. And to defend you, your barrister will have to say that His Grace was considering remarrying for the purpose of getting a son."

Jack leaned his cheek against her hair. "We'll just have to see that it doesn't come to trial. I do have a few ideas remaining, you know."

"As do I," she said, the words muffled against his shoulder.

"Splendid. Let's hear them." Hopefully they would be more substantial than his own.

She hesitated, then lifted her head to look up at him. "I'm going to spend more time with my betrothed."

"No, you are not," Jack growled, concerned anger coursing through him. He pulled free and strode across the room to turn on her. "Absolutely not."

"He's very arrogant and proud, Jack," she insisted, following him. "And he thinks very little of women. I believe I can get him to talk."

Jack shook his head. "No."

"You can't stop me, you know."

"He beats his female servants, Lil. And worse. I don't want you anywhere around him."

"If we can't prove him a murderer, then I have to marry him, Jack." She sighed. "What a hole we're in. And I don't know how to escape without completing the damage to this family that my mother began."

Jack took a short breath. "Dolph's butler has gone

missing. I've got someone trying to track him down, and Richard's creeping about to see what he can come up with.'' Slowly he reached out and caressed her cheek with his fingers. "But please don't think you're alone. I . . .'' The marquis paused, never having made any sort of honest declaration before. He wasn't certain, given the circumstances, that it was the wisest time for one, anyway. His own future was swiftly becoming rather dubious. "I certainly have no intention of abandoning you,'' he modified. "In fact, you may not be able to get rid of me even if you wanted to.''

"Well,'' she replied, a slight smile touching her soft lips, "it's certainly not a respectable offer, but I don't think I've ever heard a more honorable one.''

Jack would have contested that, but when she leaned against him and softly touched her lips to his, he decided that she had understood what he meant. "I should go,'' he whispered.

"Do you want to?'' she asked softly.

Jack had never wanted to stay somewhere, with someone, so badly in his life. "No.''

Lilith slid her hands up his shoulders and under his greatcoat, snaking it down his arms with her fingers. "Then stay a while longer,'' she replied.

The marquis slid his hands down her back to her waist. He shouldn't stay; he shouldn't even be in her house; but he was painfully aware of just how much he wanted her again. And he was also aware that if Dolph were to win this game, tonight would be the last time he would ever hold Lilith in his arms.

While she unfastened his waistcoat and breeches, her hands much more confident this time, he trailed his fingers down her chest to caress her breasts through the thin cotton of her nightgown. Slowly he gathered the material of her shift in his hands and lifted it over her head. Jack kissed her, running his hands along her warm bare skin and reveling in the thought that she was his, that she wanted him as much as he wanted her. For now, he could let that be the only thing that mattered. For now, they were together.

"Jack," she moaned as he leaned down to suckle her breast, "I'm still going to picnic with Dolph tomorrow."

He lifted his head, scowling. "No, you're not. I told you, he's dangerous."

Lilith smiled, running her hands down his chest and then lower, to grasp his aroused manhood. "I won't let you do this by yourself," she said shakily, her tentative exploration making him burn. "And besides, you can't have all the fun."

Jack groaned as she ran her tongue over his nipple. The chit certainly learned quickly. "Fun? I thought you hated deviousness."

She chuckled, obviously seeing the effect she was having on him. "Lately I've changed my mind. And I'm going to help."

"I don't like it," he returned, pulling her hands free and lifting her in his arms to carry her to the bed.

"Jack—"

He settled himself along the length of her body, kissing her deeply. At the same time he entered her, and she moaned again. "I admire you for your courage, though."

"And you could use the assistance," she gasped, lifting her hips to meet him as he surged into her.

"And I could use the assistance," he agreed unsteadily, holding her gaze as he moved inside her. He thought he knew her, but she continued to amaze him at every turn. A lifetime would barely be long enough to know her, and he would be lucky if they ever had another night. He wanted to stay inside her, part of her, forever.

He slowed and deepened his thrusts, and felt her tensing beneath him. Jack kissed her as she came, muffling her cry against his mouth. Her pulsing seemed to pull him in deeper, and he shuddered as he filled her with his seed.

Slowly he removed himself and settled on his back beside her, and she curled up against his side, resting her head on his chest. He wanted to tell her that he loved her. He wanted to tell her that he was doing his damnedest to find a way for them to be together, and that he wanted to bring something more to her life than trouble.

"Jack," Lilith said quietly, her breath warm across his chest, "tell me about Genevieve."

He took a slow breath. "Lil, don't you have enough aggravations without adding mine into the pot?"

She smiled. "I'm beginning to like aggravations. Please tell me."

Jack sighed resignedly. "Stubborn chit. Genevieve was our contact in Paris."

"Yours and Richard's?"

"Yes. But I had no idea that her loyalties really lay with Bonaparte—not until I awoke one morning to find her holding the door open for a dozen French soldiers, all pointing their muskets at my head. Richard, Peese, and Martin broke me out of the garrison prison the night before I was to be hanged, and we spent a week hiding in the catacombs beneath Paris."

She shuddered against him. "The catacombs where they moved the bones of Christians when they ran out of room in the cemeteries?"

He ran his hand possessively along her shoulder and twined a strand of her hair around his fingers. "Those exactly—not an experience I would care to repeat. Bonaparte had already headed north, and Wellington was looking for a chance to smuggle us back to England when we received word that Genevieve was on her way to Boney with Wellington's battle plans, and a list of his spies. We went after her.''

It was a relief to finally tell the tale to someone who cared enough to listen, someone who would wait until the end before she judged him. ''I found her first. She'd been traveling with a pair of soldiers, and when I cornered her alone, she started making so much noise I was certain she'd wake them and the entire garrison down the street. I kept warning her to shut up, but she was more concerned with seeing me dead.'' He closed his eyes for a moment. ''So I beat her to it. I keep thinking I could have done . . . something. Something else, so she wouldn't have had to die.''

''You did what you thought you had to do,'' she said, lifting her head to study his face closely. ''Torturing yourself about it for the rest of your life—Jack, you can't do that to yourself.''

He snorted. ''I *chose* to kill her. Not the bravest thing I've ever done. And it's not something I actually care to forget.''

''And Lord Hutton thought you killed her for revenge?'' she asked softly, running her fingers in lazy circles about his chest.

''I can hardly blame him. I know what it looked like.'' Jack covered her hand with his own, stilling her fingers over his heart. ''When I returned to London, I did some rather unsavory things. There didn't seem to be any point of trying for propriety any longer, and I'd never been very proficient at it, anyway. But I never regretted any of that, until I set eyes on you.''

''You wanted revenge on me for slighting you.'' She chuckled.

She knew him better than he'd realized. ''Well, perhaps. At first. If you knew that, why did you bother ever to speak to me?''

For a long moment she held his gaze, then slowly leaned forward to kiss him. ''You're the most alive person I've ever known,'' she said finally. ''I could no more ignore you than I could my own heart beating.''

She did love him, then. She truly did. ''Lil,'' he said, reaching up and curling her dark hair behind her ear, ''if by some highly improbable chance our little schemes come to naught, would you consider . . . escaping as an alternative to wedding Dolph?''

''Escaping?'' she repeated, sudden tension tightening her body. ''I could never—my father—it would kill—''

Jack put his fingers over her lips. ''Never mind,'' he whispered. ''It was only a thought. Dolph hasn't a chance against us, my dear. No worries.''

So she might love him, but her damned family would still come first. She would wed that monster Dolph Remdale, rather than risk the scandal of fleeing. Jack wanted to be angry at her, but her loyal, compassionate heart was what had attracted him to her in the first place. He could hardly fault her for it now. Instead, he pulled her close and made love to her again, making it last as long as he could, holding her as long as he could. Finally he stood to gather his things together, while Lilith lay curled on her bed and watched him.

''Jack,'' she whispered as he pulled on his boots.

''Yes?''

''We will win, won't we?''

He looked over his shoulder at her. ''I hope so, Lil. With all my heart.''

''So do I.''

Chapter 17

⌒◯◯⌒

It took some digging, but Lilith finally found what she sought.

The Benton House attic was full of discarded furniture, odds and ends of outdated fashions, and mismatched knickknacks. Cold and damp and dusty, the narrow, peaked room was also very dark. Lilith carefully lifted the candle she'd brought with her and made her way through the clutter toward the tall, shrouded object against the far wall. The telltale corner of a painted wood frame peeked out from the worn sheet covering it, and she shoved aside a crate of old Christmas ornaments and stopped before it.

Setting the candle on an old, water-stained chest, Lilith carefully began pulling at the sheet. It gave way reluctantly, stiff and musty, but she finally tugged it out of the way.

"There you are," she whispered, looking down at the painting she had exposed.

It still wasn't right, for they'd left the thing upside down, and with a grimace at how dirty she was getting, Lilith tilted it forward until she could grasp it. The painting was big and heavy, and it took some maneuvering to turn it around until it leaned right side up again. She shifted the candle closer, then stepped backward to perch on the edge of a three-legged occasional table.

"That's better," she breathed with a small smile. "Hello, Mama."

Her wavy black hair coiled into long, perfect curls draped artistically over one shoulder, Elizabeth Benton sat on a wicker chair beneath a towering elm tree, a scattering of spring flowers growing at her feet. In her hands was a bouquet of the same flowers. Lilith remembered the painting, remembered the faint, easy smile on her mother's face and the good-humored tilt of her green eyes—though when last she had seen the painting, before its exile to the attic, she had thought it a cold, evil expression fitting the evil Lady Hamble had done her family. Now she sat still for a long time, studying the face that so closely resembled her own.

The painting had been done shortly before her parents' marriage, and Lilith wondered that she had never seen such a smile on her mother's face in real life. Perhaps Elizabeth Benton had found marriage to someone who cared nothing for her heart and character to be as repugnant as Lilith was now imagining it must be. Perhaps Lady Hamble hadn't had anyone to show her the mistake she was about to make until it was too late.

Last night, when Jack had suggested that she run away with him rather than marry Dolph, she had realized that her mother had faced the same question, though too late to save her good name. Lord Greyton had asked her to flee with him rather than spend another day in a marriage that, given her wild, passionate nature, she couldn't have helped but detest. Greyton had deceived her mother about his own feelings, but Lilith didn't believe Jack had lied to her. And she *had* been tempted to go away with him—more than tempted.

"Mama, what am I going to do?" she whispered, the sound muffled in the close, quiet room.

She knew what she wanted—that was simple. She wanted Jack Faraday. What she didn't know was whether she would have the courage of heart to make the same decision her mother had if things went wrong, even when society said it was too late. And it *was* courage, she realized, because the idea of going against her father, her family, terrified her. Even with Jack waiting at the other end.

Lilith sighed. She tried to tell herself it would have been easier if she'd never met him, but Dolph would still have been as repulsive. The only difference would have been that she probably wouldn't have realized it until after they were married. Just as her mother had been happy enough to smile for her portrait before she'd married Lord Hamble.

Well, she did know what sort of monster Dolph was, and she hadn't lied to the marquis when she'd said stopping the brute would be fun. Deviousness was much more amusing and interesting than it used to seem. She had the best teacher in London showing her the finer points, after all.

With a long, last look at her mother, Lilith stood and covered the portrait again, then lifted the candle and made her way back to the narrow attic entrance. Finally she understood why her mother had acted as she had— and she intended to do everything in her power to avoid becoming trapped in the same kind of miserable existence. Whether that meant she would be willing to flee with Jack, she wasn't certain. Not yet.

Back in her bed chamber, she summoned Emily and swiftly changed into her patterned peach and yellow muslin. Her nerves jangled, even knowing that what she was about to do was for her and Jack's own good. After all, exciting and necessary as it was, she had little experience in trapping dukes into confessions of murder. When Aunt Eugenia pranced into the room, Lilith stifled an irritated sigh. "Good morning."

"What are you doing still practically to bed?" With an exaggerated frown, Eugenia strolled over to the window. "You should not keep His Grace waiting, dear."

Lilith motioned for Emily to finish putting up her hair. "He isn't here yet, Aunt Eugenia."

"He will here at any moment. Remember to smile, Lilith, and to comment on the loveliness of the day—and to mention that you missed his presence at the Mistner'."

"Yes, Aunt," Lilith agreed. She intended to be completely pleasant and flattering and dimwitted, so that she could convince him to give away more than he realized when she began asking questions.

"And for heaven's sake don't get into one of your flights. You've tried his patience far beyond understanding, already."

"Yes, Aunt."

Actually, it was he who had tried *her* patience, but it would never do to get into an argument with Aunt Eugenia over it. The less anyone in her family knew of her true feelings for the Duke of Wenford and for the Marquis of Dansbury, the better it would be for her. She'd hoped for their understanding, but at this point she could only pray that they wouldn't interfere until after she and Jack were able to stop Dolph. After that—there would be time to explain things and to let them know that she was in love with someone else. And while he might not be the man they had envisioned for her, he was everything she'd ever wanted.

Lilith only wished she knew whether Jack had found what he truly wanted in her. She smoothed away her small frown as her aunt glanced in her direction. When he'd suggested flight last night, it was clear that he meant them to flee together. Whether the idea of marriage had entered his unconventional mind, she didn't know, but there was time to decide what remained for them after she was certain he wouldn't hang.

At the sound of a coach clattering up the drive, she jumped and stood to let Emily wrap a warm shawl across her shoulders. Aunt Eugenia followed her downstairs, her single-minded advice on pleasing behavior increasingly annoying. If her aunt had shown the least bit of compassion over Lilith's turmoil, or if she had even bothered to notice that her niece was troubled, Lilith wouldn't have minded her constant lecturing so much. But Aunt Eugenia was nearly as obsessed as her father over the Benton family reputation.

Lord Hamble had gone out to greet Dolph in his barouche, and Lilith heaved a sigh of relief that the duke hadn't come for her in a closed carriage. His Grace didn't bother standing until she reached the side of the carriage and stopped beside her father, but she refused to be affronted or annoyed. The more lightly he regarded her, the more chance her plan had of succeeding.

She curtsied as he offered her a hand up into the barouche. "Good day, Your Grace." She smiled, gripping his fingers and stepping up into the carriage beside him.

"Miss Benton." He nodded and gestured her to sit opposite him.

Again she was relieved. They would have to spend the ride looking at one another, but the further away she was from him, the better she liked it.

He was dressed to the height of fashion, though she didn't consider that a particular compliment to her presence. Dolph Remdale always dressed impeccably, just as he always comported himself with the utmost dignity and charm—so long as anyone who mattered happened to be a witness. She'd already glimpsed what he could be like when there were no consequences, and she would be careful.

"I thought we might venture to the north of town, if you've a mind," he said politely, resuming his seat.

A twinge of uneasiness ran through Lilith. She'd hoped they might picnic in one of London's parks, where they would not be entirely alone. Dolph's blue-eyed gaze met hers, his expression changing slightly to a less pleasant and better-remembered one, and she nodded. "That would be delightful."

With her father waving happily and urging them to spend a pleasant day together, the barouche trundled back down the drive and then turned north. Lilith sat facing backward, which always served to unsettle her stomach, and after a few moments spent gazing out at the familiar streets, she was nervous enough to want to begin setting things in motion.

"You've chanced on a lovely day for a picnic, Your Grace," she offered with a smile, gesturing at the blue sky and its scattering of windblown white clouds.

"Yes, I have," he agreed, looking down at his pocket watch and then favoring her with a glance before he returned to his perusal of their surroundings.

She kept the bright smile on her face. "You were missed at the Mistners' the other evening."

"No doubt I was," he returned, looking at her again, his expression aloof. "Not by you, though."

"Of course by me, Your Grace," she protested. "We are betrothed, after all."

He laughed, and a responding shiver of uneasiness ran down her spine. "We are betrothed because I will ruin you if you refuse to marry me," he said. "Don't pretend you like this match."

"Your Grace, you have misjudged my connection with the Marquis of Dansbury, but the result is that we are to be married." She forced a smile back onto her lips. "The match is made, and I am to be the Duchess of Wenford." He thought her dim; he might as well think her greedy, if it would convince him that her own morality was as lacking as his own.

"Hm."

Eventually they passed out of the city and through Highbury, and she began to worry that he was going to take them all the way to Cambridge. Once they reached Wood Green, however, the driver turned them into Alexandra Park. Lilith breathed a silent sigh of relief. Although there was no one about whom she knew, at least it wasn't some empty glade in the woods.

She glanced at Dolph as he rose and stepped down from the barouche. She wondered why he *hadn't* chosen a place where it would be just the two of them. And whether perhaps he wasn't quite as confident as he wanted her to think. Evidently he wanted witnesses about—so long as they were witnesses who wouldn't dare speak against him.

For a moment she thought she was going to have to make her own way to the ground, but as she stood, Dolph returned to hold up a hand and help her down the pair of steps.

"Thank you, Your Grace."

He released her hand and otherwise ignored her. "Beneath that tree, Finter."

The driver hopped to the ground and removed a picnic basket and blanket from the seat beside him. He opened the blanket and set it out on the grass, placed the basket on one corner, and then returned to the carriage.

"Wait for us by the road."

"Yes, Your Grace." Finter climbed back into his seat

and guided the team toward the edge of the park.

Lilith wished the driver had stayed, but wasn't surprised that Dolph had sent him away. There were other picnickers and riders in the park, but none close enough to overhear any conversation, or even to take much note of the pair of them sitting in the grass. Even so, Lilith searched out where the closest chance for assistance lay, just in case she needed to flee.

"Sit," he ordered, and gestured her toward the blanket.

Swallowing her annoyance, Lilith obediently stepped forward and sank down onto the spread covering the grass. Whatever he felt toward her, he had to at least desire her. He had been the one to suggest the marriage, after all. The thought of him touching her and holding her as Jack had, left her nauseated. But this was *for* Jack, and deep in her heart, she hoped it was for the two of them.

"Your Grace," she began, as he seated himself beside her and opened the picnic basket, "I know that you have been angry at me, but I beg you to give me the opportunity to prove myself to you. I do not believe that either one of us could look forward to a hostile relationship, however badly it may have begun."

"Very smooth," he commented, handing her a peach. "Just what I would have expected you to say."

"Why should you not?" she pursued. "It is a logical request, is it not?"

Dolph narrowed his eyes, but continued handing out the contents of the basket. "I suppose."

It wasn't nearly as much as she had hoped for, but Lilith was relieved even at that small concession. She needed to reassure him, to set him more at ease so that his arrogance and pride would make him want to gloat. "My father tells me you've applied to Canterbury for a special license, and that we may be wed by the end of the month," she said conversationally.

"You expect me to forget your hysterics?" he returned bluntly. "Don't think to make a fool of me, girl. I know you don't want to marry me, but I don't care. Dansbury thinks he's so bloody clever, but he's going to lose both you and his head."

"I am not his to lose," Lilith said stiffly. "He has been hounding me, and I find him to be a great annoyance. And lately I have seen nothing of him at all, thank goodness." She was gratified to hear her voice pronounce the lie with such calmness and certainty that she could almost believe it herself.

"Indeed. And the earring?"

"His Grace, your uncle, was always demanding baubles from me," she answered calmly, shrugging. "I can only presume that he snatched my earring without my knowledge."

"*I* can only presume that you're lying, Miss Benton. And from this moment on, you'd best behave. Whatever you say about your damned earring, it's still enough to ruin you."

"I don't know why you feel the need to protect yourself from me," she commented. "I am no threat to you."

"And I intend to keep it that way." He looked over at her, then unexpectedly reached out to take her hand in his. "You'll be a good, dutiful wife, won't you?"

"Of course, Your Grace." She smiled agreeably, the skin of her hand crawling where he touched it.

"You are beautiful," he said almost grudgingly, running his fingers across hers. "My uncle was right about that, anyway."

"You and your uncle discussed me?" Lilith encouraged him to continue.

"My uncle was obsessed with possessing you, and with getting sons on you." Dolph smiled. "A task I look forward to, myself, I must admit."

"Then we can have an amicable relationship," Lilith declared, keeping the naive smile plastered on her face while another jolt of horror went through her.

"Amicable as long as you prove yourself worthy of being the Duchess of Wenford," he commented. His fingers crept slowly up her bare arm, like a spider stalking a trapped insect. "No fits of temper, no hysterics, no rebellions."

"Is that why you asked me out here? To set the rules by which I may become your bride?" Lilith tried to extricate her hand, but couldn't do so without a struggle. "I assure you, this is what my family wants. I will not go against their wishes."

"And what about Dansbury's wishes?"

"I know nothing of them." Lilith took a breath and leaned closer into his embrace, wondering at her own boldness. "I do think it's clever that you've managed to outsmart him. My brother says no one even speaks to him any longer."

Dolph turned his gaze toward the nearest of their fellow picnickers. Abruptly his open palm caught Lilith across the cheek in a stingingly hard slap. She blinked, stunned, while he tightened his grip on her arm and jerked her closer.

"Don't try your games on me, girl," he hissed, his eyes hard and ugly. "I don't know what you think you know, and I don't care. But don't doubt that I can and will ruin you, or that I have enough evidence to get Jack Faraday hanged." He smiled grimly. "And if that doesn't work, finding an enemy to finish the task will be easy enough."

"Let me go!" Lilith cried, trying to wrench her arm

free. Jack had said Dolph abused his female staff, but she had never thought he would dare strike *her*. No one had ever hit her before! And even more horrifying was the thought that if he felt free to hit her now, nothing would stop him from doing worse once they were married. But they would *not* be married. If she'd had any doubts on that count at all, Dolph had just answered them.

"Do you understand me?" the duke murmured, pulling her closer still, so that her face was only a few inches from his.

"I will not marry you!"

He shook her harder. "Be grateful I chose marriage for you." Dolph grabbed her chin and then shoved her face away. "There are other alternatives. Understand, my dear?"

"Yes," she rasped, shuddering. Killing her, or Jack, would be nothing to a man who'd murdered his own kin.

"Then sit quietly and finish your luncheon," he ordered, and abruptly released her.

"Never touch me again!" She moved farther away from him.

"I'll touch you whenever I please, and you'll thank me for preserving your reputation," he returned.

"I'll thank you for taking me home."

"I thought you were anxious to become the Duchess of Wenford," he said mildly, as though he hadn't just hit and threatened her. "Unless you were lying again." He held out the Madeira.

Her fingers shaking a little, she accepted the glass and stopped herself from throwing the contents into his face. "I was not lying," she lied.

He actually laughed. "I know you, Lilith," he said. "I know how important it is that you make a match according to your father's wishes.'' His smile broadened. ''You have the look of a duchess, and I can't wait to get between your legs and teach you about being a woman. So behave yourself, and we'll both have what we want.''

A few weeks ago Lilith would have been shocked and embarrassed at his words. As it was, what he'd said only made her more angry. He was right about her—or at least, he *had* been right, before she had met Jack.

Dolph was ignoring her, calmly eating his luncheon and humming a waltz. She glanced sideways at him. *He had actually dared to strike her.* As far as the rest of the *ton* was concerned, the new Duke of Wenford was the epitome of propriety and grace. This was the Dolph Remdale the rest of the peerage had never seen. This was the Dolph Remdale who had killed his uncle to keep from losing the inheritance. And this was the Dolph Remdale she had to stop before he was able to get Jack Faraday and herself killed. Or worse.

She jumped whenever he moved, but the duke seemed satisfied that she had been sufficiently intimidated. His mood became increasingly lighter, and Lilith began to wonder whether he was truly a monster, or whether he was as mad as his uncle had been. Neither supposition was reassuring.

Unable to choke down more than a few mouthfuls, she was relieved when Dolph motioned for his driver to bring up the barouche. The man silently gathered the remains of their lunch together, his avoidance of her gaze the only sign that he might have witnessed his employer's misbehavior.

Lilith was silent on the ride back to London, and thankfully, Dolph seemed content to sit back and watch her. The morning had not gone remotely as she'd hoped in all of her stupid self-confidence. She wanted to see

Jack with a wild yearning so intense it was almost frightening. She'd never thought to have the opportunity to fall in love and had resigned herself to a friendship with the husband her father chose for her. Now she was beginning to think that living without the Marquis of Dansbury would be worse than death.

As they entered Mayfair, Wenford sat up straighter. "Join me, my dear." He smiled and gestured at the seat beside him.

"And if I don't?"

He glanced down at his pocket watch. "Then I will become angry."

While little shivers of dread and hatred went down her spine, Lilith gingerly stood and turned around to sit beside him. She shifted as close to the corner of the carriage as she could, putting as much distance as possible between herself and Dolph. As they turned into the Benton House drive, her father emerged from the entryway and came down the steps to greet them. Lilith wanted to jump from the carriage and flee into the house, but she forced herself to remain seated while Dolph stepped down to greet her father. After a moment he turned with a smile to offer her his hand. With an angry, frustrated sigh, she allowed him to help her to the ground.

"Thank you, Your Grace," she said, unable to summon a smile in response to his bright one. She knew the game he was playing, but doubted her father would care. If he ever heard what had happened, it was more likely he would blame her for behaving improperly.

"A delight, Miss Benton. Or should I say, Lilith?"

"Of course, Your Grace."

"Wonderful." Lord Hamble beamed, taking her hand and patting it between his own. "Wonderful."

"Excuse me." Lilith freed her fingers and backed toward the door.

"I'll see you soon, Lilith," Dolph called after her.

She escaped into the house, where Bevins took her shawl. "Is William about?" she asked, beginning to shake.

"I believe he is in the stables, my lady."

"Thank you."

Fighting the sudden urge to cry, Lilith hurried out to the stables. William stood watching as Milgrew groomed Thor, and Lilith stopped at her brother's elbow. "William?"

"Lil," he said, turning and granting her a grin. "How was your picnic? His new Grace didn't bore you into slumber, I hope."

She shook her head tightly, glancing at Milgrew. The groom met her gaze, then cleared his throat and went back to brushing the big stallion.

"William, I need you to do something for me."

"I'm meeting Ernest Landon for billiards at Boodles," he said, motioning Milgrew to continue when the groom paused again.

"I need to see Jack," she blurted abruptly, flushing.

"Jack?" he returned, lifting an eyebrow. "Look, Lil. I know His Grace don't like Dansbury, but you don't really believe Jack murdered old Wenford, do you? Just leave it be."

"You don't understand, William. *I need to see Jack.*" Her voice shook, and she couldn't help the tear that ran down one cheek.

William stepped toward her, his expression immediately becoming concerned. "What's wrong?"

"Please, William. Just go tell him I need to see him, and let me know what he says."

"Father'll kill me if I go near Dansbury. And you, as well."

"It's important," she pressed, her voice breaking and tears flowing freely down her face. She clutched her brother's arm tightly, willing him to show some sense just this one time.

"Master William," Milgrew said, straightening, "I'll get his lordship, if you'd like."

William glanced at the groom, then returned his gaze to his sister. "That's not necessary," he said slowly, his eyes searching hers. "But it may take me a bit of work to find him."

She nodded, acute relief flooding through her. "Thank you."

Immediately Milgrew retrieved her brother's tack and went to work saddling Thor. William continued to watch her, curiosity and speculation on his face, while Lilith tried to pull herself together enough to return to the house. It would never do if her father or Aunt Eugenia saw her like this. They would never understand, never sympathize, and certainly never help her.

Finally Milgrew stepped back and handed William up into the saddle. Her brother pulled Thor around, then hesitated. "Lil?"

"I'll explain later, William," she said. "I promise."

He nodded. "All right. I'll be back soon."

She watched him out the door, hugging herself and trying to stop shaking. Milgrew gathered up his grooming brushes into their box, then returned to stand beside her. "You all right, lass?" he asked quietly.

"I will be," she answered in the same tone.

"Master William'll find the marquis. Don't you worry."

She smiled and wiped at her face. "Thank you, Milgrew. I hope so."

*   *   *

Jack was beginning to become considerably aggravated. His butler had been gone for the better part of a day, and then had sent a note that he was headed for Gloucester and would send further word as soon as he had any. So Jack had gone prowling, looking for any friend of Wenford in whom the duke might have confided. Unfortunately, it seemed more likely that he would be turned away from clubs where in the past he had been a favorite, than that he would actually find someone, friend or enemy, willing to speak to him.

It had been this way before, when he had first returned from France with the rumors of his killing a woman running through the gilded halls of Mayfair. Back then, he had buried himself in his black reputation, making certain everyone knew that he had earned it, and that he welcomed it. He'd nearly managed to convince himself that he did enjoy it. Until he'd met Lil. Now, all he could think of was that if he couldn't correct things, he would never have her.

He finally tracked down Donald Marley at the Navy Club, and with a stifled sigh of relief, took a seat beside him in one of the chairs clustered around the large, soot-blackened fireplace. Dolph Remdale's closest crony was occupied with reading the *London Times* and smoking a cigar, and it was a moment before Jack's calculated fidgeting caught his attention.

"Dansbury," he said, lowering the paper, a look of surprised dismay crossing his features.

"Marley," Jack acknowledged in the same tone.

Marley stared at him for a moment, then folded up the section of the paper he'd been reading. "If you'll excuse me," he muttered, and stood.

"You certain it's me you don't want to be seen

with?'' Jack asked offhandedly, sitting back and crossing his legs at the ankles.

"Yes, I believe I am," Donald Marley returned, glancing back at him.

"A second poor choice."

"And what was the first poor choice, pray tell?"

At least Marley had stopped his retreat. "Becoming acquainted with Dolph Remdale."

"I'd have to disagree with you, Dansbury. And considering what Antonia St. Gerard's done for you, perhaps *you* should be the one concerned with whom you become acquainted."

Alarm bells began going off in Jack's head, and he frowned. "Antonia?" he repeated. It seemed his troubles hadn't yet finished accumulating.

Marley nodded. "Still only rumors, of course, but I hear she's gone to swear out a statement against you. Says you told her you were looking for information about Lilith Benton, and that you deliberately won Dolph's pin to encourage a break between him and his uncle."

For a moment Jack sat silently, his gaze on his hands. He'd underestimated Antonia. When he'd discouraged William from seeing her, he'd expected her to be angry. He hadn't expected her to move to get him arrested. It didn't make sense, for it certainly wouldn't gain her William back. Jack pursed his lips. It only made sense if all she wanted was revenge.

"Well, you'd best run along, then," he said, waving a hand at Marley. He needed to think. Rumors and accusations from a lifelong enemy were one thing. Antonia, though, was considered to be a friend—anything she said would be taken seriously.

Donald Marley was halfway through the door when he had to sidestep to avoid another man bursting into the parlor. Jack straightened as William Benton looked about, saw him, and strode forward with a look of relief.

"Jack, thank God," he muttered, dropping into the chair Donald Marley had just vacated.

The marquis looked at him. "Tell me, William, did you win or lose our little wager concerning Antonia?" He was unable to keep the anger and bitterness out of his voice, but William didn't seem to notice.

"Oh, I lost. But we'll worry about that later." The boy looked about the room, then leaned closer. "Lilith sent me."

Jack's heart jolted. He had no idea how much William knew, and he certainly didn't want to give away anything that hadn't yet been discovered. "She did?" he asked, as mildly as he could.

"Don't act so surprised," William murmured. "She was in tears, begging me to go find you and tell you she wanted to see you. Correction—she *needed* to see you."

Jack stood. If Dolph had done something to her, there were going to be two dead Remdales. "Where is she?"

"Not so fast, Dansbury," her brother returned, unmoving.

That didn't bode well. Slowly Jack retook his seat. "Yes?"

"Why did you take up with me?"

"What sort of question is that?" Jack said, lifting an eyebrow. "And hardly the time for it, don't you think?"

"I'd heard about you, you know," William continued, undaunted, "and I didn't expect you'd want anything to do with a simpleton like me. After seeing Lilith earlier, though, I'm beginning to suspect why you allowed me to tag along. I'd just like to hear you say it."

Jack looked at his companion. "I'll admit," he said after a moment, "initially I considered that befriending you would get me your sister's attention."

William's jaw twitched. "I see."

It annoyed Jack to realize that hurting the boy's feelings bothered him. He was becoming so sentimental he hardly recognized himself. "It took me a very short time to realize that I'd made an error in my initial perception of your sister, and that in addition, she rather detested me."

"At the least." William glanced about the room again, noting the distance between their party and the rest of the club's patrons. "So why didn't you cut me, after you realized your plan wasn't going to work?"

"Because—and at the moment to my surprise—I like you," Jack said flatly.

"I heard Price calling me your whipping boy the other day."

"You're no fool, William. Initially I may have thought so, but I was mistaken."

"But—"

"William, I'm likely about to be arrested for killing the Duke of Wenford, and your sister is in tears and asking to see me. We don't have time for this."

"Yes, we do. You know how important this Season is to Lil. So now that you apparently have her 'attention,' what do you plan to do with it? For God's sake, Jack, she's to be married. And she's not used to your type, or to your games. You could hurt her very badly."

"I wouldn't hurt Lilith," Jack returned indignantly. "And as for her being betrothed, you might have taken her part and told your father how much she hates Dolph Remdale before such a damned stupid thing could happen."

Her brother blinked. "I know she thinks Wenford's a dull pot, but she doesn't hate him."

"She hates him," Jack repeated. "And I intend to get her out of it." By any means necessary.

For a moment William looked at him. "And then what?"

Jack gritted his teeth irritably. "I have no idea. If you attempt to delay me any further, though, you won't be alive to find out. So may we go?"

Finally William nodded and stood. "You can't call on her at home. Where do you wish to meet her?"

Jack pulled out his pocket watch. It was well into the afternoon, a little late for shopping, but not unfashionably so. "I'll meet her on Bond Street, by Brook, in forty minutes."

William likewise glanced at the watch. "All right." Jack started to leave, but William put a hand out and stopped him. "Jack, I'm trusting that you won't pull her into more trouble."

"I won't," he promised, though he wasn't certain whether he was trying to convince William or himself. "I'm trying to pull myself out."

William gave a slight smile as he lowered his hand. "If it matters, I thought from the beginning that you were the right one for her. You're the only man she's encountered who actually makes her forget what she's supposed to be doing for everyone else."

"I'll take that as a compliment," Jack said dryly.

He made his way to the appropriate corner of Bond Street and hid Benedick so Lilith's aunt wouldn't see him. It would be difficult to get Lil away from her escort, especially when he couldn't show himself first, but short of starting a fire or a stampede, he had very few ideas. Jack looked up the street, then smiled. Speaking to Penelope Sanford was almost as risky as seeing Lilith, but at least the accompanying innuendo was absent. And Miss Sanford had helped them before.

Arranging to collide with her wasn't difficult, given the crowded streets. She dropped one of her packages as he bumped into her, and with an apology he bent and retrieved it for her. "Beg pardon." He smiled, handing it back.

She blushed. "Quite all right, my lord," she returned, glancing at her mother.

"I need to pay more attention to where I'm going," he continued, then leaned closer on the pretext of helping her rearrange the bundles in her arms. "Lil will be here in a few minutes," he murmured. "I need to see her, over in the alley off Brook Street. Can you get her over there?"

She looked at him for a moment, then licked her lips and nodded. "She won't get in trouble?" she whispered.

He gave his head a slight shake. "She asked to see me."

"All right."

With a polite nod to Lady Sanford, Jack strolled down the street. Penelope and her mother disappeared into a shop on the corner, and Jack immediately turned and made his way back to his post at the entrance to the alley. With a slight scowl he checked his pocket watch again. Ten more minutes. He found himself pacing, and sternly planted his feet by the wall. Nervous and worried, he spent the time wondering what had happened to make her need to see him as soon as she returned from her picnic. She might have news about Dolph's guilt, but he thought she would have been more subtle in getting the information to him if that were the case.

He stood about kicking his heels, fretting like an old woman and wondering if he would have to storm Benton House to see her after all, until finally the Hamble coach appeared. Jack ducked back into the narrow alley to wait, trying not to feel like the skulking criminal he was doing a sterling impression of.

She appeared sooner than he expected, resisting as a

giggling Miss Sanford led her down the street and into the alley's entrance. "Pen, stop it," she was whispering. "I have to meet..." She saw Jack and stopped. "Jack," she muttered, her tense expression easing, and rushed forward.

Jack opened his arms and pulled her into a tight embrace. "Are you all right?" he murmured into her hair.

"I am now," she returned shakily, her shoulders heaving as she began to cry.

"I'll be right around the corner," Penelope said, and with a last, compassionate look for the two of them, vanished.

"I like your friend," Jack offered, looking after her.

Lilith raised her tear-stained face. "She knew?"

"I ran across her, and asked her to lead you over here." He held her gaze. "What happened?"

"Oh, I suppose it's silly, but... I just needed to see you," she said, her arms still wrapped tightly about his waist.

"It's not silly," he stated. "And you don't panic. What happened?"

"He did it," she stated. "I know he did it, and he threatened me about it, but I still can't prove anything."

She tried to duck her head into his shoulder, but he shifted his grip to hold her away. "What do you mean, he threatened you?"

Lilith looked at him, then shook her head. "I don't want to tell you."

Now he was worried. It was serious, and she had not kept secrets from him before. "Lil, you wanted to see me. Please tell me why."

She sighed shakily. "It's just that—well, you warned me that he abused his female staff, but I never expected—" Lilith stopped, her face flushing, and roughly moved his hand aside so she could rest her cheek against his shoulder. "I never expected," she repeated.

"*He hit you?*" Sudden black fury coursed through Jack.

"He slapped me," she admitted.

"I'll kill him for that."

"No, you won't, Dansbury, because then no one will believe you didn't kill his uncle, too."

Her tone was matter-of-fact, and a slight smile touched Jack's face. She was still more concerned for him than for herself. "Probably not. But no one believes me, anyway."

"I do."

He kissed her. "I know."

"It really didn't hurt, anyway, but it surprised me. But that's how I knew for certain that he killed his uncle. The look on his face was frightening." She looked up at him again, tears welling in her eyes. "But how can we prove it, Jack?"

For a moment, the marquis rested his cheek against Lilith's hair and allowed himself to consider just how slim his chances of escaping Wenford's trap were. "I don't know." He took a slow breath, trying to contain his anger. "I should never have let you go off with him."

"I wanted to help," she protested. "I still want to help. And I'm supposed to marry him, remember?"

He gave a bitter laugh. "How can I forget?" Jack tightened his arms around her shoulders. "We could just run away, you know, you and I. Spain, or Italy. You would like Venice, *ma chère*."

For a long moment she was silent, her breath warm on his shoulder. Finally Lilith took a step back and lifted her hands to cup the sides of his face. "Is leaving England the only way to save you?" she asked.

Jack met her gaze. She would go with him—and part

of him was elated. At the same time, he knew he couldn't do that to her, couldn't hurt her by making her desert her family as her mother had done. "No," he answered slowly, rocking her in his arms. "It's not. Tomorrow, Lil, I want you to go see Alison. Stay with her, until Richard or I tell you otherwise."

"And what will you be doing?"

He gave a grim smile. "Hunting."

Chapter 18

"**A**unt Eugenia, please?"

Lilith watched her aunt out of the corner of her eye, saw her frown, and tried to keep the pleasant expression on her own face. She had expected her task to be a difficult one, but even though Lilith had been pestering since breakfast, Aunt Eugenia was showing no sign of weakening.

"I have accepted an invitation for tea with Lady Neuland. One does not cancel an invitation to chat with Lady Neuland," Eugenia said.

"But I have accepted an invitation for tea with Lady Hutton." *And I promised Jack I would spend the day with his sister.*

"She is only a baron's wife," Eugenia sniffed. "Lady Neuland is a marchioness. Don't be ridiculous."

This was not going well. "Papa?" Lilith appealed in desperation.

Lord Hamble looked up from his perusal of the morning newspaper. His irritated expression did little to boost her confidence. "Your aunt is correct, Lilith. You're to be a duchess. Don't waste your time with inferior relations of unacceptable persons."

"That is not fair!" Lilith burst out, frustrated beyond bearing and angry at the jibe sent at Jack.

Her father looked up from his paper again, then folded it and set it aside. "Beg pardon?"

Lilith recognized the tone. She'd heard it every time she displeased him with her behavior over the past six years. "I'm only asking a small thing, Papa," she said, in as calm and reasonable a voice as she could muster. "I want to spend the morning with a friend. Is that so terrible?"

"It is if you have no one to escort you. Which you don't," Aunt Eugenia broke in.

The morning room door opened, and William stepped abruptly into the room. Looking sheepish, he cleared his throat and walked over to drop onto the couch beside his sister. "I was thinking of going over to see Richard Hutton this morning," he said brightly. "You know Lady Hutton, don't you, Lil?"

He had been listening through the door, obviously. Lilith wanted to kiss him. "Yes, I do. As a matter of fact, I was planning on going to see her this morning. Would you mind escorting me?"

He grinned. "Not a bit."

"What's going on?" the viscount said, scowling at the two of them.

William shrugged. "All right, so I overheard you a moment ago. Lil deserves a little fun before you leg-shackle her to that big oaf Wenford, and I've no objection to being her escort if our aunt has a previous engagement."

"Oh. *You've* no objection," Lord Hamble retorted caustically.

"What is your objection then, Papa?" Lilith asked carefully, trying to keep her anger and frustration in check. It was painful to realize how little he truly did

care for her, after she'd spent every waking moment of
the last six years trying to please him. "I have nothing
else scheduled for this morning, and I did give my
word."

"You shouldn't have done so without getting our approval first," Aunt Eugenia pointed out unhelpfully.

Unexpectedly, her father waved a hand at his sister.
"Let her go, Eugenia," he said. "I don't want her
storming off in another selfish fit." He lifted his paper
again and resumed reading.

Lilith quickly stood, unwilling to give anyone time to
change their minds. "Thank you, Papa," she said, and
quickly left with William.

Her brother caught hold of her arm as she shut the
door behind them. "Where's Jack this morning?" His
expression and his tone were serious, and another jolt of
worry ran through Lilith.

"He was going to find Wenford. I think he knows the
only way he'll be able to prove his innocence is if he
gets a confession."

He looked at her for a moment, then nodded. "Do
you love him?" he asked quietly.

"With all my heart," she answered.

"Then get your wrap, and I'll take you to the Huttons'. I won't be staying, though."

"Where are you going?"

"To find Jack."

Lilith hesitated. "Why, if you don't mind my asking?"

"I owe him some assistance. Don't ask, but I have
my reasons."

"All right. And thank you."

"Don't thank me yet. I happen to think we're all
doomed."

*   *   *

Jack Faraday ducked behind an ice cart and swore. Tracking someone in Paris, where he had been unknown, had been difficult enough. The infamous Marquis of Dansbury following the Duke of Wenford through Mayfair without arousing suspicion, though, was a near impossibility.

He wasn't certain confronting Dolph would work, anyway. As Richard had said, all the blasted duke needed to do was keep his silence, and he had won. And not only did Jack need him to confess, the marquis needed him to do it in front of witnesses. In private, it would be as useless as the near-confession Lil had heard. Dolph had known that, had known that Lilith wouldn't be able to pass on anything she discovered, but Jack was encouraged by the fact that the duke hadn't bothered disguising his animosities and motivations. Hopefully his confidence and arrogance would make him careless.

As plans went, he considered confronting Dolph a poor one, for it left him little room for subtlety or for error. And with Lilith's reputation and well-being at stake, he had to tread more carefully than he was used to. Jack counted to ten, then stepped around the cart and up the street. Dolph had made his way into Stanton's, and was no doubt exercising his newly substantial purse in the purchase of the most expensive cigars in London. Jack tilted his hat lower over his eyes and settled back against the bakery wall to wait. It was cold again today, and he was grateful for his heavy, dark greatcoat. In addition to the warmth, it provided a convenient hiding place for the brace of pistols resting in its deep pockets.

"Dansbury."

Jack turned quickly. "Price," he acknowledged, relaxing a fraction. "I thought you'd gone to visit your brother in Sussex. Or was it your sister in Devonshire?"

"Don't expect me to apologize," Price countered,

stopping before him. "Your ship is sinking, my friend. I'm merely an insightful rat."

"That saves me the trouble of calling you names, anyway," Jack said, glancing toward the tobacco shop. "So what brings you here now?" Price was in his evening clothes, and obviously hadn't been home since last night. That wasn't unusual, except by this time of the morning he should have been looking for a bed, rather than traipsing about the shopping district of Mayfair.

"Actually, I was looking for you. I happened to breakfast with Landon this morning, at Boodle's. A pair of Bow Street Runners came in, if you can believe their gall, and ended up at my table, asking me if I happened to know where you were."

For a moment Jack was silent. "And you said?" he finally prompted.

"I told them you'd sailed to China on Tuesday. I don't believe, however, that they were convinced."

"Thank you." If Bow Street was after him, it was either for questioning, or there was a warrant out for his arrest. In either case, he had more individuals to hide from than Dolph Remdale, and if he couldn't end this today, he would end up jailed in Old Bailey.

"If you've any sense, you *will* make for the Orient, Jack, posthaste. Face it, my friend, you lost this one. And playing as deep as you do, you lost everything."

Amused despite the fact that Price was likely correct, Jack grinned and clapped his friend on the shoulder. "Your degree of faith in me is truly astounding, my dear. But don't try to collect your wager yet. I'm not finished."

Price looked at him. "You don't need to put on a front for me, Jack. Just get out of London, before you get arrested."

"I can't do that." Jack hesitated, trying to decide how

much he could tell Price. Thus far his friend had shown himself to be loyal—more loyal than he'd expected, in fact—but it wasn't just his own freedom, or his own reputation, at stake here. "Perhaps you'd best make yourself scarce for a day or so. Not as far as China, but Sussex might be wise."

"What do you think to accomplish?" Price persisted, searching his gaze.

Jack could see in his companion's face the speculation about whether he had actually killed old Wenford or not. At least he still wasn't certain, which set him apart from most of the rest of their fellows. He shrugged, trying to make as little of it as he could. "Justice, I suppose. Or at least retribution."

"You're mad, Jack—but then, I've always said so." Price gave him a jaunty salute. "Best of luck, and I'll be skulking about. Wouldn't want to miss this." He sauntered back down the street in the direction of his townhouse.

Jack shifted impatiently. He enjoyed a challenge, but this was becoming ridiculous. He looked up the street, sudden suspicion tugging at his insides. His Grace had been in that shop for a very long time. With a wary glance around him, Jack pushed away from the wall and strolled toward Stanton's. He paused in the doorway, peering into the relative darkness, then with an aggravated sigh stepped inside. It was a small shop—and Dolph was not there.

"Wenford?" he barked at the flustered-looking attendant.

"Ex—excuse me, my lord?"

"Where the bloody hell is Wenford?" Jack repeated, ducking around the far side of the counter and making his way toward the clerk.

"Haven't seen him, my lord."

Jack shoved him aside and continued on into the back of the shop. He'd kept his eye on the front door while he'd been speaking to Price; Dolph had not left that way. In the back room, Jack stopped, staring at the door leading out into the alley. Either Dolph had managed to turn himself into the rat he was and scuttled away, or he'd known he was being followed and had gone out the back door. With a curse, Dansbury pushed through the doorway into the narrow, dirty alley. China was beginning to sound better with every passing moment. He wondered if Lil would like it there.

"I don't think this is what Jack had in mind when he asked you to stay with me," Alison Hutton whispered.

"You said you wanted to get out of doors," Lilith reminded her, taking Beatrice by the hand as the three of them crossed the street toward her favorite dress shop. "And here we are."

"He wanted you somewhere safe, Lilith. This is not safe."

"Of course it is, Alison. Besides, London's a big place. He may not even be able to find Dolph on his own. This way, there're three sets of eyes looking for him." She sighed, irritated at the useless role she'd been relegated to play. "I can't sit about and do nothing. I would go mad from worrying."

"About my brother?"

"Of course about your brother."

Alison smiled. "Good."

"I hope so."

"You know, I think there may be four sets of eyes about," Alison said thoughtfully. "Someone came pounding on the door this morning, and Richard vanished just after breakfast." Her eyes narrowed. "He didn't look very happy about whatever it was."

Lilith looked at her, far more alarmed than relieved. "William said Richard would be the one to arrest Jack if a warrant was signed."

Alison shook her head, her expression worried. "He wouldn't. They may not get along, but he would never do that."

"Are you certain?"

Alison thought over her answer for a moment. "I don't know," she said finally. "Lately, over the past few days, Richard and Jack have actually conversed with one another. They haven't done that in five years. But I don't know. I don't know."

"I need to warn him." Lilith reversed her direction, and Beatrice looked up at her.

"Are we helping Uncle Jack?" she asked.

Lilith shook her head. "No. *I* am helping Uncle Jack."

"Lilith—"

She looked up to meet Alison's gaze. "*You* are going home."

Alison sighed. "Jack will kill me for this. Please be careful."

"I will. Don't worry." It sounded brave and determined. As Lilith turned and made her way down the street, though, she began to realize just how large London was, and just how small the odds were of her finding Jack before Lord Hutton did.

She rounded the corner and froze. The Duke of Wenford stood looking in a shop window only a few feet away from her. With a strangled curse, Lilith ducked back around the corner, nearly colliding with the Earl of Manderly. "Beg pardon," she said in a rush, stepping back against the wall.

"Miss Benton," he returned, lifting both his eyebrows and his hat, and continued on his way.

Lilith took a quick breath, her heart beating fast and hard. She frowned, trying to calm herself and think clearly. Abandoning the duke to try to find Jack could be disastrous for both of them. But following Dolph would leave Jack unaware that Lord Hutton was likely after him.

"Oh, damnation," she whispered. Then she mentally shook herself. Jack was rarely unaware of events. He would be cautious—or at least as cautious as he was about anything.

And if it was too late, and if they couldn't stop Dolph or Richard Hutton, then she would go away with him. She shut her eyes for a moment, missing him with a physical ache, missing his voice, his touch, his warmth and passion. Her family would hate her, but she couldn't imagine living without him. And though she didn't know whether he felt the same or not, she thought that perhaps he did. He had twice asked her to flee with him, and she had seen the look in his dark eyes when he held her. She would go.

Determined to do everything she could, Lilith leaned back around the corner. Dolph was still in sight, several shops farther down the street. He paused in the crowd, looking into another window, and then slowly wandered away in the opposite direction. She looked up and down the street. As the duke turned up the next street and vanished, Lilith stepped out onto the walk and hurried forward.

She stayed half a block behind Wenford for nearly an hour, ducking into doorways when it seemed he would turn around, and trying not to be too obvious. Several of her fellows gave her odd looks as she passed by, but she pretended not to notice and kept her attention on her quarry. Jack was obviously much better at this sneaking about than she was, but she thought she was doing a very adequate job of it. Twice she caught herself grinning as she evaded detection with particular skill. No wonder Jack had agreed to become Wellington's spy: this was rather exhilarating, really.

They traveled well south of Mayfair, apparently heading for the Thames, and Lilith wondered what in the world would bring the Duke of Wenford into this part of London. She looked about uneasily. There were no peers around to wonder what she was doing alone on the streets, but then again, there was no one to help her in case something should happen. And there was no sign of Jack at all.

Dolph stopped again, and she ducked into the doorway of a cobbler's shop. Flexing her tired toes in her thin shoes, she counted to ten and then leaned out again. The duke had vanished. "Blast." Lilith scowled, leaving her shelter and hurrying forward. She glanced into the shop windows as she passed, making certain he hadn't stopped to make a purchase somewhere.

She passed a narrow alley between two shops and immediately sensed someone there. Before she could do more than turn her head, the duke had wrapped one arm about her waist and arms, and the other across her mouth.

"Good day, my dear. And what are you doing here alone, so far from home?" he whispered in her ear, and dragged her backward into the alley.

Lilith tried to shriek, but only a strangled whimper came from her muffled mouth. She kicked as hard as she could, and was rewarded by the sound of Dolph's grunt. He tightened his grip and jerked her roughly sideways, making her flail about to keep her balance. She wrenched one of her hands free, and frantically reached back and yanked at his hair.

The hand across her mouth let go. Before she could

scream, he slapped her hard across the face. "Stop fighting, or I'll break your neck," he growled, replacing his hand.

Lilith blinked, dazed by the blow. Suddenly it made sense. Dolph hadn't been wandering about aimlessly while she followed him. He'd known she was there and had been leading her away from assistance. Which meant he had to know that Jack was after him, as well.

His tight grip was cutting off her air, and she stopped struggling to conserve what little breath she had. At the far end of the alley he yanked open the back door of what looked like two stories of clerk's offices. Dolph shoved her against the foot of the stairs, then turned and locked the door behind him. Lilith scrambled to her feet and ran toward the front of the building. Immediately the duke was after her, grabbing her shoulder before she could dodge out of the way. He pushed her into the wall, and she stumbled and fell.

"Leave me alone!" she shrieked, kicking him again.

Dolph hauled her back to her feet and yanked her toward the stairs. "You were the one following me," he said calmly, half-dragging her up the stairs behind him. "What sort of gentleman would I be if I let you wander these dangerous streets alone?"

"You're no gentleman," she gasped, grabbing for the bannister. "You're a monster!"

They reached the top of the stairs, and Dolph pushed Lilith through one of the two doorways there. She stumbled into a large loft, half-filled with old desks and chairs and cabinets, faded from weather and covered in dust. Pale sunlight glinted through both of the dirty windows on either side of the near corner. With a shudder she watched him lock the door behind them and pocket the key.

Dolph crossed his arms over his chest and leaned back

against the door. "*I'm* a monster? Do you mean to tell me that it was merely a coincidence that I noticed Dansbury following me earlier, and that ten minutes after I evaded him, you began trailing me? Not very subtle, my dear. And not very wise. You don't want to make me angry, you know. I have a rather black temper."

Lilith looked at him, another shiver running through her. The risks she had taken that morning had been unwise in the extreme, but for perhaps the first time in her life, she hadn't thought about the consequences of her actions. Jack had needed assistance, and she'd done her best to render it.

"Where are we?" she asked, swallowing her distress and her anger. At the moment, she needed all of her wits.

He pursed his lips, then shoved away from the door and came forward a few steps. "The office of my late uncle's solicitor. I didn't like him, so I turned him away. In a happy circumstance, the Duke of Wenford owns the building. And I am the Duke of Wenford."

Lilith did not like the predatory look in his eyes. She pressed herself closer into the corner between the windows. "Was the solicitor cheating you?" she asked, to keep him distracted. She glanced sideways. Both windows were latched tight.

Dolph shrugged and advanced another step. "I didn't like him," he repeated. "You are lovely, stupid or not." He reached out and touched her cheek with his fingers.

Lilith flinched at the caress and edged away toward the door. "Don't."

The duke turned to keep her in sight, a slight smile on his face, reminding Lilith of a cat stalking a mouse. "Why not? We are to be married, after all."

"You can't be serious," she protested. "You still think to marry me?"

He shrugged, following her again. "Why not? Dansbury is certainly in no position to wed you. And if a scandal breaks over your attachment to him, which will happen if you refuse me, no one else will have you."

The duke strode forward and grabbed her by the shoulders. Before Lilith could do more than gasp, he lowered his head to force a hard, wet kiss on her. He held them together, shoving her arms down to her sides when she began to struggle, and mauled her for a long, dreadful moment. Finally he lifted his mouth away from hers and thrust out his tongue to slickly lick her cheek.

Revolted, Lilith shoved herself backward away from him. She grabbed for the door handle, but it didn't budge under her frantic flailing. Desperate, she looked around, and for a heartbeat, froze. Jack looked at her through the dirty window, then ducked sideways out of sight again. For a fleeting moment Lilith wondered if she'd gone mad, and then Jack leaned into view again. A pistol in his hand, his lips stretched in a thin, angry line, he motioned her to move away from Dolph.

If she moved, he would kill Wenford. And then Jack would hang for certain. There had to be another way. "If you insist that we must marry," she said to Dolph, stopping her retreat so suddenly he nearly ran into her, "then why do you make it so impossible for me to care for you?"

"Dear Lilith, you are the object of affection of the Marquis of Dansbury. And from your foolish activities of this morning, you bear him considerable affection as well. What sort of bride consorts with her husband's worst enemy?"

The urge to look toward the window again was nearly overpowering. "The marquis is ruining my brother," she said. "I do what is necessary to prevent that."

Dolph cocked his head, his expression skeptical.

"You say your loyalty to Dansbury is in truth only loyalty to your brother and your family?"

At least he had stopped mauling her. "Yes, Your Grace. William's ruination would be more than my father could bear. Once the marquis realized how much trouble you had him in, he insisted that I use my connection with you to assist him, or he would destroy my brother."

The disbelief on his face didn't lessen in the slightest. "And did you not consider that I would see him arrested, so that he would not be able to threaten you any longer?"

Lilith ducked her head, feigning shame and embarrassment. "No, I did not." She looked up at him again, thankful he thought her an idiot. "I was frightened. I hadn't realized that you were more than a match for him."

"Flattery, sweet Lilith?" Dolph approached again, and this time she closed her eyes and didn't protest when he kissed her. He tried to tease her mouth open, but she pretended not to understand what he was attempting and kept her lips locked together.

"I can't like the way you've treated me," she said, wanting to wipe his foul taste from her mouth, "but I suppose what he did was even worse. At least you promise me a title. All he did was threaten me." Lilith wondered how bold she dared to be. Dolph was self-centered and arrogant, but he wasn't stupid. "So I suppose that, ungentlemanly as you are, I owe you a debt of thanks."

With a smile, Dolph reached up to run his hands over her breasts through her green muslin. "If you truly want to thank me for rescuing you from Dansbury, I can think of a way." He leaned forward again, licking the base of her throat and the line of her jaw.

Jack could touch her like that, but no one else. She

was supposed to be maidenly and pure, so she flinched wildly and backed toward the door again. "Your Grace, we are not yet married!" she protested.

"But what of the debt you owe me?" he pursued, grabbing her wrists and jerking her up against him.

"That is hardly reason enough to anticipate our vows, Your Grace!"

She could feel his growing arousal through her skirt, and fought down an expression of loathing. She glanced toward the window again, but there was no sign of Jack. With all her heart she hoped he was listening, and that she could get him the confession he needed.

Pretending to be swayed by his rough embrace, Lilith said breathlessly, "But I certainly prefer you to your uncle—I couldn't stand to be touched by that old man."

Dolph nuzzled her neck wetly, his hands roaming down her back to her buttocks. "Then you owe me an even larger debt, my dear—I did save you from being mauled by him." Dolph lifted his head to look her in the eye. "But don't think you'll be able to do anything with that," he growled, his expression going ugly for a moment. "You're about to be ruined. If you say anything before our marriage, I'll make certain the entire *ton* knows what a whore you are."

He shoved her backward, shifting his leg so that she tripped over it. Flailing, Lilith lost her balance and fell to the floor. The duke knelt between her legs and licked his lips wetly.

Glass shattered into the loft, and Dolph barely had time to turn his head as Jack burst into the room and threw himself on the duke. Lilith shrieked and scrambled out of the way as the two men slammed into the floor beside her.

Jack struck Dolph hard in the face with his closed fist. "Does that hurt?" he snarled.

The duke shoved him away and scrambled to his feet. Blood welled at one corner of his mouth, and he wiped at it with his hand. "Dansbury! What in God's name—" He stopped, turning to look at Lilith. Fury touched his light blue eyes. "You harlot! You whore! You think you can—"

Jack hit him again. "I was going to shoot you," he said in a black, angry voice Lilith had never heard from him before, "but I decided that beating you to death would be more satisfying."

With a snarl Dolph swung at him, but Jack dodged out of the way and landed another blow. The duke staggered backward and hit the floor hard. Jack advanced on him again, and Dolph dug into his greatcoat pocket. He pulled free a pistol and pointed it at the marquis.

Lilith screamed.

Jack skidded to a halt, his eyes not on the pistol, but on the face of the man holding it. "Very gentlemanly of you, Wenford."

Dolph smiled nastily, blood turning his teeth red. "I told you I wouldn't kill you," he returned. "Perhaps I was in error about that." He glanced over at Lilith and turned the pistol in her direction. "I do mean to ruin you first, though. I know you're armed, Dansbury," he said, his gaze staying steadily on Lilith as she crouched against the wall. "Put your weapons on the floor."

"No, Jack," Lilith sobbed, terrified for the marquis. "He confessed. There's nothing he can do."

"And who's going to believe a whore and a killer?" Dolph wiped at his mouth again, glancing down at the blood on his fingers. "Especially one who's just tried to murder me. You're going to hang, Dansbury. Drop your weapons!"

Lilith looked at Jack, to find his gaze on her. Slowly he reached into his pocket and removed his pistol, bending to set it down on the floor. A second pistol followed.

"Jack, no," she whispered.

"I'll not make the wrong choice this time," he returned quietly. "All right, Wenford. Now leave her be."

"Move away," the duke instructed, and Jack slowly stepped back from his pistols.

"I'm your prisoner, Wenford," Jack said in a more forceful voice. "Leave her be."

"My prisoner," Dolph repeated, finally returning his full attention, and the pistol, to Jack. "My prisoner. You know, I do hope they wait to hang you until after my wedding."

"I'd kill you myself before I'd marry you," Lilith snapped. She edged closer to Dolph, her eyes on the pistol. If she could wrench it away from him, Jack would have a chance.

"You'll not be fit to marry anyone else," he retorted, glancing at her. "I'll have you, and I want him to know it. I'd thought to take care of that here, but I suppose I'll have to wait until I get him to Old Bailey. Perhaps this evening, dear."

Lilith moved closer still and took a deep breath. Then she screamed at the top of her lungs, and in the same second, hefted a three-legged chair as hard as she could sideways into Dolph's chest. He jumped at the sound, then stumbled as the chair thudded heavily into his sternum. Jack swung in to grab Dolph's hand and wrenched the pistol free.

"I don't think you're going to be doing anything this evening," the marquis snarled, tossing the pistol into the corner.

Dolph launched himself at Jack. The two men crashed into one of the old desks, knocking it over and breaking one of the legs off. Lilith scrambled out of the way, kicking the duke hard as he rolled past her. He grunted and turned on her. Jack hurled himself into Dolph's shoulders, knocking him back to the floor. Grabbing a handful of the duke's perfect blond hair, Jack slammed his head into the wooden planks. Then he did it again. And again.

It didn't look as though he intended to stop. "Jack, that's enough." Lilith climbed to her feet, alarmed at the black fury in the marquis's eyes.

"Not if he's still breathing." Again Dolph's head smacked into the floor, and he groaned.

The door handle behind them rattled, and she started. Something heavy thudded against the door. It creaked loudly, but didn't budge.

"Oh, no," she hissed. Either Dolph wasn't alone, or Lord Hutton had found Jack. "Jack, stop! Stop!" She stumbled over and grabbed Jack's arm, trying to pull him off the duke. "Don't kill him! Please!" With only her and Jack to speak against Dolph, it would be almost impossible to convince the law. If Dolph was dead, Jack was done for.

The door shuddered with another blow. Once more something pounded against it, and it rattled and burst open. Her nerves frayed, Lilith shrieked as Richard Hutton and a half dozen Bow Street Runners charged into the room. It was the nightmare she'd had for the past few nights—Jack, trapped and arrested, and nothing that she could do.

"Dansbury, that's enough!" Richard bellowed. He threw an arm around Jack's neck to haul him backward off Dolph's limp body.

The duke shuddered and coughed, then began crawling slowly for the door. Blood dripped from an ugly gash in his forehead and trailed onto the wooden floor.

"Just one more minute, Richard." Jack gasped, pulling free and going after Dolph again.

"Jack, please don't," Lilith sobbed. "Please don't."

"I let it go too long already, Jack," Richard said forcefully.

The marquis slowed, then stopped. He ignored his brother-in-law, slowly turning to look at Lilith. "All right," he murmured. "It's over. For you."

"Thank God," Richard muttered, taking a deep breath. "You'll have to come with me."

"No, he won't." Lilith leaned down and picked up Dolph's discarded pistol. Her hands shaking, she pointed it at Richard. "We're leaving."

"Lil? Lil, put the gun down," Jack said quietly, moving toward her.

She shook her head, keeping her eyes on Lord Hutton and the stunned Runners. "I have some money with me. We can be in Spain by nightfall."

Jack began to grin.

"Miss Benton," Richard said, eyeing the wavering pistol uneasily, "you may not believe me, but I'm on your side."

"You came to arrest Jack."

"Lil," Jack said, stopping beside her, "it's all right. They're here with me."

She glanced over at him. "What?"

"I lost Wenford about an hour ago. I ran across Richard, and we all caught up to you at the last moment— saw him drag you off. They were in the other room, listening. I climbed out the window so I could see what was going on. I didn't want him to hurt you again."

"They heard him?" she repeated, slowly lowering the pistol. "They heard him say he killed his uncle?"

"Yes, we did," Richard nodded, breathing a sigh of relief as Jack gently took the weapon from her fingers.

"But Alison said you were unhappy when you left her this morning."

"You'd be unhappy, too, if a damned nine-fingered butler dragged you out of a nice, warm breakfast room and tossed you into Dansbury's stables to 'interview' some other blasted butler he had tied up there."

Lilith looked at Jack again. He was smiling, his lip cut, and his hair and clothes disheveled. "You found him?" she asked.

He shook his head. "Peese found him. I wasn't home, so he went to get Richard. Frawley reluctantly verified that old Wenford stopped to see his nephew and shared a brandy before he headed off to propose to you." Jack glanced at Richard. "That's the reason I wasn't hauled off to prison. I'd hire him, if he wasn't so stuffy."

For a moment Lilith shut her eyes. "Thank goodness." Then she snapped them open again, looking suspiciously at the men hauling Dolph to his feet. "But what about them?"

One of the Runners stepped forward and doffed his hat. "There'ie still some questions we need answered, but if Lord Dansbury's willing to come with us, I don't think there'll be much more trouble."

Jack nodded. "I'll go, so long as Lord Hutton accompanies me."

"Try to keep me away," Richard muttered.

Two of the Runners headed with Dolph down the stairs. Jack handed over the pistol he'd taken from Lilith, then turned to face her. "Thank you," he said quietly.

There was so much she wanted to say to him, but with Richard and the other men standing about, she was suddenly shy. "You're welcome, Jack," she returned.

He looked at her for another moment, something she was almost afraid to put words to in his eyes, then visibly shook himself. "We need to see Miss Benton home," he told Richard, who nodded.

"It's on the way. We'd best get moving, before Prince

George sends the Royal Grenadiers after you.''

"Jack?" Lilith whispered.

He gave another slight smile. "We'll talk later," he returned in the same tone. "After I get this straightened out."

His words were reassuring, but Lilith was not calmed. She had seen the expression on his face—he was feeling noble. And abruptly she was worried. He had never said that he loved her, and Jack being noble could deny her the one thing she truly wanted for herself. Him.

Chapter 19

It was, William decided, the moral thing to do. After all, Lilith had spent her entire life making sacrifices that caused her unhappiness, for the sake of pleasing their family. He could make a small sacrifice for her.

He ran his fingers through his light hair to tousle it, and marched up the front stairs of Antonia St. Gerard's townhouse. What she'd done to Jack was inexcusable. If Dansbury hanged because of her lies, William would be to blame for it, as well.

He pounded on the door, then rushed in as Linden pulled it open. "Where's Antonia?" he barked, heading for the stairs.

"In her bed chamber, Mr. Benton," the butler answered calmly, shutting the door again. "I was instructed to allow no one but you entry."

"My thanks, Linden."

William charged up the stairs, and without knocking first, barged into Antonia's bed chamber. As usual, it gave him pause, because try as he might, he had never been able to get used to the black decor she favored. Previously he had thought it exotic, but for the first time, it seemed a bit absurd. Antonia was seated at her writing desk, and looked up from a letter she was composing.

"William, *mon amour*. Whatever is the matter?"

"We have to get you out of here," William rushed, striding over to her wardrobe and pulling out several gowns suitable for traveling.

Antonia came over to stand beside him. "Are we eloping?" She smiled, running her hand along his shoulder, then reaching into the wardrobe to select a blue muslin.

"Haven't you heard?" He shook his head, continuing to throw clothes out onto the bed. "No, of course not, you've just risen, haven't you?"

"I do stay up rather late," she continued, her sharp eyes watching him closely. "So what has happened?"

"They found a note. Old Hatchet Face killed himself."

For a moment she stared at him, her sensuous mouth opening and then closing again. "The Duke of Wenford? That's absurd, Will—"

He shook his head. "The writing's been verified by Dolph Remdale. Dansbury's been cleared, and he's apparently in a black fury about what you told the law." William clutched her hand over his heart. "I'm worried he'll come after you, Antonia. You know how he gets when someone crosses him."

"Yes, I know." Antonia freed her hand and turned away to walk slowly toward the window. For a moment she stood looking outside, until finally she turned to face him again. "Are you certain of this, William?"

He nodded. "Got it from Price."

"Jack wouldn't dare do anything to me," she said, mostly to herself.

"You came within a whisper of getting him arrested and hanged, Antonia! And he killed that woman in Paris for less than that. Now, please—get your things together! Once you're gone, I'll try to reason with him, tell him it's my fault, or something.''

"You should come with me. William, we could live in Paris." She stretched out her hand and smiled. "It would be *merveilleux*.''

This was going to be the difficult part. He nodded distractedly, then jumped at an imagined sound and glanced toward the door. "I could join you there, after I talk to Dansbury and convince my father not to cut me off.''

She lifted an eyebrow. "Whyever would he cut you off?''

He shrugged, glancing toward the door again. "Oh, I spoke out against Dolph Remdale, told him the new duke was an old bore and Lil could do better. Put that on top of my gambling debts and my running off to the Continent with you, and I don't have a chance." William sighed, then grinned. "I suppose we could open a faro parlor in Paris. Then we wouldn't need my income.''

Antonia spent a moment looking at him, then walked to the chamber door and pulled it open. "Linden!" she called. "I need my traveling trunks, *immediatement*." She closed the door again, and leaned back against it. "You are right, *mon amour*. I will go ahead, and will send you word when I have found a residence. Jack can be reasoned with, but your odds of pacifying him are better than mine right now.''

William was just barely able to keep the triumphant grin from his face. He nodded solemnly. "I'll attempt to reason with him," he agreed, then scowled. "Devil take it, Antonia, I'll miss you.''

She smiled and leaned up to kiss him. "I shall count the days.''

"So shall I.''

William lifted her hand and kissed her fingers, then backed from the room as Linden descended from the third floor with another footman, a wardrobe trunk between them. With a nod to the butler, William headed downstairs and out the front door. Outside he swung up on Thor and turned for home. It hadn't been as difficult as he'd thought. Though he was disappointed that Antonia was everything that Jack had hinted she was, he was relieved to have escaped her clutches uninjured. And now, one less witness would be available to testify against Dansbury if it came to a trial. He smiled. Perhaps the pupil had learned something from the master, after all.

Bevins pulled open the front door, and Lilith stepped inside. "Is Papa here?" she asked, listening as the carriage bearing Jack, Lord Hutton, and Wenford pulled out of the drive.

"He and your aunt went to luncheon with Lord and Lady Neuland, Miss Benton. I expect them to return within the hour."

She nodded. "And William?"

"He has not returned either, Miss Benton."

"Thank you, Bevins. I'll be in the library."

"Very good, my lady."

Lilith was relieved that no one was home. It gave her time to consider how she would tell them the news. She imagined her father would be angry and embarrassed— after all, he'd forced her into a betrothal with a murderer; it was hardly the type of upstanding match he had sought for her. And then she would finally tell him that someone else had caught her heart. Someone who had risked a great deal to protect her reputation, and her life.

She sighed and sat in one of the comfortable chairs before the hearth. Jack had been in such an odd mood after he'd stopped Wenford. He'd barely spoken to her and had seemed anxious to go off with Richard and swear out a statement of his own against Dolph. When she had offered to do the same, he had adamantly refused and told her she needn't be involved any longer.

His game was over, and he'd won. And she had to wonder if he'd decided he no longer had any use for her. That hurt—a deep, hollow ache in her chest that made it hard to breathe. Still, though, she could hope that he was trying to be noble and proper, that he did care for her as much as she cared for him. She had to hope, because it was too painful to consider anything else. He had done so much for her, and for her heart. He'd shown her how to be free.

The front door opened, and she stiffened. She did not relish the conversation that the next few minutes would bring. Hurriedly she grabbed a book off the table and opened it, pretending to read.

"Lil?"

Lilith sighed in relief and lowered the book. "William. Where have you been?"

He shrugged and dropped into the chair beside her. "Taking care of things. Why are you home? I thought you were staying with the Huttons."

She ignored his question, focusing instead on his answer. "What things, brother? You didn't do something foolish, did you?"

Lifting his hand to his chest, her brother lifted both eyebrows. "Me? Foolish?" Seeing the suspicious expression on her face, he grinned and shook his head. "No. I . . . saw the error of my ways with Antonia. She's taking a trip to France. Be gone for quite a while, I imagine. Any news from Dansbury?"

Lilith looked at him. "I heard that she'd spoken out

against Jack," she said slowly. "You knew that, didn't you?"

"Well, yes, I suppose I did." He leaned forward and took the book from her. "Johnson's *Dictionary of the English Language*?" he asked, glancing up at her. "Jack told you to stay with Lady Hutton until you received word that it was all clear. What's happened?"

It seemed that William was not quite so lightheaded as she thought. He'd done Jack a great service. "Wenford confessed."

William shot to his feet. "What?"

The front door opened again, this time with greater speed. "Lilith!"

"In here, Papa," she called, scowling at the strident bellow. He'd heard something.

Stephen Benton shoved the library door open and strode into the room, Aunt Eugenia, white-faced and tight-lipped, on his heels. "That damned Dansbury!" he snarled, then caught sight of William. "You encouraged his friendship. I can't believe it!"

Lilith took a deep breath. "Papa, I—"

"This is a disaster!" he ranted. "No way to escape the scandal. Everyone knows you were engaged. Damn Dansbury!"

"But Papa," Lilith broke in, unwilling to hear Jack's name further disparaged, "Dolph Remdale is a murderer."

He stopped his pacing and turned to look at her. "So you *have* heard. How did you know?"

Lilith remained seated, her hands folded on her lap so they wouldn't shake. "I assisted Lord Dansbury and the Bow Street Runners in stopping His Grace," she said quietly.

The other three occupants in the room stood frozen,

staring at her. "You . . . you did what?" her father finally rasped.

"From what he'd said to me, and the way he acted toward me, I was certain that Lord Dansbury was correct, and that it was His Grace, and not the marquis, who killed old Wenford."

"You were certain," the viscount repeated. "You weren't even to speak with Dansbury!"

Lilith frowned. He didn't even seem to care that Dolph Remdale had killed his uncle to gain the title. "Well, I did speak with him," she responded. "And I wouldn't be married to a man who would kill for a title, or a man who would hit a woman."

"He hit you?" William asked, his light green eyes indignant and angry.

"William, silence!" Lord Hamble, his face flushed and furious, stalked over to stand directly before Lilith. "I am speaking to your sister. By God, girl, do you think I'm a fool? You didn't want to marry Wenford, so you conspired to ruin him." He slammed one fist against the other palm. "Only now you've ruined your best—ha— your only—chance for a respectable marriage. No one will touch you now!"

Lilith shot to her feet. "Papa, he hit me! He threatened to kill me! He killed his own uncle! How can you be angry that I won't be marrying him?"

He jabbed a finger at her. "You are selfish, girl! Selfish! You knew how much our family needed this match, and you went and destroyed it because you were displeased with the husband I chose for you. And now you've ruined everything! We'll have to go back to Northamptonshire, and we'll never be able to show our faces in London again."

Lilith took a deep breath, trying to calm her outrage

at his continued abuse. She had done nothing wrong. "Papa—"

"By God, I should disown you for this. Just like your bedamned mother, thinking of nothing but yourself."

Aunt Eugenia sniffed in agreement, while William looked as though he wanted badly to throw something.

"For six years, I have done nothing but think of you, and of this family," Lilith said quietly, her voice shaking with fury. He didn't care for her. He didn't care at all. "You have given me nothing in return but your contempt. So I agree. I should be disowned, because I no longer wish to be your daughter." She turned to her brother. "William, will you help me transport my things to Penelope's home? I will not spend another night under this roof."

William stared at her for another moment, astounded, then shook himself and nodded. "Yes, of course I will."

Her father sputtered, his complexion growing alarmingly red. "If you leave this house, you will never be allowed to return! You'll have no money, no friends, no home. Nothing!"

Lilith turned her back so he wouldn't see that he was still able to hurt her. "I will become a governess, if necessary," she said coolly, though she couldn't help the tremble that touched her voice. She walked toward the door, William following close behind her. Abruptly she stopped and turned around again. "And I would like the portrait of Mama you hid in the attic. If you had been kinder to her, I don't think she would have left you. Now you've lost us both."

Aunt Eugenia gasped. "Insolent girl!"

Viscount Hamble turned his back. "Good riddance," he growled toward the fireplace. "Bevins! Gather the staff. Inform them that we're closing up the house, and we'll be returning to Northamptonshire tomorrow!"

Lilith left the library and headed up to her room, summoning Emily to help her gather her essentials. A harried-looking Bevins and William appeared with one of her traveling trunks, and another pair of footmen with a second.

"You don't have to go, Lil," her brother said, seating himself on the edge of her bed. "Father'll be ready to pretend nothing happened if you lie low for a day or so." He forced a grin. "After all, you're still his best chance at respectability."

Lilith shook her head, surprised that she wasn't more upset about the whole thing. Mostly what she felt was relief. She would never again have to listen to her father or her aunt ranting about how ill-mannered she was, or what a disappointment she was, or how much they relied on her not to shame them. "I can't do this anymore, William. I just can't."

He sighed, and nodded. "Truth be told, I'm surprised you've put up with as much as you have."

"I would appreciate it if you would put my books into storage somewhere, so Papa won't burn them. And my things back at home."

Her brother nodded. "Anything else?"

Lilith thought about it. She had friends back in Northamptonshire, but with the scandal that would break over her departure, they likely wouldn't want to have anything further to do with her, anyway. "No. When I find a position, I'll write you and let you know where I am."

"What about Jack?" he asked quietly, his eyes searching her face.

Finally tears gathered in her eyes. "I don't know, William."

He stood. "Well, I do. Perhaps I'll have a word with the old boy."

"Don't you dare," she protested, embarrassed. She'd had enough of matchmaking to last her a lifetime. "I won't have him prodded into anything."

Her brother snorted. "Doubt I could sway him about anything, anyway." He headed for the door. "I'll have Milgrew bring up the coach."

They had spent such a short time in town that Lilith actually had very little in her bed chamber that needed to be transported. Before nightfall she and William were in the coach, on their way to the Sanfords' residence. Neither her father nor Aunt Eugenia had shown themselves as she'd left the house, which only served to confirm to her that she was doing the right thing. If they'd cared about her at all, they would have come out and asked her to stay.

As they stepped down from the coach, Lilith felt the first wave of trepidation. If Lord and Lady Sanford refused her, she wondered if she dared go to the Huttons'. They were the only other family she could think of who would possibly take her in. Her father had seen to it that she had no idea where her mother's parents were, or even if they still lived. William seemed to sense her hesitation, for he offered her his arm and escorted her to the door. "No worries, Lil. We'll see you safely somewhere."

His words didn't sound all that comforting, but the Sanford butler pulled open the door before she could tell him so. "Is either Miss Sanford or Lady Sanford to home?" she asked politely.

The butler bowed. "Both are in, Miss Benton. This way, if you please."

Both ladies were in the drawing room, and Pen leapt to her feet as Lilith and William were shown in. "Lil! We heard about His Grace. Did you have any idea that he killed his uncle?"

Lilith nodded. "Yes, I did." She cleared her throat as Penelope dragged her over to the couch, and then motioned for William to take a seat, as well. "Actually, that's why I'm here."

Lady Sanford rang for tea. "What's happened, Lilith?" she asked, her expression serious.

"Well, I suppose I should tell you the entire tale."

"I'd like to hear it myself," William interjected. She glared at him, and he shrugged and gave her a sheepish smile. "I didn't exactly have a chance, earlier," he pointed out.

Lilith looked at Lady Sanford, the one she would have to convince. "Because of . . . certain circumstances which I can't go into, both the Marquis of Dansbury and I had reason to suspect that the old duke was killed by Dolph Remdale. I asked my father not to force me into a match with Dolph, but he did it anyway."

"I didn't think you were pleased," Lady Sanford murmured.

"No, I wasn't. Anyway, the evidence became stronger against Dolph, and I had to make a choice between assisting Jack—Dansbury—in something I knew to be right, or to risk allying myself with a killer. I happened to see Dolph this morning, and since I knew that Dansbury was looking for him, I followed him myself."

"You didn't," Pen gasped, covering her mouth with one hand, her eyes wide.

Lilith nodded. "I did, until Dolph grabbed me, and I realized he'd been leading me away from assistance. You don't need to know all the sordid details, but Jack, Lord Hutton, and several Bow Street Runners caught up to us. I realized that Jack was there, listening, and I . . . tricked, I suppose, Dolph into confessing."

"By Jingo, Lil, you're bang up to the mark," her brother said admiringly.

Penelope giggled.

"Papa doesn't think so," she returned, then looked back at her hostess. "My father was very upset that I'd spoiled my chances for a good match, and that I'd brought more scandal down on his house. He refused to listen to reason and threatened to disown me, so I told him to go ahead, and that I would not spend another night under the roof of someone who obviously didn't care a fig for me." She took a slow breath. "And so I came here. If you'll allow it, I—"

"Oh, Lil, you must stay here!" Penelope burst out, clutching her friend's hand.

William looked at Miss Sanford and smiled. Pen blushed.

"It's about time," Lady Sanford cut in, leaning forward to pat Lilith's leg. "You're a fine, compassionate girl, Lilith, and a very good influence on my daughter." She glanced at Penelope. "I hope you will stay with us for as long as you like."

"There will be a scandal," Lilith warned, fighting off tears of gratitude. "I'm certain of it."

"Posh." Lady Sanford smiled, and flipped her hand. "This household could use a little excitement."

"Are you certain?"

"Lil," Penelope exclaimed, "we'll be like sisters! It'll be top of the trees to have you here."

"It will only be until I can find a position as a governess," Lilith assured them, a tear finally running down one cheek.

"Governess? But Lil, what about . . ." Pen looked over at her mother. "What about you-know-who?"

"He's being noble," William broke in again, grinning at Penelope. "I'm certain he'll get over it. It's not a natural condition for him."

"And you, Mr. Benton?" Lady Sanford queried.

"Have you parted from your father, as well?"

"Oh, no, my lady. I've an inheritance to look forward to. And someone needs to make certain Lil gets her things."

"That's kind of you," Penelope said.

"Not at all. Lil's put up with my nonsense since she was born. I'm only trying to make things up to her, a little." William sat forward, his expression becoming earnest. "You're the one who's being kind, Miss Sanford."

Penelope ducked her head demurely, while her mother glanced curiously from one to the other of them. "Well," Lady Sanford said after a moment, "do you have your things with you?"

"Yes, my lady."

"Then let's get you into a bed chamber. We've the Delmore ball to attend tonight."

"Oh, I couldn't," Lilith protested. Everyone would know! Everyone would look at her, and mutter about her—and even worse, Jack might be there. A sudden tremor of excitement ran through her. Noble old Jack might be there. And whatever else happened, she wanted an explanation for his odd behavior of earlier. If William was correct, she had several ideas about how to assist Jack Faraday in getting over his uncharacteristically proper behavior.

"I think it's a splendid idea," William countered, but his eyes were again on Penelope.

Lilith stifled a smile. Perhaps her brother wasn't as daft as she sometimes thought, after all. "If you're certain," she conceded to the Sanfords. "Why not?"

Chapter 20

Jack Faraday jumped down from Benedick and walked toward the front entrance of Benton House, lit against the early evening gloom. He should never have left Lilith that morning. Her father would have been furious, and someone needed to put Lord Hamble in his place. He should have taken the opportunity to march in there with Lil and tell the viscount that he'd made a mistake in selecting Dolph Remdale for his daughter, and that he, the Marquis of Dansbury, meant to rectify it. And he didn't care whether her father approved the match or not—if Lilith wanted him, then he fully intended to marry her.

Instead he had gone off with Richard to swear out his statement, telling himself that he needed to take steps to control the damage and minimize Lilith's role in order to save what he could of her reputation. After five hours of interrogation and argument, he admitted to himself that it wasn't merely chivalry that had driven him from her side.

It was because he was overwhelmed by the realization that Lil, for all intents and purposes, was now available. He wanted Lilith, wanted her in his life for the rest of his life. But she had to know what a poor choice he was for a husband, and once the initial din died down, she would have her choice of every other eligible bachelor in London. And every blasted one of them had a better reputation than his own.

He rapped the ornate brass knocker against the door anyway. If he weren't a gambler by nature, he would have been dead a long time ago. Nothing happened for several moments too long, and then Bevins pulled open the door and peered out.

The butler's jaw dropped. "Yes, my lord?" he asked, glancing back over his shoulder.

"Is Miss Benton receiving guests?" he asked, trying his damnedest to be polite, when he much rather would have kicked open the door and gone storming in, looking for her.

Bevins cleared his throat. "No, my lord."

Jack eyed him. "Would you please inform her that I am here?" he requested, his voice becoming less friendly.

Again the butler hesitated. Just as Jack was considering throttling him, Bevins glanced over his shoulder again. "I can't do that, my lord," he said in a low voice.

"And why in damnation not?" Jack took a step closer. "Don't forget that I saw you carting the Duke of Wenford's body about. You wouldn't want anyone to know about that, now, would you?"

The butler stiffened. "No, I would not. But she is not here, my lord."

That, and the butler's extremely odd behavior, stopped him. Perhaps she'd merely gone out for dinner, though. "When will she be returning, then?"

Again the butler glanced back into the house. "She will not be, my lord."

"Bevins, if you don't wish my fist to remove your

teeth, you will tell me exactly where Lilith is. Immediately.''

"I don't know where she is, my lord. And please, keep your voice down. I don't wish to lose my position for speaking to you.''

Jack attempted to contain his temper. "What happened?''

"I'm not certain, my lord. I believe she and the viscount had a disagreement. She left with her trunks.''

"She didn't return to Northamptonshire, did she?'' That hadn't occurred to him—that her father might pack the family up and head back home to hide, as he had done six years ago. If so, Jack had a long ride ahead of him.

"I don't believe so. Her father and aunt will be returning to Hamble tomorrow.'' To Jack's surprise, the butler leaned farther out the door. "I mean that she left her father's house, my lord,'' he whispered. "And her father.''

"What?'' It was so uncharacteristic of Lil that Jack could scarcely believe it. Yet he knew how strong she was, and how far events of the past few weeks had pushed her. Apparently, she had decided it was time to push back. "I'll be damned,'' he muttered, giving a slight smile. "I'll be damned.'' He looked at the butler again. "Is William about, then?''

"He accompanied her to wherever it was she was going. Now please, my lord, go away.'' When Jack didn't protest, Bevins quietly shut the door.

For several moments Jack stood on the steps. The last grand ball of the Season was tonight, and he hoped to high heaven that Lilith would be there. He hadn't been invited, but no doubt word of Wenford's arrest had spread throughout the *ton*, so he should have no trouble gaining admittance. His presence should serve to distract everyone, and to make certain any fingers that might be inclined to point in Lilith's direction were turned back toward him. If she wasn't there, he would find her.

He returned home to find Peese and Martin celebrating their victory with one of his best bottles of brandy, and sat with them for a drink. Finally he had Martin join him upstairs, and requested his most somber-looking ensemble. His valet obligingly dressed him out in stark black breeches and coat, with a gray waistcoat beneath a snowy white cravat. He declined any other ornamentation, though tonight the outfit made him feel rather like an undertaker. "A pity I don't own a coach-and-four with black horses," he commented, accepting his gloves from Martin.

"T'would be a sight, my lord." The valet grinned.

"I'll have to look into it," Jack agreed, picking up his hat and heading for the door.

When he arrived at the Delmore soirée, the hostess hesitated only a moment before she graciously welcomed him into her home. Jack thanked her just as politely, and apologized for misplacing his invitation. When he strolled into the ballroom, he came to an abrupt halt.

Lilith was still in London—and she didn't look particularly sorrowful over parting from her father. Completely the contrary. She looked radiant. Adorned in her daring emerald gown, she stood in the center of a group of her friends, each one clamoring for her attention and congratulating her on her bravery. Jack smiled to himself. It appeared that the story he and Richard had "amended" seemed to be the one that had circulated throughout the *ton*.

Lilith had truly blossomed. Over the past weeks, and especially after the perils of the morning, she had become a spirited, laughing creature, her green eyes alight with humor and excitement. It certainly made everything he'd gone through more than worth it, but at the same time it was disheartening. Such a creature of light could hardly want to be leg-shackled to him. Living without her would kill him, but he wasn't willing to coerce her into doing what *he* wanted, as every other man she knew had tried to do. With the burden of being perfect removed from her shoulders, her natural wit and charm, which he had sensed from the beginning, were finally allowed to shine. She was a fool if she even considered risking her new popularity by being seen with him. And she was no fool.

In addition to his skills at gambling and subterfuge, Jack Faraday was evidently a proficient storyteller. When Lilith had stepped into the ballroom, she'd expected to be cut by every respectable female present. Instead, she had been greeted by an enthusiastic round of applause, and she and Pen were immediately surrounded by their usual circle of friends, joined by several others who'd never before bothered strengthening their acquaintance. For a moment she was baffled by the attention and the approval—until she heard the current version of the morning's happenings.

"Lil, you should have said," Mary Fitzroy chastised with a giggle.

"Well, I couldn't, really," Lilith answered, trying to figure out what the devil was going on.

"But to think that all along you knew His Grace was a dangerous madman, and the prime minister himself asked you to assist in stopping him!"

Lilith blinked, but immediately realized what had happened. Jack was being noble again, and apparently he'd recruited Lord Hutton and the Earl of Liverpool as well. She avoided answering most questions until she had determined exactly what the story was. Even after she heard it, she could scarcely believe it. It seemed that Dolph was being secretly investigated, and that once his interest in her was noticed, she had been approached and asked to lend her assistance. Thus it had gone until this morning, when the law feared that Dolph would make a run for it, and so they'd asked her to lead him to a location where he could be safely arrested without rendering harm to anyone else.

"I hadn't realized I was so heroic," she said in a low voice to Pen, during a momentary lull around them.

"That's not the story you told Mama and me," Penelope noted, her brow furrowed.

"Infinitely easier on my reputation than the truth, though, don't you think?" Lilith smiled. Jack was wonderful.

"Lilith?"

For a heartbeat she thought it must be Jack, and whirled around. The face before her, though, belonged to Lionel Hendrick, the Earl of Nance. "My lord." She curtsied, the sudden elation leaving her heart.

"May I speak to you for a moment?" He gestured at the dance floor. "A quadrille, perhaps?"

"Yes." Lilith allowed herself to be led out onto the polished floor. The music began, and she and Lionel bowed to one another.

"Lilith, I wish . . . I wish you had told me that your betrothal to Wenford was a sham," the earl said earnestly.

So that was what he wanted. He certainly didn't waste any time. "I was not at liberty to do so," she answered. The dance parted them, and she reflected that no one knew that she had no dowry to speak of. She wondered if once they found out, it would change the way they all looked at her. And she wondered why she no longer cared.

"Even so," he continued, as he returned to her side, taking her hand to turn her about the room, "the fact of the matter is that you are now . . . how shall I say, available once again."

Lilith nodded as they turned around one another. "Yes, I suppose I am," she admitted.

Then she caught sight of Jack. He was halfway out the door, but as though sensing her gaze, he stopped and turned around. Her breath caught as their eyes met, and she couldn't help the smile that touched her lips. He smiled in return, tilting his head sideways, and returned to lean against the wall and watch her. He had come, and he hadn't left yet. There was hope, after all.

"I see you are pleased," Lionel noted, misinterpreting her sudden delighted expression. "Then I hope you will agree to be my wife."

Lilith surveyed her dancing partner for a moment. Lionel was handsome and considerate, and while not the wittiest man she'd ever come across, at least he didn't seem the type to strike his spouse. But her heart was taken, and if she couldn't have Jack, she didn't want anyone. "I thank you for your kind offer, Lionel," she said as he approached again, "but my circumstances have recently changed somewhat, and I have decided that only love will induce me to marry. So I apologize, but I cannot accept your proposal."

For a moment he looked at her, slack-jawed, until Mr. Nanders bumped into him from behind. "Uh, beg pardon, Nanders," he stammered, and hurried to catch up to the dance. "But I would make you a good husband," he protested *sotto voce,* as they passed one another.

"But I would not make you a good wife. I am not nearly so proper and gentle as you may think."

"Surely not."

"I do not wish to marry you, Lionel. Please do not press me further on this, or I will be forced to be even more blunt."

Again he hesitated for a moment, his complexion darkening with either anger or embarrassment. "Quite right. You may be correct, Miss Benton. I beg your pardon."

To Nance's credit, he did finish out the quadrille, and then escorted her back to Lady Sanford. As soon as he'd done his duty, he swiftly departed.

"Trouble, my dear?" Penelope's mother asked, looking from her to the vanished earl.

"Just a misunderstanding," Lilith answered. She could sense Jack somewhere behind her, like an excitement pricking at her skin. Trying to gather her senses together, she looked about. "Where's Pen?"

Her mother smiled. "Over there."

Lilith spied her friend by the refreshment table, being handed a glass of punch by William. Both were laughing, and Lilith sighed. At least something was going well for someone. The orchestra struck up a waltz, and as several male acquaintances began heading in her direction, she made up her mind. She had to know, one way or the other. "Will you excuse me for a moment?"

Lady Sanford followed her gaze, and Lilith thought she might even have smiled a little. "Of course."

Lilith began walking determinedly toward Jack. A few murmured whispers started around her, but she ignored them. As she expected, the marquis looked startled, but he immediately pushed away from the wall and came forward to meet her.

"Lilith," he said, taking her hand and bringing it to his lips. "Are you all right?"

"No," she returned, deciding she could spend forever

trying to decipher what lay behind his dark eyes. "You abandoned me this morning."

He hesitated. "I had to swear out a statement."

"And quite a statement it must have been, Dansbury. I seem to be the heroine of the hour."

He grinned. "Good. You deserve to be."

"It feels good, for a change," she admitted, meeting his smile and relaxing just a little. She was familiar with this Jack Faraday, and was quite fond of him. "And what role did you play?"

"Me? I was merely out to save my own hide. Quite typically black-hearted of me, actually."

"I see." Lilith sized him up, watched him watching her. "You know what I think?"

"Never," he replied promptly.

"I think you're being stupidly noble about my reputation. That's what I think."

He lifted an eyebrow. "As I recall, your reputation was at one time quite a concern of yours, my dear."

She smiled. "I've learned that pleasing myself is more important." Lilith sighed, then held out her hand. Swiftly he took it in his own. "Will you dance with me?" she asked.

"Of course."

Jack led her out onto the floor, and swept her into his arms. She loved being in his arms, loved the strength and gracefulness of him, and the way he was currently attempting to hold her at the proper distance from himself and failing badly.

"What are your plans now?" she asked.

"That depends," he returned. "What were you and Nance discussing so intently a moment ago?"

Lilith grinned. He was jealous. "He asked me to marry him again."

Jack's eyes darted in the direction Nance had disappeared. "Ah. And you decided . . ."

"I decided that no one but you, Jack," she murmured, "has ever cared about me, about my opinion, and about my happiness."

"Lil," he said, swallowing and looking quite ill at ease for a rakehell, "I heard that you left your father. I hope it wasn't because of me."

"It was because of *me,* Jack. And because of you, I suppose. But I need to know something from you."

He scowled, his eyes uncertain. "I'm a terrible match for you. I gamble, I drink, I have no scruples—"

"The reason you risked your life to save me, I assume?" This was not going to work. As long as he was able to convince himself that the most noble choice would be to let her go off and make a wretched match with someone other than himself, no matter how miserable that would make the two of them, she hadn't a chance. She needed to get him somewhere where she could be more . . . persuasive. "We can't talk here."

"Lilith—"

She cut him off again. "Meet me in the library in a few minutes, will you?"

"I shouldn't," he said, his eyes holding hers.

"Yes, you should, if you don't want me to marry Nance."

Again a slight scowl touched his face. "He'd be a good match."

"All right, never mind, then. Shall I invite you to the wedding?"

The marquis glared at her, reluctance and yearning clearly vying with one another on his face. "Baggage," he finally growled. "I'll meet you in the damned library."

He did want her! Well, that decided it. The only detail

was, as William had said, to return Jack to his natural
state of scoundrelhood. By the time the waltz ended,
Lilith had decided on just how she might accomplish
that—if she had the courage.

Jack returned her to Lady Sanford, and then excused
himself. The evening couldn't be all that easy for him,
considering the way his fellows had treated him over the
past few days, but he appeared to be enjoying their momentary discomfiture, and made a point of going about
greeting all of his acquaintances. Lilith tried not to watch
him, failing utterly as he slowly made his way along
toward the stairs and then vanished.

"I think I'd best go chaperon Penelope and your
brother before we have another scandal on our hands,"
Lady Sanford said after a moment, and smiled as she
glanced in Jack's direction and then back at Lilith. "Neither of them can boast subtlety as their strong suit."

"I'm afraid not," Lilith agreed with a grin, and
watched her hostess make her way over to where Pen
and William sat against the wall, chatting and laughing
and completely oblivious to everything going on around
them.

As soon as the next dance began and everyone was
distracted, she slipped out of the ballroom and up the
wide staircase. The butler passed her, looking at her curiously, and Lilith raised a hand to her hair, as though
trying to fix her curls. He must have believed that she
was headed to a bed chamber to repair her coif, because
he continued on his way.

The library door was halfway open, and Lilith slipped
inside. Jack stood gazing out the tall window into the
darkness. He turned as she entered and locked the door
behind her.

Jack lifted an eyebrow. "A bit suspicious, don't you
think?"

She shrugged, strolling over to the door on the far side of the fireplace and locking it, as well. "I want to be with you, Jack."

This time he looked truly startled. "Here?"

"Yes." She stepped toward him, but he lifted a hand as if to hold her off.

He drew a ragged breath. "I'll give you one minute to retract that statement, Lil," he said gruffly, remaining planted by the window as though by sheer willpower alone. "Because you shouldn't think I'll be noble and refuse your request. I'm not remotely that much a gentleman."

She gave a slight grin and tilted her head at him, heard him draw a quick breath in response. Lilith reveled in the power she had over this cynical, fiercely intelligent man, for she'd never had such a thing before. Yet with Jack Faraday, her slightest change of expression sometimes seemed able to distract him from everything else until he had deciphered and responded to it. "Your lack of restraint is rather what I was counting on, my lord," she whispered.

Slowly she stepped forward again, not stopping until she was able to slide her hands about his waist. Lilith leaned up and brushed her lips across the base of his jaw, trailing kisses along his chin and over to his ear. Jack stood very still, his eyes closed and his breathing uneven. Knowing she must be wearing him down, Lilith trailed the tip of her tongue along the rim of his ear.

The marquis drew a harsh breath. "Lil, if someone catches us, you'll be ruined."

"Shh," she whispered, slipping her hands under the shoulders of his coat and sliding the garment down to the floor. She raised up on her tiptoes and very gently touched her lips to his. Before he could respond, she backed away a little, noting that he followed. Again she kissed him, and this time he met her mouth hungrily.

Her fingers drifted down to slowly open the buttons of his gray waistcoat, and she pushed that to the floor as well. Almost as if against his will, Jack's hands lifted to slide about her waist and pull her closer.

"This . . . this is completely improper," he commented, drawing another breath as she pulled his cravat loose and tossed it to the floor.

Lilith smiled as she pulled his shirt free from his breeches. "I know."

"May we at least move away from the window?"

That made sense, anyway. She kissed the exposed base of his throat. "If you insist."

A country dance began to play downstairs, the sound muffled by the closed doors. Lilith took Jack by the hands and led him over to the deep, overstuffed couch. This time she didn't have to coax him into kissing her as he pulled her close. She slid her fingers up under his shirt, running her hands over his well-muscled abdomen and chest. Small shivers of excitement and anticipation ran down her spine and her arms. As her hands moved down to the fastenings of his breeches, he lifted his face away from hers.

"Lil, are you certain you know what you're doing?" he asked softly, his hand caressing her cheek.

She finished working and let the trousers slide down his hips. He was clearly aroused, and she took a quick breath. "Stop being such a bore, Dansbury," she murmured, pushing him backward onto the couch.

Before she could change her mind, she removed her shoes and stockings. Gathering her emerald skirt and her shift in her hands, she straddled Jack's hips and slowly eased herself down over his erect member. She moaned at the tight slide of their flesh together and lowered her head against Jack's shoulder.

The marquis made a ragged sound of his own, chuckling breathlessly. "For God's sake," he muttered into her hair, "don't leave me like this."

Lilith raised her head to look down at him and grinned back. She kissed him deeply, then tentatively lifted her hips and lowered herself on him again. "How is that?" she asked.

"Splendid," he groaned.

Gripping tightly around her hips, he guided her movements until she felt more confident about what he wanted and what she wanted from him. Jack began lifting his own hips to meet her, and she placed her hands on his shoulders and threw her head back. As the tension inside her exploded, Jack clutched her hips and held her close against him, sucking a breath in through his teeth as he erupted as well.

Lilith leaned against him, panting, and he gently wrapped his arms around her. "Lil?" he said quietly after a few moments.

"Hm?"

"I love you," he murmured.

Lilith shivered, her eyes closed tightly. He'd said it. He'd said it when she had begun to think he never would.

As soon as she could breathe normally again, she raised her head. "Well, that settles it, then," she said in what she hoped was a matter-of-fact voice.

He furrowed his brow. "Settles what?"

"You'll just have to marry me."

Jack's eyes met hers with a startling intensity. "Beg— beg pardon?"

"I've completely ruined you," she continued. "No doubt someone saw us both enter the room. If you don't agree to wed me, I'm afraid no one else will have you."

Slowly the wary look on Jack's face slid into a smile.

His eyes dancing, he reached up to brush a straying hair from her eyes. "Is that so? You wouldn't mind being leg-shackled to a poor excuse for a gentleman such as myself?"

"Not a bit," she replied promptly. "If you don't mind being married to a respectable chit who's far too concerned with propriety."

The marquis laughed. "I think you've cured yourself of that, my dear." He pulled her face toward his and gently kissed her. "I suppose," he said softly, "if you can become a bit more scandalous for me, then I can become a bit more proper for you." He kissed her again. "Lilith, will you marry me?"

A tear ran down her cheek. This must be what absolute joy felt like. "Yes, Jack, I will marry you."

Jack shut his eyes for a moment. When he opened them again, they were twinkling merrily. "And the sooner the better, I might add," he continued, sliding his hands down her arms to entwine his fingers with hers. "You've already had seven proposals this Season. I don't want to risk your finding someone more qualified."

Lilith laughed through her tears. "Shut up, Jack," she warned him, holding his hands tightly, "and kiss me."

The Marquis of Dansbury was more than happy to comply.

Avon Romances—
the best in exceptional authors and unforgettable novels!

Avon Romantic Treasures

Unforgettable, enthralling love stories,
sparkling with passion and adventure
from Romance's bestselling authors

LADY OF WINTER *by Emma Merritt*
77985-4/$5.99 US/$7.99 Can

SILVER MOON SONG *by Genell Dellin*
78602-8/$5.99 US/$7.99 Can

FIRE HAWK'S BRIDE *by Judith E. French*
78745-8/$5.99 US/$7.99 Can

WANTED ACROSS TIME *by Eugenia Riley*
78909-4/$5.99 US/$7.99 Can

EVERYTHING AND THE MOON *by Julia Quinn*
78933-7/$5.99 US/$7.99 Can

BEAST *by Judith Ivory*
78644-3/$5.99 US/$7.99 Can

HIS FORBIDDEN TOUCH *by Shelley Thacker*
78120-4/$5.99 US/$7.99 Can

LYON'S GIFT *by Tanya Anne Crosby*
78571-4/$5.99 US/$7.99 Can

Discover Contemporary Romances at Their Sizzling Hot Best from Avon Books

RYAN'S RETURN   *by Barbara Freethy*
78531-5/$5.99 US/$7.99 Can

CATCH ME IF YOU CAN   *by Jillian Karr*
77876-9/$5.99 US/$7.99 Can

WINNING WAYS   *by Barbara Boswell*
72743-9/$5.99 US/$7.99 Can

CARRIED AWAY   *by Sue Civil-Brown*
72774-9/$5.99 US/$7.99 Can

**LOVE IN A
SMALL TOWN**   *by Curtiss Ann Matlock*
78107-7/$5.99 US/$7.99 Can

HEAVEN KNOWS BEST   *by Nikki Holiday*
78797-0/$5.99 US/$7.99 Can

FOREVER ENCHANTED   *by Maggie Shayne*
78746-6/$5.99 US/$7.99 Can